Stuart Jonathan Wakefield was born and lives in Reading with his wife of thirty years, Susan and their three grown-up daughters. Stuart is a qualified printer and print finisher, having studied and gained a city and guilds from the London college of printing. He spent thirty years as a print finisher, manufacturing paperback books.

Stuart is also a qualified swimming instructor, having spent eight years coaching at Reading swimming club, and the last five years working for Swimexpert and Hydrokids swim school.

Stuart is a keen sports fan, follows Chelsea football club, and names Sir Ian Botham as his sporting hero.

In the memory of my father, John William Wakefield
(26/06/1932–17/09/2013)

Stuart Jonathan Wakefield

SINS OF OUR PAST

AUSTIN MACAULEY PUBLISHERS™

LONDON ∗ CAMBRIDGE ∗ NEW YORK ∗ SHARJAH

A CIP catalogue record for this title is available from the British Library.

ISBN 9781528964883 (Paperback)
ISBN 9781528965460 (ePub e-book)

www.austinmacauley.com

First Published (2021)
Austin Macauley Publishers Ltd
25 Canada Square
Canary Wharf
London
E14 5LQ

I'd like to thank my wife, Susan; my daughters, Joanna, Gemma and Amanda and my mother. Thank you for believing in me.

Synopsis

Chief Inspector Johnny Allen always knew one day his past would catch up with him. Jane Woods was the love of his life, his sin. The murder of Jane and his daughter, Megan Davis, would bring Allen's past back to haunt him.

Alison Woods was murdered on September 24, 1988; she was aged eighteen. Norman Denman was convicted of her murder, but this never sat right with Allen.

Norman had a mental age of eight. He was madly in love with Alison. He wouldn't kill her; he couldn't kill her. Norman was no more a killer than he was. Alison Woods' body was found up in the woods, near the river in Pangbourne. She'd suffered multiple stab wounds. But Alison had a secret; she was pregnant. But who was the father? Surely it had to be Billy Reynolds.

Billy Reynolds loved Alison. He was Johnny's best friend; the pair were like brothers. But Billy changed once they'd met Jane Woods; he wasn't Billy anymore. Billy and his older brother Jackson had problems; both suffered from dissociative identity disorder. Jackson Reynolds was just plain straight evil. He was convicted and sent to life in prison for the murder of Sian and Kevin Van Dalen. Again, the murder never sat right with Allen.

Billy and Jackson had another problem, their sister Grace. She was very clever, very manipulative. Grace had just lost the love of her life, Joan Denman, Norman's sister. Joan was sexually abused by her father and her brother. Unable to take in what they'd done to her, she took her own life. Grace knew what Norman had done, and swore revenge.

Grace had also found out that Jackson was the father of Alison's baby, not Billy. On telling Billy what she knew, he went after his older brother. He found both Jackson and Alison down by the river. A fight broke out; Jackson pulled out a knife. In the struggle, Alison was stabbed in the stomach. Billy, unable to take in what had happened, ripped her to bits.

Having witnessed what her brother had done, Grace decided to frame Norman, blackmailing him into moving Alison's body.

Alison's diary was found and read by Jane's youngest daughter, Melissa. She had found out that Jackson, not Billy, was the father of Alison's baby. She confided in her best friend, Maddie Clarke. The two girls were heard by Maddie's brother and the boyfriend of Megan Davis, James.

James, who had met Jackson through selling drugs, sent him a text from Megan's phone, saying he knew about his secret. Believing it was from Megan, the Reynolds siblings knew Megan had to be silenced.

James was unable to remember what had happened to Megan. Believing he'd murdered her, he took his own life.

Allen, along with Inspector Walsh, knew that both Billy and Jackson had trouble with their different personalities, working out that both the brothers' personalities had murdered. Billy wanted to be dominant. So by murdering Megan, he'd proved to William, his other personality, that he was the stronger.

Chapter 1

We all have a past—some good times, some bad times—so our problems today are shaped by our past. A friend of mine…well, when I say a friend, I haven't seen him for years, but we were friends as kids. Well, this person has DID, dissociative identity disorder, has had for years. So their past must have been bad, and their problems today are their past. But from what I can remember, no, it wasn't. It was like any normal childhood. So were their problems in some way shaped by others?

He stood looking out of his bedroom window. Summer had just about gone. September was always a hard month for him. Not only was it the month his father had died, but what happened on September 24, 1988 and the murder of Alison Woods, that day sits long in his memory.

'Come on, baby. I want to dance,' she said, grabbing him by the hand.

Bloody hell! Why do girls act so stupid when they get drunk? he thought to himself. Have a good time, yes, but let's not act up about it. He laughed to himself as he remembered what his mum said about dancing around handbags in the middle of the dance floor.

The young couple started to dance. She thought it was funny he danced like an old man.

'What's so funny?' he asked, snapping at her.

'You. You dance like my dad,' she laughed.

He pulled a face at her. *Funny, very funny,* he said to himself, forcing a smile.

The music was loud, a lot louder than normal. The place seemed more crowded than it had been in recent weeks.

The nightclub itself was set mostly underground. It looked strange. From the outside, it looked small, but once you got inside and went downstairs, it was massive. The music tonight was brilliant. The DJ was amazing; the best in the business. He knew just how to get the whole place jumping.

'Oh, for God sake! Why does he have to show his face?' she said to her boyfriend.

'Who?' he replied with a lack of interest.

She turned him around, pointing at a man who was standing over by the main bar. 'Him,' she shouted angrily.

'He's okay. He's a mate, that's all,' he replied dragging her off the dance floor.

He walked over to the man; he was a lot older than he was, maybe early fifties. From what he could understand, he'd been inside for a while.

'You alright mate?' asked the man.

'Yeah, not bad, not bad at all,' he replied shaking the man's hand.

She eyed him up and down in a distasteful way. To be truthful, she found him to be a bit annoying. He seemed way too sure of himself, a bit cocky.

'Not here; over near the toilets, alright? Your girlfriend seems a bit pissed off,' he laughed, smiling nervously in her direction.

'She'll be okay. Don't worry.' He turned to his girlfriend and gave her a stern look, as if to say, at least try and be friendly. She rolled her eyes at him, giving him a forced half-smile and walked over towards the man.

'What goodies have you got tonight then?' she said, putting her arm around the man's shoulders.

'See, told you, didn't I?'

The man gave the young couple a small, clear plastic bag. 'This will get the party going,' he smiled.

'Oh shit, what the hell does he want?' she said, hiding behind her boyfriend.

'What? What's wrong?' he asked, his voice conveying a degree of anxiousness.

'My dad, he's here,' she said nervously, pointing to a grey-haired man standing near the dance floor.

'Shit, that's your dad then,' he added.

The man looked over towards the dance floor, 'I know him. Well, I knew him when we were younger. Look mate, I'll see you later. See you later, love.'

'I'm not your love,' she shouted at him, irritably.

The man turned around and smiled at her. As he did, he blew her a kiss.

What an idiot, she said to herself.

He stood and watched as the man walked across the dance floor, over towards his girlfriend's father. On greeting him, he placed one hand on his shoulder. He turned around quickly. The pair shook hands and started talking. He'd never seen or met her father; story goes he walked out on her mother about four years ago. He seemed different to what he'd imagined; he seemed older. One thought that went through his mind was, 'What's he doing here?' She'd always said he lived in Leeds.

'You, you shouldn't be taking that, Meg-Megan. It will make you sick,' said a strange man, struggling to get his words out.

'Who the hell are you?' she screamed angrily, 'You're not my dad,' she said, giving the strange man a dirty look.

The strange man disappeared very quickly. He seemed out of place, but looked familiar. She'd seen him somewhere before.

'You alright? Who was that?' James asked with concern in his voice as he put his arm around his girlfriend's waist.

She glanced quickly over towards the direction the man had disappeared in and said, 'I don't know. I've seen him somewhere before, but I'm not sure where.'

'Don't worry about it. Come on, let's get a drink.'

'No, come on, I want to go. I don't want him to see me,' she shouted at him.

She hurried off towards the toilets and the underground exit that led out by the taxi rank and the train station. He followed her, calling after her to slow down. 'Megan, stop,' he called out.

She turned around and glared at him, 'What?' she shouted.

'Where you going?' he asked her, holding out his hands and arms in protest. Well, he was pleading, more than protesting with her.

'To the toilet. Want to come and watch?' she replied sarcastically.

James walked over towards the main bar. He couldn't see either his mate or Megan's father. He was worried about her; she seemed on edge and very irritable, had been for the last few days.

'You alright, mate?' he said, patting him on the back.

James turned around, 'I thought you'd gone. What did Megan's dad want?' he asked.

'Nothing much. Don't worry about it; just two old mates catching up, that's all.'

'Where's he gone?' he asked the man.

'Little boys' room. Right, I'm off,' he said.

He stood outside the nightclub. He looked skywards as the rain started to fall a little bit heavier. His phone vibrated in his pocket, making him jump. He didn't recognise the number, but the text message more than got his full attention. 'Oh shit. Not that, not now,' he said out loud.

Megan came out of the packed toilet. It was always the same, too many people trying to get into too small a space. She bumped into a man who was standing near the exit to the men's toilet. 'Sorry,' she said, not bothering to look at him.

'Stop, Megan,' he called after her.

She stood and just glared at him; she didn't say a word. Truthfully, he was the last person she wanted to see. He tried to speak to her again, but there were just too many people around. By the time it had cleared, she was gone.

He continued to watch the world go by from his bedroom window, his mind still remembering the years gone past. 'What I am today, has that been shaped by my past?' he thought to himself. One thing he knew was that one day his past would catch up with him.

He closed his bedroom curtains and sat on the end of his bed. The bed was cold and empty, uninviting, lonely. He lay back down and checked his clock, 12:15 am. He closed his eyes, but he knew he wouldn't sleep, too much going through his mind. He started to remember that day in September 1988.

Alison Elizabeth Woods was found murdered on 25 September, 1988. Her body was found at around 06:30 am. She was found up in the woods along by the river in Pangbourne She was aged eighteen years old. The images of Alison's ripped-up body started flashing into his mind. She was stabbed over fifty times. She was also found half-naked, but wasn't raped. He slowly felt himself drifting off. His eyes started to get heavy, but found himself trying to fight it.

'Megan, Megan, don't run off, Megan,' he shouted after her.

Oh, for God sake, why doesn't she just listen? he said to himself. He checked the time, 12:23 am. He was tired; he felt sick and dizzy. He watched as the taxi turned around and disappeared into the distance. He started to lose focus. He slumped down on the side of the road. He was sweating but felt cold. He cried out her name, but nothing. Struggling to his feet, he felt unsteady; everything was going in and out of focus. He started staggering along the road, but he stopped again after only a few yards.

James slumped to his knees. He felt out of control. He had no idea where he was or what he was doing. He wiped the sick from his mouth. Blood was dripping from his nose and onto his shirt. He could sense someone standing over him. Trying to stand again, only to feel too weak to even get to his knees, he slumped to the ground as he glanced up at the shadowy figure that stood in front of him.

'Help me, help me,' he said, as he blacked out.

'James, James, oh come on. God, you're no fun at all,' she screamed out.

She carried on walking up towards the old pub that led towards the river and the woods. All she wanted was to have fun, a good time. 'I'm done with boring people. James is boring; everyone's boring,' she shouted out loudly.

Megan started to see shadows in the woods. Was it her imagination playing tricks on her or was it the drink starting to take effect? She turned around quickly; the noise came from behind her. She could sense someone or something was near her.

She stopped dead in her tracks. It felt like the dark was right on top of her trying to grab hold of her. She felt scared.

'James, come on. Please, James, this isn't funny anymore. Just stop pissing around.'

She started walking slowly, past the old pub and up through the woods. She called out her boyfriend's name again, but nothing. She had the horrible feeling she wasn't alone. Strange thoughts kept flashing through her mind. She'd always felt scared up around these parts. Her mother's cousin was murdered around here some thirty years or so back. She turned around quickly as something brushed past her, but nothing. Again, it felt as if the dark was trying to grab hold of her.

'Come on, James. I'm sorry. I didn't mean what I said. Oh please, James. I'm scared now.'

'Now you know what I want. Just do it right. Don't mess it up.'

'Don't listen. Don't do it. Why? Don't kill her, not her. He'll find out, then we'll be in trouble.'

'Oh God, I might have known you'd show up. Just go away and leave me alone.'

'Why can't you just leave us alone? We don't need you. We don't need weak people.'

She felt someone behind her grab her by the arms. She struggled trying to free herself, but it was too strong. She kicked out at its legs. It screamed out in pain.

'BITCH,' it screamed at her.

It spun her around quickly, hitting her repeatedly in the face. Blows rained down on her. She tried to cover up as she fell to the ground.

'Please leave me alone. Please don't hurt me,' she screamed.

'Come on, just do it. Just do it.'

It stood over her and looked at the blooded mess that lay on the ground. It smiled as it kicked her time and time again in the face, blood and teeth splattered everywhere. It knelt down beside her, and in a frenzied attack stabbed her repeatedly. It stood up, dropping the knife. It looked down at the lifeless young body that lay on the ground. It felt good.

'I knew I could do it; told you I didn't need any help. I knew I wouldn't let you down.' It shouted at the top of its voice.

Doubts entered its mind as the enormity of what had happened started to flash through its imagination. 'What have you done? Why? Why her? He'll come for you. You know he will.'

'JUST LEAVE ME ALONE,' it screamed.

'Oh God,' he shouted as he sat up in bed.

He could hear a phone ringing, 'Bloody hell, the phone,' he shouted out loud.

He felt on his bedside table for his phone. 'Yes, Allen,' he said sleepily.

'Sir, sorry to wake you, Sir, but someone's found a body,' said the voice on the other end of the phone.

'Okay, where?' he asked.

'Up near the woods in Pangbourne, you know, by the river.'

'Have you called Inspector Walsh?'

'Yes, Sir, he's on his way right now. Shall I tell him you're on your way?'

'No, I'll tell him. Thanks, Richard.'

He lay back down on his bed. He checked the time, 05:15. He again started thinking back to Alison Woods. Another face came into his mind, that of Jane Davis.

Detective Inspector Walsh looked skywards. *Oh great, just great, rain. Why do murders always happen when it's raining?* he said to himself.

Inspector Walsh looked down at the body lying on the ground, a young girl no older than sixteen to seventeen years old. *Bloody hell, what a waste of a life,* he thought.

'Morning, Peter! Lovely morning for it. No, I'll say that again, lovely night; it is still the middle of the night and a Sunday at that.'

'Are Johnny, at last. I've been standing here for the last half hour or so, cold, wet and freezing my nuts off. The only two people I've had for company are this poor girl here and that poor old sod over there.'

Inspector Walsh pointed over towards an old man who was sitting on an old wooden bench.

Chief Inspector Johnny Allen turned and looked at the old man. He just sat there staring into space. Allen could see he looked shocked and visibly upset.

'Do we have a name?' Allen asked.

'Yes, an Alfred Webster. He rang the station about 5 o'clock, been out walking his dog.'

Allen walked over to the old man and smiled as he sat next to him. 'You okay, Sir?' he asked.

The old man looked at Allen and shook his head. 'Bloody hell, I've had better starts to the day. It was the dog that found her, poor girl. Can't be any older than about sixteen. Scared the living daylights out of me.'

'I'm Detective Chief Inspector Allen. Do you walk these woods much?' he asked.

The old man looked out over towards the river, 'Every day, Chief Inspector, have done for years. I've lived here all my life, seventy-eight years, man and boy; know these woods like the back of my hand.'

'Did you see anyone else around, Mr Webster?' Allen asked.

'No, no one; never is at this time. Peaceful you see, that's why I come early in the morning.'

'Okay, Mr Webster. I'd like you to give me any contact details, just in case we need to talk to you again.'

Mr Webster just looked over towards where the body was and nodded. He could see the old man was upset and in a state of shock. 'Is there anyone at home who can stay with you?' he asked.

'Yeah, my wife. And I'll call my daughter; she'll come around.'

Inspector Walsh checked his watch, 05:48. He knew it wouldn't be long before Doctor Westlake and the rest of the team got here. Walsh watched as

Allen patted the old man on the back. He felt sorry for the poor old sod. *What a horrible way to start your day,* he thought.

Allen looked back towards Inspector Walsh and the body of the young girl, *What a horrible way to die,* he said to himself. All he could think of was Alison Woods; same time, same place. It went over and over in his mind as he walked back towards Inspector Walsh.

Allen looked Walsh in the eye. He could see in Peter's face that this murder wasn't nice, but then again what murders are? He knelt by the girl and looked at her ripped-up body.

'Bloody hell, Peter, what a mess,' He said as he looked at the young girl in front of him.

Walsh hated this part of the job, a young life taken before it had even started.

'Right before—' Allen stopped midsentence, 'Oh bloody hell, not like this, not this way.'

'What's wrong, Johnny?' Walsh asked with some concern.

'This girl, I know this girl.'

'Who is she, Johnny?'

He stood up and turned to look at Walsh, 'Her name's Megan Davis, and going back over the last thirty-odd years, I've been having an affair with her mother,' Allen said, looking at the shocked expression on Walsh's face.

'Bloody hell, Johnny, she isn't your—' He stopped and then with a shocked trembling voice said, '—daughter by any chance?'

He stood just looking at Megan's ripped-up body, 'I don't know. To be truthful, it's something I've never really thought about.'

Allen turned and looked out towards the river. He wasn't sure…well, not one hundred percent anyway, was Megan his?

'I'm right in saying that there's a lot more to this story than the fact you've had an affair with this poor girl's mother?'

'Yeah, a hell of a lot more,' replied Johnny.

'Good morning to you both.'

Allen turned around and smiled at the man standing behind him. 'Morning, Chris. Lovely day for it,' he said, looking skywards.

'Right then, Johnny, what have you got for me then?' asked Doctor Westlake.

'This poor young girl found by an old boy walking his dog. Her name's Megan Davis. She's aged eighteen years old.' Allen watched as Doctor Westlake examined the body. She was half undressed, and what was left of her clothes were wet and muddy. She also had one shoe on, and the other was nowhere to be seen. Her face was covered in dried blood; she had blood on her top, a hell of a lot of blood.

'What we got then, Chris?' asked Allen, almost scared of the answer.

Doctor Westlake stood up, took off his glasses and rubbed his face, 'Don't know where to start, to tell the truth. This poor girl's had the best part of her insides ripped out. In over thirty years as a doctor, I've never seen anything like this, never.'

Allen looked at Doctor Westlake. He'd never seen the Doctor so shook up. Allen put his hand on the doctor's shoulder. He then bent down by Megan's body. You couldn't tell anything was that wrong to start with as she was half-turned on one side. He carefully lifted her mudded blood-stained top, his heart starting to beat faster and faster. He felt his hands starting to shake. Allen looked at Megan's ripped-up body. 'Oh bloody hell. Oh my God!' he said standing up, 'Who in God's name would do something like that?'

Inspector Walsh started to walk forward to look for himself. Allen stood in front of him putting his hand on his arm. He just shook his head, 'No, Peter.'

Inspector Walsh looked into Allen's eyes. For the first time, he could see fear in them. Walsh knew what he meant about evil; he could see it in his face. Detective Chief Inspector Allen had just seen what evil could do to another human, and maybe for the first time, even he was scared. What made Allen even more fearful was evil was still out there somewhere.

Walsh remembered what Allen had said the other day, 'Evil's out there, and it's only a matter of time before we come face to face with it.'

'You okay?' asked Walsh.

'No, not really. Don't worry, I will be,' he said as he turned to see what Doctor Westlake was doing. As professional as ever, the doctor had regained his composure and was examining the girl's body.

'If you ask me, Johnny, this poor girl was hit in the face at least four or five times. Wouldn't be surprised if her jaw was broken.'

'Anything else of interest?' asked Allen.

'Well, she's lost at least four to five teeth as well. I've never seen so many injuries; she's just been ripped apart. Look, Johnny, I'll get this poor girl moved, and I'll do a post-mortem as soon as possible.'

'Okay, thanks Chris.'

Allen watched as Megan's body was moved. No one said a word. He could see the shock on people's faces; he could see it in their eyes.

'I've no idea where to start with all this, Peter. I just don't know.'

Inspector Walsh looked at Allen. He seemed stressed and tired. It wasn't the case, not even a murder case; he had done hundreds in the past. However, he could see the look of shock and horror in his eyes at who the victim was. Was she his daughter?

'Do you want me to tell the family, Johnny?' Walsh asked, knowing it could be a hard and painful problem for Allen.

'No, I'll do it. It has to be me.'

Allen's thoughts turned to Jane Davis, Megan's mum. He hadn't seen her for about two years or so.

Well, to say he hadn't seen her wasn't true; they hadn't spoken to each other for a while. He'd seen Jane and her daughters around over the last couple of years or so. He knew how hard it was going to be telling her that Megan had been murdered. Maybe Peter was right, maybe he should tell her. It wasn't going to be easy coming from him, not with the history between the two of them.

Inspector Walsh knew there was much more to this story than Johnny was going to let on. He knew he wouldn't tell him everything, but maybe just bits of it, so he could make some sense of it.

'You going to talk then, or am I going to be left in the dark?' Walsh asked smiling at him.

Allen smiled and said, 'You're right. You need to know. But saying that, there isn't that much to tell. I first met Jane Woods as she was back then when I was fourteen years old. Not much happened to start with. In fact, it wasn't until a year or so later that we got together. You should see her, Peter, she's stunning; the most beautiful girl I'd ever seen. Back then, I was very shy, but as time went by and our relationship grew stronger, we ended up with a bigger problem, her father.'

'What about him?' asked Walsh.

Allen's eyes conveyed a look of fear. Turning to Walsh, he said with nervousness in his voice, 'He's ex Chief Constable Simon Woods.'

Walsh looked at Allen with a stunned expression, 'Bloody hell, Johnny, wasn't he your boss?'

'Yes. Truth is he didn't find out about the two of us until we were both in the police force. Fact is, until the day her father did find out, no one really knew.

Even as kids, we didn't tell a soul. We went on for about twenty-five to thirty-odd years, but by then we were both married to other people.'

'How did he find out?'

'Don't know for sure. Someone told him, or maybe someone saw us together and told him. Fair play to him, he didn't tell a soul. All he did was rip into the two of us, that's about it.'

Allen looked at Inspector Walsh and smiled. He could see what was going through Peter's mind. He didn't say a word. He didn't have to; his eyes said it all. Why Johnny Allen? Why? Very good question why. He'd never done things by the book. Most Chief Inspectors he'd worked under were not only good detectives but very good policemen as well. He himself was a great detective, but as a policeman, no; hated police work, hated every minute of it. He always remembered what Davidson once said, 'You're a bloody poor policeman. You'll never make an inspector the way you're going on.' And as ever, Davidson was right, but he did go on to say, 'You have one thing, one massive advantage over almost ninety nine percent of every policeman who's ever been in the force. Your mind. You see things others don't. You have just about the best mind I've ever seen.'

'What's wrong, Peter?' Allen asked.

Inspector Walsh half smiled, 'This is a right mess. I mean, bloody hell, Johnny, Chief Constable Simon Woods' daughter. I've only met him once, and he scared the shit out of me.'

'Tell me something I don't know,' Allen said, as he turned around just in time to see the small very rounded figure of Chief Superintendent Davidson rolling towards him.

'Oh great, what the bloody hell does he want? And things were going so well this morning,' Allen said sarcastically.

Chief Superintendent Davidson was a small tubby man, only about 5 feet 4 inches in height, but about 16 stone in weight. He always seemed to have a red face, and he sweated a lot, even in winter.

However, what made Allen laugh more about Davidson was he seemed to have no hair, not even body hair. But saying all that, William Davidson was a very, very good policeman.

Allen could see Davidson wasn't happy. Maybe he already knew it was Megan Davis. Davidson and Simon Woods went back a long way, have been friends for years. Both families were, in fact, very close. Allen knew this would hit Davidson hard.

'Morning, Sir,' Allen said as Davidson stood in front of him.

'Are, Chief Inspector.' He always started a sentence like that, always said 'are'.

'Is it true then?' Davidson asked sharply.

'By that you mean Megan Davis?' replied Allen.

Davidson didn't reply. He stood looking out into the distance. His mind must have been on Megan Davis and her family, and how the hell he'd tell Chief Constable Simon Woods.

'How was she killed, Johnny?' he asked, his gaze still taking him out towards the distance of the river.

Allen looked hard at Davidson. He looked visibly upset; his voice sounded shaky. He had trouble looking Allen in the eye; the past clear in his mind, all the trouble and the problems. Allen turned away. He didn't want to tell Davidson. He didn't want to tell him she'd been ripped apart, slaughtered like an animal. He just couldn't tell him. He didn't know how.

'I'm sorry, Sir, sorry,' Allen said. He turned away, unable to look Davidson in the eyes.

'Bloody hell, Chief Inspector, come on let's get this out the way right now. I told you years ago your past would catch up with you,' he shouted at him.

'How the hell did either me or Jane know her daughter would turn up murdered?' he replied angrily.

We're going to have a massive problem with all this, Johnny. Look, I don't want the press to find out about you and Jane. Do you understand?' he said. 'They'll have a bloody field day with it, a bloody field day,' he continued.

Allen knew Davidson was right. The press would love this. Even though he had some friends in the press, there were some of them that would love to see him fall.'

'Are, right then, I'll tell the Chief Constable, you can tell Jane. And Chief Inspector, go careful. It's been a long time. There's a lot of painful memories.'

Allen didn't say a word. He just watched as Davidson walked away from him. This is a nightmare; his worst dream wouldn't be this bad. Even though Davidson was right about the press, he knew it wouldn't be long before they got a whiff of a story—a story that could see the end of his career.

Allen turned to see what Inspector Walsh was doing. Maybe he'd let Peter lead the case. He knew he was way too close to it, but he knew Peter would want his help.

'Johnny, over here a minute. I've found something,' shouted Walsh.

Allen walked over to Inspector Walsh and held out his hand as Walsh dropped a gold chain into it.

'What do you think?' asked Walsh.

Allen looked at the chain, 'I'd be surprised if it's Megan's. This is a man's chain.'

Inspector Walsh knelt down near to where he found the gold chain, 'Bloody hell, Johnny,' he said as he stood up.

'What's wrong?'

Inspector Walsh handed Allen a gold Saint Christopher. He knew what it was straight away. Turning it over in his hand, he read the inscribed message on the back. 'To Johnny, all my love, Jane.'

Allen looked down at the Saint Christopher lying in his hand. He hadn't seen it for years. Couldn't remember how he lost it or even where or when.

'You alright, Johnny?' asked Walsh.

Allen gave the Saint Christopher back to Inspector Walsh, 'Read what it says on the back; read it out loud.'

Walsh looked at the inscription on the back and read what it said, 'To Johnny, all my love, Jane.'

Walsh looked open-mouthed at Allen; he found it hard to say anything.

'It's okay, Peter. I know what you want to say, and no, I've no idea how it got here either. She gave me this as an eighteenth birthday present. I thought I'd lost it, but it looks like it was stolen.'

'How long since you last seen it?' asked Walsh.

'I don't know. I've no idea.'

Allen knew Davidson would start to ask questions, but right now he didn't have any answers. No idea who would want to kill Megan and no idea why. The question that had got his mind going at a hundred miles an hour was his Saint Christopher. Who the hell had it all this time? And why place it by Megan's body? Something else that came into his mind was maybe Megan had it, but he found himself asking the same question, *How? And Why?*

'Come on, let's get this over and done with. I'll go and see Jane. You start the search down here. Let me know if you come up with anything.'

Walsh watched as Allen walked away from him. He seemed in shock, even scared. For the first time in the five years he'd known Johnny Allen, he could see fear in his eyes. Not just the fear of a killer being on the loose, but the real fear that the killer was after him.

Chapter 2

Jane Davis had just tried her daughter's phone for the sixth time in the space of about 15 minutes, but nothing. It hadn't even gone to voicemail. Oh, that girl. *What's the point of having a mobile phone if it's switched off,* she said to herself.

Jane looked at the kitchen clock on the wall, 07:12 in the morning. She'd been out all night, but nothing, not a word, despite trying some of her friends. All said the same thing, Megan left for home with her boyfriend James at around midnight. Jane was starting to get worried, even more so since speaking to James's mum; she hadn't seen or heard from him either. It was strange; both Megan and James always told them what they were doing, where they were going and what time they'd be home.

Jane looked at the clock again which seemed to have stopped. She walked into a large living room.

The room was well-decorated with bright colours. She liked bright colours; made her feel happy, made the room feel inviting. But today, the room seemed dark and uninviting. Even the large photograph of Megan and her other daughter Melissa seemed strange; they looked unhappy as if they knew something was wrong. She walked over towards a large bay window; the slatted blinds were half open. She opened them fully and looked outside. She didn't really expect to see anyone; it was more in hope than anything.

Jane sat down on a large light brown corner sofa. She looked at the phone that was on the glass coffee table. Maybe she should ring the police. She stopped with her hand hovering over the phone. *I'll ring just as Megan walks in,* she said to herself.

Jane sat unsure as what to do, thoughts going through her mind. She's okay. She's not a child anymore. She could hear Megan in her mind saying, 'Oh, Mum, you don't need to treat me like a baby. I'm grown up now.'

Jane stood up and walked back towards the kitchen. *I'll ring Megan, one more try,* she thought. She was just about to pick up her mobile phone, which was on the kitchen work top, when it rang.

'Hello, Megan, is that you?' she shouted.

'No, sorry Jane, it's Catherine. I've just had a phone call from the hospital. They've got James; an elderly couple found him unconscious about a mile from your house.'

'Is Megan with him?' Jane asked more in hope than expectation.

'I don't know. The hospital didn't say. Look, do you want me to come and pick you up?'

'No, I'll make my own way. You go to James. I'll see you later at the hospital.'

Jane walked back into the living room and looked out the window again. As she did a car pulled up outside her house. She didn't recognise the car, but she more than recognised the man sat in it.

'Oh my God, Johnny,' she said out loud, placing her hands over her mouth.

Her heart started beating faster and faster. She hadn't seen him for nearly two years. Her thoughts turned back to all the great times; they had been lovers for years since meeting as teenagers. She had never really gotten over Johnny Allen. In all the years, her thoughts were always on him. He was all she ever really wanted. She knew something was wrong; despite their past, why was he here? It had to be about Megan.

Allen sat in his car outside Jane's house. All the memories started flooding back, the excitement, the thrill of the affair, the thrill of not getting caught. He knew it was wrong, they both did. After all, they were both married.

Allen laughed to himself. It only seemed like yesterday; he'd missed Jane despite the fact it had only been two years. They'd always gotten on so well, always had a good laugh with each other. His mind turned back to Megan's murder. He knew telling Jane was going to be hard, very hard; not only seeing her for the first time in two years but telling her Megan had been murdered.

Allen stepped out of his car and walked slowly up the garden path. The garden looked like a picture as always, unlike his. Jane loved gardening, whereas he hated it. Allen stopped as he got to the front door. He felt his heart racing faster and faster. He rang the bell and turned away from the door. She took one last deep breath and opened the door. He turned back just as it was opened.

Standing in front of him was a lady. She was small in height with shoulder-length blonde hair and the loveliest light blue eyes you'd ever seen. Allen looked at her and smiled. She hadn't changed a bit, still as beautiful as ever.

'Hello, Jane.' Seeing her made him feel like he did when he was a teenager.

She looked at him open-mouthed, smiling shyly. He hadn't changed much, maybe a little older. His dark brown hair was maybe a little greyer, but not much. His brown eyes still had that sparkle, but she could see fear in them, as if he wanted to tell her something.

'Hello, Johnny, it's been a while. How are you?' she asked him nervously.

'I'm fine, and you?' he asked. He felt awkward. He was the same when they first met. It took him a good month to even speak to her.

'I'm good. I've been trying to find that oldest daughter of mine, but you know what teenagers are like.' She could tell by the look on his face that this wasn't a social call.

'What's wrong, Johnny?' she asked anxiously.

'Can I come in please, Jane?'

She smiled and walked back into her living room. He followed her in, his heart beating faster and faster.

'What's she done now then? Don't know what's got into that girl,' Jane said shaking her head.

'I'm sorry, Jane. I'm sorry, but we've found Megan, I'm sorry.'

'If only we can find that girl. Maybe I'll ring around some of her friends again, someone might have heard from her.'

'Jane, please listen to me. We've found Megan, I'm sorry.' But she didn't seem to hear him. She just carried on looking for phone numbers.

'Jane, please.' Allen walked over to her and placed his hands on her shoulders. He looked into her stunning beautiful blue eyes and whispered softly to her, 'I'm sorry, I'm sorry.'

She looked at him with tears running down her face and rested her head on his shoulder. 'I knew she was dead the moment I saw you in your car outside. I could see it in your eyes. How did she die, Johnny?'

'It doesn't matter now, Jane. It doesn't matter.' Allen held Jane close to him. It had been a long time since he'd held her in his arms. He'd missed her over the last two years.

'Johnny, Johnny, I need you. I'm sorry, I'm sorry. It's only you I love, and I've only ever loved you. I need you now. Please don't leave me.'

'Oh, Jane, my Jane, my darling girl. Look, I need to find out what happened to Megan, and to do that I need your help. God, I know this is going to be so hard for you. Look, is there anything you can remember, anything Megan might have told you or someone you've seen hanging around?'

She tried hard to fight back the tears. 'There is one thing,' she sobbed. 'About a week or so back, I was in town with Melissa. I can't be sure, but I think I saw Billy Reynolds. But it couldn't be Billy, could it?'

Allen looked surprised. He hadn't seen or heard from Billy in over twenty-odd years. 'Billy, I haven't seen or heard from him since he went to New Zealand.'

Allen's mind turned back to why he left so suddenly. He never said why. He just up and left; no note, no goodbye, he just left.

'Did Billy ever tell you why he left so suddenly?' asked Jane.

'No, but it was soon after Sian and Kevin were murdered. He was never the same after Alison was killed.'

'You were never convinced about Alison's murder, about Norman. I know he had his problems, but he was never a killer. He loved Alison, he wouldn't kill her. Oh, Johnny. Why? Who would want to kill Megan, my beautiful daughter?' She started sobbing.

He wanted to ask her about Megan, ask her if she was his, if Megan was his daughter, but he knew now wasn't the right time.

'What about Melissa? You're going to have to tell her, Jane.'

'Oh my God, Melissa. She's at a friend's house, been on a sleepover. Oh, Johnny, my poor baby. How do I tell her? I can't tell her. They were so close, always have been.'

'I'll be here if you want me to. You okay?' Allen said giving Jane a hug.

'Yes, yes, I'm with you. I've always been okay when I'm with you.' She felt guilty, but she wanted him so badly. The idea of loneliness and depression filled her heart with fear.

'You need to tell her father, Jane; Alex has a right to know his daughter's dead.'

'I know, I haven't seen him in about four years, haven't even spoken to him. He has written to Megan and Melissa, but not me.'

'When was the last letter?' he asked.

'About two weeks back. It's strange, his last two or three letters to the girls have been really cold, you know, no feeling, like it was written by someone else.'

'Does he still pay you money to help with Megan and Missy?'

Jane walked over towards a small cabinet. She opened a drawer and pulled out half a dozen bank statements, 'The 1st of every month, £400.'

Allen looked at the statements Jane had handed him. 'He was a good man, Johnny. Maybe I did love him in some way, but it was always you; it's only ever been you.'

Allen smiled, 'Same with me, I shouldn't have married Debbie. I never really loved her.'

Jane held his face softly and said, 'Since the day we first met, from that day to this, you're the only person I've ever loved.'

'Debbie knew about us, well, in the end she did. I had to tell her. Did Alex know?'

'Look we both tried to get over each other with other people, but however hard we tried, we were both still in the way. I don't know how much Alex knew about us. If he did, he never said anything.'

'Do you have any contact details for him?'

'Just an address, that's it. No phone numbers. I'm not sure if the girls had a phone number. He just up and left, you see; I woke up one morning and he'd left a letter on the bedside table. It wasn't a long letter. It just said, 'Sorry; I'm sorry, Jane. I do love you, but I know you don't love me; I've always known. Say sorry to the girls for me. Tell them I love them.

Allen found it strange. It sounded like Alex Davis didn't want to be found. He just sends the money each month and that's it. But any father surely would want to see his kids. He knew he would.

'Would you like me to find Alex for you?'

Jane didn't say anything, she just nodded and smiled. Walking over towards him with tears running down her face, she looked at him and put her arms around his waist and her head on his chest.

'Stay with me, Johnny. Stay with me tonight. I need you. I need you so much.'

He knew what he wanted to do. God, he wanted her so much, just to hold her, kiss her, even make love to her. 'Jane, I don't know. I've got a lot on. I get home late and I'm up early.'

She looked at him and held his face again. 'I understand, Johnny. It's okay, my darling.'

'Look, I'll come back later on, make sure you're okay. Do you want me to come with you and tell Melissa?'

'No, I'll be okay.' He looked at her. Even under the greatest stress of all, being told her daughter had just been killed, she still looked so beautiful.

'Jane, I'm sorry, so sorry about Megan, sorry about us. Every day, every second of every day, you're all I have ever thought about. I love you with all my heart.'

'Johnny, it's okay. I know. I know you do. Please catch this man for me; find out who killed our baby.'

Allen sat in his car for a minute or two. His mind was racing and his heart just as fast. He couldn't believe how gorgeous Jane looked. Both still had so much love for each other, so much passion. Allen was just about to drive off when his phone rang.'

'Yes, Allen.'

'Johnny, it's me,' came Inspector Walsh's voice.'

'Peter, what you got?' he replied.

'Not too sure, but any chance you could get over here?'

'Okay, on my way.'

It didn't take Allen long to get over to the woods where Megan's body was found. He pulled up outside an old pub which was on the main road; the river and the woods ran behind it. Once, it was nice here; it had a lovely garden; you could come here sit and watch the river and the world go by. Now it was just a broken-down old building.

Allen looked out towards the river; he could see the search was still ongoing. How could such a beautiful place become the scene of such horror? He loved coming down here as a kid, playing in the river and the woods. He laughed to himself when he remembered the old boat he and his friends would play in. Allen's mind turned to what Jane had said about seeing Billy Reynolds. Billy was his best friend; they'd been friends since the age of about four years old. Billy one day just up and left, no word, no letter, nothing. He only found out some five years later that Billy had moved to New Zealand.

'Johnny, how did it go with Jane?'

Allen turned around, 'Peter, about as well as can be expected. Hard part for her will be telling her youngest daughter Melissa that her sister has been killed. How are things down here?'

'Davidson wants the whole area searched, so I reckon we're here for at least another day or so.'

'Fair enough, if that's what Davidson wants, that's what he'll get. What have you found then?'

Walsh didn't say anything at first. He just started walking over towards where Megan's body was found.

'Come on, Peter, what is all this?'

Inspector Walsh stopped by a large tree about ten to fifteen feet away from where Megan's body was dumped.

'This Johnny, this is what all this is about,' Walsh said pointing at what at first looked like a necklace.

Allen walked over to where Walsh was pointing. Hanging on a tree was indeed a necklace, but hanging on it were four teeth.

'Bloody hell, Peter, what in the name of God is this?'

'Do you remember what Doctor Westlake said about Megan's teeth?'

'Yes, yes, I do. She had at least four to five teeth knocked out. Are you thinking what I'm thinking?'

'Yeah, but that's not all Johnny. He left a message…well, one message and a scribbled note. He inscribed the message on that tree.'

Allen looked at the large tree. Inscribed on it in capital letters were, JANE WOODS LOVES… then nothing. Allen looked puzzled at the inscription, 'Why this? Why not finish it? Why just leave it like this? What does the note say?'

Walsh pointed to the bottom of the tree. 'It's down there nailed to the tree.'

Allen bent down and read the note: 'MEGAN'S BLOOD IS ON YOUR HANDS, JOHNNY,' 'Bloody hell, Peter, it looks like it's written in blood.'

'We've got an even bigger problem with all this.'

'Which is what?'

'This wasn't here when we found Megan's body; this was placed here within the last half hour.'

Allen looked down at the message written in blood. He knew he was being watched. He had that feeling earlier; he felt uneasy. He stood still looking way out over the woods and the river. He felt strange. The whole situation felt strange.

'He's out there, Peter. He, evil, evil's out there. He's watching, waiting, playing games.'

'You okay, Johnny?'

'I don't know, don't know what to think. He's not after Jane or even Megan. It's me he wants, not them. All this, this isn't a random killing. He knew her, he knew Megan, but he's done it for one reason and that's to get at me. Megan just happened to be a pawn, a pawn in a chess game.'

'Who knows about you and Jane?'

'Not that many people, to tell the truth. Jane's mum and dad, my parents, my sister, Jane's brother, you and Davidson, that's about it. Billy Reynolds, an old school friend of mine, he knew, but Billy moved to New Zealand when we were in our late twenties. Truth be told, I haven't seen him from that day to this. Not sure how much he knew, to be truthful; if he did he never said. It has to be someone I know, someone who knew the secret between me and Jane.'

Allen's mind turned to Billy. The two were best friends, like brothers. He found it hard when Billy left for New Zealand. 'Billy was like a brother to me; we did everything together. But when we met Jane, Billy changed; he wasn't the same person. One day he just up and left, off to New Zealand.'

'Look, I'll stay here for a bit. When I've finished, I'll come back to the station, then we'll go over what we've got.'

'Okay, there's something I need to look over anyway,' Allen said as he walked back towards the old pub and his car.

Allen sat in his car and started driving. He started thinking about the murder of Alison Woods again.

Alison Elizabeth Woods was murdered on 24 September 1988. Her body was found at around 06:30 on the 25th. She was found in the woods along by the river in Pangbourne. She was eighteen years old. The images of Alison's ripped-up body started flashing into his mind. She was stabbed over fifty times. She was found half naked, but wasn't raped.

Norman Denman was arrested on the morning of 29 September 1988. His camera and bike were found near to where Alison's body was dumped. The police also found two knives; one was covered in Alison's blood but didn't have any fingerprints on it, the other had a trace of Alison's blood on it and Norman's fingerprints. What the police didn't take into consideration was Norman was always leaving his camera and bike lying around. He was always losing it;

anyone could have picked it up, but the only fingerprints found were his. Allen started thinking about Norman's interviews. Poor sod didn't have a clue. They just told him he was guilty, and he believed them.

Allen stopped his car and picked up his phone, 'Hi Robert, it's Johnny. Couldn't do me a favour could you, and dig out Norman Denman's interview tapes for me?'

'Bloody hell, Johnny, that's a name from the past. Do you need all the paperwork as well?'

'Yes, please, Rob, I'll be back in about ten minutes or so. Put them on my desk. And Rob, don't tell Davidson. Thanks.'

Allen knew Davidson would do his nut if he found out he was going back over the Alison Woods murder case. Who the hell would want to set Norman up? Okay, he was simple, but Norman wouldn't hurt anyone. He would get upset when Billy started teasing him, but it was all in good fun. His mind then turned to Billy's older brother Jackson. Jackson Reynolds was just plain straight horrible. He was a nasty piece of work, always in trouble. Jackson also seemed to take great pleasure in picking on Norman; he would get on at him all the time. Only person who ever stood up to him was Alison. He laughed to himself as he remembered one time when Jackson was having a go at Norman. She just walked up to him and hit him in the face; not a slap, a proper punch.

Allen suspected Jackson was more than likely Alison's killer. Something wasn't right. It had never sat right with him that maybe Jackson killed Alison. Anyway, he couldn't have killed Megan as he's still inside. He couldn't remember where Jackson was, but he could more than remember the case. Jackson Reynolds was sent to life in prison for the murder of Sian and Kevin Van Dalen.

Sian Andrews, as she was back then, was a dark-haired girl who lived three doors away from Jackson. She and Jackson were girlfriend and boyfriend. Jackson, however, made Sian's life hell. He would beat her up, verbally abuse her; he never seemed to take her out or buy her flowers. One afternoon, Sian and Jackson were out walking up near a park in Reading, when Jackson started on her. He was stopped by a man out running, Kevin Van Dalen. Van Dalen not only stopped Jackson from hitting Sian, but put him in hospital. Jackson was going to press charges against Van Dalen. He dropped the charges after Sian said she'd press charges against him.

After all this died down, Sian and Kevin got together and married about two years later. Jackson, on the other hand, had a massive problem with Kevin Van Dalen. He just couldn't take it, couldn't take the fact that Sian fell in love with Van Dalen. On the morning of 5 April 1996, Jackson Reynolds broke into the Van Dalens' house and just butchered them to death.

Allen sat at his desk just looking at the tapes and the notes from Norman's case. He wasn't really reading it, just looking at them. *How the hell could three of the most experienced policemen in the force at the time get it so wrong,* he thought. *Bloody hell, Norman was no more a killer than he was.* He picked up the first tape and placed it carefully into the tape machine.

'I'm Chief Constable Simon Woods. Also with me is Superintendent Davidson. The time is 07:30 on 29 September 1988.

Chief Constable Woods: 'You are Norman Stephen Denman of 18 Northcote Road, Reading?'

Norman Denman: 'Yes sir.'

Chief Constable Woods: 'Do you like girls, Norman?'

Norman Denman: 'Yes, Sir, I like Alison.'

Chief Constable Woods: 'Just Alison, no one else?'

Norman Denman: 'Alison and Jane are my friends.'

Superintendent Davidson: 'Both very pretty girls, Norman. Did they make you get excited?'

Norman Denman: 'I don't know, don't understand.'

Superintendent Davidson: 'Come on, Norman, you know what I mean? You remember? You went for a walk with Alison down by the river, and you tried it on with her, didn't you? You tried to kiss her, didn't you? But she pushed you away.'

Norman Denman: 'NO, NO, NO.'

Superintendent Davidson: 'Yes, yes, yes, Norman. Then you wanted to take pictures of her. Come on, you must remember that?'

Norman Denman: 'Yes, I remember. I did take pictures. I take lots of pictures.'

Chief Constable Woods: 'Norman, you then asked Alison to take her clothes off, didn't you?'

Norman Denman: 'Yes, Sir, she did. She wanted to swim in the river. I tried to stop her, but she didn't listen.'

Chief Constable Woods: 'You then got excited, didn't you? You then lost control seeing her like that. You tried to touch her. Again, she pushed you away, so you hit her and carried on hitting her. Then Norman, you stabbed her repeatedly.'

Norman Denman: 'NO, NO. SHE WAS MY FRIEND. SHE WAS MY FRIEND.'

Superintendent Davidson: 'Come on, do yourself a favour, son. Tell us the truth. You killed her, didn't you? You just couldn't help yourself, seeing her naked body like that. You got really turned on. When she said no, you just couldn't take it, so you just kept on hitting and stabbing her.'

Norman Denman: 'No, no, I didn't kill her, I didn't kill her. I love Alison. She was my friend. I ran away; I just ran away.'

Chief Constable Woods: 'Yes, Norman, you did run away, but only after you killed Alison. She got you so excited, sexually, you just couldn't control yourself, could you?'

Allen stopped the tape, just as his phone rang. 'Johnny, we've got an extremely beautiful lady down here for you, by the name of Jane Davis.'

'Okay Rob, calm down, calm down. I'm on my way.'

Allen showed Jane into his office. She half smiled as she looked around, 'This was my dad's office. God, it takes me back. He'd bring me in sometimes. I'd sit on a swing chair and just swing around and around, until either I got giddy or dad got fed up. Strange, only seems like yesterday.'

'Time flies, Jane.' Allen watched as she looked around his office. She was still so pretty. He couldn't get over how beautiful she still looked; but then again, he never could.

It was strange; when he first met her he was scared of her. Not because of who her father was, that would come later, but it was how stunning and beautiful she looked. He smiled to himself. Every red-blooded man from eight to one hundred and eight, everyone she ever met, even women, all said the same thing. Jane Woods, as she was back then, was just so beautiful. He often wondered what it would have been like if things had worked out differently between them, if her father had accepted him.

'Afternoon, Johnny,' Inspector Walsh said as he entered the office.

'Are, Peter, you okay?'

Walsh looked at Allen and laughed.

'What?' Allen said, looking puzzled.

'You sound like Davidson,' Walsh said with a smile on his face. Allen, for once, was lost for words, Peter was right. He'd been doing it a lot over the last few weeks or so. Starting a sentence with the word, 'are'.

'Peter, I'd like you to meet Jane Davis. Jane, this is Inspector Peter Walsh.' Walsh turned and smiled at Jane. She was stunning, so beautiful. He could see what Johnny meant when he said she was just about the loveliest girl you'd ever seen. She was about late-forties but only looked about mid-twenties.

'I'm sorry about your daughter, Mrs Davis,' Walsh said smiling at her.

'Thank you, Inspector, and please it's Jane. Are the toilets still in the same place, Johnny?'

'Just as you left them, Jane. To tell the truth, they're exactly as you've left them,' smiled Allen.

Both men watched as she left the office. Walsh turned to Allen and smiled.

'Bloody hell, Johnny, she's stunning, so beautiful. Her eyes, bloody hell, those lovely blue eyes, oh my God, what an angel.'

'You okay, Peter?' laughed Allen. 'I did tell you she was beautiful.'

Walsh looked at Allen and smiled. What he couldn't understand was, why if both Johnny and Jane had such strong feelings for each other, why not just be open with family and friends, then just get married. 'Why Johnny? Why not just be open with people about how you felt?'

'Two things, Peter. One, Johnny was very shy when we first met. I knew the first time we met he liked me, and to tell the truth I liked him, but it took him a while to tell me. Funny thing was, he did drop so many hints, and trust me, I gave him so many opportunities.'

Allen smiled and even went a bit red in the face. He watched her as she sat back down. 'It took me about a year to ask Jane out, and as for not telling anyone, well—'

'We enjoyed the excitement; you see it was our secret as teenagers. We just carried it on as we got older—once Johnny got over his shyness that was that.'

'I'm sorry to have to do this, Jane, but we need to find Megan's killer. Do you have any ideas why? Or who would do this?' asked Allen.

Jane looked at Johnny. She was finding it hard to fight back the tears. 'I'm sorry, Johnny, I don't know. I've no idea.'

'What about a boyfriend?' asked Walsh.

'Yes, she did, a lovely young man named James Clarke. They met at school. James also has a sister, Maddie. She's best friends with my youngest daughter, Melissa.'

'Did Megan and James go out last night?' he asked her softly.

'Yes,' she said, tears running down her face, 'to a nightclub with friends. It's called the J2, I think?'

'What about Melissa, would she know anything?' asked Allen.

'Not sure how important this is. About two weeks or so back, Missy was coming back from school, when she saw this strange man.'

'What did he say or do?' asked Allen.

'That's it, nothing. He was just standing by the bus stop; all he did was look at her. He didn't say anything, but she said he was having a good look at her. She also saw the same man standing on the other side of the road opposite our house.'

'Would she recognise him again?' he asked.

'Knowing Missy, yes, very much; she doesn't miss a thing. I'll bring her in over the next day or so.'

'You told me earlier about seeing Billy Reynolds.'

'The more I think about it, the more convinced I am it was Billy. I was walking in town with Missy, and this man just walked into me. As I turned around, he looked at me. He was older, yes, but yeah, it was Billy, I'm so sure about that.'

'I haven't seen or heard from Billy for over twenty years. He just up and left; no word, no goodbye, nothing. I don't know why.' Allen said.

'Look, Johnny, I've got to go. I need to get back to Melissa. Also, I said I'd find out how James is; he ended up in hospital, but I don't think he's too bad.'

'Can you let me know if he's back home? I need to speak to him as soon as possible.'

'Okay, will do. I'm not sure you'll get much out of him. He's taken it very badly; says it's his fault Megan was killed. Please come and see me, Johnny. I need to see you.'

Allen smiled at her. As he stood up, he gave her a kiss on each cheek, 'I will, Jane. I'll come around tonight.'

Jane turned to Inspector Walsh and smiled. 'Nice to meet you, Peter. Look after him for me. Keep him safe.'

'I will, Jane. It's been lovely to meet you.'

Allen watched from his office window as Jane pulled out of the station car park. He knew he had to find Megan's killer, not only for Jane but for himself.

'You okay, Johnny?' asked Walsh looking up from his computer.

'I'm fine, just thinking that's all.'

'About Jane?'

'Just thinking what might have been, that's all.'

Chapter 3

The room was dark, well, dimly lit at best. It was cold and damp. The room was small but not that cramped, a chair, an old table, and in a small box room an old metal bed—not that well-furnished. The damp smell wasn't that pleasant, but the smell of whiskey, good old whiskey, that's all he could smell. He looked at the bottle in his hand, his best friend. It would never, never walk out on him and leave him with nothing. It would never tell him he was his best friend, then when he needed a friend never be there for him. He looked at the bottle. It was as good as finished. He downed the rest and dropped the bottle on the floor. He tried to stand, but even for an alcoholic the drink had an effect on him.

Just about managing to stand, he looked at the wall in front of him. Most of the paint had just about peeled off it. It was the same with the others. This one was different, different in one way, for on the wall were pictures, hundreds of pictures of two people: Jane Davis and Johnny Allen. He picked up another bottle from off the table, opened the top and drunk a toast.

'To you Jane, the lovely Jane, and the great Johnny Allen.' He held up the bottle, pointed it towards the wall and threw it at the pictures. The bottle smashed against the wall, shattering into pieces.

'Now look what you've made me do. You've made me upset her, upset my true love.'

He fell on the floor and started smashing his hands on the broken glass. Even when he started bleeding, he didn't stop. It wasn't for at least another twenty to thirty seconds that he stopped. He knelt on the floor looking at the blood on his hands. Staggering to his feet, he started laughing uncontrollably, hysterically.

'Her blood's on your hands, Johnny, your hands. Megan's blood's on your hands. Soon it will be on Jane.'

He smeared blood on a picture of Jane, 'You see, Johnny, this is your blood on Jane, and soon her blood will be on you.'

He sank to his knees again and started crying, angrily at first, then uncontrollably. He looked at a picture in front of him. It was of Jane and Johnny aged sixteen years old. He laughed at it through the tears. He touched the picture. 'I loved her as well, Johnny. I loved her as well.'

Allen sat reading the case notes on the Reynolds murders. Jackson Reynolds stabbed and killed Sian and Kevin Van Dalen on 5 April 1996. She was twenty-six years old; he was twenty-nine years old. Kevin Van Dalen suffered thirty-eight stab wounds. Sian Van Dalen suffered forty-six stab wounds and a broken jaw. She was also so badly beaten facially that her own mother didn't recognise her. Both were pronounced dead at the scene.

Allen's mind flashed back to the bloody mess that confronted him that April morning, he'd never seen so much blood. One thing from that day that had stayed with him every day since, was a message written in blood on the dressing table mirror, 'FACELESS BITCH.'

Sian Van Dalen was an ex-girlfriend of Jackson Reynolds when the pair were in their late teens, early twenties. Jackson was however violent towards Sian, and often would beat her up. Kevin Van Dalen was Dutch born, to a Dutch father and a South African mother. The Van Dalens had moved to England when Kevin was eight years old.

One afternoon in the late summer of 1990, he put Reynolds in hospital. He was out running in a park in Reading when he came across Reynolds and his then girlfriend Sian Andrews. Van Dalen had just witnessed Reynolds hitting Sian in the face. As she fell to the ground, he slapped her twice around the head. Van Dalen confronted Reynolds and an argument started. Reynolds pushed Van Dalen over. As he got to his feet, Reynolds went for him again. Van Dalen then hit Reynolds four times, breaking his jaw and an eye socket.

Both Reynolds and Van Dalen wanted the other charged, but both dropped the charges. The police only became involved after Van Dalen had taken Sian to the hospital, where he admitted to a doctor what had happened. Reynolds was found on the steps of the Royal Berkshire Hospital in Reading; he had somehow managed to walk to the hospital but collapsed outside. Kevin and Sian started dating from that moment and married in January 1993.

'You alright, Johnny, you seem miles away?'

'I was just thinking about Kevin and Sian Van Dalen.'

'Jackson Reynolds, tell me about him. From what I can figure out, so far he sounds a right head case.'

'You're right there, Peter, he is. He was and still is a nasty piece of work, always in trouble. He's a year or so older than Billy. There's also a sister, Grace. She's two years younger than Billy. Billy and Grace were close, but Jackson didn't seem to have any time for either of them.'

Allen remembered their poor old mother: 'Their mother was a lovely lady, she was kind and would help anyone, but both Billy and Jackson would run her ragged. Billy in a fun sort of way, but Jackson was just plain straight horrible to her, but then again he was like that with everyone.'

'I've read up on the Van Dalen case. Bloody hell, talk about a revenge killing.'

'He'd planned it for years, Peter. He swore revenge once Van Dalen put him in hospital. After that it was just a matter of time. Jane hated him. She couldn't stand him, but she was good friends for a while with Grace. I believe she felt sorry for her.'

'Any chance he could have killed Megan?' asked Walsh.

'I don't know. I know this will sound strange, but it's not his style. Okay, yes, he fits the profile, but no, Jackson Reynolds didn't kill Megan, but Jack Reynolds may have. Anyway, I thought he was still inside.'

'No, he's out, has been for about a month or so. Any ideas where he may be living?'

'I don't know, probably giving his mum hell.'

'What about the sister Grace?'

'Not that sure, last I heard she was living in Oxford. Tell you what, you could check for me.'

'Right on it, boss,' smiled Walsh as he left the office.

Allen started thinking about Grace Reynolds. She was about two years younger than he was. She was painfully shy when she was younger, but nice. She was very fond of Jane; they both got on well.

Allen wondered if Jane had kept in contact with her at all over the years. It was worth asking her, especially if Peter didn't come up with anything.

Allen opened his draw and pulled out an old picture. It was of Jane; she was aged about sixteen years old. Her golden hair was worn down over her shoulders, her smile that made her light blue eyes light up like diamonds. She hadn't changed that much. He placed the picture back in his desk draw, looking up as he did, and seeing a very worried PC Simon Rogers stood in his office doorway.

'Sir, I think you need to come to the front desk.'

'What's wrong Simon?' asked Allen.

'It's a letter, Sir, in a big brown envelope, but there's a hell of a lot of blood on it. It's addressed to you, Sir.'

'Blood? Who the hell would put blood on a letter? How was it delivered, Simon?'

PC Rogers looked at Allen with a concerned look, 'Sir, it wasn't delivered as such. It's on your car. It's been placed under the front windscreen wipers.'

Allen followed PC Rogers down to the car park. He stood in front of his car and glared at the large brown envelope that was covered in blood. 'Simon, can you go and find Inspector Walsh for me?'

It took a couple of minutes for Inspector Walsh to get down to the car park. 'What's up, Johnny?' asked Walsh with some concern.

Allen looked at Walsh and pointed to the envelope that was placed under his car windscreen wipers. 'That's what's up,' he said uneasily.

'That's blood, bloody hell. Do you want me to take it off your car?'

Allen nodded; Walsh could see by the look on Johnny's face that this wasn't going to be anything cheerful. Inspector Walsh put on a pair of rubber gloves so not to get any blood on his hands or destroy any evidence. Carefully opening the envelope, he pulled out a white piece of paper. On it was a note written in blood.

'What does it say, Peter?' Johnny asked nervously.

Walsh looked at the piece of paper and read it out loud: 'HER BLOOD'S ON YOUR HANDS. MEGAN'S BLOOD'S ON YOUR HANDS.'

Allen looked at Walsh with fear in his eyes. 'What else is in it?'

Inspector Walsh pulled out not one but two photographs. 'Oh bloody hell,' shouted Walsh, throwing the pictures on the floor.

Allen picked up the photos. One was of Megan's ripped-up body, the other was of Inspector Walsh showing Allen the necklace with Megan's teeth on it.

'Bloody hell, Peter, I knew we were being watched, this morning when we found her body and that necklace. This evil son of a—' Allen stopped mid-sentence. He looked over towards the street that ran through the main town centre. He ran over towards the big iron gates that led into the station car park. Walsh followed Allen out into the street.

'What's wrong? What is it?' he shouted after him.

Allen shook his head and said, 'He's here. He's watching us. He's laughing at us, Peter.'

Allen looked up and down the street. He stood out in the middle of the road, looking at the rooftops and at the tall buildings.

He could feel the rage in his body. He could feel the anger building up inside. 'He's here. He's here,' he shouted. 'Come on then, come and get me. Come on, it's me you want, not Jane, not poor Megan, me; come on.'

Walsh looked over at Allen. He could see he was angry, maybe even scared. In the five years or so he'd been working with him, he'd never seen him like this. 'You okay?'

Allen turned to Walsh, and said, 'I'm fine. He's playing games with us. I know he's watching us. He's here.'

'Come on, let's get these pictures checked out. You never know we might find a blood match,' Walsh said as he looked at the pictures.

Allen took one last look around, but nothing. No one stood out, no one acting strangely. He slowly started to walk back inside. He started to wonder who this person was. It had to be someone he knew, someone who knew the truth about Jane and himself.

'Chief Inspector, Chief Inspector,' came a voice that echoed around the car park.

Allen didn't even turn around. He knew who it was. 'Great, now what?' he said to himself.

'Bloody hell, Peter, he always does it. He always turns up just at the wrong bloody moment. It's like a sixth sense,' whispered Allen.

But this time Davidson looked concerned. He didn't look angry or red in the face; he wasn't even sweating, which was something he did even in mid-winter.

'Johnny, you okay?' Davidson asked as he approached Allen.

'I'm fine, Sir. I'm okay.'

'Chief Constable Simon Woods is here. Any chance of your presence?'

'Yes, Sir.'

Allen watched as Davidson walked away. *That's going to be fun and games,* he thought.

'Now what?' asked Walsh.

'Great, if this isn't enough, Simon Woods wants a word.'

'Now, now ex-Chief Constable Simon Woods, if things had worked out different between you and Jane, he would have been your father-in-law.'

Allen looked at Walsh and smiled, 'Tell me something I don't know.'

'Look, I'll get these pictures checked out. Enjoy your meeting with daddy,' laughed Walsh.

'Ha ha ha, very funny.'

Allen stood outside Davidson's office door. He knew this wouldn't be fun, especially with Jane's dad, Simon Woods, being in attendance. Allen sighed. Part of him just wanted to tell Davidson, 'I'm done, I can't do it. Let Inspector Walsh handle the case.' After all, Peter was more than capable. He took a deep breath and knocked the door.

'Come,' came a booming voice from beyond the door.

Allen opened the door. Both Davidson and Woods were standing up looking out the window. The moment Allen walked in, Simon Woods turned around and glared at him. Time seemed to stop; the world at that point just froze. Woods didn't say anything; he didn't have too. Allen could see the displeasure in his eyes.

'Are, Chief Inspector Allen, please do sit down,' Davidson said pointing at a chair.

Allen sat down, glancing up at Simon Woods. The two had never seen eye to eye, even when he was younger. When he first became a policeman, Woods made his life hell. He was the main reason he couldn't marry Jane; it just wouldn't have worked. He wouldn't have let it.

No one was ever going to be good enough for his daughter, not even Jane's husband Alex; although he did accept Alex, but that was more to do with his well-to-do family. Woods looked at Allen not in a friendly way, but like a parent ready to tell a naughty child off.

Allen smiled to himself as he glared back at Woods. He remembered once when he and Jane were about sixteen years old and nearly got caught upstairs in Jane's bed. He just about stopped himself from laughing out loud as he thought about that afternoon. Both he and Jane had very little clothes on. In fact, he just had his underpants on, and Jane a pair of white laced knickers. The best part was, when they heard the front door open, you'd never seen two people get dressed so fast in all your life. The look on Woods face that day was the same as the look now.

'Okay, Chief Inspector, what have you got so far?' Davidson asked.

Allen knew he couldn't lie, maybe just not tell them everything. 'To tell the truth, not that much. So far we have a letter that was left on my car, and that's about it.'

'Any ideas who might have sent it?' asked Woods sharply.

'No, Sir. If I knew that, I would have found the killer by now.'

'Norman Denman; Chief Inspector, remember him?' Woods said angrily.

'Yes, Sir, I remember Norman, but what's this got to do with him?'

'He's killed once before, my niece Alison. Remember her, Chief Inspector?'

Allen remembered all too well the murder of Alison Woods. 'Come on, Norman Denman didn't kill Alison.'

'What?' shouted Woods. 'That man murdered my niece, Chief Inspector, and you'll do well to remember that. Tom Jameson did a good job; he was a good detective.'

'Sir, poor old Tom was well out of his depth; you know that, I know that, and anyone who had anything to do with the case knew that.'

'He was the only Chief Inspector here at the time, Johnny,' Davidson added.

'Yes, okay, but he was six months from retirement, and his drinking by that time had gotten out of hand. The press made him and this police station a laughing stock. Norman fitted the bill and that was good enough, good enough for you and the press.'

'I take it, Allen, you've seen my daughter again. You'll do well to leave her alone. Just do your job that's all. Find this killer. Find the bastard who killed my granddaughter.

'I'll do better than that. I'll find him and the person who killed Alison. As for me and Jane, yes, I've seen her again. We love each other, always have, always will, and you'll do well to remember that.'

Allen could tell he'd angered Woods. The two of them had never gotten on. It was okay to start with, but once he found out that he was in love with his daughter, that was it. He often wondered how much Woods knew about his relationship with Jane.

'Just one more thing, just between you and me; you've always known about Jane and me, haven't you?'

'Yes, I have; I could see it a mile off. The likes of you have never been good enough for my daughter, and you never will.'

'Not good enough. You pushed your own daughter into a loveless marriage. You have no idea, no idea at all, sins of our past.'

Woods didn't respond; he just stood glaring at Allen. In fact, both men just sat staring at each other for at least twenty seconds or so; both with as much hate in their eyes as the other, both refusing to look away.

'Okay, right you are, Chief Inspector, keep me up to date with any developments,' Davidson said ending the stare down.

Allen nodded, stood up and walked over to the door. 'And Johnny,' added Davidson, 'by the book, just do your job.'

Allen stood outside Davidson's office. Maybe he should have told them about his Saint Christopher that Inspector Walsh had found and that note on the tree. At the moment, he didn't think it important. At this point in time, he'd just keep it to himself.

'Are, Johnny, there you are. How did your meeting with Davidson and Woods go?' smiled Walsh.

Allen looked at Walsh and laughed, 'Peter, that's getting a bit boring now. As for the meeting, shit as always. 'Johnny, just do it by the book,' that's all the man has to say. Anyway you look happy with yourself. Tell me it's good news, please.'

'Well, I've found Grace Reynolds, and she's living in Newbury. She did live in Oxford, moved there to be closer to her brother. She said she found it hard going visiting him in prison. She wants to talk to you.'

'Do you remember me telling you about a man by the name of Norman Denman?' asked Chief Inspector Allen.

'Yes, wasn't he convicted of killing that girl...what's her name?' asked Walsh, tapping his hand on his head as he tried to remember.

'Alison Woods; she was found ripped apart in the same place Megan was found.'

'That's right. Didn't the press nickname him Norman Strange?'

Allen started thinking back to what happened that September day in 1988. He remembered it was hot, bloody hot. In his own mind, he was convinced Norman was innocent.

'Poor Norman had no idea what was going on, not a clue. He was simple you see. Okay, he was an adult, but he had a mental age of an eight-year-old.'

'You didn't have that much to do with this case, did you?' asked Walsh.

Allen shook his head, 'No, it was poor old Tom Jameson. Poor old sod was well out of his depth. The press and the public wanted someone caught and Norman fitted the bill to a tee.'

'Didn't the press hound Norman for days?'

'Yeah, mostly after they got hold of the story that poor old Norman was hopelessly in love with Alison.'

'But being in love doesn't make him a killer.'

'It wasn't so much he was in love with her; it was more a case of who she was.'

Allen looked up at Inspector Walsh. Reaching down he took out a newspaper cutting from his desk draw and handed it over to him. Walsh looked at the headline on the cutting dated 30 September 1988. GOT HIM, the headline said. Inspector Walsh read on: Norman Denman arrested for the murder of Alison Woods. 'Bloody hell,' said Walsh.

'I take it that from your reaction, you know who Alison Woods is?'

'Yes, I've just put two and two together. She was related to Jane, right?'

'Yes, you've got it in one. Cousin, she was Simon Woods younger brother Roger's daughter, only daughter at that. I knew her really well. She was nice, fun; you could have a good laugh with Alison.'

'What was the age difference between Alison and Jane?'

'Jane was about six months or so older. That's why Simon Woods wanted someone, anyone, for her murder. You should listen to Norman's interviews; God, two senior policemen, what a joke.'

'What about Norman, how old is he?' asked Walsh.

'Norman, he's about a year older than me. He's had a hard life, you know. His father, Norman Senior, was just horrible to him, wouldn't leave him alone. He was always on at him. He had a sister as well, Joan. She was about two years older than Norman. He'd do anything for her. She committed suicide; she hung herself. Story goes…now how true this is I don't know, but it was said that Norman raped her. But like I said, I've no idea how true it is.'

'Was he capable of something like that?' asked Walsh.

'Maybe, who knows? Norman had three things in his life, his sister, photography and Alison Woods. Alison wouldn't look twice at him, not in that way. He was a child in an adult's body. God knows what went through his mind.'

'In the report on Alison Woods, it said she wasn't raped. Surely if Norman had it in him, he would have raped her.'

'That's what I believe. You see, he's strong, very strong. Alison wouldn't have stood a chance. If he wanted to rape her, she wouldn't have been able to fight back, or so it was said.'

'Okay, but if he did kill her or rape her, she would have at least put up some fight; she would have struggled.'

Allen smiled and said, 'You've got it in one, Peter. As far as I know, Norman didn't have a mark on him, not even a scratch. You see, Woods and Davidson played on the fact that Norman was very strong and said he overpowered Alison. But I don't get it. As you said, she'd put up some sort of struggle.'

'Something else I don't understand. If he has a mental age of a child, he wouldn't have loved her or had feelings for her, as say we would, you know, sexually.'

'Norman saw Alison, and Jane, for that matter, as friends. You are my friend, he would say. He was always saying it. And if he saw you as a friend, he told you he loved you. If Norman did murder Alison, there's no way in hell he could have planned it. The only way he had anything to do with her murder was to have someone tell him, force him to do it. Someone who could control him, *You'll be in trouble, Norman, if you don't do as I say. It's you or her.*'

Allen stood up. Just as he was about to walk out of his office, his phone rang. 'Hello, DCI Allen.'

'Johnny, it's Jane. Megan's boyfriend James Clarke, well, his mother has just called me. He's back home and he wants to speak to you.'

'Okay, do you have an address?'

'Yes, it's 106 Sulham Close. It's only about a five-minute walk from my house.'

'Right, thanks darling, I'll come and see you later.'

'Okay, honey, bye.'

'Don't tell me, that was the lovely Jane.'

'No, it was Davidson,' Allen laughed.

'Okay, whatever takes your fancy,' Walsh said laughing.

'No, it was Jane. James Clarke, Megan's boyfriend, well, he's out of hospital and wants to speak to us. Come on.'

Walsh stopped and looked at Allen with a strange look on his face as if to say haven't you forgotten something.

'What?' Allen said holding his hands out.

'Just before Jane called you, you were on your way somewhere?'

'Was I? Oh yeah, toilet, I nearly forgot. Old age you see, losing my mind.'

Catherine Clarke looked at her son with concern, the concern that only a mother would have for a son. She wanted to know what happened, but James hadn't said anything, not a word. He just sat in a chair staring into space.

'I know it's hard, James, but you need to talk. The police will be here soon.'

Catherine stood in front of her son, but nothing. He just sat there; no expression, no emotion.

'James, it was you that said about talking to the police. It's your idea.'

'I will,' he mumbled.'

'Now's your chance then, because here they are.'

Catherine opened her front door as the two detectives got out of Allen's car. *So that's Johnny Allen then,* she said to herself.

Allen half smiled as he looked at Mrs Clarke. He'd seen her before, out with Jane. She was taller than Jane, which wasn't that hard. She had dark brown eyes and light brown hair. She looked worried and anxious, understandably so.

'Hello, you must be Chief Inspector Allen. I'm Catherine Clarke.'

'Hello, yes, I am, and this is Inspector Walsh.'

Catherine Clarke showed the two detectives in. Allen looked around. The house was the same as Jane's, same layout. A teenage girl aged about sixteen looked at him and smiled.

'Hello, I'm Maddie. Do you know Jane Davis?' she asked.

Before Allen could speak, James looked at him, smiled and said. 'Oh yeah, that's right. Megan told me about you and her mum.'

'Yes, I do. I've known Jane for years,' replied Allen.

'She's beautiful, so pretty,' Maddie said with a big smile on her face.

'Come on now, Maddie, I'm sure Chief Inspector Allen doesn't want to hear about all this. He's a very busy man,' responded Catherine, giving her daughter a look only a mother could give.

'Yeah, boghead, we all know you love Jane, or shall I say Princess Jane,' James sneered at his sister.

Maddie turned around, looked at her brother and poked her tongue out at him. Allen turned to Inspector Walsh and smiled, 'You've got all this to come, Peter.'

'How old are your children, Inspector?' asked Catherine.

'I've got twins, a girl and a boy aged nine years old, and it's great fun,' Inspector Walsh said smiling.

'I'd like to ask you some questions, James, about last night. What time did you and Megan go out?'

'Well, I met up with Megan about 7:30 pm.'

'Where did you meet up?' asked Allen.

'Outside her house. It's only five-minutes around the road, but you already know that,' James said smiling.

'After that, where did you go?' Walsh asked.

'Well, we got a bus into town, number 15. We then met up with some mates, ended up in Pizzaland. After that, we went to the J2 nightclub.

'Was that you, Megan and your friends?' asked Allen.

'No, just the two of us. Some of the others got there later. We got there around 9:30 pm, stayed until around 12ish.'

'Is that not a bit early? Surely nightclubs don't get going until 11 o'clock time,' Allen said.

'Megan didn't feel that well. She was, to be truthful, a bit drunk. Look, Mr Allen, I'm sorry about this, but you'll probably find this out anyway; she took drugs.'

'Oh, James, why? You bloody kids, stupid boy,' shouted his mother.

'I'm sorry, Mum, sorry,' he said looking at the floor.

'Bloody hell, boy, you won't find the answer on your shoes. What's Megan's mum going to say? She's my best friend, Oh sorry, Jane, but my idiot son gave your daughter drugs.'

'What did she take?' asked Allen.

'Not sure, Sir. This man came up to us and gave us them. He was older than us, about your age. I'm sorry, it happens a lot in clubs, I think I'd recognise him again.'

'Okay, good. What happened after you left the club?' asked Walsh.

'Well, Sir, she had an argument with someone. You see, this man came up to Megan and said she shouldn't be taking drugs. But it was strange. It was as if he knew her. He didn't say "oh Miss" or "sorry love, but you shouldn't be taking that," he called her "Megan". He seemed a bit thick, you know, slow.'

'Maybe he did know her,' Allen said, turning and looking at Walsh.

Walsh could see by the look Allen gave him that he knew who it was.

'I asked Megan if she knew him, but she didn't have a clue who he was, no idea. One thing, Megan turned around and said, 'What the hell has it got to do with you, you're not my father.' He then just stood there gawping at her, not saying a word. Then he just disappeared.'

'Was he old or young?' Allen asked.

'Old, older than me, again, about your age. But he looked strange; he looked out of place.'

'After that what happened?'

'Megan got upset. That's when she wanted to go home, but I wanted to stay. We then had an argument. She stormed out. I followed her out of the night club, but I lost sight of her. After about five minutes or so of looking for her, I walked over towards the taxi rank, but she'd gone. After that, I can't remember much, only waking up in hospital.'

'Okay, James, look, I'll need to talk to you again. So I'd like you over the next day or so to come down to the station to check over any CCTV tapes that we may get from the nightclub.'

'Yes, Mr Allen, and I'm sorry about the drugs. It won't happen again.'

'I hope not, James. Anyway that's not my priority; finding Megan's killer is.'

Allen and Walsh were stopped outside by Maddie Clarke just as they were about to climb into Johnny's car. She was holding a white plastic bag. Allen could see the young girl looked really anxious and very nervous.

'Maddie, you okay?' asked Allen.

'No, not really. This was given to my mum earlier when she was at the hospital with James. I don't believe she even looked at it. I was doing some washing, it's one of my chores, so I checked in the bag and found this.' She handed Allen the plastic bag, he opened it and took a look.

'I take it this is James' shirt?' he asked. Inside was a light blue shirt that was covered in blood.

'I think so, yes. Look I don't want to get my brother into trouble, but I'll be honest with you, I was going to hide it, but—' the young girl looked at Allen with tears in her eyes.

'Look, don't worry, Maddie, you've done the right thing. Thank you.'

Maddie quickly ran back inside. She seemed really scared, unsure whether or not she may have got her brother into trouble.

'Job for forensics, me thinks,' Walsh said, looking at the shirt.

Allen sat in his car. He didn't say anything. He didn't even start the engine. He just sat staring into space.

'You okay?' he asked.

Allen turned and looked at Walsh; Peter could tell something was wrong. Johnny was way too close to this case, too close to make the right decision. 'Why don't you take some time off, Johnny? I've got this. Go and clear your mind. You may see thing's different in a couple of days or so.'

'No, I'm okay.'

'Look, Johnny, ask her. Ask Jane about Megan. Even if she's not your daughter, at least you'll know for sure.'

'Maybe, I don't know yet. Come on, let's go and do your most favourite thing in the whole wide world.'

'And what's that?' he replied.

'Watching telly,' smiled Allen.

'Oh joy, what's on today then? No, don't tell me; drunks and people acting bloody stupid,' laughed Walsh.

Chapter 4

He looked back at the person looking back at him. He pointed at him and said. 'You see what you've gone and done now? You killed her. You killed that girl, Johnny's girl. He'll come and get you for it.'

'Are you so bloody stupid? Allen doesn't know anything; he doesn't even know she's his daughter. You've had your moment, now it's my time. Thirty years I've waited for this, thirty years of being second best to you.'

'That's shit. You've had your chance over the years. You've gone and done it now; not Allen, not Johnny Allen.'

'You're scared of him. the great "I am", scared of a bloody copper. You've always been weak, the weaker one of us. But me, I'm strong, and you'll bloody well do as I say, weak, fucking weak.'

'NO, NO, NOT ALLEN,' he screamed. Tears started to run down his face. He looked at the person who was now laughing at him, shouting at him, 'WEAK, WEAK, WEAK.'

'NO, NO, NO.' He picked up the half-drunk whiskey bottle and smashed it against the mirror. The bottle and the mirror shattered into hundreds and hundreds of pieces.

'Now look what you've made me do.'

But the laughing didn't stop. 'WEAK, WEAK, WEAK,' it laughed.

'NO, JUST LEAVE ME ALONE. JUST LEAVE ME ALONE,' he screamed.

Allen walked into his office. He sat at his desk and rubbed his eyes. He knew Peter would be some hours with the CCTV tapes. He looked at his tape machine which had a tape from Norman Denman's murder case interviews. He knew what would be on the tape. The whole case was a joke from start to finish. He reached forward and pressed play. The first voice he heard was that of Norman.

Norman Denman: 'No, Sir, I didn't. I don't do that.'

Chief Constable Simon Woods: 'So you're telling me you're not like other men. A pretty girl starts taking her clothes off and you don't get turned on?'

Norman Denman: 'Alison was my friend. She was my friend.'

Superintendent Davidson: 'Do yourself a favour, come on we know what you've done; you know what you've done, Norman. The sooner you tell us the truth, the sooner we can help you.'

Chief Constable Simon Woods: 'Right, no more shit, Norman. You went into the woods with Alison. You wanted her, but she didn't want you. You then lost control when she started to undress. She just wanted to go swimming, but you wanted more. Then you started taking pictures, but you wanted more. You wanted to touch her, didn't you, but she pushed you away. You then started hitting her. Then you ripped her apart. You're a sick bastard. She was my niece, you sick, sick bastard.'

Superintendent Davidson: 'SIR, SIR, that's enough, Sir. Norman, we've found your camera and your bike. Come on son, she said no, and you lost it. Then you killed her. That's right, isn't it?'

Norman Denman: 'Yes, I did, Sir, YES, YES, YES. YOU'LL HELP ME NOW?'

Allen turned the tape off. *Bloody hell, this is a joke. I can't listen to any more of this. I've got to get out of here.*

'Hi Johnny, what's wrong?' Walsh said, answering his phone.

'Look, I've got to get out of here for an hour or two,' replied Allen.

'No problem, where are you going?'

'To see a friend,' Allen laughed.

Walsh smiled to himself. He stood at a small window as he watched Allen pull out of the car park. He knew where he was going. He knew he was going to see Jane. Deep down, he wanted them to get back together, make a real go of it. It was so obvious they still had strong feelings for each other. He could tell by the way they looked at each other. But he couldn't understand why they didn't marry. Maybe they enjoyed the secret, added to the fun.

Allen knew what he had in his mind was wrong, but he couldn't get the feeling out of his head. He looked into her stunning blue eyes. She looked as beautiful as ever. He wanted to touch her, touch her body, make love to her. It had been too long, way too long.

'This is so bad Jane, but—'

54

'Don't say a word, darling,' she said putting a finger to his lips.

She didn't need words at this point; just having him here was enough. Pulling her close, he kissed her passionately on the lips. All the passion came flooding back. She took hold of his hand and led him upstairs. As he followed her, he started to remember the first time they'd made love, aged sixteen; first time for both, and scared to death.

He remembered at first they both just lay on the bed looking at the ceiling, neither saying a word. Both didn't have a clue what to do or what to expect.

She stopped at the bedroom door; he knew what she wanted him to do. He smiled at her as he picked her up in his arms. He carried her and lay her down on the bed. It was something he'd done hundreds of times before.

'You okay? That was really nice,' she said with a naughty glint in her eyes.

'Yeah, fine,' he said smiling at her.

She turned and looked at the clock. *Oh God,* she thought to herself, *it's 4:45 in the afternoon, how bad is that?* 'Johnny, it's quarter to five, Melissa will be back soon. She's still at Maddie's, thought it best. I can't believe she's gone Johnny, my poor, poor baby. God, I feel so guilty. My daughter's dead and here we are in bed.'

'Oh, Jane, don't. You'll make me feel guilty as well. Look, I need to speak to Melissa, just to find out who she might have seen, you remember, at the bus stop and outside here.'

'Okay, I'll bring her in tomorrow morning.'

'I'm worried, Jane. This madman's not going to stop until I catch him. Just be careful, okay. Tell Melissa the same; anyone you're both not sure about you ring me, okay?'

'I will. Can you stay with me tonight, please?' she asked him softly.

'Okay, okay, I will,' he said.

Allen popped his head around the door which led to a small office; an office which had a video recorder, a desk and a chair, and one very tired looking Inspector Walsh.

'Morning, Peter, a bit early for this kind of thing, even for you. Hey, does Amy know what you watch on telly?' Allen said as he looked at the small screen.

'This is great, just bloody brilliant, the things some people do. This bloke just brought this young girl a kebab. He then handed it over to this girl, and then he just threw up all over the girl and the kebab. Bloody brilliant.'

'Best thing for it really. Have you seen what's in these kebabs? Besides, if someone was sick in it, who the bloody hell would notice anyway.'

'Amy's sister loves the bloody things. Picked them up after a night out the other week, and there's Rachel, kebab in hand. Spent about a week trying to get the smell out of my car.'

'I'm surprised at that; Rachel has a lovely figure,' smiled Allen.

Walsh looked at the expression on Allen's face. His mind then raced to his sister-in-law, the very lovely Rachel. 'Yes, she has. We went around to her house the other week, and she was doing some telly workout video when we got there. Oh my God, Johnny, you should see what she was wearing; didn't know where to put my eyes or what to look at first.'

'I must go and see your sister-in-law sometime soon. What time of day does she do this work out video? Anyway, what have we got then?'

'Not much really. No one stands out.'

'Maybe we'll get James Clarke to have a look. Right, come on. I'd like you to meet someone,' Allen said with a smile on his face.

Inspector Walsh stopped the video tape and followed Allen out of the small office and up two flights of stairs. He'd often wondered why he and Johnny were put on the top floor. Every morning, well, most mornings, he'd walk up three flights of stairs. Some days not once or even twice, sometimes six to seven times a day, up and down.

'Tell you what, who the hell needs a workout video; up and down, up and down,' laughed Walsh as he puffed out his cheeks.

Walsh followed Allen into his office. Sitting at Allen's desk, swinging around and around on his swing chair, was a young girl aged about fourteen to fifteen years old. The girl stopped swinging around as the two detectives entered the room. As she stopped, Inspector Walsh could see that sitting at Allen's desk was an angel. She had long golden hair, and Walsh could see that like her mother, she had just about the loveliest light blue eyes you'd ever seen. Walsh looked at her open-mouthed. If her mother was beautiful, then this young lady was every bit as.

'Peter, I'd like you to meet Melissa Davis. This is Jane's youngest daughter, as you can probably see.'

'Yes, I can see that. Good morning Melissa. You are every bit as lovely as your mother.'

The young girl smiled and said, 'Thank you.'

'Melissa seems to think she may have seen the man from the nightclub, you know, the one who spoke to James and Megan. You see, I spoke to Jane and Melissa last night and asked if she remembers seeing anyone hanging around. Jane couldn't remember, but Missy seems to think she can.'

'It was about a week ago. I'd just got back from school, which was around quarter to four time. I noticed this man; he was standing over the road from our house. It was strange as he seemed to be just staring straight at it, you know, like he was watching it.'

'What did he do when he saw you?' asked Allen.

'Well, he saw me just as I got to the corner of the road; it was like he knew who I was. Then he watched as I went in. He then stood there for about a minute or two, then he went. It was like I just said, it was as if he knew me, but I'd never seen him before in my life.'

'Can you remember what he looked like?' asked Walsh.

'I can do better than that,' she smiled. 'I've drawn a picture of him. You see, art's one of my best subjects. I'm doing 'A' level a year early.'

Missy reached down beside Allen's desk and picked up a black art folder. She pulled out an A4 art pad and held it up for both Allen and Walsh to see.

'Melissa, have you ever thought about being an artist? This is brilliant. But then again, your mum was very good at art,' replied Allen.

Melissa smiled, 'She still is. I've seen the oil painting she did of you. It's very lifelike, I can see that now,'

'I remember that painting, had to sit for hours. Okay, I'd like you to go with Inspector Walsh and WPC Stevens. What we're going to do is, first, I'd like you to look through a video, just to see if you can spot anyone you might know. After that we're going to do a photofit picture with the help of your drawing, okay?'

Allen looked at Melissa and smiled. Poor kid; must be so hard to lose a loved one so young. Yet, even at the age of fifteen years old, she seemed so grown up and so very much like her mother. He couldn't get over how much like Jane she was, not only in looks but in mannerisms.

He watched from his office door as WPC Stevens walked Melissa down to the video room. His mind was full of memories about Jane. Seeing Melissa took him back to when they first met.

Inspector Walsh walked up behind Allen and placed his hand on his shoulder. 'You okay, Johnny?' he asked.

'I'm fine,' he said, turning around. 'Well, what do you think of Melissa then?'

Walsh smiled, 'She's lovely, so very much like her mother. She's going to be a real heartbreaker, Johnny.'

'Going to be? She already is, Peter,' Allen said laughing.

Melissa sat watching the video, but so far, she'd seen nothing or anybody she recognised, only Megan and James. It amazed her what people got up to on a night out. She thought it funny what people did when drunk.

'Seen anything as yet?' asked Walsh.

'Sorry, Inspector, so far not much. Is this really what people do on a night out?' Melissa asked pulling a face.

Inspector Walsh laughed, 'I'm afraid so, Melissa. Trust me, I've seen some real sights on these videos.'

'I don't think I want to go out or get drunk, if this is the mess that people get into.'

'Glad to hear it,' smiled Walsh.

'Oh, that's…no,' she seemed confused. *Was it who she thought it was? No, that's silly,* she said to herself.

'What's wrong? Have you seen someone you know?' he asked.

'No, it's nothing. Just this man reminded me of someone, that's all. Hey, that's him; that man just going into the nightclub, that's the man in my picture,' Melissa shouted excitedly.

Walsh stopped the video and looked at the man who was just about to enter the nightclub. *Bloody hell,* he said to himself, *it's the same man.*

'Are you sure about this, Melissa? You one hundred percent sure it's the same man in your picture?'

'Yes, Inspector, it's him. It's the same man who was standing outside my house.'

Walsh looked hard at the man on the video. Who the hell was he and what was he doing? Walsh turned and looked at Melissa. She was drawing the man on the video. She was drawing the same man she'd seen outside her house. He was amazed at just how good she was; not just good but brilliant.

'There you are, that's him,' she said holding up the picture. 'Do you know who he is?' she asked.

'Okay, what's new then?' Allen asked as he entered the video room.

Walsh looked up from the video, 'Johnny, right. First off, Melissa has recognised someone from the CCTV video, and she drew this.

'Let me look?' asked Allen.

Walsh handed Allen the picture. He looked closely at it, 'Melissa, can I have a look at the other picture you drew?'

'Yes, sure,' Melissa smiled, as she handed Allen the other picture.

Looking at both pictures carefully, he suddenly smiled as he realised who it was. 'That's it. It's been going around in my head all night. All I could think of was Norman's photos, which were brilliant by the way, then this, brilliant pictures.' Allen held up both pictures, and said, 'Norman Denman.'

'I've never met the man, but he doesn't sound like someone who'd go to nightclubs,' replied Walsh.'

'Thank you, Missy, you've been brilliant.'

'No problem. I just want to help Megan. I loved my sister. She was brilliant, so kind, so caring.'

'Okay, how are you getting back home?' he asked the young girl.

'I don't know. To be truthful, Mum's at the doctor's,' she replied.

'Okay, I'll get someone to take you. I don't want you to go home on your own.'

Allen watched as WPC Stevens took Melissa down to a waiting car. He had questions to ask, but he didn't want to ask them in front of her. One question going through his mind was, *What was Norman doing in a nightclub?*

'Anything else?' Allen asked.

'Megan's post-mortem, nothing much in it that we didn't already know. She lost six teeth and suffered a broken jaw. She also had a massive blood loss. There are signs of sexual activity, but what with her relationship with James, that answers that question.'

'I'd be very surprised if there was anyone else. She wasn't raped, besides that's not our killer's style. He's not in it for anything sexual. That's not how he gets his kicks.'

'We've also got a blood match back from the note that was left on your car, also, for the note left near Megan's body. And guess what? He used Megan's blood.'

'No surprises there then. I believe he did all these notes there and then.'

'What? Seconds after he murdered her?' asked Walsh.

'Yes, he had all this in mind. I know this sounds strange, but it's me he wants, not Megan.'

'So why not just come after you?'

'He wants me to suffer. Come on then we're going to see James Clarke again. I'm going to show him the pictures of Norman, see if he recognises him.'

'What about James as Megan's killer?' he asked.

'It had crossed my mind; after all, he was closest to her. Yes, he may have loved her, but people in love do kill.'

Mrs Clarke was worried about her son; he seemed lost, not surprising, considering what had just happened. 'James, James, are you planning on getting up sometime today?' she shouted at him.

'No, what's the point? Leave me alone,' he shouted back.

Allen pulled up outside Mrs Clarke's house.

'He's hiding something, Johnny; he knows more than he's making out.'

'About what?' asked Allen.

'Leaving the nightclub. Remember he said he lost sight of Megan? Sorry, I can't believe that.'

Allen didn't reply. He rang the bell and waited. 'Sorry to bother you again Mrs Clarke, but I'd like to talk to James again.'

'No problem, Chief Inspector. Hopefully, he'll tell you the truth, as he certainly hasn't been very truthful with me.'

Allen seemed a bit surprised at what Mrs Clarke had just said. Most parents go out of their way to protect their kids; some even lie to protect them.

'James can you come here, please? It's the police.'

'Bloody hell, what now? Can't these people just leave me alone?' he shouted.

'James, James, did you hear me?' she called up to him, 'God, that boy.'

'Okay, okay, I'm coming,' he shouted. As he entered the living room, he looked straight at Allen. He didn't take his eyes off him the whole time.

'How's the lovely Jane then Chief Inspector? Did you have fun last night? I overheard Maddie talking to Melissa. She said you stayed the night.'

Allen didn't respond. He didn't say a word. He just stood there staring at him.

'James, don't be so rude. Look, I'm sorry, Mr Allen,' Catherine said apologetically.

'I'm sorry, Sir. I didn't mean to upset you. I'm sorry,' James said sheepishly.

James didn't look at Allen. He just sat staring at the floor. Allen knew he didn't mean anything by it. He was just trying to be clever.

'That's okay, James, don't worry about it. It's okay. Right then, I'd like to show you these pictures, just to see if you recognise anyone,' Allen said handing James the two pictures.

'Melissa drew these, didn't she?' he asked, smiling at the pictures.

'Yes,' Allen said, nodding.

'She's brilliant at art, always has been,' he added.

James looked hard at the pictures, 'Yeah, that's him. That's the man from the nightclub, you know, the man who said to Megan about taking drugs. Is he the killer? Did he kill Megan?'

'I don't know yet, James. Have you seen him around anywhere over the last few days or so?'

'No, the first and only time I've seen him was at the nightclub, that's it.'

'He was spotted outside Jane Davis's house about a week or so ago by Melissa, that's when she did the drawing. She also recognised him from CCTV videos, as he was just about to go into the nightclub.'

'Can I take a look, Mr Allen?' asked Mrs Clarke. Allen handed the pictures over. She looked closely at the two drawings.

'Hey, I've seen this man before. I know who he is. I saw him the other day. I'd been into town with Maddie; he was standing at the bus stop when we got back home.'

'Which stop is that?' asked Walsh.

'The one just over there, just by the corner where the two roads meet,' Catherine replied pointing out the window at the bus stop.

'What made you remember him?' asked Walsh.

'It was Maddie really, Inspector. She turned around and said to him, 'Are you having a good look at me?' He seemed transfixed by her. She called him an old pervert.'

Allen turned to Inspector Walsh, 'Peter, can you do me a favour. Ring a lady called Alice Denman, she's Norman's mother, and check if he's okay?' Allen said handing Walsh his phone, 'It's under, A. Denman.'

'That name Denman, I've heard that name before. Yes, that's right. Didn't he kill Jane's cousin, Alison, Alison Woods?'

'Yes, you may well be right, Mrs Clarke. It may well be Norman Denman you've seen, but we need to check. James, I'd like to ask you about the night

Megan died. You said yesterday that you lost sight of Megan in the nightclub. I'd like you to tell me what happened.'

'It was just after we saw that man, you know, Norman. She said she felt a bit sick. I assumed she went to the bathroom. She was gone an age, a couple of minutes turned into five, then ten, and after about fifteen minutes, I went looking for her.'

'How long did you look for?' asked Allen. He could see by now that James was starting to get upset and angry. 'It's okay, James, take your time,' he said, reassuring the young man.

James sat staring at the floor. He didn't say anything for a while. 'I don't know. I'm not that sure; seemed like an age.'

'What then?'

'I then went outside, that's when I felt a bit strange myself.'

'Can I ask you a question? We haven't got you or Megan leaving the club, nothing on CCTV.'

'Underground, Chief Inspector, you can leave by the underground exit. It then takes you right up near the taxi rank.'

'Did you check?'

'Yes, I asked at the door, but they hadn't seen her. After that, I went and asked at the main entrance, but again nothing, no sign of her. I looked around for about five to ten minutes again in the club itself, but couldn't see her anywhere. After that I went to the taxi rank, asked around, but I got the same answer. It was like she just disappeared.'

'Johnny, we've got a problem,' Walsh said as he entered the living room.

'Sorry about this, Mrs Clarke,' Allen said as he followed Inspector Walsh outside.

'What's wrong, Peter?'

'It's Norman. I've just rung Alice Denman. She had a phone call just after 10:30 this morning. Norman never made it to work today. His boss rang to see if he was okay.'

'Tell you what, go around to his workplace and see his boss. Probably come up with nothing, but he may well be able to shed some light on Norman's mood over the last week or so. Take my car. I'll finish up here, then I'm going around to see Jane. It's only a five-minute walk.'

'Okay, see you later. What about Norman's mum? She seemed very upset when I spoke to her.'

'Don't worry, I'll give her a ring.'

Allen watched Inspector Walsh drive away. He was concerned about Norman; he had that nagging thought in the back of his mind that he was in trouble. *What's Norman up to?* he said to himself. *Why would he follow James and Megan into a nightclub? Why did he turn up outside Jane's house? It didn't make any sense.*

Allen walked back up to Mrs Clarke's house. Something else that was playing on his mind was James. He wasn't convinced he was telling the whole truth.

'Everything okay, Chief Inspector?' asked Mrs Clarke.

'Nothing we can't handle. Okay then, James, answer me this question please. Can you remember who gave you the drugs?'

James didn't say a word. He just gazed into space; tears started to fill up in his eyes. He seemed worried and confused.

'James, don't worry about getting this man into trouble. We'll look after you, I promise.'

James looked at Allen shaking his head. 'No, sorry, Sir, I don't know who he is,' he said, tears running down his face. 'I've never seen him before, and that's the truth, Sir.'

'Would you recognise him again?' asked Allen.

'Maybe, yeah, I think I would,' James responded quietly.

Allen started to believe that this time James was telling the truth. Plenty of teenagers get sold drugs by faceless drug dealers, especially in a nightclub.

'Would you be able to describe him so we can do a photofit picture?' asked Allen.

'Yeah, I think I would. You should get Melissa to draw him,' James said through a half-forced smile.

'Maybe I will,' Allen said smiling. 'Look, I will need to ask you more questions, James. If there's anything else you remember, I'd like you to ring me as soon as possible.'

'Trust me, Mr Allen, I'll make sure he does.'

Chapter 5

Inspector Walsh peered through the glass door of the photo shop where Norman worked. He tried the door which was locked; he carried on knocking for what seemed like an age. He was just about to give up when a small grey-haired man wearing glasses appeared, holding the biggest bunch of keys he'd ever seen. The man started to unlock what seemed around a dozen locks. *Can't be too careful, not today anyway,* Walsh said smiling to himself. After what seemed like five minutes of finding the right key, then the wrong key, lots of head shaking, the door was finally opened.

'Good afternoon, I'm Inspector Walsh. You rang a Mrs Denman earlier concerning her son, Norman?'

'Yes, that's right, he works here for me. Good worker, very unlike him not to turn up though. I'm Mr Richardson, David Richardson.'

'Can you tell me, Mr Richardson, is Norman usually very punctual?' asked Walsh.

'Yes, he's usually here at 8:30 am on the dot.'

'Can you tell me, Mr Richardson, what's Norman been like over the last week or so?'

Mr Richardson showed Walsh into the shop. He could see he looked concerned and worried about Norman.

'To be truthful, Inspector, I've been a bit worried about him. He's not been his usual self for a while now. He's been very distant. It's like he's worried or upset over something. And before you ask, I know about Norman's past, that's how I met him.'

'How was that?'

'Through my brother Michael; he worked with Norman at the hospital. He's a doctor you see, a psychiatrist. Michael told me about Norman and his love for pictures. He's very good Inspector, very good. So I went to see him just before he was released and promised him a job. I don't know much about his case, Inspector, but the Norman Denman I know isn't a murderer.'

'Have you seen him with anyone strange, someone you've never seen him with before?' asked Walsh.

'Well, there was one man, he only came in once. He wanted some photos blown up. These pictures were about thirty-odd years old. One was of two boys aged fourteen to fifteen years old; the other was of the same two boys but with two girls around the same age. One of the girls was very beautiful, really very stunning, blonde hair and the most stunning light blue eyes I'd ever seen. I'm a professional photographer, Inspector. I've taken pictures of many beautiful women, but this girl was something else.'

'What was Norman's reaction when he saw the photographs?' Inspector Walsh was one hundred percent sure he knew who the girl was. It was Jane. It couldn't be anyone else but Jane Woods.

'He just stood and glared at the pictures shouting, 'no, no, no,' over and over again. In the end, I did the job. I may still have a record of it. I'll check.'

Inspector Walsh had a very good idea about who one of the two boys may have been. It was none other than Johnny Allen. Who the other was, he'd no idea; maybe Billy Reynolds, but until he saw the picture he couldn't tell.

'Do you keep any copies of the pictures at all, Mr Richardson?'

'No, sorry. Here we go, a Mr Derek Dickinson, came in on 19 July, which was a Monday.'

'How much can you remember about the other three people in the picture?'

Mr Richardson laughed, 'Not much, to tell the truth. Once I saw that girl, that was it. I didn't really notice the others.'

Walsh smiled. He knew what he meant. Once you've seen Jane it was very hard to look at anyone else, she's that stunning.'

'One more thing, Inspector. Norman seemed to know the man; he seemed to recognise him. He seemed a bit scared of him like it was a face from the past.

'Your CCTV camera, how long do you keep the tapes?' Walsh asked hopefully.

'Sorry, Mr Walsh, it would have been wiped over long time ago. Sorry about that. I hope Norman's okay. I do hope he's not in any trouble.'

'I'm sure he's okay. Thank you, you've been very helpful.'

Allen walked the short distance from Mrs Clarke's house around the corner to where Jane lived. He started wondering how Peter was getting on at the photo shop. He was starting to worry about Norman He knew he had to find him, and fast. Something else that went through his mind was, what if Norman didn't want to be found? What if Norman had heard about Megan's death? After all, it would bring back so many painful memories. Allen didn't feel right; he felt strange. This whole case felt strange.

'Now if I knew you were into gardening, I would have got you to do mine,' Allen said as he stood in front of Jane's garden.

Jane looked up and smiled, 'Since when have I ever been a gardener? Just thought I'd do something positive. It's been a hard day today; I've done nothing but cry.'

She stood up and smiled at him. She had tears in her eyes. He walked over to her putting his arms around her.

'Oh, Jane, it's okay to cry, my darling. You've just lost your daughter,' he said, smiling and kissing her on the forehead.

'Hold me, Johnny. You will stay with me again tonight, won't you? Oh, please stay with me,' she cried.

'I will, I will, my darling.'

'Promise me, please, don't leave me. I love you. I love you so much.'

Allen held her tight in his arms as he whispered, 'I love you so much more.' Jane smiled at him. He always said that, 'I love you so much more.' She felt happy and safe in his arms. When she was younger she'd spend most of the day at school daydreaming. Her friends would tease her by saying, 'Jane loves Johnny,' It didn't upset her for one reason, it was true.

Allen looked around at the garden, 'Shall we leave the gardening for a while. Oh, now what?' he said as his mobile phone started ringing. Maybe though, just for once, it was going to be good news.

'Hi, Johnny, it's me. Listen up, I've found out something very interesting. I've just had a chat with a David Richardson, he's Norman's boss. Well, he said that about a month or so back a man called Derek Dickinson came in with two photographs he wanted blown up. He also said that Norman got very upset about it.'

'Why was that?' asked Allen.

'One was of two boys, and the other was the same two boys and two girls. By the way he described one of the girls it sounds very much like Jane, and I'd say one of the two boys was you.'

'And the others were Alison and Billy. I remember the photos being taken. Norman must have gotten upset seeing Alison. Also, did he say if Norman recognised this Mr Dickinson?'

'No, he didn't say, but he said by his reaction he well might have.'

'Derek Dickinson. You see, Norman not only might have recognised this man, but also the name. Derek Dickinson was his uncle; Uncle DD, that's what Norman called him. But it couldn't be his uncle; he died some months back, and this man knew it would upset him.'

'Any ideas who he might be?'

'No. Okay, I'm at Jane's at the moment. Come around and pick me up. How do you fancy a trip to Oxford?'

'Okay, then, what or who's in Oxford?' asked Walsh inquisitively.'

'We're going to have a chat with Norman's doctor,' replied Allen.

'His name wouldn't be Michael Richardson by any chance?'

Allen laughed, 'Go on then, how did you know that?'

'He's Norman's boss' brother. That's how he got the job at the photo shop. I'll see you in about half an hour.'

Allen started to wonder who this man was. Was he involved? Who else would have these photos? Who else would know who Derek Dickinson was? It wasn't any wonder Norman got upset.

'You okay, darling?' Jane asked.

'Do you remember Norman Denman taking photos of me and Billy, you and Alison?'

'Yes, that's right. Didn't he also take a photo of just me and Alison? He framed them as well; hung them on his bedroom wall. Why?'

'Well, we've got a problem, Norman's gone missing…well, I think he's missing. You see, he didn't turn up for work this morning. He works in a photo shop. Peter went around to see his boss, just to see how he's been. He said ever since a man came in a month or so back, he's been acting strangely. The man gave his name as Derek Dickinson.

'Oh, Uncle DD,' she responded surprisingly.

'Anyway, this man wanted these photos of us blown up, you know, enlargements made. But it was only two of them: the one of the four of us, and the one of Billy and me.'

'Norman never gave his pictures to anyone; he had hundreds of them. The only other two people who were there, besides you and me, were Alison and Billy. Alison's dead, and Billy's in New Zealand. Or is he? Like I said yesterday, I saw him, Johnny. The more I think about it, the more positive I am it was him.'

'Look, I'll see you tonight,' he said giving her a kiss.

'Okay, I'll be waiting for you. Enjoy your trip to Oxford,' she smiled.

Inspector Walsh pulled into the hospital car park, 'This is a mental hospital, isn't it?' he asked.

'Yeah, Norman spent over twenty years here. Come on, let's find Doctor Richardson.'

'Good afternoon, you must be Chief Inspector Allen and Inspector Walsh. I got your message, Chief Inspector; saw you pull into the car park. Come, follow me.'

Doctor Richardson led them up a flight of stairs and into his office, 'Please sit down, gentlemen.'

'Thank you for meeting us, Doctor. Haven't we met before?' asked Allen.

'Yes, I believe we have, the Jackson Reynolds case. He was released some two or so months back,' replied the Doctor.

'I understand you looked after a Norman Denman. Tell me, in your opinion, could Norman have done what he was convicted for?'

'Well, you'd have to say if pushed then, yes, he could. I, for one, believe Norman did kill Alison Woods. But not on his own; he would almost certainly have had and needed help. He wouldn't have been able to have planned it himself.'

'Does Norman, in your opinion, have a split personality?'

'No, not in the classic case, but he did have, does have two sides to his character. Norman doesn't have dissociative identity disorder. He could get very depressed, even get very angry. He'd let little things get to him. But he couldn't comprehend or understand the meaning of death.'

'In what way?' asked Walsh.

'To Norman, people were asleep, not dead. It's my belief, in Norman's mind, Alison isn't dead; she's just sleeping.'

'Did he say much about what happened? Did he ever admit to killing Alison?' asked Walsh.

'No, not really. He wouldn't talk much about it. He'd go very quiet, very withdrawn. I understand he had a sister, Joan?'

'Yes, that's right,' replied Allen.

'He told me she committed suicide. Is that right?' asked Richardson.

'Yes, sad case really, Norman would do anything for Joan. They were very close.'

'He told me something one day that Alison looked like his sister. I'm not sure what he meant by that'

'No, not at all. Alison was a blonde, Joan had dark hair,' said Allen.

'That's what I believed. I took it that he saw them as both being asleep, and not dead. He said he found her; he said he found her asleep. How long before Alison was murdered did Joan commit suicide?'

'Just over a year. He was never the same after that. He changed. At the funeral, he just lost the plot. He just screamed and screamed, 'Wake up Joan. Wake up Joan,' it was heart breaking.'

Allen thought back to Joan's funeral. It was a horrible day. Norman was just uncontrollable. Allen remembered at least five grown men trying to get him to calm down. At one point, he even went and lay by her coffin. It was then he started shouting and screaming for Joan to wake up.

'Tell me, whose decision was it to release Norman?' Allen asked.

'It's up to the parole board. We give them the information about the prisoner, then it's up to them. You see, Norman wasn't a danger to himself or anyone else anymore. The one reason he stayed here so long was his lack of understanding about what happened to Alison Woods.'

'Tell me, Doctor, did Norman and Jackson Reynolds ever talk? If so did they get on at all?'

'Look, Chief Inspector, as you know, they knew each other beforehand. Norman was scared to death of him. Jackson spent the best part of twelve years in here trying to get inside Norman's head.'

Doctor Richardson looked straight at Allen. He could see by the look in his eyes, that the name Jackson Reynolds bothered him.

'Trust me, gentlemen, how the hell Jackson Reynolds was ever released is beyond me. That man is truly evil.'

Allen knew there was a pattern to both the Alison Woods murder and that of Megan. Was the pattern the same in the Jackson Reynolds case? All victims were ripped apart, but something wasn't right. It just went over and over in his mind, *Same killer, but different killers.* He wondered how much of a part, if any, Reynolds played in Megan's murder. After all, he more than fitted the profile.

'Tell me, does Jackson Reynolds have a split personality?' Allen asked.

'Yes, very much so. Reynolds' is a strange case. You see, both his personalities are evil, but one side of him is eviller than the other. You can reason with Jackson, but Jack, as he calls himself, he's the killer. Jackson just went along for the hell of it.'

'Dominant and submissive. Would he still have one side dominant the other submissive?' asked Walsh.

'You would think so; that's the way it goes with a split personality. But not with Jackson; both are dominant, both trying to outdo the other.'

'One more question, have you ever met Grace Reynolds, Jackson's sister?'

'No, sorry. I have heard the name, but no, I've never met her.'

'Thank you for your time, Doctor Richardson. We may well meet up again.'

'No problem, Chief Inspector. Inspector, I hope I've been some help. As for meeting up again, that's the line of work we're both in. You catch them, I'll try and help them.'

'Come on, Peter, I need to think. I need to get all this straight in my head.'

James felt strange. He could sense he was being followed. He stopped and looked back at the man following him. He'd seen him before, but where? His mind flashed back to the night Megan was murdered. It was him. He'd remembered where he'd seen him. He closed his eyes for a brief moment; another flashback, he could see someone kneeling over Megan's body. He started to walk again, each step, he'd glance behind him. He was still there, getting closer and closer.

'Hello, James, remember me?'

James stared at the man stood in front of him. He remembered him now, all too well. He started to quicken his stride to try and get away. 'Leave me alone. Just go away,' he screamed.

James stopped, turned around and stood right in front of the man. 'What do you want? What do you want from me?'

The man laughed. 'Oh, James, don't tell me you've forgotten poor Megan? Remember? You do remember your girlfriend, don't you?'

James had another flashback to the night Megan died, but it was still too muddled. He could remember some bits, but it was still such a mess. He could see that figure again knelt over Megan's body, but this time the figure turned around. James put his hands on his head. He started crying and shaking. He knelt down on the ground screaming, 'NO, NO, NO.'

The man looked down at James and started laughing. 'Oh, James, do you remember now? Remember what you did to poor Megan? Slaughtered like an animal.'

James pleaded for help. He reached up, grabbing hold of the man's left hand, and sobbed uncontrollably. 'I didn't kill her, I didn't kill her,' he cried out.

The man placed his hand on James's shoulder. 'I knew you'd remember.' He started laughing, then just walked away.

James lifted his head. He watched as the man walked away and then just disappear. James struggled to his feet, wiping the tears away from his eyes. He could now remember what happened. It was all so clear now. 'NO, NO, WHAT HAVE I DONE?' he screamed.

'Look, drop me off here, Peter, I'll walk the rest of the way, I need to think.'

'You sure?'

'Yeah, I just need to get things straight in my mind.'

Allen started thinking about Norman Denman. Why would Norman murder not just Alison, but Megan as well? As Doctor Richardson said, he didn't understand the meaning of death.

'Alison isn't dead, she's just asleep.'

'Alison looks like my sister.'

If Norman didn't murder Alison, then he must have seen what happened. He after all found his sister.

'I can't wake her up, Johnny. Wake up, Joan. Wake up, Joan.'

He remembered Norman telling him that he couldn't wake his sister up. How easy would it have been for someone to get Norman to do what they wanted?

It was easy enough when they were young. You could ask him to do anything, and he'd do it. 'Norman, go around the shop for me,' some kids would send him off to buy cigarettes and drink, or play knock-down ginger. Billy once sent him around to his Uncle's garage to ask for a long wait; Norman would just go off and do it. But murder, would he do something like that if asked? Not the Norman he knew.

Norman could get very angry. When upset, he was as good as uncontrollable. Did Alison upset him enough to murder? Sexually maybe? Norman didn't really understand about sex and girls, but he must have got turned on, especially if she stripped off in front of him.

No, Norman wouldn't have killed Alison; not in that way. He wouldn't have ripped her apart. He would maybe have hit her once and then run away. Norman never really had a fight with anyone when they were young. He only remembered one fight he had. Norman hit this boy once then just ran; it scared him too much.

The months after Joan died, Norman would often be found sitting or lying by her grave. But he didn't understand why she was there. He wouldn't have understood that that's where Joan's body was. Another question going over in his mind was, what was Norman doing at the nightclub? After all, nightclubs were hardly his scene. Why was he watching Megan? What did he know? Did he know who was selling Megan and James drugs?

James Clarke, what was he hiding? What does he know that he hasn't told me? He knows more. A lot more that's for sure. Could James have killed Megan? If so, why? What was the reason? But like Norman, he wouldn't have murdered like that. He wouldn't have ripped her apart. It would have scared him too much.

Two killers; same killer but different killers, it went over and over in his mind, but what does it mean? Two murders, Alison and Megan, killed by two different people, submissive, but controlled by one person, dominant.

'But not Jackson. Both are dominant, both trying to outdo the other.'

He said it over and over to himself, unable to make any sense of it.

'You could reason with Jackson, but Jack as he calls himself, no, he's the killer.'

Jack murdered Alison; Jackson watched, controlled him, told him what to do. Jackson murdered Megan; Jack watched, controlled him, told him what to do. Same killer but different killers…no, no, that's not right. It doesn't fit. Both dominant, both would want to kill.

Jackson Reynolds could plan, plan his murder; the Van Dalen murders were planned years in advanced. But who killed? Jack or Jackson?

'Jack, he's your killer. Jackson just went along for the hell of it.'

Were both Jackson and Jack controlled by a dominant person? Told him what to do, said you can both murder. Both murdered the Van Dalens. Jack killed Kevin; Jackson killed Sian.

Allen walked into the police station, his mind still going over and over. Two killers; same killer but different killers, dominant and submissive.

'Sir, Sir, Chief Inspector.'

'Oh sorry, miles away.'

'Sir, this has just been delivered.' Sergeant Rogers said as he handed Allen a large brown envelope. Written on the envelope was, FOR THE ATTENTION OF JOHNNY ALLEN, in big bold capital letters. Allen looked down at the envelope as he walked back to his office. He was almost too scared to open it, after what was in the one left on his car.

He sat at his desk. His mind in an instant turned to Norman and the pictures that upset him. He ripped open the envelope like an excited child on Christmas morning. He knew in an instant what he'd find: two photos, one of Billy and himself, the other of Billy, Jane, Alison and again, himself. He laughed out loud when he looked at the photos. He couldn't believe how young they all looked.

He turned the photos over, and written on the back of the one of just him and Billy was, MEGAN'S BLOOD'S ON YOUR HANDS. On the other of the four of them was written, LOOK INTO THE BACKGROUND.

'Johnny, you okay?' asked Walsh as he entered Allen's office.

Allen looked up at Inspector Walsh and smiled, 'CCTV tape from outside the nightclub, do we still have it?'

Walsh nodded, 'Yeah, of course we do.'

'Come on, Peter, follow me; I'll explain when we've looked at the tape.'

Inspector Walsh smiled and said, 'Okay, if you say so.'

Allen started watching the tape just as Megan and James entered the nightclub. 'Come on, where are you? I know you're here. Come out, come on, Johnny will see you now.'

Allen stopped the tape and smiled. 'Okay, first off, I got this delivered to me about ten minutes or so ago.' Allen handed Walsh the brown envelope. 'It's the pictures of me and Billy, then of me, Jane, Billy and Alison. On the back of the one of the four of us is written, LOOK INTO THE BACKGROUND. Look at the photo, Peter, and tell me what you see.'

Inspector Walsh studded the picture, 'Well, I see you and Billy, Jane and Alison, and in the background a blurred figure.'

'You've got it in one, and that blurred figure is none other than Jackson Reynolds. The second I saw him triggered something in my mind. You see, I didn't see the connection at first when I looked at this tape. I must have seen him for my mind to register it, but it wasn't until I saw the photo, I then remembered who I'd seen.'

Allen pointed at the screen. Walsh looked at a figure of a man standing outside the nightclub.

'And that, Peter my friend, is the same said Jackson Reynolds, but about thirty-odd years older.'

'And I bet I can guess what he's doing there.'

'It wouldn't be selling drugs by any chance?' Allen said smiling.

Allen looked at the figure on the screen. *Come on then Jackson, why now? Why this? Did you kill Megan? Kill my little girl? No, you didn't, did you? You can't. You're not strong enough are you, Jackson. But Jack, you could. You could kill my little girl, kill my daughter.*

'Jackson didn't kill Megan, but Jack, I'm not so sure. He could, could have killed.'

'Johnny, remember, you still haven't seen Grace Reynolds yet. She wants to talk to you. She called again to see when you were going to see her. She seemed very on edge, said she moved to Newbury to be near Jackson. She then said she hated going to visit him, especially when on one visit she met Norman.'

'I've just remembered something about Grace I haven't told you. She accused Norman of raping her.'

'What, Norman?'

'Well, that's the story anyway, but it was never proven.'

Walsh looked at Allen. He knew what he was thinking. What if Norman did rape Grace, then maybe he could have killed Alison.

'Right, I'm off to see Grace Reynolds. Can you do me a favour? Take a trip down to the nightclub. I want to see if any of the staff members can remember anything about that night.'

'Okay, I may also start asking some of the taxi drivers. You never know someone might have seen Megan or James.

'Okay, good idea. I'll see you later.'

He started thinking as he drove. His mind started racing. Are we like the people we meet and see every day? Especially those we admire, do we in some small way try to imagine life as them? I have sat many times watching people, trying to work out what makes them act the way they do.

Who are you? What's your name? Your likes and dislikes? Do you think the same as me? If so, why? But then again, it's the same question, if you don't, why? You, that man over there, are you like me? Do you think like me? Act like me? Do your actions shape your world and the world around you? Or even shape the world of other people around you? So why do you ask? Simple, you killed my Megan, killed my daughter. But what's your name? Who are you? Dominant or submissive? You have to be one or the other. Why do I? Why do I have to be one or the other? Good question, because only one can kill, not both, that's impossible. What about Jackson Reynolds? Jack killed, but Jackson is just as capable.

But they didn't kill Megan, it's impossible. But how is that? Why is that? Simple, one wouldn't let the other, both are dominant.

Look, if I told you Jackson or Jack Reynolds didn't even kill Kevin and Sian Van Dalen, what would you say? You'd say, no way, that's madness. He got put away for it. No, for once you're wrong, but are you? Look, it's any easy answer, like I said before, both are dominant, neither one nor the other would let it happen.

In a split personality with one dominant, one submissive, dominant could kill; even submissive could if dominant would let it. But which one? Which one killed Megan, killed my daughter? Was it you?

Allen wondered what Grace looked like now. When she was younger, she was a pretty girl, dark haired, big brown eyes. She maybe wasn't in Jane's league, but then again, who is?

He found it strange that she'd moved near to where Jackson was; as children, the two seemed to hate each other. She always seemed troubled as a child, never seemed to laugh that much or have fun.

He stopped for a moment outside a block of flats. He looked around the area. It seemed nice. It hadn't been built that long, maybe only ten years ago. He looked at the names on the buzzers. He pressed number 14; above it read the name Miss Grace Reynolds.

He found it hard to believe that Grace had never married. Maybe too many bad relationships, perhaps she never met the right person. It seemed like an age before the buzzer was answered. He was just about to buzz again when a lady's voice answered.

'Hello, sorry it took me a while to answer.'

'That's okay. Miss, you wouldn't be Grace Reynolds by any chance?'

'If that's what the name says above the buzzer, then I guess I must be.'

Allen laughed to himself, still the same old Grace. 'Hello, Grace, it's Johnny, Johnny Allen.'

'Well, well, Johnny Allen. It's been a long time, Johnny. Push the door and come on up. I'm on the second floor, flat in the corner to your right.'

Allen pushed the door and was met on the landing by Grace. She hadn't changed that much, still had her long dark hair which didn't have any grey in it. She still had those lovely big brown eyes as well.

'Hello, Grace, you haven't changed a bit. You still look the same. How are you?'

She smiled at him, tucking her hair around her right ear, a nervous habit she had from childhood. The light caught her diamond earrings, making them sparkle like stars in the night sky. She'd never admit it, certainly not when she was younger, but she had a massive crush on him. He still looked good, but she remembered the history he had with Jane Woods. She smiled to herself. She herself was pretty, always had many men ask her out. But Jane Woods was just stunning. If she was truthful with herself, she even had a crush on Jane.

'You haven't changed much, Johnny; you still look good. Not sure I should ask you this, but do you still see Jane?'

He felt awkward; the silence seemed to last an age. He wondered how much Grace knew, how much she knew about his relationship with Jane. 'It's partly because of Jane I'm here. I'm not sure if you've heard, but her daughter Megan was murdered the other day. I'm just following up links.'

'Yes, I've heard. These links wouldn't be anything to do with my brother by any chance, would it?'

He wondered if Grace would be protective towards Jackson. Then again, the pair hated each other, especially as children.

'Johnny, what Jackson did was beyond anything any normal human would do. You know, each and every day since, I've paid for what that sick evil bastard did. But he's my brother, and yes, I do love him. I know it sounds stupid. I know

76

what you're thinking, and you're right; I hate him, hated him as a child, hate him today.'

'Have you seen much of him since he's been released?'

Grace tried hard to hold back the tears, but however hard she tried she just couldn't. 'I'm sorry, Johnny, but it's been so hard, so hard I can't even hold down a job let alone a relationship. I have had so many different jobs, then I meet someone I like. Even when Jackson was inside, the second I say, 'Oh, by the way, I'm going to visit my brother. He's in a mental hospital,' that was that. 'Oh yes, your names Reynolds. Didn't your brother kill that couple?' After they found out, no one wanted to know. As for the last time I saw Jackson, that was about three weeks back.'

Allen looked around Grace's flat. It was well spaced out. Two pictures that hung on the walls took his notice. One was of just Grace; she looked older in that one, aged around mid-twenties. The other was of Grace, Jackson and Billy, when in late teens, early twenties. Both pictures were taken years ago. The one of the three of them really took his notice. At the bottom of the picture were the initials ND, Norman Denman.

'Nice pictures, Grace. Norman took one of them, I see.'

'Yeah, it was one of the only times the three of us were not at each other's throats. He didn't want to take it at first. It was about the only thing he was good at. God, I look so young. I can't be any older than sixteen, seventeen.'

'You thought he was strange, didn't you?'

'Who, Norman? Tell you what, Johnny, maybe he did murder Megan. After all, he's killed before.'

'You don't need to answer this if you don't want to. But do you really believe your brother killed Kevin and Sian Van Dalen?'

Grace half smiled through the tears in her eyes, and said, 'To tell the truth, I've never been that sure. I know what Jackson's like. Is he capable of murder? Yes, yes, he is, well, capable.'

'As kids you hated each other. He was horrible to you. Yet here you are still paying for his crime.'

She looked at him, tears streaming down her face, 'Like I said, every day I've paid for his sin, but do you know what my biggest sin is?'

Allen said nothing. He in some way or another knew what was coming. He'd known for years about Grace having a crush on him. 'Don't Grace, don't say a word. I know, I've always known.'

'And here's me thinking it was my big secret.'

'Oh, Grace, you're a lovely lady, and you were very sweet as a little girl. But there's only ever been one girl for me. You know that.'

Grace smiled through the tears. She knew he was right. She'd always known. 'I know it's only ever been Jane, the beautiful gorgeous Jane, the most beautiful girl in the world. I know how much you love her, and I love her as well, always have.

'It did cross my mind many times. I could tell by the way you'd look at her.'

Grace smiled, 'You see, Johnny, I've only ever loved four people, and each one of those people, well, didn't love me back.'

'Tell me who the others were, Grace? Who else did you love?'

The tears had made her eyes red and swollen. 'One was real, she was mine; six months, the best time of my life, the only time I was ever really happy. But it couldn't work. He just wouldn't let it.'

Allen looked puzzled. 'Who wouldn't let it, Grace?'

'Jackson, my brother, my evil bastard of a brother. He didn't want or love her, but I did.'

'Bloody hell, Grace, it was Sian Andrews, wasn't it? You were in love with her.' He now understood why Jackson and Sian had that fight the day she met Kevin Van Dalen. He'd found out about her affair with his sister.

'You knew what Jackson would do when he found out. And that made you feel happy. Why? Because she'd told you it was over between the two of them. You then thought you could have Sian to yourself. Sian then met and fell in love with Kevin. That was something you didn't bank on, was it?'

Grace said nothing. She didn't need to. Johnny was right.

If Jackson couldn't have Sian, in his mind no one could. Not Grace, not Kevin, no one, so he murdered them, and Grace has suffered ever since.

'Why wouldn't Jackson let you be happy? After all, it was clear to everyone that knew him he didn't love Sian.'

She laughed and said. 'That's the way he is. 'I can't have her so why should I let my lesbian little sister have her,' or Kevin for that matter. I believed he hated me being gay more than anything, well, bisexual anyway. You see, yes okay, I had a crush on you, but I've always known I was bisexual, ever since I was young. Don't get me wrong, I've had affairs with a few men, but I much prefer women.'

'I know Grace, I could see it. You said four people; who's the other?' he asked.

'Oh no, that's my little secret, my sin you could say.'

Allen looked at her and smiled. He wasn't going to press her on it. He knew she'd tell him in her own time, if at all.

'This girl that was murdered, Megan, answer me this question, Johnny, is she your daughter?' she asked with a half-smile on her face.

'Why do you ask?' he replied.

'I could see it in your eyes the moment you walked in. She has your eyes, Johnny.'

He knew Grace was right. He could see so much of himself in Megan. 'To be truthful Grace, I'd never really admitted it to myself, let alone anyone else.'

'I never understood why? Why you and Jane just didn't admit your love for each other. We could all see it; the whole world could see it. I would have laid down my life for Jane. You should have done the same.'

'Tell me, Grace, at Jackson's trial he claimed he was with you when the Van Dalens were murdered. How true is this?'

'Like I said at the time, he got to me about 9:30 am and left me about 10:00 am. What he did before or after, I've no idea. All I will say is when he got to me, he was in a strange mood, or should I say a stranger mood than usual. You don't believe he did it, do you?'

'Jackson murdered the Van Dalens. But a lot about these murders doesn't make sense. But one thing I am sure is Jackson didn't kill the Van Dalens, not on his own anyway.'

'You're telling me he had help?' Grace said in surprise, 'Who would help Jackson murder?'

'I don't know for sure, Grace. One more thing, when was the last time you saw Billy?'

'I haven't seen Billy since God knows when. It's been years.'

'Come on, Grace, you can tell me. You were, after all, the last person to see him before he left.'

Grace tried hard not to cry again. She stopped, took a deep breath and sighed, 'The last time I saw Billy was the day Kevin and Sian were murdered. The day after, he was gone. No goodbye, just a note, 'Gone to find a new life, make a fresh start. I'll write soon. Love you, love to mum and dad,' that's it.'

'Surely, Grace, you don't believe Billy had anything to do with the Van Dalen murders?'

'He would for me. If it meant getting back at anyone who'd hurt me, he would.'

'What? Even murder?'

'If it meant getting back at Jackson as well, then yes, even murder.'

'Billy would do anything for you, Grace, anything at all. But not murder, no, not the Billy I knew.'

'Oh, Johnny, Billy changed after Alison was murdered. He just wasn't the same person. I believe what happened with Kevin and Sian, and what Jackson did, well, he just couldn't take it.'

Grace looked at him. She touched his face, smiled and said, 'Billy changed; maybe we all have. We all change, Johnny, that's life. It's just the way it goes. You think you know someone, but you don't.'

Chapter 6

Inspector Walsh stood outside the nightclub. He tried the main door, but it was locked. In fact, the whole place was locked up; no sign of anyone. He peered through a glass window, but he couldn't see much; it was too dark inside. The nightclub didn't look that big from the outside. It was a bit like the TARDIS out of *"Doctor Who"*, bigger on the inside than the out. A lot of the club was set underground. It was very popular, especially with the teenagers and the early twenties. He peered through the window one last time, but nothing; no sign of life.

'No one in at this time of day, mate,' came a voice from behind him.

Walsh turned around to see a very tall, very well-built gentleman standing behind him.

'I work the doors here. I'm head doorman, Robert Murphy.'

'I'm Inspector Walsh,' he said showing the man his warrant card. 'Were you working here on Saturday night?'

'Yeah, I was here. I'm here most weekends. Is this about that girl? Heard it on the news. Bloody horrible that. Sends shivers through my body, things like that,' he said shaking his very thick set shoulders and arms.

Walsh showed Murphy a photo of Megan, 'Do you remember seeing this girl at all on Saturday night?' he asked handing him the photo.

'Yeah, I know her and her boyfriend, James. Yeah, that's his name. Nice kids, never any trouble.'

'What about this man?' asked Walsh showing him the picture of Norman Denman that Melissa had drawn.

'No, sorry mate, never seen him before. Remember most of the youngsters, especially those who come most weekends. But some people just come once or twice.'

'Do you have much trouble with drugs in here?' asked Walsh.

'Look, Inspector, you get that sort of problem in most clubs. We try and keep it under control. This club is one of the best in the south east. We're always on the lookout.'

'Have you ever heard of a man named Jackson Reynolds?'

'No, sorry, I'll ask some of the other lads and let you know if anyone knows anything.'

'I understand this club has an underground entrance, is that right?'

'Yeah, but it's only an exit. It's quicker to get to the taxi rank. But you have to come in through this entrance first. You can only leave by the exit downstairs.'

'I've seen the CCTV cameras for this entrance, and the tapes. We haven't had anything for the underground exit. Do you have CCTV cameras for this?'

'Yes, we do, but slight problem; someone smashed both cameras. Came here Friday last week and noticed it, both smashed; bloody kids.'

'Okay, thanks for your time, Mr Murphy.'

'No problem. I've got to wait here for about an hour now. Left my keys at home, so I can't get in. We've got a do on here tonight, something to do with the local council,' he said laughing.

'You can hire this place out then?'

'Yeah, parties, wedding receptions, that sort of thing.'

Walsh smiled at him, 'Enjoy your wait.'

Walsh headed off in the direction of the taxi rank. He still couldn't work out what Norman was doing in a nightclub. He'd look so out of place. He looked at a long line of taxis. *Surely someone here must know something*, he thought. He approached the first taxi in the line. All the taxis were black cabs. He flashed his warrant card at the taxi driver, who proceeded to just sit in his cab reading his paper. It was as if he hadn't seen him.

Walsh knocked on the cab window. The driver reluctantly wound it down. Inspector Walsh showed him his warrant card again.

'Yeah, what?' replied the driver still not making any eye contact.

'Hi, I'm Inspector Walsh. Have you seen this girl? She may have been here in the early hours of Sunday morning,' Walsh said as he thrust the photo of Megan under the driver's nose.

'See loads of people don't I? Just faces, mate, that's all.'

'So you can't remember picking this girl up?'

The driver took the photo and shook his head, 'No mate, can't remember. Ask Lenny over there. He'll remember a pretty girl like that.' The driver pointed behind him in the direction of four drivers who were standing over by the train station drinking cups of tea.

'Okay, thanks.' Inspector Walsh walked over towards the other drivers. *Hopefully, these guys will be more cooperative,* he said to himself.

'Hi, I'm Inspector Walsh,' he said flashing his warrant card. 'Which one of you is Lenny?' he asked.

'That'll be me,' said an old grey-haired man.

Walsh looked at the old man. He looked as old as time itself. He had a cigarette hanging out of his mouth that had more ash hanging off it than cigarette.

'Any chance you may have seen this girl in the early hours of Sunday morning?' Walsh asked as he handed the old man Megan's picture.

The old man looked at it. 'Yeah, I remember her. She looked, well, out of it. She was shouting and raging at her boyfriend. Well, I take it he was her feller. She was going at him for the whole journey.'

'Where did you take them?' asked Walsh.

'Just past the train station up near Pangbourne. He just said, 'Stop here, mate,' paid up, and that was that. If you ask me, he'd had enough of her nagging.'

'What time was this?'

'Around 12:30, no later than that.'

'When you dropped them off, did you notice anyone else, anyone just hanging around?'

'No, not really. Streets were empty, Inspector. Has this got anything to do with that girl that was found murdered? That's her, isn't it? Bloody hell.'

Walsh looked at the old man. He looked in a state of shock. He looked visibly upset. 'You okay, Sir?' he asked.

'Yeah, fine, just a bit shocked that's all,' he replied, trying to light another cigarette with very shaky hands.

'Okay, just so I've got this right, you picked up both of them?'

'Yeah, that's what I said, mate.'

'Any chance you can give a statement. Just pop into the station and ask for Inspector Walsh. I'll give you my card.'

'Okay.'

Allen read the name and dates on the headstone. Alison Elizabeth Woods 25 July 1970 – 25 September 1988. Forever loved, forever missed. What happened, Alison? Who killed you? It wasn't Norman, of that I'm sure. He loved you, not sure if you knew that. Was it Billy? Did Billy do this to you? No, not the Billy I knew. What about Jackson? But we were all just kids. We couldn't kill, could we?

'Why Alison? Why?' he said out loud.

'I ask that question every day.'

Allen turned around and looked at the man stood behind him. 'Roger, is that really you? Well, well, Roger Woods.'

'Yes, and you must be Johnny Allen?' Allen smiled, nodded and shook Roger's hand.

'You and Alison were friends as kids? Am I right in saying that?'

'Yes, that's right. I met Alison through Jane.'

Roger smiled and nodded, 'That's right. I remember.'

There was a silence for about thirty seconds or so as Roger placed some flowers on his daughter's grave. 'He didn't kill her, you know, the man who got sent down, Norman Denman. My brother was wrong.'

'What makes you say that?' asked Allen.

'Look, Johnny…you don't mind if I call you Johnny, do you?' Allen nodded. 'My brother wanted someone, anyone, and this Norman fitted the bill. She was hanging around with some not very nice people. You remember Jane's husband Alex Davis, don't you? Well, his cousin Graham Ashford for one. And let's be fair, Alex was no saint when he was younger.'

Roger stopped to wipe away a tear from his eye. 'But it's strange that one person who, shall we say, was not all there, was a young girl called Grace. I can't remember the surname.'

'Reynolds, Grace Reynolds. Why? What makes you say that?'

'I didn't really know her or her brothers. But the times I did meet her, she was very domineering; it was her way or no way. Jane would always say, leave her alone, she's okay.'

'If you don't mind me asking you, how much do you remember about the day Alison was killed?'

'It was like any other normal Saturday. Alison didn't get up until about midday. She spent about an hour or so getting ready, then she met up with Alex Davis and Graham Ashford.'

'What time did she meet up with them?'

'Must have been around one, just after one o'clock.'

'None of this was ever brought up, not in Norman's interviews or his trial. Story went that Alison met up with Norman up near the woods. No one else was mentioned.'

'That's right, she did meet up with Norman, but she also met up with Alex and Graham.' Roger sighed and shook his head. 'Look, I told my brother over and over again who Alison went out with. But all he'd say was don't worry, that doesn't matter. We've got Norman.'

'You do know it was Alex Davis who found Alison's body?' Allen said.

'Yes, I know, and that was something else that my brother kept quiet.' Roger looked at Allen and smiled, 'She loves you, you know that? She always has— Jane I mean. That was something else I couldn't understand about Simon. He didn't want you to marry Jane, but he let Alex Davis.'

Allen laughed, 'I don't think either of us would be any good for his daughter. In fact, no one would.'

'Look, Johnny, one last thing. All this with Megan has brought back so many bad memories. Find out the truth. Find out who killed Megan and Alison.'

Allen watched as Roger Woods walked away. His mind turned to Alex Davis, Jane's ex-husband, and something else that came into his mind about Alex and an ex-girlfriend.

Inspector Walsh walked up the three flights of stairs that led to his and Johnny's office. He knew Johnny would want to speak to James Clarke again. He couldn't understand why he'd lie.

Walsh sat at his desk and rubbed his eyes. He picked up the case report of Alison Woods murder that was on his desk and started reading through it. Walsh looked at the map of the woods and the river. He compared where both Alison and Megan were found, same place; in fact, exactly the same place. Alison's body was found by a man out running. No mention of who found her, just a man out running. Why wasn't his name mentioned? Who found her? He said to himself. Who'd know? Johnny, yes? Davidson?

'Yeah, Davidson, he'd know,' Walsh said out loud.

'Davidson would know what, Inspector?'

Inspector Walsh looked up from his desk, 'Sir, sorry, didn't know you were there. It's just, well, it doesn't mention in Alison Woods report who found the body.'

'Are yes, look Peter, she was found by Alex Davis. As you probably know, he was Jane's husband, and as you may well have guessed, he may not be Megan's father.'

'I take it he's Melissa's father?' asked Walsh.

'As far as I know, yes. Alex, when he was younger, got into a lot of trouble. Let's just say he had a very bad habit of taking things that were not his. He and Johnny didn't really get on that well, as you could well understand. Jane and Alex got together, married within about three years of meeting.'

'How did Johnny take it, do you know?'

'Well, he didn't say that much. In fact, he at one point wanted out of the police force. He just wanted to move right away from here. He nearly got suspended. It was only because of my intervention that he didn't.'

'What happened?'

'Well, it was soon after Melissa was born. Johnny, for some reason, couldn't take it that Jane had a child with Alex. One night, he got very drunk and went out looking for Alex, and when he found him, all hell broke loose. I'd never seen him like that before or since. He just snapped. You, more than most, Peter, you know Johnny Allen. He sees things that we don't.'

'I'm surprised Jane's father let someone like Alex marry Jane and not Johnny.'

'You and me both, but let's just say he wasn't best pleased. But I'll give Alex his credit. Once he married Jane, he changed for the better. He was a good husband and a good father.'

'He must have known about Jane and Johnny?'

'He knew Megan wasn't his. Well, I believed he did. Maybe he knew Johnny was her father, I don't know. Look, Jane may have cheated on him with Johnny, but he had an affair with another woman.'

'Do you know who?' Walsh asked.

Davidson took off his glasses and wiped his forehead. 'Yes, I do, Grace Reynolds. Peter, Alex Davis may have been a troublemaker when he was younger, but he's no killer.'

'And neither is Norman Denman,' came a voice from the office doorway.

Both Davidson and Walsh turned around to see Johnny standing there.

Allen smiled at them. 'You could say, Peter, I owe my career to this man on both occasions. For that, Bill, thank you.'

'How long have you been standing listening then?' Davidson asked.

'About five minutes or so,' he said smiling.

'How did it go with Grace Reynolds then, Johnny?' Walsh asked.

'Okay, she's suffered for her brother's crime, that I do know. As for her affair with Alex Davis, that does surprise me.'

'Why's that, Johnny?' asked Davidson.

'Well, for one, I had no idea they even knew each other. How did you get on at the club and with the taxi drivers?'

'James Clarke lied about not being able to find Megan. Both got in a taxi around 12:30 am. Old boy named Lenny said he picked them up and dropped them off near the train station in Pangbourne.'

'Bloody hell, Lenny Smith, he can't still be driving. He's about eighty if he's a day,' laughed Allen.

'That man should never have been allowed a driving licence. For one, he can't see two feet in front of his own eyes. As for his sense of direction, well, he could get lost coming out of his own driveway,' laughed Davidson.

'You didn't get to talk with old "Smiler" Jones by any chance?' Allen asked, smiling at Walsh.

'Grey hair, reading a paper, very uncooperative,' Walsh said shaking his head.

'That's Dave "Smiler" Jones,' Allen laughed.

'Okay, gentlemen, I'll leave you too it,' Davidson said as he left the office.

'Thanks, Bill,' Allen said as he watched him leave.

'Right then, what do you want to do?' Walsh asked as he clapped his hands together.

'Come on, let's go and talk to James Clarke. I knew he wasn't telling the truth, well not the whole truth anyway. This time I want answers.' Allen knew James was hiding something. But he could also see that he was scared, scared of what happened to Megan or scared of someone.

'I didn't get much out of anyone at the nightclub. I spoke to the head doorman. He remembers Megan and James, but nothing on Norman or Jackson Reynolds.'

'I take it Davidson told you that Alex Davis found Alison's body. Well, he should have found her; he was out with her all afternoon. After I left Grace, I had a chat with a man named Roger Woods, Alison's father. I met up with him at the cemetery. Well, he said that Alison had been hanging around with Davis and his cousin, a man called Graham Ashford. She met up with them down by the woods the afternoon she was murdered. I also take it you know who Alex Davis is then,' Allen said turning and looking at Walsh with a half-smile on his face.

'Yes, Jane's ex-husband. Alex was a troublemaker when he was younger, according to Davidson.'

'Yeah, nothing big, he would just take things that weren't his, things like cars. He's done some house breaking, that sort of thing.'

'Davidson also didn't have him down as a murderer,' Walsh said.

Allen shook his head. Alex was a petty thief, nothing else. Davidson was right, Alex was no murderer. As for Graham Ashford, he couldn't remember what happened to him, but again, he was no murderer either.

'Neither of them was capable of murder. Again, it would have scared them too much. As for what happened between me and Alex, well, I just lost the plot. You see, he was rubbing my nose in it; I couldn't take it that he had a child with Jane.'

'What did you do to him?' asked Walsh.

'Well, I was drunk, out of my head. To be truthful, I can't really remember that much about it. You see, I found him in a pub, and we just had a little fight that's all. He hit me, I hit him, that sort of thing. Okay, I smashed a chair over his head.' Allen stopped and forced a half-smile to himself. 'He then rang his father-in-law. He was all for having me out the force. If it wasn't for Davidson, I'd have been out.'

'I'm surprised you weren't charged. He must have done something for you to do that?'

'He did. He first smashed my car windscreen. Then he put a brick through my front room window. That's what really set me off. You see, I'd been having trouble with my marriage to Debbie. That night we'd had a massive bust up, so I got drunk. Then my car alarm goes off. Just as I got up to take a look, a brick comes through my window. I knew it was Alex, saw him drive off.'

Walsh gave Allen a sideways glance. He didn't say anything; he didn't have too.

'How did you get on with Grace, then? I got the impression there was something else you wanted to say, but as Davidson was there you didn't.'

'Well, not much really. I know why Jackson and Sian split up; you know the afternoon Kevin Van Dalen put Jackson in hospital? Sian and Grace were having an affair. You see, Grace is bisexual and Sian…well, I don't know why Sian did what she did. But you see, Jackson found out. After that it was just a matter of time before he killed Sian and Kevin. Grace wanted Sian, but she didn't bank on Sian falling in love with Kevin.'

'Both had a motive to want to kill the Van Dalens. Jackson because of what both Sian and Kevin did. But I believe he wanted revenge on Kevin more than Sian; Grace, because Sian didn't want her. Could both Jackson and Grace have murdered the Van Dalens?'

Allen didn't say anything, but he knew Peter could be right. It was something he hadn't really thought about. Grace and Jackson Reynolds, who would be dominant? Who would be submissive? What was it Roger Woods said about Grace? It was her way or no way.

Grace couldn't and wouldn't murder. This was a frenzied attack. Sian's face was a bloody mess; both had multiple stab wounds. He couldn't see Grace doing this, not the Grace he knew as a child or the Grace he'd just met.

'I've just been on to forensics, and the blood on James Clarke's shirt wasn't Megan's. I guess it's more than likely his own, maybe a nosebleed or something,' Walsh said, replacing his phone back into his jacket pocket.

Allen and Walsh pulled up outside the Clarke household. *Right,* he said to himself, *I'm getting the truth from this young man, if I have to take him down the station to do so.*

'Okay, I'll give him ten minutes to tell me the truth, if not we'll take him down the station,' Allen said as he walked up the garden path.

Mrs Clarke opened the door before either Allen or Walsh could ring the doorbell.

'Hello, again. I take it you want to speak to James,' she said shaking her head. 'Tell you the truth, Chief Inspector, I've had it with him. He's in a real mood, banging around, shouting and screaming.'

The two detectives followed Mrs Clarke into the living room. 'James, James, down here, right now.'

'Hello, again,' said Maddie, 'Hopefully, you can get some sense out of him,' she added.

'Has he not said anything to you at all, Maddie?' asked Walsh, smiling at the young lady.

'No, he just screams at me. Only thing I get out of him is, 'Go away boghead.' That's his nickname for me. Lovely isn't it?' she smiled.

Maddie sat down opposite Allen and Walsh. 'You know, some little sisters get called, 'Oh, this is my kid sister,' or, 'This is Madeleine,' or even, 'Maddie.' No, I get, 'Oh, this is boghead.'

Allen turned to Walsh and laughed, saying, 'I love kids, just love them.'

'But you couldn't eat a whole one,' Walsh said trying hard not to laugh.

Maddie looked over at Walsh and laughed, 'I like that. I'll remember that when I have children.'

'One thing, Maddie, the blood on James' shirt wasn't Megan's.'

Maddie looked at Allen and smiled nervously. She seemed relieved. He could still see fear in her eyes, fear that her brother was in trouble.

James came down into the living room. Slumping down on the sofa, he put his feet on the glass coffee table and sat just staring into space. He looked as if he'd been crying. His eyes were red and blood shot.

'Look, James, whatever trouble you're in, I can help you. But you've got to tell me the truth. No more lies,' Allen said, looking at the young man.

'We know you and Megan got into a taxi up by the train station. One of the taxi drivers remembers picking you both up. He said you had an argument. You stopped him up near the train station in Pangbourne, that's where you both got out. I've spoken to the taxi driver myself. He recognised Megan's picture,' Walsh said shaking his head.

James didn't seem to hear him. He just stared at the wall on the other side of the room. 'Sorry,' he mumbled.

'James, get your feet off the coffee table and speak up,' shouted his mother.

'I'm sorry,' he cried. 'We did get a taxi, but she was so out of it. By that time, I wasn't feeling too clever myself. You see, we had a fight over the drugs. She thought it would be a laugh. But I don't do drugs, neither had Megan up to then. You see, I tried to stop her, that's when she ran off. I reckon I had my drink spiked by the same man who gave Megan the drugs.'

'What happened after that?' asked Allen.

'Well, it was like I said, to start with, I couldn't find her. After a while, I found her sitting on the floor near the front entrance to the train station.' James stopped and wiped the tears away from his eyes.

'What happened next, James? You're doing okay, don't worry. Like I said, I can only help you if you tell me what happened?'

'Well, after about ten minutes of Megan calling me every name under the sun and trying to run off again, she said she wanted to go home as she felt unwell.'

'How long did you have to wait for a taxi?' asked Walsh.

'Not long, about a couple of minutes. Driver was an old man, grey haired; he looked like my grandad. He looked too old to drive.'

'Can you remember after you got out of the taxi what happened next?' Allen asked.

'Now this is the truth. By the time we got out of the taxi, I was really starting to feel unwell. I can't really remember much. I do remember Megan running off into the woods. She wanted to play hide and seek. She kept shouting, 'Come on James, come and find me.' I didn't find her. I just can't remember what happened. She just disappeared.'

'Did you see anyone around when you got out of the taxi? Any other cars? Or other taxis?'

'No, sorry, Chief Inspector, if there was anyone else around, I can't remember them,' James said looking at Allen with tears running down his face.

'The man who gave you drugs, you said you've no idea who he was?' Allen asked.

'No, never seen him before. I'll try and give a description. I might be able to remember him.'

'We've got a man we'd like you to have a look at on the CCTV tape we got from Saturday night.'

'Okay, when would you like me to come in?' asked James.

'What about 10 am tomorrow morning?' replied Allen.

Mrs Clarke nodded and smiled. 'I'll make sure he's on time,' she said.

'One last thing, James, we have a shirt belonging to you. It had blood on it. Any reason why?'

'Yeah, I get a lot of nosebleeds. Had one in hospital, always getting them.'

'Okay, thanks,' replied Allen.

Chapter 7

Allen lay in bed unable to sleep, the body willing, but the mind was not. He watched Jane as she slept. She seemed peaceful; maybe she felt safe with him being here. He laughed to himself, it seemed strange. This is what they'd both wanted—to be together. It was the only thing they both wanted, even as teenagers.

Norman Denman was missing, or was he just hiding? Maybe he didn't want to be found. What with Megan's murder, maybe it was all too much, too many painful memories. Allen checked the time on his phone, 01:32 am in the morning. Two words entered his mind, dominant and submissive. He couldn't get it out of his head, over and over it would go.

In a split personality, one would be dominant the other submissive. Dominant would kill, submissive would just watch, hide away. Could submissive kill? Be told by dominant, 'Go on you kill'? Surely in a split personality that wouldn't work. Dominant wouldn't let it work; he wouldn't be the dominant one anymore.

Now with two people, one dominant, one submissive, this could and would work. Dominant would still be the dominant one, still the one in charge. Could, in a split personality, submissive become dominant? Would and could this happen?

Norman didn't or doesn't have a split personality. If he was one of the two people, he'd be submissive, his personality would show that. He'd be scared, frightened. Norman would do whatever his dominant partner said. After all, he was a loner, didn't have many friends, couldn't socialise very well. So if it meant him having a friend, being liked, being told, 'Well done, you've done well today. I'm pleased for you and with you,' he'd do anything, anything at all to be liked, even murder. But would he?

Norman Denman's no cold-blooded murderer. But he could kill if dominant told him. He couldn't have ripped Alison apart. It's not in his makeup, not in his personality.

Another name that kept coming into his mind was Joan Denman. Something about her suicide bothered him. What happened in that old boathouse? Something that set all this off, but what?

Norman found his sister, 'I couldn't wake her up. Wake up, Joan, wake up.'

Catherine Clarke was starting to worry. She was worried about James. He was very down last night, in a real strange mood, very on edge. She knew it had been hard on him losing Megan, but it had hit everyone hard. One minute he'd be okay, then he'd just flip. Last night, he seemed visibly upset, even panicky as if he was still hiding something.

'Maddie, I take it you heard James shouting and screaming last night?'

'Yes, I did. He kept me awake. Mum, can I have some ice cream?'

'Yes, yes, Maddie whatever, but you'll have to get it from the big freezer in the garage.' *Bloody hell, ice cream at this time in the morning,* she said laughing to herself.

Maddie stood up and grabbed the keys to the garage and skipped outside, singing, 'I love ice cream.' She unlocked the door and pushed it open. She stopped dead in her tracks transfixed on what was in front of her. She was unable to move or speak. Time seemed to just stop. She couldn't catch her breath. She reached and grabbed for the garage door. She tried to scream, but nothing came out.

Catherine stood in the doorway to James's bedroom. *Bloody hell, if he was in here you wouldn't be able to find him; what a mess,* she said to herself.

'Maddie, Maddie,' she called out to her daughter as she walked down the stairs, but nothing, no reply. *That girl, bet she's got her headphones on, music fall blast.* Catherine ran down the last few stairs, still calling out her daughter's name, 'Maddie, where are you?'

Catherine walked out into the garden and then over towards the garage. She stopped dead in her tracks as she saw her daughter holding the garage door. Maddie had tears running down her face, her gaze transfixed on whatever was in the garage.

'Maddie, whatever is wrong?'

Maddie turned to look at her mother and screamed, 'MUM, MUM.'

Catherine walked up to the garage door where Maddie was standing and followed her daughter's gaze. As she did, she screamed out her son's name, 'James, James.'

Inspector Walsh answered what seemed to be a never-ending stream of phone calls, ring, ring, ring. *Bloody thing's going out the window if it rings again,* he laughed to himself.

'Sir, we've just received a phone call from Mrs Clarke. It's concerning her son, James. I think you should find Chief Inspector Allen. She's just found her son dead; he's hung himself in their garage.'

Walsh didn't say anything for about twenty seconds or so. He found it hard to take in what he'd just been told.

'Sir, you okay, Sir?'

'Yes, sorry Richard, I'm fine. I'll find him, thanks.'

Walsh slumped back in his chair still unable to take it all in. Why? What the hell's going on here? Why would James take his own life?

Allen lay on Jane's bed. He turned on his side and smiled at her, 'Morning, sleepy head.'

'Hi, what time is it?' she asked sleepily.

He checked his phone, 'Oh God, it's 08:26. I need to be in by 08:30. Oh well, Peter's always in early. Tell you what, I didn't sleep much last night. When I did, all I could dream about was my Saint Christopher and photographs. There was this photograph of it, nothing else.'

'You were very restless last night,' she said smiling at him.

He looked at her again and kissed her on the lips. He looked at her amazing blue eyes. She still looked so beautiful. He could spend all day looking at her and into her eyes.

'What are you thinking about?' she asked, smiling at him.

Allen laughed, 'Do you remember the first time we made love? We just lay on my bed looking at the ceiling for about half an hour. I was scared half to death; you know that, don't you?'

'You were scared, I was terrified. I didn't have a clue what to do. Not to mention the fact we could have been caught,' she replied excitingly.

'You didn't have a clue, like I was anymore clued up,' he said, laying on his back. He lay with his hands behind his head and smiled.

'Nothing's changed there then,' she said resting her head on his chest.

'Oh, very funny, Woods. Hey, that doesn't sound right anymore. I remember reading your diary, what was it? Oh yes, the Diary of Jane Allen. Maybe one day soon how would you like to be Jane Allen?'

'Are you asking me to marry you at last then?'

He was just about to answer when his phone rang. *Oh great,* he thought, *and I was just getting somewhere.*

'Hello. Yes, Allen.'

'Johnny, it's me. James Clarke's dead. He hung himself. His mother and sister found him in their garage.'

Allen found it hard to take in what Inspector Walsh had just told him. He was in a state of shock.

'Bloody hell, Peter. Okay, I'll meet you there. I'm only about five minutes around the corner.'

Allen slumped back down on Jane's bed. He put his hands over his face.

'Johnny, what's wrong? Baby, you okay?' Jane asked with concern. She knew something was wrong by the expression on his face.

He sat back up and just stared into space shaking his head in disbelief. He turned and looked at Jane, 'It's James Clarke. He's dead. He hung himself.'

Allen looked at Catherine Clarke as he entered her house. He was unable to find the right words to say to her except, 'Sorry.' That was it. That's all he could say.

'Why Inspector? Why? I just don't understand. Please help me to understand all this,' she said, grabbing hold of his arm.

'I wish I could, but I'm struggling to understand it all myself. What was he like last night?'

'Last night, he seemed strange, on edge. He didn't say much, only to shout at poor Maddie.'

Allen could tell Mrs Clarke was struggling. She was trying to remain composed, but the tears just came. His concern turned to poor Maddie, bloody hell, poor kid having to walk into that.

'Johnny, please help me. Please? Jane said you're the best. She said if anyone can understand all this, then it's you,' she said squeezing his hand.

'Is your husband not here Mrs Clarke?' Allen asked softly.

'No, he's away on business in America. He left last Friday. I've rang him and left a message, but it's still the middle of the night.'

'I take it he'll come straight back?'

'I hope so,' she said as she burst into tears.

'Morning, Johnny, how are things?' Inspector Walsh asked as he entered the living room.

'Not good, Peter, not good at all. I just don't know what to say. Look, I know it must have been hard for him. After all, he's maybe lost the love of his life. But to take your own life, I just don't get it. He must have been desperate to do that.'

'How's Maddie?' asked Walsh with concern in his voice.

'Maddie has been taken to hospital; she just went hysterical. Mrs Clarke needs to be with her. Mr Clarke, well, he's away on business in America. I've got a car for Mrs Clarke to take her to the hospital. She wouldn't go to start with, wanted to be here with James, which I suppose is understandable.'

Allen watched as Mrs Clarke was driven away to the hospital. He knew it was the best place for her. He stood outside the house and looked up and down the road. He felt uneasy. He felt strange; he felt the same way the other day. He had the strange feeling he was being watched again.

'Come on, Johnny, smile you're on camera. Two more to go. Now then, who's next? Now let me think. That's it, Norman, simple old Norman. Then the end Johnny, it will all end with…no, no, now that would be telling. Can't give the game away. That would be too easy, wouldn't be any fun whatsoever.'

'Why? Why don't you just say? Just bloody get it over and done with.'

'I knew you'd show up. What's wrong? Scared, are we? Why, why?' he screamed. 'Why do you have to do this? Why do you have to interfere and put doubts in my mind?'

'Just saying, that's all. Bloody well get on with it. Just get it over with.'

'Oh, just go away and leave me alone,' he screamed.

Allen looked up and down the street again, but he couldn't see anything or anyone out of place.

'What's wrong, Johnny?' asked Walsh with concern.

'He's here. We're being watched. Come on then, show yourself.' Allen turned around quickly. He saw it, a flash of light. 'Come on, where are you? Who are you? I know you're here.'

Allen walked over towards the other side of the road. Up the road about one hundred meters was an alleyway that led to a park.

'Did you see it, Peter? Over there, it came from over near those trees, by that alleyway and the park.'

'See what?' replied Walsh.

'A flash of light, like a camera flash going off. He's here, the man who's been watching us, he's here. I know he is.'

'Who? Who is he, Johnny?'

'Dominant. It wouldn't be submissive; he wouldn't and couldn't get this close. No, he'd be too scared, too frightened in case he got caught.'

'Why now? I don't get all this. Why just at this moment?' asked Walsh.

'He knew James would take his own life. He's playing games with us, and now it's just starting to make sense.'

'What next?' Walsh asked as he looked up and down the road. He turned around and looked back towards the alleyway, but nothing.

'Back to the office, I want to go over everything we've got: Alison Woods, the Van Dalens, Megan and James, Norman, Jackson Reynolds, everything. There's a link here and I want to find it.'

'Okay, I'll meet you there,' replied Walsh.

'Okay, I'm going back to Jane's to get my car. Tell you what, meet me down by the river. I want to have a look around again.

Inspector Walsh stood outside the old pub waiting for Johnny. *It must have looked nice here once,* he thought to himself. He turned around as he heard a noise from behind the old pub. It sounded like someone stepping on some old twigs or old branches. He turned back quickly as he heard a car pull up behind him. *Bloody hell, Simon Woods,* he said to himself.

Walsh watched as Woods and, what he took to be, his wife slowly got out of the car. He smiled to himself. He could see where Jane and Melissa got their looks from. And it wasn't from their father or grandfather.

'Hello, it's Inspector Walsh, isn't it?' Woods asked as he walked over towards the Inspector.

'Hello, yes Sir, it is.' He smiled nervously at him. He then turned and looked at the very elegant lady that was stood by Simon Woods.

'This is my wife Susan. We've come to place some flowers where Megan's body was found.'

She looked like an older version of Jane. Walsh could tell she'd been crying; her eyes were red and the skin around her them was red and blotchy.

I'm so sorry about your granddaughter, Mrs Woods. Would you like me to show you where she was found?' he asked politely.

'No, but thank you, Inspector, we'll be fine,' she replied smiling at him.

'Thank you,' added Woods.

'No problem, Sir,' Walsh said smiling. He watched the elderly couple walk arm in arm slowly up through the woods and over towards the river. Must be so hard to lose someone so close. *God, what a wicked world we live in,* he said. He was glad in some way that Johnny wasn't here and that Woods didn't ask what he was doing.

Walsh walked slowly out towards the main road. In the distance, he could see a silver coloured BMW speeding towards him. He laughed to himself, *he'll get done for speeding one day.*

Allen flashed his lights as he turned into the old car park by the pub. He noticed the black range rover parked by Inspector Walsh's car. *Oh great, Simon Woods,* he said to himself.

'I take it you've spoken to the ex-Chief Constable?' Allen asked as he got out of his car.

'Yes, I have, and his lovely wife Susan.'

'You can see where Jane gets her looks from then. Susan's half Swedish; her mother Anna was from Sweden.'

'What's she like then?' asked Walsh.

'Susan? She's really nice. I've never had any problems with her. In fact, I believe she knew about me and Jane before we did,' Allen smiled.

'They've gone up to place some flowers near where Megan was found.'

'Okay, right then, we'll head off down towards the river. We'll go through this way. I'd like to show you something.

Walsh followed Allen through the woods and down towards the river. They were quite away from where Megan's body was found. Allen stopped and looked back towards the old pub, which was almost in line with where they'd walked. The river was no more than fifteen to twenty feet away from where they were standing. An old boat, which looked as if it had been there for years, was turned on its side and propped up against an old tree.

Allen looked at the old boat and laughed to himself. *God,* he thought, *can't believe it's still here.*

'Bloody thing was falling apart when we were kids. You'd get about five feet from the riverbank, and the old thing would fill up with water. You'd end up with your socks and shoes wet through. Also, say about two hundred metres over towards those new houses, was an old boat house, but it was knocked down some years back.'

'I take it you haven't just brought me here to show me this old boat and talk about an old boat house,' Walsh laughed as he looked over towards the old boat.

'No, you're right, I haven't. Look, I believe this is where Alison was murdered. Her clothes were found right where that boat is, and Norman's camera was found just over there by that tree, so say about ten feet away. Again, I believe there were two of them, not one. It would have taken two people to carry Alison's body over to where she was found, which is at least three quarters of a mile away.'

'Could Norman have carried her body that far on his own?'

'I'm not sure. Yes, he's strong enough. If he had murdered her right here, then that's where we'd have found her.'

Allen could picture in his mind Alison's body lying on the ground. 'She was murdered here alright.'

'If she went swimming in the river, as they said, then it makes sense. You think about it, Johnny, if you went over in that direction, it's at least a mile or so before you get down to the river side.'

'Another thing, on Norman's camera were three pictures from that afternoon. One of just the river, the other two were of Alison.'

'Where were they taken from?'

'In one of the photographs of Alison, you could see the shadow of another person. Those photographs were taken from this spot right here,' Allen said pointing down at his feet.

Allen looked out over the river. Why move the body? What was the reason? Surely if she was left down here, she'd had been harder to find, you could have hidden her more.

'What about Megan? Do you believe she was murdered down here?' asked Walsh.

'No, she was murdered where we found her. On that necklace, how many of Megan's teeth were on it?'

'Four,' replied Walsh holding up four fingers.

'Okay, she lost six teeth. Now unless our murderer has kept them, I believe the other two are around here somewhere.'

'That's a long shot, Johnny. They could be anywhere by now.'

'Yeah, I know. You searched down here, is that right?'

'Yeah, we found nothing, not a thing. Megan's clothes were scattered around all over the place, but down here, no, nothing.'

'It can't be that simple. He can't have kept the teeth. This killer isn't a trophy taker,' Allen said as he started looking around. He had that feeling again, the feeling he was being watched.

Walsh suspected Allen was up to something, playing games, playing the killer at his own game. He felt uneasy as if he was being watched. He looked around but couldn't see anyone.

'He's watching us, isn't he?' Walsh said uneasily.

'Oh yes, he's here.'

'But he wouldn't have known we'd be down here?' Walsh said, making a gesture with his hands as if to say, how.

'No, you're right, but he followed us. Well, he followed you. I wasn't followed down here from Mrs Clarke's house; I made sure of that,' Allen said.

'Bloody hell, I remember. Thinking of it, yeah, you could be right. First off, when I was driving down here, an old black mini sped by me.'

'Registration number? Allen asked hopefully.

'No, sorry. But just before Simon Woods pulled up, I heard something, sounded like someone stepping on old branches, came from behind the old pub.'

'How do you know he followed us down here?'

'I didn't, I took a guess. I had a feeling, a sense. He's placed something down here; he knew I'd come down this way.' Allen stopped and smiled as he looked at Walsh. 'That's it, of course, the old boat. Come on, help me turn this thing over.'

Walsh followed Allen over towards the old boat. It was more holes than boat, the wood in some places had just about rotted away, *but fun to play in as a child,* he thought to himself.

Allen took hold of one end and Walsh the other. The boat was about ten to twelve feet long and about three to four feet wide. The two detectives turned the boat over. Lying in the boat was an old oar that had broken in half. Pinned on the oar was a brown envelope. Allen looked over at Walsh. Peter could see that Johnny was almost too scared to even touch the envelope, let alone open it.

'Not again,' Allen said puffing his cheeks out.

'Do you want me to open it?' Walsh asked as he walked around the boat to where Allen was standing.

Allen handed Walsh the brown envelope. This time it had nothing written on the front. Walsh paused briefly, then opened it. Inside was a photograph of Johnny and Jane standing outside in Jane's front garden. Walsh looked inside the envelope, but nothing; it was empty.

'Let's have a look at that photograph?' asked Allen.

Walsh handed over the photograph, and noticed something written on the back. 'On the back, Johnny, he's left you a note,' he said pointing at the photograph.

Allen turned the photograph over and read the note. 'You didn't think it would be that easy did you? After all, the postman only knocks once. Do parents keep their children's teeth these days?'

'What the hell does this—' Allen stopped mid-sentence, 'Bloody hell. Jane…he's sent Megan's teeth to Jane.'

Allen frantically fished around inside his jacket pocket for his phone. 'Jane, it's me, you okay?' he asked her softly.

'Oh, Johnny,' she sobbed down the phone, 'these are Megan's, these are Megan's teeth. Oh, my poor baby,' she cried.

'Okay, I'm on my way back to yours,' he said with concern in his voice.

'No, no, my parents are coming. I'll be okay, darling. What's going on?'

'It's okay. Don't worry, darling. Are you sure you don't want me to come back?' he asked.

'No, it will only start an argument between you and my dad. I'll call you later. Love you.'

'Bloody hell, this guy always seems to be one step ahead of us. When was this picture taken then?' asked Walsh, looking at the photograph.

'The other afternoon, I went around to see Jane, she was outside doing some gardening. Come on, let's have a little look around where Megan was found, then back to the station.'

Walsh followed Allen back up through the woods and back to where Megan was found. He started thinking about the photographs. He wondered where, if anywhere, this man was getting these pictures developed.

'I'm going to check to see if anyone remembers getting these photographs developed. You never know, we might get lucky.

'Good idea. She was just about here, wasn't she, turned on her side, feet pointing down towards the river. Alison was in an almost identical position. So this person or persons knew how Alison's body was placed, placed deliberately, not dumped. No, no, Alison was dumped. Her body was carried up to here and then just dumped. Megan was placed here deliberately.'

'When Alison was murdered, was anything found, like pictures or a necklace?' asked Walsh.

'No, nothing. Alison's murder wasn't planned, Megan's was. She was given drugs in the nightclub deliberately. James and Megan were followed here, Megan killed. And James, not sure about James.'

Same killer, but different killers, he said to himself. 'Come on Peter, I need to think. I need to get this straight in my mind.'

'Norman, oh Norman,' he sneered at him.

The room was dark and damp. He could only just about make out the shadow of someone standing over near a doorway. Norman Denman slumped off an old metal camp bed and on to the floor. He drew his knees into his chest holding them at the same time and started too rock backwards and forwards.

'What's wrong with you?' the shadow asked him sharply.

'No, I want to see Johnny. He'll help me,' Norman sobbed.

'Oh yeah, right, I forgot, big mates with the great detective. Johnny Allen knows shit. He'll play the game my way; my game, my rules,' laughed the shadowy figure.

'Just leave Norman alone. He's done what we've asked of him, now leave him.'

Norman looked over towards the door, but could only see one figure. There was no one else. 'Who are you talking to?' he asked.

'Norman, oh Norman, don't worry about him. He'll be like you soon, a puppet for me to play games with.'

'But you were talking to yourself.'

102

The door slammed shut. It went pitch black. Norman sat rocking backwards and forwards again. He held his knees and buried his head between his arms and screamed, 'NO, NO, NO.'

She sat just staring at her daughter's teeth that were on the coffee table. Who? Who in hell's name would do something like this? She picked them up and held them tight in her hands, *my poor baby girl, who did this to you?* She slumped back in the sofa, tears running down her face. She started having flashbacks to when Megan was first teething as a baby. She would keep her up all night, but she didn't mind. She'd lay downstairs on the sofa singing her songs and nursery rhymes. She started to remember Megan's excitement at losing her first baby tooth.

Jane closed her eyes. She woke with a start, *oh God, how long have I been asleep?* She checked the time. *Oh my, only five minutes, but it seemed longer,* she thought. *Oh my God, I shouldn't be falling asleep at this time of day. I slept like a log last night,* she said to herself.

Her thoughts turned to Johnny. She felt safe with him here last night, lying in his arms and falling asleep. She knew she'd have to tell him, tell him her secret, but she was scared, scared that she'd lose him.

Despite sleeping well, she felt washed out. The stress had gotten to her. She knew that she needed to grieve for Megan. She spent years trying to work out how to grieve for Alison, but it was so hard. She had thoughts that she was being punished for her sins. Was Johnny her sin?

She closed her eyes again. The thoughts in her mind turned back to Johnny, all the love, the passion, the excitement. She could feel herself drifting off again, deeper and deeper. This time she didn't fight it.

She looked down at the blooded mess in front of her. She wasn't sure who it was. It was the body of a young girl. She wanted to touch her, help her. Her face was hidden. She took a deep breath and knelt down beside the body. Her heart started beating faster and faster. She found it hard to control her breathing. With some trouble, she turned the body over and screamed out, 'JOHNNY, JOHNNY.'

She jumped. She could hear a ringing noise. *Oh God, the doorbell. I need to get a grip,* she thought to herself. Slowly getting up from the sofa, she rubbed her eyes and sleepily walked over to the front door. She smiled wearily as she opened it.

'Hello darling, you okay? You look half asleep,' said her mother giving her a kiss and a hug.

'Oh, Mum, I am half asleep. I shouldn't be; I slept really well last night, but I keep dropping off.'

'Grandma, Grandad,' Melissa said as she bounded down the stairs.

'Hello darling, at least someone's got some energy.'

'I'm always full of energy, Grandma,' she said with a beaming smile, giving her grandparents a hug and a kiss each.

'We've just been up to the river, laid some flowers down. We met…who was he?' she asked her husband.

'Inspector Walsh, Peter, good man, very good detective,' he replied.

'Yeah, he's really nice. Johnny speaks very highly of him,' Jane added.

'I take it you've been seeing a lot of Johnny Allen then?' he asked his daughter sharply.

'Oh, dad, don't start. Look, I'll see who I like. I'm not a child anymore. I'm 48 years old,' she snapped back at him.

'What about Alex? Does he know about Megan?' he asked bluntly.

'I've no idea, and to be truthful, I don't care,' Jane said as she stormed off into the kitchen. He made her angry. She started banging cupboard doors about. *God, why can't he just leave it alone,* she thought to herself.

'Well, he has a right to know his daughter is dead,' he shouted.

'Oh, he does, does he?' Jane shouted back as she stormed back into the living room.

'Yes, he was Megan's father.'

'Mum, Grandad, can't you just stop it? This is all you two do, you argue all the time. Just stop it,' screamed Melissa.

'Have you been in contact with your father?' he asked his granddaughter.

'Yes, but I've heard nothing. I left a message, but he hasn't replied.'

'I really don't understand you, Jane. You had a good marriage. You and Alex have two lovely children, but you continued to chase Johnny Allen.

'Oh yeah, a really great marriage. You made me marry a man I didn't even love. To be truthful, I didn't even like him that much,' she screamed at him.

'But he's still Megan and Melissa's father.'

'NO, HE'S NOT,' she screamed.

'What?' he shouted angrily. 'Who is then?'

'Oh, for God sake,' she said, throwing her arms up in the air. 'Johnny Allen. There you go, yes, at last I've said it. Johnny is Megan and Melissa's father; I'd made sure of that.

He looked stunned, almost shocked. He sat down on the sofa shaking his head in disbelief.

'I only ever let Alex make love to me once, on our wedding night. After that I couldn't even bear to sleep in the same bed.'

Melissa looked at her mother and smiled at her through the tears. 'Oh, Mum, I always had a good idea Megan was Johnny's daughter, but not me. Does he know?'

'He must have guessed about Megan, but not you. I'm sorry, my darling, so sorry. I've always wanted to tell you both, every single day, but I just didn't know how.'

Melissa walked over to her mother and put her arms around her shoulders. The two hugged each other, tears running down their faces. 'I bet we look a right mess,' she said giving her mother a kiss. 'Do you think Johnny will love me like a daughter,' she sobbed.

'Oh yes, my darling, oh yes.'

'Come on Susan, we're going,' he said angrily.

'Oh, come on Simon, it's no great secret. I've known for years. I could see it a mile away, a mother always knows,' she said, giving her daughter and granddaughter a hug each.

'Jane, Melissa, Johnny Allen is a good man. He loves you so much, always has, and I know you've always loved him. I used to watch you both, oh yes, even when you were both married. I'd often see you both out walking in the park, or in his car.'

'I'm surprised, Mum. I did wonder how much you knew,' Jane said wiping the tears from her eyes.

'You've got to tell him, my darling,' she smiled.

'Grandad, why don't you like Johnny? He's great, really nice,' Melissa asked her grandfather.

He sighed, 'Some people you get on with, some you don't.'

'I'm sorry, Dad. I love Johnny, and he loves me. We're going to spend the rest of our lives together, something we should have done years ago.'

'Well, I don't have to like it. Come on Susan, we're going.'

Jane gave her mum a hug and a kiss. 'I'll ring you later, Jane. Don't worry, he'll come around to the idea. As for you, my darling girl,' she said giving her granddaughter a hug and a kiss.

'Love you, Grandma.'

Melissa turned and looked at her grandfather. She held her arms open. She wanted to give him a hug, not just for herself, but for him as well. 'I'm still your granddaughter, that won't change. I still love you, it doesn't matter who my father is.'

He looked at the tears running down her face. He walked over to her and gave her a hug and a kiss. 'I'm sorry, Melissa, I'm sorry.'

'Do I get one as well?' Jane asked her father.

She could see it in his eyes. She felt it when he hugged her. He seemed angry with her, almost disappointed at what she'd done. She knew he never really accepted Johnny, never liked him. She didn't care anymore. She wished she'd stood up to him years ago, told him, *I love Johnny, you'll just have to deal with it.* She stood by the front door and watched as her parents as they drove away. She felt her daughter's arms around her waist. She smiled at her youngest daughter. She didn't want Melissa to make the same mistakes. If she loves someone then it's her choice. She wasn't going to make the choice for her.

'You okay, Mum?' Melissa asked giving her mother a kiss on the cheek.

'I will be, my darling. I'm sorry you found out this way,' she said smiling through the tears.

'It's okay, don't worry. I know this may sound strange, but I need to find Alex. He needs to know about me and Megan. We owe him that much.'

'Any ideas where he may be?' she asked her daughter.

'I don't know, to be truthful. I don't believe he still in Leeds, maybe he's here.'

'Right, I'm going to the hospital to see Catherine and Maddie. You coming?'

'Yeah, I will. Oh, poor Maddie, my poor Maddie. Oh, this is such a mess.'

Allen sat at his desk looking into space. He thought about ringing Jane, just to make sure she was okay. He held his phone in his hands just looking at it. He was about to ring, but stopped himself, no, no, her parents would still be there.

Blowing his cheeks out and sighing, he placed his phone back into his inside jacket pocket. 'Right, let's make a start,' he said out loud. He laughed to himself, and said, 'Should be, where do I start?'

'Johnny, I've just been checking to see if any cars have been reported stolen. That car that sped past me earlier, well, a black mini was reported stolen this morning.'

'Okay, where from?' Allen asked.

'Now this is the good bit. It was reported stolen by a Mrs Cook, she's Mrs Clarke's next-door neighbour,' replied Walsh looking at the surprise on Allen's face.

'Bloody hell, he must have nicked it this morning. I take it the car hasn't been found yet?' he asked rubbing his eyes.

'No, all patrols are still on the lookout for it,' replied Walsh.

'Okay, right, I've been thinking, let's start to get this in order. Alison Woods, now two things; first, I believe she was murdered by at least two maybe even three people. No way in God's world did Norman Denman murder Alison on his own, if at all. Second, now this may sound strange, but this started with an accident. It wasn't like, Megan's, a planned murder. This is different.'

'In what way? What makes you believe this was an accident?' asked Walsh.

'I don't know. I'm missing something in all this. Something isn't right, but what? Anyway, okay, Alison, as we've decided, was murdered down by that old boat, and her body was found by, of all people, Alex Davis.'

'Do you reckon he knew something about it?' asked Walsh.

'I'm not sure, to be truthful. If he did, I'm still not sure he had anything to do with her murder. Alex was many things, but he's no murderer.' Allen smiled to himself when he thought about Alex. He was so smug when he got together with Jane, but he knew she wanted him and no one else.

'Now you told me Alison hated Jackson Reynolds. Was there enough dislike or hatred between the two for Jackson to want to kill her?'

'Good point. Maybe that's how he thought, that's the way his mind worked. Only thing is, and it's always been in the back of my mind, Jackson as with the Van Dalens would have and did murder. But to plan a murder like Megan's...no, no, he wouldn't have even planned Alison's murder.'

'What makes you say that, Johnny?' replied Walsh.

'He wouldn't have moved the body. He would have just killed Alison and then just left her there. As I've said, I believe her murder started off with an accident.'

'I've also been thinking about James Clarke and what part he may have played in Megan's murder. I also believe someone may well have got to him.'

'In what way?' asked Allen.

'Well, got inside his head, told him what happened. Then maybe he started to remember what actually happened,' Walsh replied.

'Yeah, you could be right. He said he felt funny before he got in the taxi once he found Megan. Didn't he also say by the time they got out of the taxi up near the river and the woods, he felt so bad he couldn't remember what happened?'

'Also, I believe he had a lot more to do with drugs than he made out. I reckon he's been pushing them as well,' added Walsh.

'Yeah, I do, and he knows Jackson Reynolds as well, of that I'm sure,' replied Allen.

Allen sat thinking about James Clarke. How well did he know Jackson? Was he working for Jackson selling drugs? What about that argument between James and Megan. Did he take the drugs? Was it her drink that got spiked? And not the other way around as he said.

'Do you remember what he said, Megan took the drugs, said it would be a laugh, and he had his drink spiked. Now what if he took the drugs, then spiked Megan's drink, she found out, and that's what started the argument?'

'How well do you think he knew Jackson Reynolds?' asked Walsh inquisitively.

'Great minds, Peter, I was thinking the same. As I've said, he knew Jackson, but how? And for how long? I'm not sure. Bloody kids, why do they make such a mess of their lives? Drugs don't make any sense to me,' he said shaking his head.

'Tell me about it. Don't understand drugs myself. I did three years on the drug squad in Bristol. Trust me some of the things you see…'

'I know, what a waste. Okay, these photographs, two questions, why send them? What's his reason?'

'I'm clever. I'm in charge. It's my game, and you'll play it my way,' answered Walsh.

'Yeah, yes. Look at me, I know what you're doing. I'm one step ahead. Look, I know this is going to sound strange, but I don't believe this guy is our killer. He's a puppet. He's having his strings pulled by someone else.'

'I thought to start with, it may well be Norman, you know, his love of photographs,' added Walsh.

'Yeah, Norman may well be taking these photographs, but he couldn't have planned all this; it would be way too much for him. When I say this guy isn't our murderer, let's just say he isn't pulling the strings.'

Allen started thinking. Alison's murder wasn't planned. It was a spur of the moment, an accident. Something triggered it off, but the question is, what? Oh, come on brain think. Alison, sin, secret.

'Do we have the post-mortem report on Alison Woods?' asked Allen with a faint smile on his mouth.

'Yes, we do,' Walsh replied, handing the report over.

'God, I'm stupid, I've been really slow on this,' Allen said as he read through the report. He looked up and smiled at Inspector Walsh.

'Go on then?' he asked, 'Also if you're stupid then that doesn't leave much hope for the rest of us,' laughed Walsh.

'Peter, my good friend, Alison Woods was pregnant,' Allen said smiling. 'I knew there was something else. I couldn't think why she was just murdered, not just for the sake of it anyway. She was pregnant. Only problem is, I don't know who the father was.'

'Maybe that's why she was murdered? She confronted the father and was murdered for it?'

'Yeah, maybe. But I believe there was way more to it than that. This is about jealousy and control. But there's still something else I'm missing.'

'Alison didn't really have a steady boyfriend, did she?'

'Not really, God knows why? She was a very pretty girl. I knew Billy liked her, and from what I could read into, it she liked him,' Allen replied looking back at the post-mortem report.

'What about Billy Reynolds being the father? Was that the reason he left so suddenly?'

'No, I don't know. Maybe? Problem with that was he didn't leave for some eight years after Alison was killed.'

Did Billy leave because of Alison? he asked himself. Surely though if he was the father, he'd have left soon after she was murdered. Billy changed soon after Alison was killed; he wasn't the same person. Truth be told, he changed after we first met Jane and Alison, did he like Jane more? Was that the reason? Allen sat thinking about Billy's friendship with Jane. They were like any other normal teenagers, good mates, not in love with each other, just friends. Alison and

Billy's relationship was different though. You could tell they liked each other. You could tell they wanted to be more than good friends.

'Billy went missing soon after Alison's murder. Not sure where he went, but he was gone for a good month or so; it hit him really hard. It was strange. Billy changed once we met Jane and Alison. Don't know why. He just wasn't fun anymore; he wasn't the same Billy Reynolds.'

'The Van Dalen murders, he wouldn't have had anything to do with that, surely not?'

'No, that was Jackson or Jack, he murdered them. But not on his own. He wouldn't have planned it. Someone else did that.'

'These photographs taken on Norman's camera at Alison's murder scene, what if Norman didn't take them? What if someone else found his camera, then took the photographs?'

'Only three pictures were found to be on his camera. If someone else took them, why just take three pictures? Why not more? No, Norman took them,' Allen replied.

'He didn't like anyone touching his camera, did he?'

'No, God no. Tell you what though, you may have something. I just remembered something about Alex Davis. He was well into photography just like Norman. It had gone through my mind that it was Norman taking these photographs of the two of us, but what if it was Alex taking them?'

'Did Alex and Norman know each other at all?' asked Walsh.

'No, I don't believe so. Well, they knew of each other, but they were not friends or anything.'

'Tell you something, we need to find Norman,' Walsh added.

'Come on, let's go and see Alice Denman.'

Chapter 8

Allen and Walsh pulled up outside an old three-bedroom terraced house. The whole area looked run down. The area itself pre-dated the Second World War. Most of the area was built in the 1920s and 1930s, where the walls would never remain straight, and the floors were uneven. Saying that, the houses seemed bigger, unlike new houses which seem a little smaller. Inspector Walsh looked up and down the long row of old houses. Some looked nice, nice tidy gardens, new windows and doors, whereas others looked old and run down.

'Tell you what, Peter, it was nice around this area once. I lived in the next road, back-to-back terraced houses,' he said smiling.

'Looks almost lost in time,' replied Walsh.

Allen looked at Walsh and smiled again, saying, 'You're right. Most of the people living around here are lost in time. Alice Denman is, that's for sure.'

Allen stood outside the front garden of number eighteen. The garden itself was untidy. An old toilet was left propped up against the garden fence. He looked around the garden, no grass, no flowers, just weeds and mud. He looked down at the old garden gate which looked as if it would fall off at any minute. He laughed to himself as he remembered the game they played as kids—who could open the Denman gate without it falling off in your hands.

He turned and looked at Walsh, then back to the gate. Walsh looked down at the gate then back to Allen, 'I know what you're thinking, and no, I'm not. The second I touch it, off it comes in my hands.'

'Well, someone's got to open it,' Allen said, trying to keep a straight face.

'Oh, come on. I mean look, there's an old toilet over there,' Walsh said, pointing towards the toilet.

'I bet it doesn't work,' smiled Allen.

'No, really,' Walsh replied sarcastically.

'Oh, no, it won't work. The one in the bloody bathroom never worked. What hope has that one got?'

'Didn't houses like this have outside toilets?' asked Walsh, trying his hardest not to laugh.

'Yeah, but not outside in the front garden. Tell you what, my old man would spend about an hour sitting in the toilet reading the paper. He only did it to get away from my mum's nagging.'

'So you're telling me he'd sit on a toilet that's outside in the cold and the snow for an hour, just so he couldn't hear your mum nagging?'

'Yeah,' smiled Allen, 'but she'd follow him outside and nag at him through the door. I'm not really sure why she did it, to be truthful.'

'Why's that then?' Walsh asked looking over at the old toilet.

'He was stone deaf.'

'Bloody hell, Davidson warned me about you. He said on my first day that your sense of humour was terrible.'

'Working with Davidson for the last thirty-odd years you need a sense of humour. Right, go on then, Inspector. Open it,' laughed Allen.

'Yes, Sir. But trust me, if this thing falls off, I'm blaming you,' Walsh said as he stood in front of the gate.

It happened in slow motion. As Inspector Walsh had hold of the gate in his right hand, just as he was about to open the lock, the gate came away in his hands. Allen and Walsh turned and looked at each other. Neither said a word, but both found it hard not to laugh. Both men hurried into the garden. Walsh placed the gate back as carefully as possible, so it didn't look as if it had come away.

Allen turned and looked at Walsh with tears running down his face through laughing so much.

'What?' said Walsh, holding his hands and arms out as if pleading his innocence.

'I'm sorry, Peter,' he said holding his hands up as if to apologise, 'I knew that would happen. It's an old joke from years back when we were kids. We'd play a game—who could open the Denman gate without it falling off.'

'Anyone manage it?' smiled Walsh.

'No, no, I don't believe anyone did. Okay, there's two things I need to tell you,' Allen said as he rang the doorbell.

'Which is?' replied Walsh fearing the worst.

'Well, as you've already witnessed with the gate, you see, a lot of the decorating and some of the rebuilding of this fine old house was done by none other than Sidney Yates.'

'Oh great, now the house is going to fall down the second that front door is opened. What's the other thing then?' Walsh asked as the door was opened.

'Alice here is blind,' Allen said smiling.

'Well, I'd know that voice anywhere,' said a grey-haired old lady.

The old lady was still in an old dressing gown that looked as old as the house. She had on her feet what Inspector Walsh could only describe as bomb damaged slippers.

'Johnny Allen, well, well. And who's your friend then?' Alice asked taking hold of Allen's hand.

'This Alice is Peter Walsh, and Peter, this is Alice Denman.'

'Nice to meet you, Peter. Now Johnny how long has it been?' she asked, as she led the two detectives inside.

'Too long, Alice, way too long,' he replied smiling.

'Now then let me look at you.' Allen stood in front of Alice. She felt around his face. She smiled to herself as she did, 'Still the same old Johnny; still as handsome as ever.'

'You still haven't heard from Norman then?' he asked her as he sat down on an old armchair.

'No, that boy, he'll be the death of me. Peter, now sit yourself down over there on the sofa.'

Inspector Walsh looked at the sofa inquisitively. He turned to Allen for help and guidance, as if to ask, is it safe to sit on. Allen just sat back in the old chair with a big smile on his face.

'I'll just put the tea on. You boys make yourselves comfortable.'

'Go on then, Peter, sit yourself down. You heard the lady. Make yourself comfortable.'

Inspector Walsh sat on the edge of the sofa. He was almost too scared to sit back in it; he moved himself slowly backwards. He was surprised that after sitting on the sofa for about ten seconds nothing had happened.

'You'll be safe on that one, Peter. It's only about twenty years old. It was her old one that was the problem.'

'Why's that then?' Walsh asked shifting around the sofa.

'Well, if you sat in the middle, you'd end up like a praying mantis. And if there were two of you sitting on either end, you needed to balance the weight up. I remember coming around here with Jane. Now as you know, Jane's five foot nothing and about a hundred pounds wet through; and I'm not a hundred pound wet through, I'm double that. Well, Jane sat on one end I sat on the other, and she almost hit her head on the ceiling.'

Inspector Walsh looked at Allen with tears running down his face, 'Bloody brilliant that,' he laughed.

'Oh God, bloody hell, I've just remembered, Alice's tea,' he said looking at Walsh with a concerned look on his face.

'I don't want to know.'

'Now Peter, you've sat in this lovely old house for around five minutes. Now look to your right and tell me that pot plants don't grow to be around seven foot tall.'

Walsh turned and looked at the pot plant that was as tall as the room, if not taller. 'I'm almost too scared to ask. That's not a pot plant, that's like something out of *The Day of the Triffids".'*

'That pot plant has drunk more tea over the last twenty-odd years since Alice went blind, than anyone on this planet. I'll let you get your tea first, then I'll tell you.'

'Bloody hell, Johnny, I've never seen anything like this. I'm almost too scared to ask what's coming next.'

Allen smiled at him and said, 'You think this is bad, we've got a trip to the Reynolds's household next.'

'You are joking, right?' Walsh could see by the look on Johnny's face that he wasn't joking. 'You're not joking, are you?'

'I only wish I was, Peter. Trust me, it's going to be an eye-opener.'

Mrs Denman came back into the living room with a tray of cups. 'Here we go, boys.' She placed the tray on a table. Walsh was surprised at how well she did.

'Don't be surprised, Peter. I can walk around this house without having any accidents. Been blind for over twenty-plus years now; I see things with my mind, not my eyes,' she said sitting down on her old armchair.

'Now Alice, tell me when was the last time you saw Norman?' Allen asked looking at his tea with some fear in his eyes.

'Now then, let's see, two days ago now. I take it he went out to work as normal, but he never made it. His boss rang me to ask if he was okay. You see, I wasn't here over the weekend. I went to stay with my sister, so truthfully I don't know'

'Mr Richardson, I went around to his shop yesterday morning,' Walsh said as he reached for his cup of tea.

Allen could see by the look on Peter's face that he just worked out why no one ever drunk Alice's tea. Walsh looked over at Allen with raised eyebrows. Allen made a gesture to pour the bloody lot into the pot plant. Walsh looked again at the watery milky liquid that Alice passed off as tea, then back to Allen.

'Tell me, Alice, what's Norman been like over the last month or so?'

'Not himself, Johnny, not at all. I would say he's been acting very strangely, almost fearful of something or someone.'

'Does he go out much?' asked Walsh.

'No, not really. Only thing he does except go to work is to go out and take photographs. Now don't take this the wrong way, but he never went on any dates, not that too many girls would want to date him. You see, Peter, Norman was hard work, very hard work, Johnny will tell you that.'

'What do you believe happened the afternoon Alison was murdered?' Allen asked.

Mrs Denman sat right back in her armchair. You could see by the look on her face that it still upset her greatly.

'He never killed her. I know he liked her; that was easy to see. But my boy was no murderer. He was gentle, a gentle young man. He changed, though, after my Joan died. It haunted him for years, still does. I've never been sure of what happened to either Alison or Joan.'

'Does he ever say much about either of them?' asked Walsh.

'No, no, he wouldn't; never said much about Alison. He would sometimes speak about Joan and what they did as young kids. You see, Peter, he was devoted to his sister. He'd do anything for her, anything at all. She was very good with him, helped him a lot. She was one of the only people who could calm him down. That's my Joan's picture on the fireplace. You can have a look if you like.'

As Inspector Walsh got up off the sofa, a loud twanging noise accompanied his movements.

'Bloody sofa, that spring's always going; had it fixed time and time again,' Alice said looking towards Johnny and winking at him. 'Do you remember the old sofa, Johnny?' she asked him smiling.

'Remember it? I'm still having bloody nightmares about it,' Allen said laughing.

Inspector Walsh stood looking at the photo of Joan Denman. She was a dark-haired girl with big brown eyes. Walsh could see a likeness to her mother in the photograph. 'She looks like you Mrs Denman.'

'It's Alice, dear. Yes, thankfully. I wouldn't have wanted her to look like her father, God no. I'll tell you, that man must have aged two years for every one that he was alive. By the time he reached fifty, he looked about a hundred.'

Allen could see the sadness in her face as she thought about Joan and her late husband. 'You okay Alice?' he asked, taking her hand.

'Oh, I'm okay, Johnny. Horrible man, what he did to that poor girl, my poor Joan. I don't miss him. I'm happier now he's gone.'

'What happened, if you don't mind me asking?' Walsh said as he sat down very carefully.

'He abused her right from the age of about ten, right through until she died. You see, she hung herself in that old boat house down by the river. He found her, Norman did.'

'Long time ago, Alice, long time,' he said softly to her.

'Find my boy. He's a good lad. Please find my Norman. I know if anyone can, then it's you, Johnny. One more thing, that girl that was murdered, ask her, you have to ask Jane,' she said taking hold of his arm.

'I will, Alice. I'll find Norman, and I'll ask Jane,' he smiled. 'One more thing, Alice, do you have a picture of Norman, an up-to-date one?'

'I'll go and get you one,' she said, smiling as she hurried off into the other room.

Once Alice had left the room, Allen quickly stood up and poured both cups of tea into the pot plant. He then placed both cups on the tray, turned to Inspector Walsh and smiled.

'Best place for it if you ask me,' Walsh said as he looked back at the pot plant.

'Here we go then,' Alice said as she handed Allen a photo of Norman.

'Thank you, Alice,' he said, giving the old lady a kiss on her cheek.

'Have you met her then, Peter, Jane I mean?' she asked him smiling.

'Yes, I have, and she's beautiful,' he replied.

'She's always been so beautiful; only had eyes for each other. You'll ask her?' she said, looking towards Allen, then towards Walsh, 'Make sure he does for me, Peter.'

'I will, Alice,' Walsh said smiling at Allen.

'Come on, let's get this over and done with; let's go and see Elizabeth Mary Reynolds. Trust me, this is going to be fun.'

'She's amazing, Alice I mean. You wouldn't have known she was blind.'

'Yes, she is. She's had a hard life, you know. Her husband, Norman Senior or old Norman as we called him, was horrible, not only to Alice but Joan and Norman. God knows what he put his family through over the years. As a child, Norman was scared to death of him. He'd hit him, you know; he'd call him stupid, thick, always on at him.'

'What about Joan, what's the story there?' asked Walsh.

'She was nice, Joan, really lovely person, very kind, would help anyone. But her father wouldn't leave her alone, sexually, I mean. As far as I can make out, Norman found out the night before Joan hung herself, what had happened. He ended up stood in the middle of the road just screaming. He just couldn't take it in. Well, old Norman did six years. Sad part about it was when he came out, Alice took him back.'

'I take it old Norman's dead now?' asked Walsh.

'Yes, he died about ten years or so back. He had a heart attack, sat in his armchair and just died. As you've probably worked out, Alice wasn't overly upset.'

'I can't believe a husband or a father would put their loved ones through that much pain,' Walsh said, shaking his head in disbelief.

'I know. I'm not surprised Joan took her own life. She must have been so desperate. If only she'd told someone before it was too late. Come on, we'll walk. It's only about five minutes around the road to the Reynolds house.'

'Did Joan leave a suicide note at all?' Walsh asked.

'I don't know, to be truthful. You see, as I've said, it only came out the night before. From what I can remember, and from other people's accounts, the story goes like this. Young Norman had been out taking photographs. It was a Saturday afternoon. Alice was out visiting her mother who was in hospital, which left Joan and her father at home alone. I'll tell you any excuse and old Norman would take it. Young Norman came back to screaming. He found her upstairs sitting on the bathroom floor just screaming. She just went hysterical. What happened after that, I've no idea. It was Grace Reynolds that had said that Joan had been abused by her father. Young Norman just couldn't take it in, but he was scared of him.

Some people have even said that it was young Norman who'd abused her, but truth be told, I don't know.'

'How did Grace Reynolds find out?'

'You see Grace has had a lot of mental problems even as a child, but she was clever, very clever. She seemed to be able to read people and situations very well, and even manipulate them to her advantage.'

'Was she the type of child that would tell tall stories?'

'Sometimes yes, but like I said, she could manipulate a situation to suit herself. She was very good at getting Billy to do whatever she wanted. She could wrap him around her little finger.'

Allen stood outside number 23 Park Road, so named as a park ran behind the row of houses. Allen smiled to himself. He'd spent many a happy time in this old house as a child. The house itself hadn't changed in over thirty years. Same front door, same colour as well, and what seemed to be the same hedge that ran right across the front garden.

'You're lucky this time, Peter, no gate. Okay, now then, as you well might have guessed having three children, and let's be truthful, all three were a handful, Beth is, let's say, very loud. She will say it as it is. The fun part is when she gets on at poor old Tom. Trust me, what that man's been through, God only knows.'

'Anything I need to know?' Walsh asked nervously.

'Like what?' replied Allen with a smirk on his face.

'Well, is it safe to sit down, is the tea drinkable, and are there seven-foot pot plants?'

'Umm, well, sort of, the hard part will be getting through the front door in one piece.'

'Why?'

'Sheba.'

'Sheba, what in hell's name is Sheba?' Walsh asked, knowing all too well he wouldn't like the answer.

'A great Dane,' Allen whispered softly enough so Peter couldn't quite hear him.

'What? You didn't just say what I thought you said?'

'A great Dane, and a bloody big one at that.'

'That's what I thought you said. How big?'

'Well, it's about the same size as that pot plant, but I don't know for sure. The last time I saw her, she was only a puppy. Even then she was about the same size as Jane.

'Oh, great, what's her name, Sheba?'

'Yes, Sheba the Second to be accurate,' replied Allen.

'So you're telling me there was a Sheba mark one?' Walsh asked nervously.

'Yes,' Allen replied with some fear in his voice.

'Okay, I've just remembered I need to make an important phone call, but I've left my phone in your car,' Walsh said as he headed out of the garden.

Allen turned and stood in front of Peter. He placed his hands on his shoulders, looked him straight in the eyes and said. 'Do it for the badge, for Queen and country, for the honour, and mostly for me and the fact that I'm scared shitless of dogs.'

'Oh, come on then. I'm going to need weeks of therapy after all this,' Walsh laughed nervously.

'Why do you think I'm like I am? I bloody well lived here. In fact, I lived three doors away at number 29, Jane lived at 31. A good story about Sheba the First. One day Jane was outside playing with her younger brother Laurence, when Sheba got out. Trust me, that girl must have broken the hundred metres world record. Laurence just stood there saying, 'Nice horsey, nice horsey.'

'Bloody hell, I think I'd have done the same as Jane.'

Allen took a deep breath and rang the doorbell. Within seconds all hell broke loose. All you could hear was loud barking, then the front door nearly coming off its hinges as the dog launched itself at it.

Allen took five steps backwards turned around to make sure Peter was okay, only to find him lying in the next door's front garden with his hands held over his head.

'Peter, Peter, you okay?' Allen asked with some concern, 'How the bloody hell did you end up over there?'

Inspector Walsh looked up at Allen took a deep breath and said, 'Tell Amy and the kids that I love them.'

The front door was slowly opened, but only enough for a head to peer through the gap.

'Hello,' came the voice from behind the door.

'Hello, Beth, I see the dogs doing well?' smiled Allen.

'Well, well, Johnny Allen, do come in. Sheba, will you get down?' she screamed at the dog.

Allen and Walsh nervously entered the Reynolds household. 'Don't worry, she only wants to be friendly.

'Friendly? Bloody hell, Beth, this one's bigger than the last one,' Allen said looking at the dog with wide eyes.

'What does she eat?' Walsh said hiding behind Allen.

'Policemen probably,' replied Allen.

'I'll put her outside in the garden. Sit yourselves down then.'

Allen and Walsh sat down on the sofa. Both turned and looked at each other, neither saying a word, but both knew what the other was thinking.

'Okay, she'll be okay out there. Right then, what can I do for you then Johnny?'

'Seen much of Billy recently then Beth?' Allen asked.

'Come on Johnny, you of all people know where Billy's living. He's not been back home since,' she replied sternly.

'You can do better than that, Beth. He's been seen by someone who knows him very well,' Allen replied.

'Okay, then, by who?'

'That doesn't matter. All I want to know is, is he here?'

Allen could tell Beth wasn't being truthful. Was she protecting him? Protecting him from what? 'Look, Beth, he's done nothing wrong, I just want to talk to him that's all.'

'If he's been back, then he hasn't been to see me, and that's the truth. Ask Grace. If he's back then he's more than likely to stay with her. Only one of my three I see is Jackson.'

'What happened to Billy? Why did he just up and leave?'

'Don't know really. Maybe he couldn't live with what his brother did. As you well know, Johnny, he changed after Alison was murdered; just wasn't the same Billy anymore. I'll tell you something, police got the wrong man for her murder; right family, father not son.'

'Why do you say that?'

'That bloody man, no wonder that boy was like he was, having a father like that. I wouldn't be surprised if he killed his own daughter, with what he put her through. Okay, she took her own life, but he put the rope around her neck.'

'I know, he was an evil man, Beth, but he's no murderer.'

120

'You reckon, Johnny?' She said shaking her head. 'Old Norman, that's who killed Alison; couldn't leave young girls alone. God knows why Alice took him back.'

'Wasn't he inside at the time?' asked Walsh.

'No, that was about six months later,' replied Allen.

'You don't see much of Grace then?' Allen asked.

'No, not much. That girl, always a troubled child. It would upset me when people called her strange, but she had problems. She was sweet as a child. I'd always wake her up the same way each morning, 'Wakey, wakey, sleepyhead. Jane was the only one who could see that Grace was struggling with life. Billy was close to her, but Jackson never helped matters much, always on at her.'

'Is Jackson living back here?' Allen asked.

'On and off. Some days he's here, other's he's…God knows, I don't know,' she said with tears in her eyes.

'I know what he did was wrong. But I'm a mother, and I love my children. If God can forgive, so can I.'

'Did Billy ever say much about Alison?' Allen asked.

'He liked her, liked her a lot; you could see that a mile away. But something happened between Billy, Alison and Jackson. Don't know what though,' she replied. 'Sheba, Sheba,' she shouted at the dog.

'When was this?' Walsh asked nervously, as the dog was trying it's best to take the back door off.

'Just before she died. Jackson and Grace had this big argument; always at each other those two. This was the night before Alison was murdered.'

'Any idea what it was about?' asked Walsh.

'No, sorry. All I heard was Grace telling Jackson that she was going to tell Billy, but what I don't know. That morning, Jackson was up and out early; no idea where he went. Then sometime early afternoon Grace and Billy were arguing. All I heard him say was, 'You better be telling the truth.' Then he said, 'I'll kill him.' After that he stormed out.'

'No Tom?' Allen asked politely.

'No, his brother isn't well. He's in hospital, had a stroke a couple of days ago. Tom's up there visiting. He's not been that good himself, heart problems.'

'Truthfully, Beth, Grace was very manipulative, especially with her two brothers.'

'Oh, yes, very clever that girl. She'd say one thing to Jackson, then something different to Billy. The boys would fight and argue; Grace would sit back and enjoy the moment.'

'So she could very well have been just winding Billy and Jackson up?'

'Oh, yes, very much so.'

'Thank you, Beth, it's good to see you again,' Allen said smiling at her.

'And you, Johnny, go careful. I saw Jane the other week. How is she? Must be so hard on her.'

'She's okay. She struggling with it all, but she's a strong-willed lady. She'll be fine.'

Allen and Walsh walked slowly back to Allen's car, neither saying much. Both men were deep in thought. What was the argument between Jackson and Billy about? Was it just Grace trying to manipulate her two brothers? After all, that's what she was like as a child, always trying to get a payoff.

'What do you reckon happened between Jackson and Billy? Remember what Beth said about Grace and Billy's argument, when she heard him say, 'You better be telling the truth,' then, 'I'll kill him'?

'Tell you what, Johnny, you said that Jackson and Alison hated each other. What if Jackson had a go at her, Grace heard this or even witnessed it, then told Billy?'

'Maybe. I can't get out of my mind that this has something to do with Joan's suicide. Norman found his sister, so he must have gone looking for her.'

'Would he have known where she would go?' asked Walsh.

'I'm not sure. We all knew of the old boat house. It was somewhere we all went.'

'Problem with Norman is, he wouldn't have understood his sister was dead.'

'Yeah, you're right, he had no idea. Remember, 'Wake up Joan, wake up. I found her asleep'? Come on, I want to speak to Grace Reynolds again.'

Allen sat in his car. He turned to Walsh and said, 'Something happened between Grace and her brothers. Trust me, I'm going to find out the truth, even if I have to arrest her.'

Allen was just about to start his car when his mobile rang. 'Let's hope this is good news.'

'Yes, Richard, what can I do for you?' he asked.

'Sir, we've got a problem here,' replied the desk sergeant.

'Go on, Richard.'

'We've got Norman Denman here. He won't come in. He's standing out in the car park; keeps calling for you.'

'Okay, Dick, don't upset him. Make sure he doesn't leave. I'll be there in ten minutes.'

'One more thing, Sir, he's holding a knife. It's got a hell of a lot of dried blood on it.'

'Okay, is Davidson there? Allen asked. He was now worried, almost scared. *What the hell has he done?* he asked himself.

'Yes, Sir, I'll hand him over to you.'

'Johnny, he won't talk to anyone else but you. I've tried to get him to come inside, but he just screams, I want Johnny.'

'Okay Bill, I'm on my way.'

Allen sped off at high speed. 'Norman's turned up at the station. He's out in the car park. He won't go inside, neither will he speak to anyone but me. Problem is he's holding a knife with a hell of a lot of dried blood on it.'

Allen pulled up outside the main gates to the police station. He could see Norman standing in the middle of the car park, holding a knife in his right hand. The knife was around twelve inches in length with a black handle.

'Right, nice and slowly. Okay, let me speak to him.'

Allen and Walsh both climbed slowly out of the car. Walsh walked slowly around to the left-hand side of where Norman was standing. He stopped around twenty feet away from him. Allen walked slowly up behind Norman and stopped about ten to twelve feet away.

'Norman, it's Johnny. I'm here,' Allen said as Norman turned around to face him.

'Johnny, you're my friend.' Norman turned to his right and glared at Inspector Walsh. As he did, he took about ten steps backwards, shouting, 'NO, NO, NO.'

'It's okay, it's okay. This is Peter; he's my friend. He'll help you.' Allen said holding his hands and arms out in an attempt to calm him down.

Norman looked at Walsh then at Allen. He nodded but still seemed very nervous of Walsh's presence. Allen knew that any little thing could and would set him off, so he needed to keep him as calm as possible.

'Norman, why don't you drop the knife, so Peter can take it?' Allen said as he slowly walked towards him. Allen looked around the station car park. By this time, the whole station was gripped by what was happening. You could, by now, cut the tension with a knife; no one was saying a word.

'NO, NO, I didn't hurt Alison. I didn't hurt her, Johnny. She was my friend,' he screamed.

'I know, I know, Norman. It's okay. Why don't you drop the knife on the ground?'

Norman looked down at the knife he was holding in his hands. Letting go of the knife, it seemed to drop to the ground in slow motion, the sound echoed around the silent car park. Norman looked up at Johnny. Then turning to Inspector Walsh, he started walking towards him. Stopping around ten feet away from him, he said, 'You're my friend, Peter. You can have the knife.'

Walsh looked over towards Allen, Allen nodded to him. He slowly walked over towards Norman and the knife. Allen made a gesture with his hands for Walsh to stop.

'Norman, Peter's just coming to pick the knife up, okay? Now can you walk slowly over this way? I'll walk over with you. It's okay, it's okay,' he said trying to reassure him.

Norman looked at Allen and nodded. Allen looked over towards Walsh. Inspector Walsh waited until Norman was some distance away. He quickly moved towards the knife as Norman and Johnny walked slowly over to the other side of the car park. He placed an evidence bag on his hand and picked it up. The knife was covered in dried blood, both on the blade and the handle. Walsh looked at it. *Bloody hell,* he thought. He knew in an instant what it was used for. This was the knife that killed Megan.

'That was okay. Well done, Norman,' Allen said smiling at him.

'I couldn't wake her up. She was sleeping, sleeping like Alison and Joan.'

'Who was sleeping Norman? Tell me?' Allen asked walking slowly towards him.

Norman looked down at his feet, then up at Allen, 'Your daughter.'

'Megan? What happened to her? Can you remember?' he asked.

'She's asleep, Johnny, just like Alison. She wouldn't wake up.'

'Where did you find the knife? Can you tell me?'

'I found it by Megan. She had it.'

'Tell you what, how would you like to come and see my office? Maybe we can have a cup of tea as well.'

'Is this where you work, Johnny?' he asked smiling.

'Yeah, it's nice here. You'll like it,' he said, placing his hand on Norman's shoulder.

'Okay then.'

'Norman, Peter's going to come with us as well. Is that okay?'

'Peter's my friend. He'll help me.'

'I just need to talk to Peter and my boss. You stay right here, okay?'

'Your boss?' he asked, 'Like Mr Richardson? He's my boss.'

Allen nodded and walked slowly over towards Walsh and Davidson. 'You okay, Johnny? Davidson asked with some anxiety in his voice.

'Yeah, I'm fine; just didn't want him upset, that's all,' Allen replied, blowing his cheeks out.

'The knife's been sent off for forensics.' Walsh added looking over towards Norman. He was standing over by three patrol cars, just staring at the ground, no emotion. It was almost a lifeless expression.

'Is he okay?' Walsh asked Allen.

Allen turned and looked at him, 'He'll be okay, don't worry. I know how to handle him. You've got to let me speak to him, no one else. He trusts me, a child in an adult body. God, this doesn't look that good, does it? I'll tell you both what you'll find on that knife, Megan's blood and Norman's fingerprints.

Allen walked back over towards Norman. He placed his arm around his shoulder and smiled at him, 'Come on then, let's go. I'm afraid we've rather a lot of steps to walk up. You see my office is right up there,' he said pointing up at his office.

Norman looked skywards, and said, 'That's high, Johnny, almost as high as the sky.'

Allen knew Davidson would want Norman charged. After all, none of this looked good for him, especially if it was Megan's blood and Norman's fingerprints on that knife. What was he doing here? He couldn't understand what made him come down to the station. Where had he been hiding? Was he even hiding? Or had someone told him to do this?

Allen knew he wouldn't understand what was going on. He'd remember from the last time; he'll remember being in a police cell. He couldn't get one thought out of his mind. It was an image, a flashback of Norman holding his sister's lifeless body in his arms. Was that where all this started? Did he kill her?

Allen and Walsh led Norman into their office. He stood in the middle of the room and looked around. He turned and looked at Johnny and smiled. 'It's nice. Where can I sit?' he asked.

Allen moved a chair that was placed by Peter's desk, and placed it in front of his. Norman looked at the chair, smiled and sat on it.

'How's that then?' asked Allen.

'It's good. Are we going to play at being policemen?' he smiled.

'That's a good idea Norman. You can help me and Peter with something really important. You told me that Megan had the knife. Can you remember where you were when you found it?'

'Yes, by the river,' he replied.

'What, where we played as kids?' asked Allen.

'Yes, Megan fell asleep. She was asleep in the same place as Alison.'

'When was this Norman? What day was it?' Allen asked reassuring him.

'It would have been Saturday, but it was dark. I told Megan that she shouldn't sleep outside in the dark.'

'What made you go there? Why were you at the river?'

'Megan, I followed her.'

'From where?'

'The music place. I didn't like it there, too loud. I saw Jackson, so I was scared.'

'Did you speak to Megan at all when you were in the music place?'

'Yes, I told her that the tablets would hurt her. Is that why she went to sleep, Johnny?'

'Maybe. Now Norman, I'm going to ask you about Joan. Is that okay?'

For the first time since Norman sat down in his office, he looked on edge, unsure. Allen knew that by asking him about his sister, it would upset him.

'Look, I need to ask you, so I can help. Remember when you found Joan, was she asleep in the boat house?'

'No, she was standing on a chair. I told her she'd fall off and hurt herself.'

'Did she fall off?' he asked.

'Yes, then she fell asleep. She had a rope around her neck.'

'What did you do then?' he asked. 'Can you tell me?'

'She was playing swinging on the rope. I watched her play, then I helped her down,'

Bloody hell, he sat and watched his own sister die, Allen said to himself. He thought she was playing a game. He sat and watched Norman. Even after all these years, he still had no idea she's dead.

'Was she asleep then?' he asked.

'Yes, she wouldn't wake up.'

'Did you see anyone else around at the time?'

'I don't want to tell you,' he shouted.

'Why don't you want to tell me, Norman?'

'No, no, no,' he screamed. He started rocking backwards and forwards. Allen could see he was starting to get very distressed. He walked over to him and put his arms around his shoulders. 'It's okay, it's okay,' he whispered to him over and over again.

'Norman, look at me. I can't help you, if you don't tell me who you saw down by the boat house.'

Norman stopped rocking backwards and forwards. He looked down at the floor and said, 'It was Grace Reynolds.'

'Did she speak to you at all?'

'No, she ran away,' he said looking up at Allen. 'I don't want to play at being a policeman anymore.'

'One more question, then we'll stop. When you followed Megan to the river, was she asleep or awake when you found her?'

'I don't understand, Johnny,' he cried out.

'Was she asleep like Alison was?'

'No,' he replied.

Allen turned to Inspector Walsh, and said, 'Peter, can you find Richard for me? Also bring PC Wilkins with you.'

He sat down and rubbed his eyes. *What a mess,* he thought. He couldn't understand how people he grew up with, people he considered not just friends but family, could get themselves in to such a mess. What went wrong? Something from the past set all this off, but what? He looked over at Norman. No way would he have come here with that knife, unless told to do so, but by whom? He'd be kept in a cell overnight, and unless he came up with new evidence, then Norman Denman would be charged with Megan's murder.

'Right, Norman, this is Richard and Gary, both very good friends of mine and Peter. Richard here, is also very good at photography, just like yourself.' Allen paused took a deep breath and said, 'I'm afraid, Norman, that you're going to have to stay here for a while. Do you understand?'

Norman stood by the chair he was sitting on, staring at the floor. He didn't say anything. He just nodded.

Allen and Walsh stood and watched as Richard and the very large frame of PC Wilkins took Norman down to the cells. Walsh could see that Johnny didn't want to place Norman down there, but he had no choice.

Allen took a deep breath and sighed. 'I'm missing something. Don't know what, but it's something I've seen. Never mind. Right come on, let's go and have a chat with Grace Reynolds. Tell you what, meet me downstairs. I'd better let Davidson know what's happening.'

'No problem, see you in a minute,' Walsh replied as he left the office.

Allen walked slowly down one flight of stairs and stood outside Davidson's office. Maybe Davidson and Simon Woods were right all along, Norman Denman murdered Alison Woods.

He knocked the door and waited. 'Enter,' boomed Davidson's voice.

'Johnny, well, what's he said then?'

'Okay, he said he followed her down to the river from the nightclub. He also said she wasn't asleep when he met her.'

'So she was alive? Is that what you're telling me, Johnny?'

'Yes Bill, it is,' replied Allen.

'So if forensics comes back with Megan's blood and Norman's fingerprints, then we've got him. Well done, Johnny, great work.'

'Thanks.' He didn't look Davidson in the eyes. He just turned and walked slowly out of his office. Well done, Johnny, great work, so why doesn't it feel that way. It still didn't feel right. He still felt something was wrong. *I've said it before and I'll say it again, Norman Denman's no murderer. He didn't kill Alison and he didn't kill Megan, no way,* he said to himself. He walked down the last two flights of stairs and into the main lobby, and over to where Peter was waiting for him.

'You okay?' Walsh could see in his eyes that he hated what he'd just done, but he didn't have a choice.

'Bloody hell, this isn't right. Norman didn't murder either Alison or Megan. Trust me, if he did, then that's it. I quit.'

'It doesn't look good for him. What do you want to do next?'

'Come on let's go and ask Grace Reynolds what the argument was between her and her brothers.'

'You believe he was set up, don't you?' Walsh asked.

'Yeah, I do. Look, he sat and witnessed his sister commit suicide, for God sake. He's no killer,' he sighed. 'You heard what he said. She was playing swinging, then she went to sleep. He just doesn't understand.'

'He wouldn't cope in prison again, would he?'

'No, not at all. Right, let's see what Grace has to say about what she witnessed that afternoon as well. You drive. I need to think.'

Chapter 9

The rain had just started to come down again. The weather matched his mood, very dark. His mind turned to Joan Denman's suicide. Beth Reynolds was right in some way; Joan's father may have well put the rope around her neck.

Oh my God, he thought, *Norman Denman didn't just witness his sister's hanging, what if he caused it?* She was standing on an old chair. Norman tells her to get down or she'll hurt herself. Did he push her or knock the chair from under her? After all, he's always been the clumsiest of people. The image flashed through his mind, *Oh no, not like that.* Did he accidently kill his sister? Is that what Grace witnessed? *Saint Christopher, photograph,* it went over and over in his mind, *but what does it mean?*

'I hope I'm wrong, but I've just had a horrible thought about Norman. He accidently killed his sister,' he said, sighing for about the one hundredth time. 'You've seen him. You've witnessed how clumsy he is. What if he accidently knocked Joan off the chair? It would have been just a game to him. No way he'd have foreseen what was to come.'

'If Grace Reynolds witnessed this, surely she would have said something?' Walsh replied.

'Not sure how she'd have taken it. She was very shy and nervous as a child, even into her teenage years. Something like that would have just freaked her out.'

'Whatever way you look at this, it doesn't look good for him,' Walsh added.

'I can't get over the feeling I've missed something blindingly obvious. I know it's in here somewhere,' he said pointing at his head.

Walsh smiled at him and said, 'I'm shocked. I thought you saw everything.'

'I do,' he laughed. 'Sometimes I see things I'm not even looking at. Then a day or so later I get these thoughts in my mind or a flashback.'

'It will come.' Walsh knew Johnny could see things others couldn't. But even his mind at the moment must be running at a hundred miles an hour.'

He sat back and closed his eyes. *Be nice to sleep,* he thought, *just block out the world. Come on, think. Saint Christopher, photograph. My Saint Christopher stolen from where? Where was I? Come on, where? Party? New Year's Eve 1990, Jane's house, I had it on.*

He didn't hear it. He was miles away, 'Johnny, Johnny, your phone,' Walsh said, smiling at him.

'Oh God, yes. Hello Allen,' he answered.

'Johnny, it's Melissa. I've seen that man, you know, Norman.'

'Where was this Missy? he asked her, surprised.

'Early this morning. He was standing opposite our house again.'

'What time was this?'

'Around half past nine – ten o'clock. It was just after mum got that parcel. Also, he was with another man, but I couldn't see his face, so I haven't been able to draw him at all.'

'Okay, Missy, look, don't worry. I know where Norman is. What was this man like build-wise?'

'He was a lot smaller than Norman in height and build. He was wearing a black fleece jacket and dark blue tracksuit bottoms, white training shoes, that's it.'

'Okay, thanks, Missy. Tell mum I'll ring her later.'

'Will do.'

'Okay, Johnny?'

'Yeah, no, it's all okay. That was Melissa. She saw Norman this morning, standing opposite their house. She said he was with another man, but couldn't see him facially.'

'Any ideas who?'

'No, could be anyone.'

Walsh pulled up outside the flats where Grace Reynolds lived. The area looked totally different to where Alice Denman and Beth Reynolds lived. Walsh quickly looked around, no toilets, no gates that were about to fall off at any moment, and so far no massive dogs or seven-foot pot plants. He followed Johnny across the car park and over towards the entrance to the flats. He watched him push the buzzer that had Grace Reynolds name above it.

'Hello,' answered a lady's voice.

'Hello, Grace, it's Johnny,' he replied.

'Twice in two days, people will start talking, Johnny.'

Allen pushed the main door open. Walsh followed him up a flight of stairs. As he reached the top stair, he could see a dark-haired lady standing in the doorway to the flat. She wasn't quite what he'd expected, having met her mother earlier. She didn't look her age. Walsh had her down at early to mid-thirties, but he knew she was somewhere in her forties.

'Grace, this is Inspector Peter Walsh, Peter this is Grace Reynolds.'

'Hello, Peter. What's he been saying about me then? What a lovely sweet lady I am,' she said as she placed both hands under her chin and battered her eyelashes at him.

Walsh smiled a slightly awkward smile, 'Nice flat,' he replied.

'Yeah, glad you like it. Should be nice, cost enough.'

'Had a lovely chat with your mother earlier,' Allen said glancing towards the big photographs she had hanging on the walls.

'What's the old bag been saying now?' she replied sharply.

'Now, now Grace, that's your mother you're talking about,' Allen said, raising an eyebrow at her.

'I know. She's still an old bag though, Johnny. Now you haven't come around to speak about my dear old mother, so come on then out with it.'

'What can you remember about the day Joan Denman died?' Allen asked as he sat down.

She smiled a half nervous smile and took a deep breath, 'I knew you'd ask eventually. You see, I'd gone down to the river to think.' She stopped and bit her bottom lip. 'You see, I'd just had my first sexual encounter, a girlfriend of mine, really sweet. I needed to clear my mind, so I went for a walk. I was down by the river. Anyway, I was confused about how I felt sexually. I was miles away to start with. Truthfully I can't remember much at all,' she said, as she stopped and wiped a tear away from her eyes. 'By the time I'd realised where I was, I was down by the old boat house. As I got closer, I started to hear voices coming from inside. To be truthful, I wasn't that sure who it was; I couldn't make the voices out.' She smiled, 'Tell you what I thought it was, you know, a couple, well, having sex. Then I heard Norman's voice.'

'What did he say, Grace?' asked Allen.

'He told Joan to get down from a chair. Well, I think it was a chair anyway. He told her she'll hurt herself.'

'What happened after that? Did you see anything? he asked.

'Well, sort of. I've never been one hundred percent sure what really happened. I heard Joan scream out Norman's name.' Grace stopped speaking. She seemed really upset. It was almost as if she wanted to tell someone for years what had happened, but didn't know how to.

'You okay, Grace?' Allen asked her sympathetically.

'Yeah, I'm fine,' she said trying her hardest to compose herself. 'I heard this crash. I'd been standing by the window, you know, the one closest to the river.'

'Yeah, I know. Carry on,' he said.

'I then walked around to the door which was half open. She was just swinging from this rope. Norman was just standing there watching,' she said as the tears ran down her face.

'Why have you never told me this before, Grace? he asked her softly.

'I didn't know how to. I was scared. You see, I thought he'd killed her. It wasn't until some months later, I realised it was just an accident. I dream about what happened. It's been with me every day since. I just can't get that image of Joan out of my head. I've even had therapy for it.'

'You now believe it was an accident then?' asked Walsh.

'Oh, yes, well, I do now. He wouldn't have killed his sister, no way. If he did knock her off whatever she was standing on, then it was a total accident.'

'He seems very clumsy,' added Walsh.

'Trust me, Inspector, that man could fall over his own feet while sitting in a chair. His legs and feet always seemed half hour in front of his brain.'

'Poor Norman, he's had it hard, trust me on that,' replied Allen.

'Tell me, Johnny, how did you know I was there that afternoon?' she asked inquisitively.

'Norman, he told me he saw you.'

'I was never sure if he saw me or not. Do you remember the old wooden bench? Well, I panicked, you see, and knocked into it. He turned around and looked right at me.'

'What did you do after that?' Allen asked her.

'I ran. I was scared out of my mind.'

'You told me the other day that Norman had killed before. I took it to believe he murdered Alison, but you meant Joan didn't you.'

'No, no, Johnny, I meant Alison. Norman murdered Alison.'

Allen studied the photograph of Grace and her two brothers. It was telling him something, but what? He looked at it intensely, but he just couldn't see it.

He turned and studied the other photograph of Grace on her own, hoping it would give him inspiration, but again nothing. He closely examined the other photograph of the three of them. She was wearing a low-cut black top, no necklaces, no chains. You could clearly see her hands and arms, but nothing, not a ring, or bracelets, nothing obvious. Chains, necklaces, it flashed through his mind. He quickly turned and looked back at the other photograph. She was wearing in this one a low-cut blue dress and around her neck a solid gold chain. He closely examined the chain. It was thick, heavy, something a man would wear.

'What can you tell me about your argument with your two brothers on the day before Alison's murder?' Allen asked. He looked at Grace, no necklace, no chain. It flashed through his mind, Saint Christopher, photograph. *I've seen it, but where?* he said to himself.

'My mother's been talking again, hasn't she? Anyway, when were the three of us not arguing,' she smiled, 'Oh, I remember that one. You see, Jackson had a go at Alison, and you know how sweet Billy was on her.'

'What do you mean Jackson had a go at her? Surely not in a sexual way?'

'No way. What? Jackson and Alison? Now that is funny, really funny,' she replied laughing.

'Is it?' he replied bluntly.

'Yeah, it is. I wouldn't have touched that if she was the last woman on earth,' came a voice from the doorway.

Allen turned and looked at the man standing in front of the photograph of Grace. 'Well, well, Jackson, long time.' He'd aged, but not in a good way. He was two years older than himself, but looked more like ten to fifteen years older. He had thinning brown hair that was very grey around the sides. His eyes looked heavy and bloodshot; years of drug taking had taken its toll.

'If it isn't the great detective. Who's your puppet then?' he sneered, glaring at Inspector Walsh.

'This is Inspector Walsh, and he's nobody's puppet. How's the nightclub scene, good business?'

'No idea what you mean. I'm a bit old for nightclubs.'

'Remember James Clarke?' Allen asked staring blankly at him.

'No idea,' Jackson replied, shaking his head.

'Maybe you can enlighten me about your sibling argument?'

'It's like Grace said, I had a go at Alison. Billy didn't like it. Anyway, we were laughing about it a few hours later. How's Jane then, Johnny? Now that's someone I wouldn't mind having a go at, if you know what I mean,' he said smiling. 'And her youngest daughter, better keep an eye on that one,' he said, as his smile turned to a smirk.

Walsh could see by Allen's facial expression that Jackson was starting to get at him. He didn't reply to Jackson's lewd comments about Jane or Melissa. He just sat staring at him for what seemed like an age.

'Tell me, either of you two seen your brother recently?' asked Walsh, finally breaking the silence.

'Who Billy? Haven't seen my little brother for over twenty years. What about you, Johnny? Jackson asked, smiling at him.

'Same, but I know someone who has.'

'What? Billy's here?' Grace asked with some surprise.

'No, no way. If my brother was back in England, he would have been in contact,' Jackson said turning and glaring at his sister as if to say, well, have you seen him?

'No, Jackson, you surely don't believe I've seen him,' Grace replied angrily.

'Tell you something, someone you need to speak to, Alex Davis. Ask him what he was doing that afternoon,' Jackson said still glaring at his sister.

'Why Alex?' replied Allen.

'He was up to something. You think about it, he tried it on with Alison, married Jane, then had an affair with my sister. If you ask me, it was Alison he wanted more.'

'He's right, Johnny, she was all he'd ever speak about. I don't know if she liked him, but they'd started hanging around with each other.'

'How long was your affair with him, Grace?' asked Walsh.

'Not long, only about a month. He said his wife didn't want him. I understand she was having an affair with a policeman of all people,' Grace replied with a wicked smile on her face.

Allen half smiled. *Not the best-kept secret,* he thought. 'When did you last see him?' he asked.

'Oh, that was years back. It was a chance meeting, and I thought, why not, a change is as good as a rest.'

'You said, Jackson, that he tried it on with Alison. Anything come of it?' asked Walsh.

'Don't know, to be truthful,' he replied.

'Tell me both of you, did either of you know that Alison was pregnant.'

Grace looked at Allen open-mouthed. Her brother turned away and half smiled. 'Any idea who the father was?' she asked.

'No, I was hoping you might have some ideas?' he asked.

'Sorry, Johnny, like Jackson said, ask Alex Davis. He might know,' replied Grace.

'He never said anything to you about it?' asked Allen.

'No, not a thing. I'm not sure to what level or how far Alex and Alison's relationship had gotten too.'

'You and Billy were really close when we were younger. Did he not say anything to you about it?'

'No. I knew he liked her, we all did, but no.' He often wondered how far Billy's relationship with Alison had gone. Maybe he tried and did a better job of keeping it quiet than he and Jane did with theirs.

'What about you, big brother, any ideas?' she asked him with a smile. She quickly glanced at Johnny, and again smiled at him, as if to say I know something you don't.

He didn't say anything. He just looked at his sister, then turned to Allen and shook his head. Both Grace and Jackson looked surprised, even shocked that Alison was pregnant. She looked more surprised than he did, but with Grace you could never tell.

'I asked you a little while back, Jackson, if you knew James Clarke. Why did you say no?'

'I've never met him, okay,' he said, laughing nervously.

'He was Megan Davis's boyfriend, wasn't he?' Grace said, looking daggers at her brother. 'I didn't know him. I've never met him,' she continued.

'Alright, maybe I might have met him once or twice, and—?' he asked holding his hands and arms out, as he shrugged his shoulders.

'He's dead,' replied Allen.

'Bloody hell, how?' Jackson responded with shock and fear in his voice.

'He took his own life,' added Allen, trying to gauge their reactions.

'Not drugs. No, not James,' Jackson said rubbing his face. 'Look, I only knew him for about a couple of months. He seemed a nice kid. Didn't want to see him get into any trouble. That's the truth.'

'What about Megan? How well did you know her?' Walsh asked.

'Not that well. She didn't say much. I got the impression she wasn't that happy with James talking to me.'

'Thank you both for your time,' Allen said as he and Walsh got up to leave.

'Don't be a stranger, Johnny,' Grace replied smiling.

She watched from her front door as the two detectives left. Once out of sight, she slammed the front door shut and turned and looked straight at her brother. Her stare was one of anger, not sibling love. 'Oh, Jackson, what have you done? Tell me you had nothing to do with that boy's death. Come on, tell me,' she screamed at him.'

Jackson turned away from his sister. He didn't answer. She walked over to him and grabbed him by the shoulders and turned him around to face her. He looked at her with tears running down his face. He couldn't look at her for more than a split second before turning away again. She shook her head and shouted at him, 'No, not drugs. Not drugs, Jackson.'

Walsh knew Allen had seen something; he could see it in his eyes, in his facial expression. He himself had studied the photographs hard, but nothing sprung to mind. Did Johnny believe Grace? Was she telling the truth about the afternoon of Joan's suicide? If not, why lie? After all she didn't do anything; she didn't kill her. Joan took her own life.

'You've seen something, haven't you?' he asked turning to him.

'Well, maybe, I'm not sure. In the picture of Grace on her own, she was wearing a gold chain, a man's chain.

'What about the other picture?'

'No, the one that Norman took of the three of them, no it's too old. He never took the one of Grace. That was taken some years later. Problem is I've no way of finding out if it's mine or not.'

'I've a very good idea who took the one of Grace on her own. Wouldn't have been one Alex Davis by any chance?'

'Yeah, great minds,' Allen smiled.

'Tell you what, I'm going to see if I can find Alex Davis. What about you?'

'Well, I want to have a good look at all these photographs we've been getting, see what I've missed. Any blood matches as yet?' Allen asked fishing his mobile out of his pocket.

'Well, as expected, the one that was on your car has Megan's blood all over it. No fingerprints on it, only yours and mine.'

137

'Hi, it's me, you alright?' he asked her softly.

'Hi darling, I'm okay now, had a bit of an argument with my dad.'

'What about?'

'Sorry, it was about you. I told him I'm 48 years old; I'm not a child anymore; I can see and date who I like. We've also got another problem, we need to talk, Johnny,' she said nervously.

'Melissa rang me earlier. She said she saw Norman standing outside your house this morning.'

'Okay, she didn't tell me. Have you found Norman yet?' she asked.

'Yes, we have and it's not good news. I'll tell you later. I'll be home in about a couple of hours. Maybe we could go out for a meal tonight.'

'That will be nice. I'll book the Indian around the corner. You'll like it there.'

'Sounds good. See you later. Love you, Woods.'

'Love you, Allen,' she said laughing.

Allen replaced his phone in his pocket. He knew what was coming. He could hear it in Jane's voice. Maybe tonight was the right time. 'I'm going to ask Jane to marry me.'

'And about bloody time too, only about thirty years too late, but never mind.'

'Bloody hell, I hope she says yes. I've got a ring. I bought it back in 1990; I should have asked her back then. I've carried this ring around with me ever since,' he said, pulling a small box out of his jacket pocket. He opened it and looked at the ring.

'She'll say yes, you've no worries on that one.'

'I should have asked her, Peter, to hell with her father. Do you know what the first thing I ever said to her was?' he smiled.

'Go on then,' Walsh replied knowing it would be something stupid.

Allen smiled as he thought about what he said the first time he ever met Jane, 'I said, oh, bloody hell, you're gorgeous. It was right in front of my parents, Jane's parents, everyone. Trust me, the look on her father's face, God what a picture.'

Both men looked at each other and burst out laughing. 'What did Jane say?' asked Walsh.

'Not much, she just went bright red. Well, she did say thank you. Great chat up line or what,' he laughed.

'How did you meet Amy?' he asked Walsh.

'On a bus in Bristol. I'd been eyeing her up over about a week or so. I managed to pluck up enough courage to write a note and hand it to her. I was devastated when the next morning she wasn't on the bus. I thought I'd lost my chance. But the following morning she got on and came and sat next to me.'

'What did you write on the note?'

'I asked her if she would like to go out for a meal. Anyway, that morning she slipped me a note which said in big capital letters, YES PLEASE. Turns out she'd been trying to ask me out, but she was very shy and nervous.'

'So it all turned out right in the end,' Allen laughed.

Allen's thoughts turned to Alex Davis. What was his relationship with Alison? Were they just close friends? Or was it more than that? If so, was he the father? Did Billy Reynolds find out? Was that the reason she was murdered? If so, how did Billy find out? She must have told him. Maybe he saw them together and confronted them both about their relationship.

Grace looked genuinely surprised about Alison being pregnant. Jackson though, his reaction was different. He gave the impression he knew. But with Grace, you never can tell.

He wondered why Alex just up and left Jane. What was his reason? What did he know? He knew about his relationship with Jane, that's for sure. He may have even known that Megan wasn't his daughter. What did he witness on the afternoon of Alison's murder? Was he involved? Was he the murderer? After all, he'd met up with her sometime that afternoon. He thought back to what Roger Woods had told him, that Alison had been hanging around with Alex and his cousin for some time, but why? If she had feelings for Billy, why hang around with someone else?

Did Jane know? Did she know Alison was pregnant? But surely, she'd have told him that, unless Alison told her to keep it a secret.

What if Alex, sometime after he married Jane, had told her about Alison, told her he was the father? 'I believe I know the reason why Alison was murdered. It has to be with her being pregnant and who the father was.'

'Maybe Alex Davis was the father. We need to find him, he may hold the key to all this,' replied Walsh.

'Tell you what we'll do, we'll go around and have a chat with Jane and Melissa about Alex. Maybe they've heard from him.'

Jane stood in her eldest daughter's bedroom. She closed her eyes and imagined Megan as a young child playing on the floor with her dolls. She smiled to herself. Megan loved her dolls, wouldn't go anywhere without at least two of them with her. She sat on the edge of the bed and stroked the bed covers. Someone else she wouldn't go anywhere without was her stuffed toy dog named 'Over.' She had no idea why or how he came to be named 'Over the dog.' The toy dog always took pride and place sitting on her pillows. She reached over and grabbed hold of the toy dog, 'Hello, my name's Over the dog,' she laughed.

Jane stood up. Still holding the toy dog, she walked over towards a large pine wooden dressing table. On the table, was a picture of Megan and James that was taken last Christmas. She looked at the picture with tears rolling down her face. They were so young, so full of life, the whole world at their feet. She stood transfixed on the picture. Her tears were running off her face and on to the glass picture frame. She sat back down on Megan's bed holding the photo and the toy dog close to her chest. She was unable to take in the fact that they were both dead.

She stood and walked over towards the bedroom window. She watched as the world went on its merry way. It never stops, never grieves its dead, just keeps on going. She watched as the raindrops started to run down the window. Her tears seemed to follow the same pattern as they ran down her face. Her thoughts turned to this evening and telling Johnny about Megan and Melissa. He needed to know the truth.

A black Mazda 6 pulled up outside Jane's house, 'Oh, Johnny and Peter,' she said out loud.

Melissa jumped as she heard the doorbell. 'I'll get it, Mum,' she shouted up the stairs.

'Okay,' she replied, 'It's Johnny and Peter. Oh, Melissa, don't say anything yet. We'll talk about it tonight.'

She never replied to her mother. She jumped up and answered the door. 'Good afternoon, do come in,' she said smiling. 'Mum, two very dishy detectives to see you.'

Allen and Walsh looked at each other and shrugged their shoulders. 'Good afternoon, Miss. Is the lady of the house in? We'd like a chat,' Allen said trying his hardest not to laugh.

'You made me jump. I was miles away. Been trying to catch up on schoolwork I've missed, but I can't seem to get my brain going.'

'What are you working on, Missy?' asked Walsh.

'English essay on the pros and cons of modern technology. So far I've got, pros, communication, and that's about it,' she said smiling.

'Johnny here doesn't understand modern technology, has no idea about computers,' Walsh said looking at Johnny with a raised eyebrow.

'Pencil and paper, can't go wrong with good old pencil and paper.'

'True, shame I've never seen you use it. Trust me, Missy, I do all the paperwork, and his lordship sits and does nothing.'

'That's not true. I don't just sit and do nothing. I sit and drink tea,' Allen replied with a mischievous grin on his face.

'Yeah, that I've bloody well made for you,' Walsh replied shaking his head and smiling at Melissa.

'I'm a Chief Inspector, that's what we do,' he said trying to plead his innocence.

'And trust me, darling, he hasn't gotten any better with age. He was the same when we were younger,' Jane said as she entered the living room.

'You two should be on stage. You'd make a great comedy act,' Melissa said wiping tears from her eyes.

Allen and Walsh looked at each other and laughed. 'That's what our boss says, 'You two should be on stage.' He then goes on to say that we're wasted as detectives.'

'I'm not sure if that's a compliment or not,' added Walsh smiling.

'I wasn't expecting you this early,' Jane added.

'I know. We've just had a chat with Grace and Jackson Reynolds. Look, I don't want to upset either of you, but we need to talk about Alex.'

'Have you been in contact with him yet?' Walsh asked.

'I've left him four voice messages and at least ten or so texts, but nothing, no reply,' Melissa replied checking her phone again.

'It's as if he doesn't want to be found,' added Jane.

'Tell me, Jane, did Alex ever say anything about the day Alison died?' Allen asked. He felt Jane's hand slip into his; she held it tight. He knew she felt nervous. He could feel it in her touch.

'I know he liked her. I wasn't sure if she felt the same way though. I know he met up with her around lunchtime. She told me just before she left to meet him. For the last two weeks or so before she died, she would say, 'Jane, I've a big secret to tell you,' but she never did.'

Allen looked over at Walsh. Both men knew what the other was thinking. Alison was going to tell Jane she was pregnant. 'I know this may come as a bit of a shock to you, but Alison was pregnant.'

He watched her as she struggled to take in what she'd just been told. 'Oh my God, so that was her big secret. Do you know who the father was?' she asked.

'No, sorry, darling, I don't; had hoped you might have known.'

'I think I may know who it might have been,' Melissa said nervously.

'Go on, Missy, you can tell us,' added Walsh.

'Well, I'm not sure, but Megan knew. You see I overheard her talking to James about it. She said she knew a big secret about Alison.'

'Did she say a name?' Allen asked.

'Yes,' she said, trying to fight back the tears, 'my dad.' She couldn't hold them back any longer. She just burst into tears.'

'You mean Alex Davis? Is that right? Are you sure about this?' Allen asked, walking over to her and giving her a hug.

'Yes—oh, I don't know. I'm sorry, Mum. I was going to say something, but I was scared. I still believe I may have got all this wrong. I only heard part of the conversation, so I may have missed part of it.'

'He would never talk about it. Thinking back, it was as if he was hiding something. There was one thing, we'd had this massive argument one night; he was drunk as always. Anyway, he was going on and on about marrying the wrong cousin, I don't love you. It's Alison I loved.' She stopped and took a deep breath, and tried to fight back the tears. 'He told me that if he hadn't seen Billy and Norman that afternoon down by the river, then she'd still be alive.'

'Did he say if they were together or not, Billy and Norman I mean?' asked Allen.

'Yes, he did, he said he saw Billy first, then Norman, but not together. He did say that Billy looked really angry. He said it was as if he didn't even notice he was there. He also mentioned when he met up with Norman, he looked scared out of his mind. You've found Norman then?' she asked him.

'Yes, we have. I'm afraid he came into the station. He was holding a knife which was covered in blood, dried blood.'

'Oh my God, no. Not Norman, not again, not my baby as well,' Jane said bursting into tears. She buried her face into his chest and arms, sobbing uncontrollably.

'Did he kill my sister?' Missy asked as she gave her mother a hug.

'I don't know to be sure, but it doesn't look good for him. If the blood on the knife is Megan's and if it's got his fingerprints on the knife, then I'm afraid unless I can get evidence to suggest otherwise, then he'll be charged.'

'What do you believe, Johnny, did he murder my daughter?' she asked, almost pleading with him for an answer.

'I'm not sure. It doesn't sound like Norman. Did you know he witnessed his sister hang herself? He just thought she was playing a game. He said he watched as she played swinging. He doesn't understand death. To him, they're just asleep. He said to me, I couldn't wake her up. Wake up Joan, wake up.'

Allen stood up and walked over to the large photograph of Megan and Melissa that hung over the fireplace. He smiled as he looked at it. 'I love this photo of you and Megan,' he said turning and smiling at Melissa.

'It's lovely, isn't it? We take lovely photos, even if I may say so myself.'

'Beautiful, two beautiful young ladies. When was it taken?' he asked.

'Christmas just gone, it was our present to mum,' she said smiling.

Allen looked closely at Megan. He could see it staring him in the face, 'I like Megan's Saint Christopher. Your mum gave me one for my eighteenth birthday. I lost it somewhere, never found it.' He never said that his had been found by Megan's body. This was his, of that he was one hundred percent sure.

'I think James gave Megan that one on her last birthday.'

'You've still never found yours then, darling?' Jane asked.

'No idea what happened to it, not a clue.' He hated lying, especially to Jane and Melissa, but he needed to know how James came to have his Saint Christopher.

'Can I take a picture of this on my phone?' he asked smiling at Melissa and Jane.

Jane smiled at him and nodded.

'One more thing, does Alex have any family, either living in Leeds or down here?' asked Walsh.

'His mother has always lived in Leeds. He's got a sister, Sarah; not sure where she lives. Last I heard, she was somewhere in London,' said Jane.

'What's her surname?' added Walsh.

'Same as mine, Davis, Sarah Davis. She's not married,' replied Jane.

'Tell you what, Auntie Sarah has a daughter, Julie. I've got a number somewhere. Worth a shot. Only problem is, she lives with her father, so we don't really know her that well.'

Melissa checked through her contact list on her mobile, 'Good God, I've got the whole world on this phone,' she laughed. 'Here we go, Julie Rogers-Davis,' she said handing her phone over to Inspector Walsh.

Walsh took the number down and handed her phone back. 'Thank you,' he smiled.

'Okay, what time are we going out tonight?' Johnny asked, rubbing his hands together.

'I've booked a table for 8:30,' Jane replied smiling at him.

'Okay, good. Are you coming, Melissa, as well?' he asked.

'Yeah, only if that's okay,' she replied.

'I wouldn't have it any other way,' he said giving her a kiss on the cheek.

'Where are you guys going then?' Walsh asked.

'Indian restaurant, it's only around the corner. Peter, I'm sorry, I'll apologise right now. Having been out with Johnny for many Indians, trust me tomorrow morning isn't going to be very pleasant for you.'

'I know. I've been there,' he said laughing.

'Why the hell do you think we get put on the top floor? It isn't to keep us fit from going up and down stairs all day long,' he smiled.

'Yeah, I understand, it's the only floor with working toilets,' replied Walsh.

'You've got it in one,' laughed Allen.

Grace Reynolds sat looking daggers at her brother. *Not drugs, not a young kid,* she thought. She was worried not only about her brother, but Johnny Allen. He'd seen something, but what? What does Johnny now know? What did he see?

'You going to give me the cold shoulder all evening?' he asked his sister bluntly.

'God sake Jackson, you're a bloody idiot. Why? What the hell are you thinking of,' she shouted at him.

'I'm sorry,' he mumbled.

'God, you've always been a waste of space. You're weak, bloody weak,' she screamed at him angrily.

'You of all people should know my problem. I can't help it, I'm sorry.'

'I've always got you out of trouble. Now it's time you helped yourself,' she shouted.

'Oh, you helped me? I spent over twenty years locked up, some help you were.'

'Yeah, I tried to help, Jackson, but as ever Jack got in the way. He always gets in the way,' she shouted at him.

'I can't help it. I can't control him. He's way too strong,' he sobbed.

'Yeah, he says you're weak, weak little boy. Oh, Jackson, don't just sit there and cry like a baby,' she said mocking him.

'I need to see Doctor O'Sullivan. I don't know how much longer I can carry on. I don't know what's real anymore. I can't remember what Jack's done. Please help me, Grace, please.' He knelt on the floor holding his sister's leg pleading with her. She looked down at her brother and stroked the side of his face. She looked up and smiled to herself.

'Oh, I'll help you, Jackson. I'll help you.'

Inspector Walsh sat at his desk and rang the number Melissa had given him for Julie Rogers-Davis. He knew it would and could be a bit of a long shot, but you never know. He sat waiting for an answer.

'Hello, can I help you?' said a lady's voice.

'Hello, sorry to bother you, but are you Julie Rogers-Davis?' he asked.

'Yes, that's me, and you are?' she asked him.

'I'm Detective Inspector Walsh from Reading CID. We're trying to find the whereabouts of Alex Davis. I understand he's your uncle, is that right?'

'Yes, that's right. I'm afraid I haven't seen him for about three years or so. Tell you what, I'll ask my mother. She may have an idea where he is. Hang on a second,' she said. 'Mum,' he heard her call out. 'She won't be a second.'

'Thanks,' he replied.

'Hello.'

'Hello, I'm Detective Inspector Walsh from Reading CID. I understand your brother is Alex Davis?' He asked her.

'Yes, that's right. I'm Sarah Davis,' she replied.

'We're trying to find the whereabouts of your brother. Have you seen him recently?'

'He's not in any trouble is he? Not that it would be the first time. I spoke to him about a week or so back. He said he's coming back to Reading to live, not sure how true that is.'

'It's very important we speak to him.'

'I'll try him again if you like. I know he was coming down to Reading last week sometime. I'll find out for you.'

'Thank you. If you get in contact with him, can you get him to ring me as soon as possible? I'll give you my phone number.' Walsh gave Sarah Davis his mobile phone number and thanked her again.

'Any luck?' Allen asked hopefully.

'Well, she spoke to him last week. She said he was down in Reading a week or so back. She's going to try and ring him again, find out where he's staying.'

'Did you see the picture of Megan and Melissa?' Allen asked looking over towards Walsh.

'Yes, yes, I did. She had your Saint Christopher on, didn't she?'

'Yes, oh yes, that was mine all right. But how did James get hold of it? I'd never met him until Megan's murder,' he said looking at the picture he'd taken of Megan and Melissa.

'Someone gave it to him maybe. He might have even found it in Jane's house?'

'If only I'd taken a picture of Grace, you know, the one in which she's wearing that gold chain. If Grace had taken it, then she must have known James and Megan.'

'Jackson knew them. Maybe he introduced them to her,' replied Walsh.

'I hated lying to Jane about it, but I'd like to keep it a secret about my Saint Christopher. Let's just say for now, Grace had it, either she or Jackson gave it to James, then he gave it to Megan.'

'They must have known it was yours. At least we know how it came to be by Megan's body.'

An image flashed into his mind, an image of Megan falling to the ground. He could see the Saint Christopher and the gold chain flying through the air in slow motion. She tried to reach for it as she fell, but it was just too far out of her reach. The Saint Christopher and the gold chain lay by her lifeless body. He could see it, touch it. He reached down and picked it up, holding it tight in his hands. He looked down at his clenched hand. He opened it; his hand was empty.

'You okay, Johnny?'

He looked at his empty hand, 'She knew it was mine. She knew who I was, her father.'

'Is this what tonight's all about?' he asked.

'Yes,' he replied. Walsh could almost see tears in his eyes. It must hit him at some point. Maybe tonight, once the truth is out for good, then the reality will hit him.

'Tell you these pictures haven't shown me anything. Can't see anything amiss or out of place. Right, I'm going to give Doctor Richardson a call. I need to ask him some questions about Norman.'

'Hello, Doctor Richardson speaking,' came the response.

'Hello, Doctor, it's Chief Inspector Allen.'

'Hi, Chief Inspector. All good, I hope?' he asked.

'Not really, I'm afraid. I've called you about Norman Denman. I'm afraid to say, but we've arrested him, and it doesn't look good at the moment.'

'Oh, poor Norman. Is it about that girl that was murdered? Is he guilty?' asked the Doctor.

'Truth be told, I'm not sure. But unless I find evidence to suggest otherwise, I'm afraid he'll be charged. I'd just like to ask you a couple of questions, if that's okay?'

'No problem, Chief Inspector, ask away,' replied Doctor Richardson.'

'Norman doesn't understand the meaning of death. To him, they're asleep, not dead. Would he be transfixed on death at all?' asked Allen.

'Well, that depends. In Norman's case, he has mild dissociative identity disorder. He suffered severe trauma, albeit not in early childhood. Norman has a mental age of a child. His trauma was seeing his sister hang herself. I've been thinking, he has it in him to kill, but it would frighten him. He would only kill if he was alone. But it would just be a game. If there were others around, he would have run away.'

'He suffered abuse as a child from his father, both physical and emotional. This, I understand would have a massive effect on him.'

'Yes, very much so. Has he told you much about what happened with his sister?' asked the Doctor.

'Yes, he did. He said she was playing swinging. He believed she was playing a game with him. He had no understanding that Joan was taking her own life.'

'From what I could understand, she was sexually abused by her father from an early age. This would surely have led to her taking her own life. I understand he was very close to his sister?' asked Doctor Richardson.

'Yes, very much so. He would never have understood what his father had done to Joan. I'm just afraid that if he murdered Megan Davis, then it may well have been just a game to him.'

'Most likely, yes. It's sad. Norman couldn't cope with being locked up again. Trust me on this, Chief Inspector, he most likely would want to play the same game that his sister did. In his mind, she's safe; she's asleep and safe from her father.'

'So by murdering Megan Davis, if she was in any sort of trouble, then he's trying to protect her. Doctor Richardson, thank you very much,' he said.

'No problem, Chief Inspector, anytime. One last thing, someone may be able to help you, a work colleague of mine, Doctor Amanda O'Sullivan. I believe she may even know Grace Reynolds,' he replied.

'Okay, thank you.'

Allen sat in his chair and turned it around and looked out of his office window. He started thinking. We pay for our sins, but surely in Norman's case he's paying for the sins of others. What were his sins? The sins of forbidden love? We all sin in some way or another. Is knowledge a sin? Surely knowledge is power. Was Megan killed for what she knew? Was Alison killed for the sin of knowledge? After all, her sin was a secret. Megan knew Alison's secret; she knew who the father was. Megan was killed for the sin of knowledge. Alison was killed for the sin of forbidden love. Joan took her own life for the sin of others.

Knowledge is power. Dominant has knowledge. He knew, knew all the sins, the sins of our past. What if Alex Davis was the father of Alison's baby? If Megan found out about who the father was, maybe even found out who her father was...but why would Alex murder Megan? Who else knew Alison was pregnant? Her parents? Billy Reynolds? Grace and Jackson knew something. If Billy was the father, he wouldn't have killed her. He loved Alison.

What, if anything, did Norman know? Would he have understood it? Norman ran away; he ran before Alison was murdered, then went back later to find her. 'Come on, I want to speak to Norman.'

'You okay, Johnny?' asked Walsh.

'Yeah, I'm okay, I was miles away. I want to ask Norman something.'

Walsh followed Allen down to the cells. Norman was sitting on his bed just looking at the floor. Again, as with earlier, no real sign of emotion, just a blank expression.

'Hello, Norman, you okay?' Allen asked, as he sat next to him.

Norman didn't speak. He just nodded.

'Can you answer me one question? Alison was asleep when you found her, wasn't she?' he asked. 'When you went back to find her, she was asleep?'

'Yes,' he replied blankly.

'Was she down by the old boat, Norman?' he asked.

'Yes, I carried her, but she wouldn't wake up. She wasn't asleep before.'

'Why did you run away?'

'I didn't like Alison's friends,' he replied.

'Who, Billy?'

'No, he married Jane.'

'Alex Davis, he was with Alison? Who else?'

'I don't know him. They told me to go away,' he replied.

'Okay, okay,' Allen said patting Norman on the back.

'He wasn't even there. He only went back to make sure she was all right,' Walsh added.

'Right, I'm off, if you find Alex Davis, text or ring me straight away.'

'Have a good evening Johnny,' Walsh said smiling.

Chapter 10

Jane was getting more nervous as the time ticked by. She was fine to start with. Don't worry, he'll be fine about it, no problem. But now, what if he gets angry, walks out? What if he doesn't want to see me again? Something else that went through her mind, how much does he know? He surely must know that Megan's his.

Melissa was excited and nervous at the same time. She liked Johnny; he seemed fun, but would he love her as a daughter? She found the last week so hard, so many different emotions: losing Megan, finding out Alex wasn't her father, then finding out that Johnny was.

Jane was unsure what to wear. She stood in her bedroom looking at three dresses she laid out on her bed.

'Melissa, come here a second, darling,' she called out to her daughter.

'What's wrong?' Melissa replied as she walked into her mother's bedroom.

'I can't decide what to wear,' she said holding up a red dress against herself and looking in her fall length mirror.

'No, Mum, it has to be the dark blue one,' she said handing her mother the dress.

'You sure,' she replied.

'Oh yes, he'll fall in love with you all over again if you wear that dress,' Melissa said smiling at her mother.

Jane held the dress up against her. She knew her daughter was right. She always seemed to know what looked good. Melissa watched as her mother got dressed. She always thought as a young child that her mother was a princess. She always looked so beautiful. She laughed to herself. Maddie always said, 'Missy, you sure your mum isn't a princess?'

'Well?' Jane asked turning around to her daughter.

'Mum, you're so beautiful, everyone says it. Everyone at my school says how pretty you are.'

'I'm beautiful, Melissa darling? Have you looked in the mirror recently?' she smiled.

'I get that at school as well. I get asked out at least ten times a day,' she said nervously.

'Oh, anyone that takes your eye?' she said.

'Well, I like Richard Perkins, but he's a year older than me, and I'm too shy to ask him out. Maddie keeps saying, 'Go on, just ask him. If he says no then he must be blind.'

'What about Stephen Hardwick? He's nice,' Jane smiled.

'Yeah, but his sister Gemma is one of my best friends, so could be a bit awkward.'

Jane checked the time, 19:15. She knew Johnny would be here any time soon. *I'm going to tell him before we go,* she said to herself. She checked herself in the mirror. *Good choice Missy,* she thought. Her thoughts turned to Melissa. She had so many boys after her. All she wanted was for her daughter to be happy and not make the same mistake she'd made.

Johnny pulled up outside Jane's house. He felt nervous, even scared. He knew what tonight was about. He checked he still had the ring. He smiled to himself as he looked at it. He paused as he reached the door. Taking one last deep breath, he rang the doorbell.

'I'll get it, Missy,' Jane said as she ran down the stairs.

'Okay,' Missy replied.

'Hello again,' she said smiling at him as she opened the door.

He smiled at her; she looked stunning. He kissed her passionately on the lips. 'Oh my God, you look amazing,' he said.

'You two need to get a room,' Melissa said, covering her eyes as she walked past.

They looked at each other and laughed. Melissa was right. They were like two love-struck teenagers. Jane walked over to her daughter and gave her a hug. She whispered to her, 'You look stunning.' Melissa smiled and gave her mother a kiss. 'Thank you,' she said.

Allen looked at the two lovely ladies standing in front of him. 'You two look absolutely amazing, so beautiful,' he said smiling.

'We scrub up well, don't we?' Melissa said as she smiled at her mother.

'Johnny, we need to talk. We've got time before we need to leave for the restaurant,' she said nervously.

She looked so nervous, even close to tears; he could see that. He knew this was going to be hard, but he understood. Truth be told, they were both to blame.

'I'm sorry. I don't really know where to start, to be truthful. I've been meaning to tell you for years, but I don't know why I didn't. I was scared I'd lose you. You see, it's only surfaced again since Megan was murdered and since I had an argument with my father this morning. You must know by now that Megan is your daughter. Truthfully, we've both known since she was born. But you see, Melissa is your daughter as well.'

He looked shocked, dumbfounded. 'I had no idea. Yes okay, I knew about Megan, but not you, Melissa,' he said as he slumped back in the chair.

She felt like a massive weight had been lifted from her mind. She wanted to tell him years ago, in fact, from the day they were both born. 'I'm sorry, Johnny, I didn't want to have children with anyone else but you. I never let Alex sleep with me, only once on our wedding night. I knew I didn't love him, I never have, and he didn't love me.'

'Oh, Jane, look, I don't know what to say. I love you so much, I always have, and I always will. I'm just in a state of shock.'

He could feel himself starting to well up; the emotion of what happened, finding Jane and Melissa again, Megan's murder. He knew he was way too close to all this. Truth be told, he shouldn't even be on the case. But he was close, close to finding out the truth about who murdered Alison and Megan.

'I only found out this morning. When you were here earlier, I so desperately wanted to tell you, but mum said no. I know how hard all this must be for you, but I don't want anyone else as my dad but you. I just want you to love me as your daughter,' she said with tears running down her face.

'Oh, Melissa, of course I love you. You're my daughter, my little girl. Come here you two.'

He held them both in his arms. He gave them both a kiss on the cheek. In some ways, it's all he really wanted, a family, children. He knew he could never bring Megan back. He wondered if she knew about him, if she knew he was her father.

'Did Megan know much about me? Did she know I was her father?' he asked wiping a tear from his eyes.

'I believe she did. She was very good at finding things out, always full of questions was Megan.' Jane laughed and said, 'She'd have made a very good detective. She never really said much about it. If she knew, then she kept it to herself.'

'One more thing,' Melissa said smiling, 'can I call you dad?'

'I wouldn't want it any other way,' he said smiling at his daughter. It seemed strange being called dad. He knew it would take some time to comprehend this, but it was something he'd always wanted.

She stood up and threw her arms around him. Looking up at him, her light blue eyes glinting in the light, she kissed him on the cheek and whispered, 'Thank you.'

Allen reached inside his jacket pocket; he knew it was the right time. Standing up, he smiled at Jane as he went down on one knee. Saying nothing, he opened the box. By now Melissa was jumping up and down screaming with delight.

'Calm down, Missy. Your father hasn't asked me yet. Anyway, I might say no,' she said smiling.

'Jane, will you marry me?' he asked nervously.

'Oh yes, oh yes, oh yes,' she screamed with delight, 'and about time too,' she said kissing him tenderly on the lips.

He slipped the ring on her finger. It fitted like a dream. He let out a big sigh. It had gone through his mind that the ring wouldn't fit. After all, he'd bought it years ago.

'Mum, Mum, can Maddie and I be bridesmaids? Oh please, oh please,' she screamed in excitement.

'What do you think?' Jane said laughing at her daughter.

'There's a story about this ring. I bought it years ago when we were younger. You see, I should have asked you back then to marry me.'

'I wondered when you bought it. So you've had it all this time.'

'I've carried it around with me for years. It became like a good luck charm. I'm just glad it fits.'

'Right you two, we'd better get going. We'll walk around,' Jane said.

Allen pulled up outside the Littlemore Mental Health Centre in Oxford. He didn't really know what to expect or what help Doctor O'Sullivan could give him. His thoughts turned back to last night. It was a very enjoyable evening, with two lovely ladies. It was strange at times when Melissa kept calling him dad, but it made him feel good. He felt loved.

'Good morning, I'm Chief Inspector Allen. I've an appointment with Doctor O'Sullivan,' he said smiling at the young receptionist.

The young girl checked the Chief Inspector's warrant card and smiled, 'I'll just call her for you, Chief Inspector.'

'Thank you,' he replied.

'She'll be with you in a couple of minutes. Please take a seat, Chief Inspector,' smiled the young girl.

Just as Allen sat down his phone rang, 'Morning, Peter,' he answered.

'Morning, I've got some good news for you. We've found Alex Davis. His sister rang back about ten minutes ago.'

'Okay, good. Is he coming in to see us?' Allen asked.

'Yes, they'll be here around 12 o'clock time. One problem, I've just spoken to Davidson, Simon Woods wants to come in with him.'

'Oh, what joy. Okay, I should be back by then.'

'Chief Inspector Allen? I'm Doctor Amanda O'Sullivan, pleased to meet you.'

Allen stood up and smiled at the Doctor. She looked younger than he'd imagined. She was a tall, slim-built lady, with dark brown hair.

'Nice to meet you, Doctor O'Sullivan,' he replied.

'Please call me Amanda,' she replied smiling at him.

Allen followed the Doctor up a flight of stairs to her office. He was very impressed with what he saw. The office was unlike his, very modern and spacious.

'Please take a seat, Chief Inspector,' she said pointing towards a large comfortable looking chair.

'Thank you, and as we're on first names, it's Johnny.'

'How can I help you, Johnny? I understand from Doctor Richardson you know Grace Reynolds?' she asked.

'Yes, I've known Grace since we were children. You've treated Grace, from what I can understand?' he asked.

'Yes, for around five years now. She suffers from depression, has had for years. Grace's depression has been brought on by a trauma. Her older brother committed a murder back in 1996. This, I'm afraid, has haunted her ever since.'

'Does she suffer from any other mental health problems?' he asked.

'No, not at all, only depression. Grace, I'm afraid, is an alcoholic, and when she drinks, she gets very depressed. It doesn't help that she's had a string of broken relationships. The worst thing you can do, Johnny, is drink alone.'

'You mentioned her brother. Have you ever met Jackson Reynolds?'

'No, but Doctor Richardson has spoken a lot about him. He suffers from DID, dissociative identity disorder. From what I can understand, he's a lot worse than his brother, a William or Billy.'

Allen looked at her. He was surprised and shocked, 'You know Billy Reynolds?'

'Yes, I've seen Billy for the last three months now. As I've said, he's not as bad as his brother, but he's in a bad way at the moment. I'll be truthful with you; your name has come up from time to time. Billy blames you for a lot of his problems.'

Billy's here, he thought to himself. So Jane was right, she did see him. *Why blame me? And for what?* he thought.

'So I'm right in saying Billy has dissociative identity disorder as well?'

'Well, I'm not sure at the moment. But if he has, then it was brought on by the death of a girlfriend some years back.'

'Alison Woods, she was murdered back in September 1988. Billy and Alison were close. It hit him really hard; it hit all of us hard. You said he blames me for a lot of his problems. Can you tell me why?'

Allen listened as Doctor O'Sullivan explained what Billy had told her. 'His main problem was your relationship with a Jane Woods. Part of him just couldn't accept it. Now how true this is, I'm not sure, but he said he was in a relationship with her. He even explained in great detail about their relationship.'

'Billy and Jane were never in a relationship, never. They got on well as friends, that's it. Would I be right in saying that he has erotomania?' he asked.

'De Clerambault syndrome, yes, it's very possible. It's more common in women than men, but yes, it's possible. You see, I asked his sister. She thought it very funny. She said Jane Woods had eyes for one person and one person only, yourself.'

'I'm shocked. This doesn't sound like the Billy I knew when we were kids,' he said, shaking his head in disbelief.

'He even went as far as telling me that he and Jane had a daughter together,' replied the Doctor.

'How real would this fantasy be?' he asked.

'Erotomania is, as I said, more common in women. In Billy's case, to him, his relationship with Jane Woods was and still is very real. Men are more likely to exhibit violent and stalker-like behaviour.'

'Would I be right in saying that Billy has a dominant and submissive personality?

'Yes, very much so. I'm afraid both of his personalities blame you, the dominant side more than the submissive. Billy is, like his sister, an alcoholic. Do, or did, either of their parents have a problem with drink?' she asked him. She could see the astonishment in his face. It was as if she was talking about another person.

'I don't know, to be truthful; I never really took much notice. I'd be surprised.'

'I only asked as something in the three of them has triggered their mental problems. Three children from the same family all with problems, maybe a family tragedy? '

'It's something I'll try and find out. Amanda, thank you for your time,' he said as he stood up.

'Any time, Johnny,' she said smiling.

Allen sat in his car. He was finding it hard to take in what Doctor O'Sullivan had told him. Why? Why would Billy blame him? They had always been so close. If either had a problem with the other, they would always sort it out. He found it hard to believe that Billy had been back in England for at least the last three months. He was shocked, but not overly surprised about Billy's love for Jane. It had always been in the back of his mind. You could tell by the way he looked at her sometimes.

What surprised him more than anything the Doctor had told him was Billy having dissociative identity disorder. He was fine as a child. Did Alison's murder trigger it off?

It flashed through his mind. He didn't want to think it, not of Billy. What if he found out that Megan was his daughter? Did it push Billy over the edge? Did he murder Megan because he was her father? Why Norman? What was his part in all this? He was an easy target, yes, and he took the blame once before, so it's just wrong time, wrong place?

Had Billy been stalking Jane? Surely she'd have noticed, realised something was wrong, then told him. He knew Jane didn't feel the same way towards Billy.

Yes, they were good friends, but that was it; that's all he was to Jane, a good friend.

His thoughts turned to what Norman had told him about carrying Alison's body from the old boat up to where she was found by Alex Davis. Did Alex witness this? Did he tell Davidson and Simon Woods what he'd witnessed?

At Norman's trial, it never came up who found Alison's body, 'found by person or persons unknown.' He just rang the station to say he'd found a body, but left no name. Davidson and Woods both knew it was Alex, but for some reason kept it quiet. What was the reason for Alex not coming clean about finding Alison's body? It was Davidson some years later that told him. Did Alex witness the murder? Was he part of it? Is that the reason why it was kept a secret? Was he scared?

Allen pulled into the station car park. He parked right next to Simon Woods. Oh great, just what I needed. He knew how his interview with Alex Davis would go. Woods would want it his way. But he wasn't going to let him. *This is my case. I'll do it my way,* he said to himself.

Allen was met down in the station lobby by Inspector Walsh. 'Davidson wants us both in his office. Simon Woods is here as well,' Walsh informed Allen.

'I know. I've seen his car in the car park,' he replied, 'Is Alex Davis here as well?' he asked.

'Yeah, he's here,' Walsh responded.

Allen and Walsh stood outside Davidson's office. He turned to Inspector Walsh and said, 'Right, I've found a few things out this morning, okay. Just go with me on this. Did you bring what I asked?' he said.

Walsh said nothing. He just nodded, knocked the door and waited. 'Come in,' Davidson called out.

The two detectives entered the Chief Superintendent's office. Davidson, Woods and Alex Davis were sitting around the large oak table that was in the middle of the room. Allen could see that Davis had a half smirk on his face as he entered. His stare wasn't a friendly one. It was one of pure hatred. He looked older than Allen had imagined. His hair was now mostly grey and thinning on top. His face was lined, especially around the eyes. He looked as if he'd put on weight as well; time hadn't been that kind to him.

'Sit down, Johnny, Peter,' Davidson said pointing towards two chairs.

'Okay, Johnny, where are we at?' asked Davidson.

'Well, Sir, we're waiting on forensics to come back with a report on the knife that Norman had with him. I'm afraid it doesn't look that good.' Allen could tell by the look on Woods face, it was as if he was saying, I told you so. He's killed before, remember Alison, my niece.

'I understand the boyfriend of Megan Davis took his own life yesterday. Is that right?' asked Davidson.

'Yes, Sir, I'm sorry to say that James Clarke was found hanging yesterday morning by his younger sister.'

'Allen, I have found out from my daughter that you are Megan and Melissa's father, and not Alex. How long have you known?' Woods asked sharply.

'Jane told me last night,' he replied bluntly.

'Ha, I've bloody well known for years. God, she wouldn't let me anywhere near her,' Alex said angrily.

Allen didn't respond; he didn't know how to. He felt guilty, but then again, the guilt wasn't all on him and Jane. Simon Woods needed to take his share.

'As much as I'd like to sit here and have a massive argument, we've a killer to catch. I've one or two questions to ask you, Alex.'

'Ask away, Johnny. The floor's all yours,' replied Davis.

'You found Alison's body. You rang the station, but you never gave your name, why?' he asked.

'I don't deny I found her. As for not giving my name, I was scared, scared that I'd take the blame for murdering Alison.'

'That's guilt talking. If you had nothing to do with her murder, then why not be truthful?' responded Allen.

'I was seen down by the river. I panicked,' Davis replied.

'Who by?' he asked.

'Jackson and Grace Reynolds. The only other person I saw was Norman Denman. Norman, I saw twice, once before Alison was murdered, then I saw him carrying her body. The second time, he didn't see me.'

'Why didn't you stay with Alison?'

'I did for about an hour. We got there about one thirty; I left her around two thirty. I left because we had an argument. I wanted to go on a date with her, but she didn't want to know.'

'What time did you meet up with Jackson and Grace?' asked Allen trying to make eye contact.

'I didn't really meet up with them. I saw them up near the old pub. This was just before I met up with Alison. They were arguing, not sure what about. Only thing I can remember is Grace telling him to leave it for a while and calm down.'

'What time did you see Norman? What did he do when you saw him?' Allen asked.

'I first saw him around half past one; it was just before I met up with Alison. All he was doing was taking photos. He didn't say anything, but he did seem angry,' he said nervously.

'What was Alison like when you met up with her?' asked Walsh.

'Well, she was undressed and wet; she'd been swimming in the river. Look, if you ask me, she'd had an argument with Norman. I believe he tried it on with her, and she pushed him away. I reckon he waited for me to leave, then went back to her. I didn't really know him that well. We didn't really say that much to each other.'

'Did you know Alison was pregnant?' asked Allen. He watched Alex's facial expression. He didn't seem that surprised. He knew she was pregnant, all right.

'Yes, I did. She told me that afternoon. That was something we argued about. I'm one hundred percent sure I wasn't the father,' he replied.

'And why's that?' asked Walsh.

'Our relationship never got that far. From what I could work out, the only person she'd slept with was Billy Reynolds.'

Allen started thinking. What if Alex found out that Alison was pregnant, knowing all too well he wasn't the father, then an argument started between the two. What if he lost control? Couldn't take it? Couldn't accept that she liked Billy better? Norman said when he went back to find Alison, she was asleep.

'You see, Alex, I've got this problem. I don't believe Norman murdered Alison. Okay, yes, he moved her body. But you see, Norman has no idea about death. To him, there just a sleep. Do you know what he told me?' Davis looked at Allen and shook his head. 'He told me he found Alison asleep, he tried to wake her up; but she was dead. Now you're saying that she was alive when you left her. Her post-mortem states that she was murdered somewhere between 14:30 to 15:00.'

'No, no way you bastard, I didn't kill her. I'm telling you she was alive when I left her,' he shouted angrily.

'Come on, for God sake, Allen. I've told you before many times, Norman Denman killed my niece. And he also killed my granddaughter,' shouted Woods.

'Johnny, listen, the only fingerprints that were found on the knives were Norman's. So unless someone either had gloves on or wiped the fingerprints off, the only evidence points to Norman as Alison's murderer,' said Davidson.

Davidson could see that Johnny still didn't believe him. He still didn't accept that Norman was a murderer. He himself over the years had some doubts. He couldn't work out what made Norman want to kill Alison, or Megan for that matter. It didn't make sense.

'Tell you what, Allen, find your best mate; find Billy Reynolds,' shouted Alex.

'Been talking to Grace, have we?' he asked.

'And what if I have? We were good friends. Problem with that?'

'Come on, Alex. I know the story between you and Grace,' Allen said shaking his head. 'Let's be truthful. She played her two brothers off against each other all her life,' he continued.

'Okay. So I had an affair with Grace Reynolds. It's not like my wife didn't have an affair as well,' he said sarcastically.

He found it hard to believe Alex had nothing to do with Alison's death. He knew something, but what? He looked hard at him. He seemed on edge, nervous. He turned and looked at Simon Woods. He seemed in a state of shock at Alex admitting he'd had an affair with Grace Reynolds. For the first time, he could see doubt in his eyes. He could almost see it going around in his mind. Is Johnny right, did I let a murderer marry my daughter?

'If you're going to charge me, then do so, but I didn't murder Alison.' He slammed his fist down on the table. He was starting to get angry. He could feel the rage building up inside his body. 'You, I blame you, no one else but you, the great Johnny Allen, the great detective. You took my wife and now my daughters. Yes okay, I was married to Jane, but I've always been the third person in my marriage. It's been hard enough being told that Megan was dead, but finding out you of all people are the father to both those girls. Megan's blood's on your hands, Johnny. Her blood's on your hands.'

It went through his mind like a firework going off. You, you sent me those pictures, but why? What would he expect to gain from it?

'Why send them to me? What did you expect to gain from it?' he asked him.

'No idea what you're talking about,' Alex replied sharply.

Allen turned to Inspector Walsh. Peter said nothing. He knew what he wanted. He handed him over the photographs. Allen laid them out on the table. He said nothing as he looked up at Davis.

'And this has what to do with me?' he said as he briefly glanced at the photographs, not really bothering to look at them.

'Come on, Alex, you took these pictures, and you sent them to me.'

Davis said nothing. His facial expression was one of pure hatred. 'I didn't send any of them, no idea.' he said as he picked up one of the photographs, glanced at it, then threw it across the table towards Allen.

'So you didn't take them, and you've no idea who did then?' asked Walsh.

'NO,' he shouted.

'You see, Alex, what you've just said to me, 'Megan's blood's on your hands. Her blood's on your hands,' that's what's written on the back of one of these photographs,' he said placing the picture right in front of him.

'No idea, maybe I heard it said somewhere,' he said staring at Allen and not at the photograph.

'One more question. Where were you Saturday night, into the early hours of Sunday morning?'

Davis smiled, 'In bed with a lovely young lady.'

'And does this young lady have a name?' Allen asked.

'Yes, but she's no one you'd know,' he replied sarcastically.

'Just give him the name, Alex, and stop playing games,' Woods added angrily.

'Don't know her name. I didn't ask. Oh yeah, that's right, I think it was Jane or something like that,' he said with a smug grin on his face.

He knew Davis was lying and trying to get at him. 'Come on, Alex, it won't do you any good. Just tell me the truth.'

'Okay, I went out and got pissed. Can't remember past 12 o'clock. There you go, I don't have an alibi for Megan's murder. I woke up on some park bench.

'Can you remember what pub you were in?' asked Walsh.

'It wasn't a pub, it was a nightclub. It was called...sorry, I don't know, I can't remember.'

'How about a nightclub called J2, does that ring any bells?'

'Sorry, I'm not sure. I don't know.'

'One more question, where are you staying?' asked Allen, half expecting the answer he got.

'With me,' replied Woods sharply.

'Was going to ask the ex-wife, but sounds to me like she's already got someone staying at night,' he said with a smug grin.

Allen didn't reply. He stood up, thanked the three gentlemen and made his way to the door. He wasn't sure what to make of it. Did Alex send him the photographs? If not, then who did? Was he at the nightclub Saturday night as well? If so, he'd be on the CCTV tape. He turned his thoughts to Norman again. He knew by now that he'd be a little bit calmer. He wanted to ask him where he was hiding, and importantly, if he took the photographs.

'I take it you don't believe him?' asked Walsh.

'No, he knows a lot more than he's making out. The photographs, I'm not that worried about. It's what happened the afternoon of Alison's murder that bothers me. Also, what was he doing at the nightclub? Surely he met up with Megan and James?'

'If what he said is true about the time he left Alison, then he must have been the last person to see her alive. I've been thinking. Now we've assumed that either Billy Reynolds or Alex Davis was the father of Alison's baby. Now I know what you've said about Jackson and Alison hating each other, but—'

'I know,' Allen said stopping Walsh mid-sentence. 'It's something that's been going through my mind since talking to Jackson. He knew. He knew alright.'

Surely it couldn't be Jackson. The pair hated each other. What if he was the father, did either Alex or Billy find this out? But why murder Alison? No, that was an accident. *I need to find Billy Reynolds and fast,* he said to himself. Maybe Grace would come clean this time about where her brother is.

'Right, Peter, I want to speak to Norman again. I want to ask him if he took these photographs and where the hell he'd been hiding.'

'I'll go and get him. Where do you want him?' asked Walsh.

'Interview room. This needs to be done properly,' he replied.

'I'll also find out if we've got any news from forensics.'

Alex Davis could see that his ex-father-in-law was angry. He'd seen that look before on many occasions. 'Go on then, let me have it. Give me both barrels. I can take it,' he said.

'You and my daughter are unbelievable. God, you could have had a good marriage, but oh no, you both decide to have affairs,' shouted Woods angrily.

'Okay, and Jane will tell you the same, we didn't love each other. It was your fault. You pushed us into getting married,' he replied angrily pointing his finger at him.

'What about Alison? Tell me the truth, were you the father of her baby?' he shouted.

'Like I said to Allen, our relationship didn't get that far. And before you ask, no, I don't know who the father was.'

'So she was alive when you left her?' Woods asked sharply.

'Oh my God, not you and all. He's got to you as well, hasn't he? Oh yeah, that's right, the great detective, never wrong is he.'

He wasn't sure. For the first time since his niece was murdered, he was starting to have doubts. Was Allen right? Was he blinded by rage after Alison's murder? Norman Denman fitted the bill, and that was that. No, he was right. The evidence pointed to Norman. He confessed. The courts found him guilty.

He watched as Alex left Davidson's office. He stood up and looked out of the office window. He knew he was too hard on Jane yesterday. All he wanted was the best for her, that's all: nice home, a good husband, children. Maybe he was wrong about Johnny. Maybe he was right for Jane. Maybe his judgement of Jonathan James Allen was wrong.

Inspector Walsh hated it down in the cells. It was cold and dark, gave him the shivers, but then again it wasn't supposed to be a hotel. He followed the duty sergeant down to the cell where Norman was being held. He watched as he unlocked the cell door, something else he hated, the sound of the cell door slamming shut. He knew Norman would be scared. After all, how much did he really understand.

Norman was sitting on the bed just staring into space. Walsh was surprised. He seemed remarkably calm. Inspector Walsh looked around the cell. It was small and felt uninviting. He'd have hated being locked up. He could understand why some people said it was like hell on earth. Norman looked up at him and smiled. He seemed really pleased to see him.

'Hello, Peter, is it time to go home yet?' he asked.

'Not just yet, Norman. I'm going to take you to see Johnny. Would you like that?' he said smiling at him.

'Yes, Johnny's my friend,' he said smiling back.

Inspector Walsh, along with PC Wilkins, led Norman from his cell along to the interview room. 'Right, Norman, PC Wilkins is going to stay with you for a while. Johnny won't be long, okay?'

Allen wanted to make sure Jane and Melissa were safe. He was worried. Had Billy been stalking them? Was he the one that was sending the photographs? His thoughts turned to the man Norman met in Mr Richardson's photo shop. Was that Billy? But Billy and Norman always got on okay, so why would he be scared of him?

'Hi, it's me. You okay?' he asked her.

'Yeah, I'm okay. I'm just off to see Catherine and Maddie. Why what's wrong?' she asked.

'I've just been speaking to Alex and your father,' he replied.

'Oh, you've found him then. And what did he have to say for himself?' she asked bluntly.

'Oh, nothing I didn't already know. I asked him about his movements for the afternoon of Alison's murder.'

'Okay, and my dad?'

'His usual self,' he replied.

'Yeah, telling us what we should and shouldn't do. You sound worried darling, what's up?' she asked with concern in her voice.

'Billy Reynolds. You were right; you did see him. He's been back for about three months or so. Look, if you see him again, ring me right away. Tell Melissa the same.'

'Okay, I knew it was him. What's going on?'

'Billy isn't well, not at all. I'll explain later. Just go careful. Love you.'

'Love you more,' she said laughing.

Inspector Walsh read through the forensics report. He knew what it would say even before he read it. Blood match to Megan Davis, fingerprints a match to Norman Stephen Denman. Walsh carried on reading, fingerprint match to unknown, another set of prints, he said to himself, but who?

Walsh ran up the three flights of stairs to his and Johnny's office. *Who was this other person? Who else was there?* he thought.

'Johnny,' he said as he walked through the office door.

'Peter, you okay?' Allen asked looking up from his desk.

'Forensics report on that knife. We've a blood match to Megan Davis, fingerprint match to Norman. And also, a fingerprint match unknown.'

Walsh handed Allen the report. *Who? Who are you?* he said to himself. 'I know one person it isn't, well two. One is Jackson Reynolds, and the other is Alex Davis. Both have done time, so their fingerprints are on record.'

'What about Billy?' asked Walsh.

'No, nothing on Billy. Oh no, I know who this is. Right Peter, I want you to go around to Mrs Clarke's house. I want something with James Clarke's fingerprints on it, but don't say why.'

'James…why? Why would he murder his own girlfriend?' asked Walsh. He looked at Allen with a puzzled expression. He didn't understand why James would murder her.

'He didn't. Oh, this is clever, very clever, placing the blame on not one, but two people, James Clarke and Norman Denman. You see, both Jackson and Alex knew we'd find out that they'd both been in the nightclub. They knew we'd check CCTV. And there we have it, an alibi for both. Davis was just being clever when he said, 'Oh, I woke up on some park bench, so I don't have an alibi for Megan's murder.' I take it the nightclub doesn't have CCTV for the downstairs entrance.'

'Yes, it does. But it wasn't working that night. Cameras got smashed some time on Friday, I checked,' Walsh said.

'So we've no way of finding out what time either left. You get two guesses, come on, who broke the CCTV cameras?'

'Yeah right, no prizes for either.'

'Right, I'm going to see Norman. I'll see you in a while. We also need to check again at the taxi rank, see if anyone picked either Davis or Jackson up. And I've one or two things to tell you.'

Allen entered the interview room. Norman was seated waiting. He looked up and smiled when Johnny walked in. He knew this was going to be hard, the questions he wanted answers for. He knew Norman had no idea whatsoever about how serious all this was.

'Norman, how are you? You okay?' he asked, smiling at him.

'I'm okay, Johnny, but I want to go home,' he said.

'Soon, Norman, you can go home soon, I promise. Right then, can you remember what you did after you left the nightclub?' he asked.

'I can remember leaving, once Megan left. I followed her and her friend up to the river.'

'Okay, can you tell me what happened once you got to the river?'

'I got out of the car. I couldn't find Megan, only her friend. He was being sick. I walked up through the woods. It took me a long time to find her. I then saw her asleep on the ground.'

'What did you do once you found her asleep?'

'I tried to wake her up, but I couldn't, so I left her there. I said to Megan that she was silly, but she didn't answer.' He stopped and looked at Allen. He looked puzzled. He seemed unable to remember what happened next.

'I can't remember what happened. I didn't wake up in my bedroom. It was dark; it scared me. This man was there and someone else, but I didn't see the other man,' he said nervously.

'The first man, can you remember him at all?' Allen asked.

'No, it was dark. The other man wasn't there. He was silly; he was talking to himself. I talk to myself.

Dissociative identity disorder, he said to himself, *Billy or Jackson or both.*

'Can you remember where you were?'

'No, but it had pictures on the wall. They were of you and Jane. This man knew you. He said your name.'

'Right, Norman, can you remember when you came here yesterday, you had a big knife with you? You told me Megan had it. Did you pick it up?'

'No, the man said that Johnny will help me if I take this knife to him, so that's what I did.'

'Can you remember what the time was when you saw Megan asleep?'

'No, I'm not sure,' he replied.

'Just a few more questions now.' He showed Norman some of the pictures, 'Do you remember taking any of them?'

'No, mine are better than these,' he replied bluntly.

'Now when you were at work, do you remember a man called Derek Dickinson coming into the shop?'

Norman looked puzzled as he tried to remember the man. 'He had the same name as my uncle, Uncle DD. He had some of my pictures. I'm not sure, but I think it was Billy Reynolds, but he looked different.'

'Norman, now I want you to think very hard for me. You were seen standing outside Jane's house. You remember Jane, Megan's mum? Any reason why?' he asked.

Norman didn't reply. He just sat staring at the table in front of him. Allen could see he was starting to get upset. 'It's okay, you can tell me. I can only help you if you tell me what happened?'

'That's where my uncle lived,' he replied.

'Who, uncle DD?' Allen asked.

'Yes. I remember the man who came into the shop. He said he lived in my uncle's house. I'm sorry, Johnny.'

'No, it's fine, don't worry.' Of course, he lived next door to Jane. He died about six months back. *No wonder Norman got so upset,* Allen thought to himself.

'I remember, because I saw Jane and her daughters. Then I saw Megan in the music club.'

'Why did you go to the club, any reason?' he asked.

'My friend Thomas Richardson works there; he makes drinks for people. He said I should come down, it's fun, but it was too loud. Thomas is my boss Mr Richardson's son, and he said it would be good for me to get out.'

'Why did you follow Megan to the river?'

'I was just going home, Thomas had arranged for a man to pick me up and take me home. On the way, I saw Megan's friend, so I got out of the car. I just wanted to help. Megan was upset in the music club. She took some tablets. Is that what made her go to sleep?' he asked.

'Yeah, maybe,' he said, smiling at him.

Inspector Walsh paused just before he rang the doorbell of Mrs Clarke's house. It must be horrible to lose a child, especially the way James died, taking his own life. He knew it would hit Johnny sometime losing Megan, but at the moment, he seemed driven to finding out the truth.

'Hello, I'm so sorry to bother you,' he said as Catherine Clarke opened the front door.

'That's okay, Inspector, please do come in,' she said smiling. He could see she'd been crying; her eyes were red and swollen.

'Hello, Peter,' Jane said smiling at him as he entered the living room.

'Hi, Jane, how are you?' he replied.

'Oh, we're okay. We're just remembering good times, but it's so hard,' she said wiping tears from her eyes.

'I won't keep you long, but we need something with James's fingerprints on it. It's just for elimination purposes, so we know what fingerprints belong to whom. If you have something that only James has touched, that would be great.' He felt awkward. Mrs Clarke seemed okay with it, but Jane knew he was fishing. He could tell by the look on her face She was after all an ex-policewoman.

'I'm not sure what you could have, Inspector,' she said looking around the room. 'Oh, his phone, he wouldn't let anyone touch it. It's in his fleece jacket pocket.'

Mrs Clarke went and fetched James's fleece. She handed the jacket to inspector Walsh. He took out a handkerchief. He reached inside the pocket and pulled out the mobile phone and placed it into an evidence bag.

'Thank you, Mrs Clarke. I'll let you have it back as soon as possible. Right, I'll leave you ladies to it then,' he said smiling.

'No problem, Inspector,' she said, clutching the fleece jacket tight to her body.

'He hasn't told you then?' Jane asked, smiling at him.

Walsh laughed, 'You should know better than most, he tells me nothing.'

'Sounds like Johnny. Well, he asked me to marry him, and I said yes,' she smiled, as she showed him her ring.

'And it's about time as well. I can't believe you never married years ago,' he replied.

'That's what I said. Anyway we need some good news,' Catherine said, as she gave Jane a hug.

Allen sat watching the video from the nightclub CCTV cameras, but so far nothing. *Come on, Alex, I know you're here somewhere,* he said to himself. Surely if he went into the nightclub, then Megan would recognise him. He carried on watching, fast-forwarding the tape as he watched.

'I didn't expect to see you in here.' Walsh said, popping his head around the door of the very small, very cramped video room.

'He's on here, I'm sure of that.'

'Bloody hell, I've just remembered something. Melissa, the other day when she was looking through this video, seemed to recognise someone. But she wasn't sure, she seemed confused.'

'Did she say who?' he asked, pausing the video.

'No, but it was just moments before she recognised Norman.'

Allen fast-forwarded the video until he saw Norman enter the club. He rewound the video slowly back about twenty seconds, and pressed play. He watched for about a second or two and stopped the video. 'Well, well, if it isn't Alex Davis. I knew it. But why? What the hell's he doing in there?'

'He must have met Megan and James in there surely,' Walsh said as he looked at the image of Alex Davis.

'Yes, he probably would have, but his main purpose was a meeting with one Jackson Reynolds. I'm not sure Norman would have recognised him. I very much doubt if he even knew he was there or not.'

'Only reason I can think of for Alex and Jackson to meet up is drugs,' said Walsh.

'True, but I'll guess another topic of conversation was Alison Woods. You think about it, either could have been the father. You can also add Billy to that list as well.'

'What did you find out from Doctor O'Sullivan?'

'Well, she's been treating one Billy Reynolds for the last three months. He's suffering from dissociative identity disorder. Apparently, according to Doctor O'Sullivan, he blames me for a lot of his problems. He also suffers from De Clerambault syndrome or erotomania. Do you know he believes he's been in a relationship with Jane? He even went into detail about having a child with her.'

Walsh looked puzzled, 'I've heard about this syndrome, more common in women than men. Surely Billy doesn't mean Megan was his?'

'Not sure, but it's like a fantasy story. People with erotomania suffer from delusions. He believes Jane is in love with him. He's not well.'

'So any idea where he's staying?' Walsh asked.

'No. Grace's flat maybe, even his mother's house. I don't know, to be truthful.'

'How did last night go? Did you ask Jane?' Walsh said smiling, confident in the fact that he already knew the answer.

'Yes, I did, and she said yes. Also, as you know, Megan is my daughter, and so is Melissa.'

Walsh was surprised. Megan, yes, he could understand and even see it. But Melissa, now that did surprise him. 'How did she take it?' he asked.

'Very well. She's already started calling me dad, which I'm finding a little bit hard to get used to, but it's good. I'm in need of a best man, do you know of anyone?'

'Well, there is someone that stands out, but I can't for the life of me remember his name.'

'Oh, I know,' he said clapping his hands together, 'Davidson,' he added smiling.

'You'd have to get married in the winter. If it was in the summer, God, all that sweat,' he said laughing.

'That man could sweat even if he lived in the North Pole. No, Peter, will you be my best man?' he asked.

'Johnny, I'd love too,' he said shaking his hand in congratulations. 'And it's about time you two got married. All you need to do is tell Jane's father.'

'Oh yeah, I forgot about him,' he said shaking his head, more in fear than excitement.

'I'm sure he'd love to have you as a son-in-law,' Walsh said.

'Yeah, right, bloody shame if he doesn't,' smiled Allen.

'You must have some regrets about not marrying Jane.

Allen knew Peter was right. he did, massive regrets. She was all he ever wanted. She was the only girl he'd ever been in love with.

'Yes, I do,' he said smiling.

Chapter 11

Alex Davis started to worry. He was worried about Johnny Allen. *What does he know?* he said to himself. Allen knew sodding everything. He could read people like a book. If he'd found out he was in the J2 nightclub on Saturday night, then he knew who he'd met up with and maybe even why? Davis found it hard to accept that Allen was the father of Megan and Melissa, but then again it was something he already knew. *I brought those girls up. I was at the birth. I looked after them when they were sick, not Johnny bloody Allen,* he said to himself. He, in some way, had regrets about marrying Jane in the first place. Yes, she's gorgeous, but that wasn't everything. He always knew that she wasn't in love with him. She was in love with Allen, and that was that. Jane's affair with Allen was the main reason he had an affair with Grace Reynolds. What's good for one is good for the other.

He knew of Grace. When the pair were younger, he'd always found her interesting. She was wrapped up inside her own little world. He met up with her again in a pub in Oxford. She made him laugh. Her first words were, 'I need to try something different. I'm bored with women.' But with Grace comes a problem, well, two problems in fact: her brothers, Jackson and Billy. Billy was okay, but Jackson was different, and at the moment he was being a massive problem.

Come on Jackson, answer the bloody phone, it's not hard, he said impatiently to himself.

'Hi, you alright?' answered Jackson.

'At last,' he said. 'No, I'm far from alright,' he said angrily

'Go on, what's wrong?' replied Jackson.

'Johnny Allen, that's what's wrong. He knows we met up in that nightclub.'

'Yeah, how?'

'He knows everything, that's how. And I've just spent the last half hour with him,' Davis said.

'You better not have said anything. Just remember to keep your mouth shut,' he shouted down the phone.

'I'm not that stupid. Anyway from what I can gather he's more interested in Norman Denman.'

'Oh right, yeah, I've heard he's in a bit of trouble again. You heard about James Clarke I take it?' Jackson asked.

'No, go on, he's Megan's boyfriend, right? I never met him, to be truthful.'

'He hung himself. If you ask me, that's guilt talking,' replied Jackson.'

'Bloody hell, so you're telling me he may have had something to do with Megan's murder.'

'Don't know, but it looks that way. Look, we'll have to keep quiet for a while, keep our heads down. I don't want Allen putting two and two together and coming up with five.'

'Okay, I'll speak to you soon,' Davis said as he hung up.

Alex was shocked about what happened to James Clarke. Two questions started to run through his mind. One was, why would James murder Megan? And the other was, had Allen already put two and two together?

'Come on, Jackson, who was that?' Grace asked her brother. She knew he'd lie; he always did. Their mum always said Jackson wouldn't know the truth if he fell over it.

'Oh, a friend of mine, that's all. No one you should worry about,' replied Jackson.

Grace looked at her brother with raised eyebrows. She had a very good idea who it was, but she couldn't understand what he'd be doing getting involved with her older brother. She was worried about him. He seemed on edge, nervous about something. Was he involved in James Clarke taking his own life?

'I know who it was, so you may as well just say so,' she shouted at him.

'Okay, it was an old flame of yours. Any ideas?' he replied grinning at her.

'Alex Davis,' she said bluntly.

'Who's been speaking with Alex Davis,' said a voice from the other room.

'Now look what you've done, Jackson. Don't start him off. He's been okay today. Just leave him alone.'

Jackson stared at his sister and sarcastically mouthed, 'I'm sorry.' He knew it was always going to be hard, the three of them living together, especially Billy being the way he was at the moment. He watched as his younger brother walked into the living room. He looked old. He hadn't shaved in about three weeks. He seemed on edge the whole time. He was genuinely worried about his younger brother. He knew they'd had problem with each other over the years, more so when younger. But Billy needed him and Grace right now more than ever. After all he was family, blood—you look after your family.

'Look Billy, you can talk to us, you know. You're my little brother. If you're in trouble, I can help you. We both can,' he said looking over at Grace.

'He's right, Billy. Come on, you've been so jumpy these last few weeks. What's wrong?' she asked. She went and sat next to him and put her arm around his shoulder.

'I don't know where to start, to be truthful. I see her. Every time I close my eyes, I see her just lying there,' he sobbed.'

'Who Alison?' asked Jackson.

'Yeah, I can't get that image of her out of my mind. It haunts my every waking second. I even see her in the street, in the pub, everywhere. I thought when I left for New Zealand things would be different, I could just get on with my life, but even that was hard.'

'What did Jessica say when you left to come back here?' Grace asked.

He laughed through the tears and shook his head. 'Goodbye, and don't bother coming back. I tried with her, I really did. We got on well for years, but I just couldn't forget the past. Three people from my past keep haunting me, Alison, Jane and Johnny Allen. Then he keeps annoying me. He's so much stronger than me; I just can't control him. I don't know what he's done.'

'Look, I know how you feel, mate. I struggle with the same problem. Jack's so much stronger-minded than I am. Have you seen Johnny since you've been back?' he asked.

'No, I can't bring myself to speak to him. He started all this. I liked her as well, but oh no, once Johnny came on the scene that was that,' he cried.

Grace knew her brother's problem with Jane. She knew he suffered from erotomania. Part of the reason he left for New Zealand was because of how he felt about her. She knew she had one choice, to go and see Jane herself and sort this out.

Davidson marched up to Allen's office. He knew what his answer would be, but it had to be done. Norman Denman had to be charged.

'Right then, Johnny, have you charged Norman Denman yet, or do I have to do it myself,' he said sharply.

173

'Charge Norman what with?' Allen replied.

'Murder, Chief Inspector, that's what.'

'You can charge him, but he's innocent, innocent of the murder of Megan Davis and Alison Woods. Look Bill, all I need is a little bit more time. I'm close to cracking this. Norman has no idea what happened to either Alison or Megan. It was just wrong time, wrong place.'

'Go on, I'm listening.'

'Norman doesn't understand about death in any way shape or form. To him, they're just asleep. He found Alison. He said he tried to wake her up. When he couldn't, he picked her up and walked around with her. It's what he did with his sister. He wasn't in hiding either, someone abducted him. He said, 'I didn't wake up in my bedroom.' Norman Denman doesn't lie, he can't. He doesn't understand the meaning of lying.'

'Okay, what do you want done with him?' Davidson asked bluntly.

'Send him home. We'll keep an eye on him. It's the best place for him.'

'Okay, you've got forty-eight hours, Johnny, that's it. I just hope you're right.'

'Hello, yes,' Walsh said, answering his phone.

Walsh listened to what forensics had to say. He already knew the answer before they even rang him. Part of him wanted it to be someone else, but as ever Johnny was right.

'Okay, thanks,' he said replacing the phone. 'Okay, that was forensics. The fingerprints on the knife are a match to James Clarke.'

'Okay, as expected. What I don't understand is the timing in all this. Norman said he saw James by the roadside, being sick. Also, he mentioned that it took him a long time to find Megan. He said he couldn't find her to start with. Right, let's say Norman met up with James by the roadside, let's say, around 12:45 am. If it took him around an hour or so to find Megan, that's somewhere near 02:00 am. What does the post-mortem say about time of death?'

Walsh read through the post-mortem report, 'Time of death 01:00–02:00 in the morning. So in that case, it's impossible for Norman to have murdered her.'

'She was dead when Norman found her. It's the same with Alison, she was already dead. Where was James found by that old couple?'

174

'In the park, near to where Jane lives, so that's about a mile or so away. No evidence to say how he got there. My guess is, after Norman left him, he couldn't find Megan, so he decided to walk home.'

'He might have believed she'd gone home without him. But it still gives him enough time to have killed her. It's more than an hour between Norman seeing him, then finding Megan. Knife…he wouldn't have got into the nightclub with a knife in his pocket.'

'Could have hidden it near to where she was murdered,' Walsh suggested.

'Maybe, bit of a long shot. Still he wouldn't have murdered her on his own, no way. He would have had help.'

'So he could have met up with someone,' said Walsh.

'Possible, but who? That's the question. I still believe both Norman and James would have run. It would have scared them to death.'

'Norman especially, not so sure about James,' added Walsh.

'James had no other traces of blood on his shirt or anything else he was wearing?' Allen asked.

'No, the only traces of blood were his own. If he murdered her he'd have been covered in it.'

'That's true. I'm going to see Mrs Clarke again; I need to find out what state of mind James had been in over the last few weeks. These fingerprints on that knife have got me puzzled.'

'That's a first, Johnny Allen puzzled. Tell you what, I'm going to see Mr and Mrs White,' Walsh said picking up his jacket.

'I know, right. Mr and Mrs White?' Allen asked.

'Yeah, the couple that found James in the park.'

'Okay, good idea. See you later.'

He must have been there. He must have seen his girlfriend murdered. How else would he have gotten his fingerprints on that knife? He sat at his desk and closed his eyes, the images flashed through his mind.

He'd lost track of time. Where was she? 'Megan, Megan,' he called out, but nothing.

Bloody hell, where the hell has she gone? He staggered slowly up through the woods. He'd been walking around for an age. He stopped suddenly. He could sense movement in the woods.

'Who's there?' he shouted.

Just about able to walk, he tripped on what he first thought was a tree stump. Steadying himself against a tree, he stopped and took a deep breath, wiping his face he looked down as he did.

'Oh my God,' he screamed out.

He fell backwards against the tree. Slumping to the ground, he reached forwards and touched her face, 'Megan, Megan, oh no, what have I done?' he cried out.

He reached over next to her body. He picked it up and looked at it, unable to remember what had happened. He dropped the knife on the ground. He managed to stand up. His body felt strange; his mind was a mess. He looked back down at the ripped-up body of his girlfriend and screamed, 'NO.'

'Oh James, oh James, what have you done?' came a voice from behind him.

He turned around quickly, then blacked out, falling to the ground.

Bloody hell, he found her body, before or after Norman? Had to have been before, he said to himself. How did he get up to the park? He was dumped there. Whoever murdered Megan dumped James in the park.

Bloody hell, no wonder he took his own life. He killed himself believing he murdered his girlfriend.

Jane walked slowly back around the road to her house. Her thoughts were a mess, her mind racing at a hundred mile an hour. Why? What possible reason would anyone have for wanting to murder Megan? Did she witness something horrible? Was she in trouble? Did she owe money to the wrong people? So many questions and sadly, at the moment, no real answers.

She could see a dark-haired lady standing outside her house. She seemed vaguely familiar. She got to within fifty metres of her when it hit her. 'Oh my God, Grace Reynolds,' she said out loud. 'Grace is that you? I wasn't sure to start with. How are you?' she asked.

'I'm okay. I just thought I'd come and see how you are. Oh, it must be so hard on you. I'm so sorry to hear about your daughter,' she said giving Jane a hug.

'Thank you, Grace. Let's just say the last few days have been horrible. I still can't take it all in. You'll come in for coffee?' she asked.'

'Yes, thank you,' Grace replied smiling.

Grace followed Jane into her house. She still looked as lovely as ever. She wondered if she ever knew that she had a massive crush on her when she was younger. As she entered the living room, she was instantly drawn to the picture of Megan and Melissa that hung over the fireplace. She knew in an instant what Johnny must have seen, not only in this photograph but in the one of her that was hanging in her flat.

She looked at Megan. She could see Johnny in her; there was no mistake whatsoever.

'Lovely, isn't it?' Jane said as she brought in the coffee.

'Your youngest daughter is so much like you. Does he know?' she asked turning to Jane.

'If you mean Johnny, yes, he does; both girls are his,' she replied.

Grace was surprised. She looked at Jane with raised eyebrows. She smiled to herself. It made sense. After all, Alex told her that Jane wouldn't let him anywhere near her.

'Okay, that's a surprise. What about Alex? Does he know?'

'Now, now Grace, you of all people should know the answer to that question. And before you ask, yes, I know about you and Alex.'

'It doesn't bother you?' she asked as she sat down.

'No, not one bit. I didn't love him, so I didn't care then, and I don't care now.'

Jane didn't hate Grace for her affair with Alex. After all, how could she? She didn't love her husband. She was surprised at how young Grace still looked, but she seemed troubled by something. It was as if she wanted to tell her, but didn't know how.

'What's wrong, Grace? You seemed troubled. You can tell me,' she said, genuinely showing concern.

'Billy, that's what's wrong. He's back in England, has been for about four months or so, but he's not well, not well at all.'

'I saw him about two weeks or so back. I was in town; I wasn't sure it was him to start with, but now you've said he's back here. You said he's not well. What's wrong with him?' she asked.

Grace didn't want to tell Jane about the dissociative identity disorder. Admitting one of her brothers has it is hard enough, but both, that's way too much.

'Well, it's part of the reason I came around to see you. Part of Billy's problem is with you.'

'Me, why?' she said, surprised.

'He suffers from De Clerambault syndrome, commonly known as erotomania. He's in love with you. It's part of the reason he left for New Zealand. I know it's a fantasy, but to him it's very real. He believes that you love him. He even believes you've had a child together.'

Grace could see that Jane looked shocked, even worried. She started to sense she was having trouble taking it all in.

'I don't know what to say. Is he having treatment?'

'Yes, he's seeing a Doctor O'Sullivan. She's very good. The problem is more common in women than men. Men, I'm afraid, tend to stalk the woman of their dreams.'

'I haven't seen him, only once in town. You said he believes we've had a child. Has he said who it may be?' she asked.

'Melissa. I'm afraid he thinks Melissa is his daughter,' replied Grace.

Jane sat in stunned silence, unable to think straight. She always got on well with Billy, but they were just good friends. Thinking back, she'd sometimes catch him looking at her, but he'd either turn away quickly or just make some joke of it. She slumped back on the sofa. She tried her hardest, but she just couldn't fight back the tears.

'I'm so sorry, Jane. The last thing I wanted to do was upset you. But I'm scared for you. Billy's not right. He's saying some very strange things at the moment, and it's scary.'

'Oh, Grace, don't worry, I'll be okay. Is he living with you?' she asked.

'No, he's in a bedsit somewhere in Reading. But I've never been there. He won't let anyone in. He's been to see me from time to time. Look, I'll leave you in peace. It's been nice to see you again; shame it's in such sad circumstances.'

Jane stood up and gave Grace a hug and thanked her for coming around. She seemed upset, even frightened. She could tell she was worried about her brother. She watched from the front door as Grace drove off. She nervously looked up and down the road, but nothing, only the neighbours going about their own business. She wanted Johnny. At this precise moment, she needed him so badly.

She hurried back inside, she struggled to hold the phone, let alone dial Johnny's number. She sat on her sofa, trying her best to calm herself down.

He felt his phone vibrate in his jacket pocket. Fishing around for it, he managed to just about hold the phone without dropping it on the floor. 'Hello, what's wrong?' he asked her worriedly.

'Johnny, I'm scared,' she cried out in panic.

'Okay, calm down. What's wrong?' he asked, trying to keep her calm.

'I've just been speaking to Grace Reynolds. She came around to see me. She told me about Billy,' she said sobbing.

'Okay, I know about Billy. I was going to tell you later,' he replied softly.

'She said he believes that Melissa is his daughter. Why would he think like that?'

'Like I told you earlier, he isn't well, mentally I mean.'

'Grace said he's suffering from some syndrome; I can't remember the name. I need you here. Where are you?' she cried.

'I was just about to go and see Catherine Clarke again. Look, walk back around to her house, I'll meet you there.'

'Okay. Oh, I've just remembered Melissa's in town with Maddie Clarke. She'll be okay, won't she?'

'Right, okay, I'll put a call in. I'll get uniform to keep a look out. Ring her. Tell her to speak to the first policeman she sees, okay?'

'Right, see you in a while. Don't be long; I'm scared. Love you,' she said as she hung up.

He was starting to get worried. Surely Billy wouldn't go for Melissa, would he? But then again if he believes she's his daughter, he'd try anything. He pondered with the idea of going to find Melissa and Maddie himself. But Jane sounded terrified. He knew she'd want him with her as soon as possible.

'Hi, Richard, it's Johnny. Put a call out to uniform, anyone in Reading Town Centre, to keep a look out for Melissa Davis and Maddie Clarke. I just need to know they're safe.'

'Okay, what do they look like?'

'Melissa is blonde haired, with light blue eyes. She's about 5 foot 3 inches in height. Maddie Clarke has light brown hair and brown eyes, again about the same height as Melissa. Both girls are aged fifteen.'

'Okay, no problem. This is your daughter, is that right?'

'Melissa, yes. I'll give her a ring myself. Thanks, Richard.'

His mind was starting to race. He couldn't lose them, not now. It's been hard enough losing Megan. It flashed through his mind, who would Billy go for first,

Jane or Melissa? Surely Jane would be safe. It was only five minutes around the road to Catherine's house. But Billy wouldn't know, unless he'd been following them, where Melissa and Maddie had gone.

'Hello, Missy, it's Johnny—sorry dad. Where are you?' he asked.

'Hi dad, I'm on a bus with Maddie. We're going into town, why? she responded nervously.

'Right, now don't worry, darling. When you're in town, I want you to go up to the first policeman you see, and let them know who you are and that you're okay.'

'Why, what's wrong? Is mum okay?' she asked worryingly.

'Nothing's wrong, don't worry. Hasn't mum called you?' he asked.

'No. Right, we're off the bus now. I can see a policeman and a policewoman.' Melissa and Maddie ran over towards the police, and told them who they were.

'Dad, the policewoman wants to speak to you,' Melissa said handing the policewoman her phone.

'Okay,' he replied.

'Sir, it's WPC Stevens. I'll keep an eye on them, don't worry.'

'Thanks, Becky. Can you put my daughter back on, please?'

'Look, Becky will keep an eye on you, don't worry. I'll see you later.'

'See you later,' she said hanging up.

Allen tried Jane's phone, but nothing. Where the hell is she? He tried again, but this time the phone went straight to voice mail. Her phone never went to voice mail, she always answered it. He knew it would take him around fifteen to twenty minutes to get over to Catherine Clarke's house. He was starting to panic and worry about where Jane was. *Peter, I'll get Peter to drive around that way. He's closer than me,* he said to himself.

'Peter, it's Johnny. How far from Jane's house are you?' he asked.

'I'm seconds away, if that. Why what's wrong?'

'I can't get hold of Jane. She was on her way back around to Catherine Clarke's house. I've rang twice, but nothing,' he said frantically.

'Right, I'm outside Jane's house. Give me a minute,' Walsh said.

He stopped his car and jumped out. He ran towards the front door and banged on it, ringing the doorbell at the same time. He peered through the living room window, but the house was quiet; no sign of anyone. He tried the doorbell again, but nothing.

Inspector Walsh ran back to his car, 'She's not here. I'll drive around to Mrs Clarke's,' he said as he sped off at high speed.

'Okay, I'm a few minutes or so away.'

'Johnny, no sign of her walking along the road. I've just pulled up outside,' Inspector Walsh said as he jumped out of his car.

He rang the doorbell and waited for an answer. He could hear Mrs Clarke coming down the stairs as he rang the bell again. He could hear her shouting, 'Okay, okay, I'm coming,' as she opened the door.

'Hi, Inspector, what's wrong?' she asked with concern.

'Is Jane here?' he asked.

'No, she was here earlier, but that was about an hour or so back.'

'Okay, look, if she gets in contact with you, ring me as soon as possible.'

'Okay, I'll try some friends of ours. They might have seen her.'

'Johnny, she's not here. I'll drive around for a while, see if I can see her.'

Allen was frantic. He sped through the traffic at high speeds, his thoughts racing through his mind as fast as he drove. He couldn't lose her, not now, not after all that's happened. What would he do? How would he cope? He pulled up outside Jane's house. He knew she wasn't there, but he had to try. He jumped out of his car. His mind was playing tricks with him. He saw her in the living room. He banged on the front door shouting her name out, but nothing. He was wrong. The house was dark and empty.

He walked out towards the road and stood looking up and down the street, but it was empty. He stood in the middle of the road. It was as if the whole world had stood still and he was the last person on earth. He rubbed his face and eyes with his hands. He slowly started walking over towards the park. *She'll be in there; she's just collecting her thoughts,* he said to himself. She'd often spend time in the park. Sometimes they'd meet up there. He stood by the entrance as Inspector Walsh pulled up beside him.

'Johnny, anything?' he asked as he got out of his car.

'No, nothing. I was just going to check in the park. She may be in there,' replied Allen.

'Johnny, she isn't there. I've checked.'

'Where the hell is she, Peter? Bloody hell, she can't just disappear. I'll try her mobile again,' he said as he rang Jane's number.

Come on ring, pick up, pick up Jane, but nothing, it didn't even ring. It was dead. Allen looked at Walsh. He didn't know what to do. For once, he was lost.

Peter could see the strain on his face. He could tell, he could see it. He knew Johnny was starting to find this all too much to deal with.

'I want Melissa. Put a call out, tell all units to find my daughter and bring her back to the station. I want my daughter,' he shouted.

Walsh walked up to Allen and put his arm around his shoulder and said, 'We've got her. She's safe, Johnny. Melissa's fine.'

She was frightened, scared to death. It was dark and cramped. She thought she could feel what felt like the motion of a vehicle on a road. She struggled to move. She tried to move her arms and feet, but both were tied: her arms behind her back, her ankles tied together. She tried to look around, but it was way too dark. She felt cramped. She tried stretching her legs out, but there wasn't enough room. Jane screamed out in fear. She knew deep down she wouldn't be heard. It then dawned on her. She was in the boot of a car. She felt the car come to a sudden halt. The boot was flung open, but she still couldn't see anything. *Why?* she thought to herself. She then realised she was blindfolded. He picked her up out of the boot, which was easy enough; she wasn't heavy, in fact, the opposite. She struggled as he put her over his shoulder. He screamed at her to stop struggling.

'Where are you taking me?' she cried out.

'Shut up, okay? Just shut the fuck up.' he shouted.

'Who are you?' she asked sobbing.

'Never mind who I am. Just stop bloody crying like a baby.'

He pushed open an old wooden door, up a flight of stairs, then through another door. The man entered a dark damp room. He threw her on to an old metal bed. She screamed out as she hit her head on a wall behind the bed. The man left her arms and hands tied together, as well as her feet and legs. He removed the blindfold she was wearing, but before she could take a look at him, he was gone.

'Hello, help me,' she screamed out, but nothing. No one answered.

The room was cold and dark. She could just about make out where the door was. Sitting on the edge of the bed, she managed to roll off and onto a hard wooden floor. Managing to shuffle to the door, she tried to push it open, but it was locked. Jane slumped down by the door sobbing her eyes out. She lay down and curled up into a ball the best she could. She started wondering if this was what Megan went through. She needed Johnny. She needed him more than ever now.

She must have dropped off for a brief while, but no more than ten minutes. She could hear footsteps getting closer and closer. She quickly shuffled back towards the bed. She sat on the floor, trying to bring her knees up close to her chest. She sat sobbing, cold and scared.

The door slowly opened. She could see a shadowy figure of a man standing in the doorway. He just stood there for what seemed like an age.

'Come on, thirty years you've waited for this. Take it then you've won. You've beaten the great Johnny Allen.

The man walked slowly into the room and stood about ten feet from the metal bed. He looked down at her. She didn't look up. She was too scared to make eye contact. She buried her face in her knees and arms, sobbing, 'No, no.' The figure started laughing, as if he was mocking her. He walked over and stood in front of her. He grabbed her by the hair and yanked her head up. 'Look at me,' he screamed at her. 'Come on, look at me,' he screamed again. She slowly opened her tear-filled eyes. As she did, he jumped back. All she saw was a blinding flash of light, then darkness.

'You go too far. You always have to go too far. He'll find us, trust me. That's what he does.'

Allen walked back through the main doors and into the lobby, his mind on two things and two things only: finding Jane and seeing his daughter.

'Right, is she here? Is Melissa here?' he shouted at the desk sergeant.

'Sir, your daughter and her friend are in your office, Sir.'

'Okay, thank you Richard,' he replied, 'Sorry.'

Allen ran up the three flights of stairs that led up to his office. He was struggling to find the right words in his mind. *What the hell do I tell her?* he asked himself. He was met outside the office door by Inspector Walsh, neither really knowing what to say. Walsh knew how hard this could be for Johnny. He knew they needed some time and space.

'Johnny, I'll give you some time with Melissa. I'm going back to see Mr and Mrs White. Do you want me to go and see Mrs Clarke, just to make sure she's okay?'

'Okay, yes. Thanks Peter.'

He stood in the doorway to his office, the two girls were sat talking to WPC Stevens. Melissa was being comforted by Maddie. You could see she'd been crying. What must this poor girl be going through at the moment? First her sister gets murdered, now her mother is abducted. Melissa looked up at him as he stood in the doorway. She jumped up and ran into his arms, burying her face in his chest. He held her tight, kissing her on the forehead as she sobbed into his chest. He held her face and looked into her eyes. He whispered softly to her, 'It's okay, it's okay.'

Allen looked over towards Maddie. He could see she was finding this all too much as well. He beckoned her over. He held both girls in his arms, telling them over and over again, 'It's okay, it's okay.'

Mrs Denman stood at her front door. She knew he'd be home soon. He'd called her about ten minutes or so back. Oh, that boy, she said to herself, trouble from day one, he always seems to be in the wrong place at the wrong time.

Mrs Denman heard a car pull up. She couldn't see it, but she knew that it was Norman alright. Norman stepped out of the police car and looked over towards his mother. She seemed upset, as if she'd been crying. Slowly walking up the garden path, he stood in front of his mother. She reached forward and touched his face.

'Oh, Norman, what have you been up to now?' she asked him.

Norman looked at the ground. He didn't know what to say, 'Don't look at the floor, boy. No answers down there,' she said.

'I'm sorry, Mum, I didn't do nothing wrong. Johnny said so,' he replied still looking at the ground.

'Oh, you're lucky he looks out for you. Heaven only knows what trouble you'd be in without him.'

Alice gave her son a hug and kissed him on the cheek. She knew she needed to keep him safe. She knew he couldn't really look after himself. She'd found it hard going with him, more so since she lost her eyesight. It was times like this that she really missed Joan. She was brilliant with her brother, always looked out for him. Many times, she'd miss out on doing things, things that all teenage girls would normally do like going out on dates, going to the pictures, dancing. She never really had a boyfriend. When on odd occasions she'd bring a boy home, it would never last. Once the boy met Norman, that was it. Once or twice he got so jealous, it even started a fight, between whoever she brought home and Norman.

He just didn't understand. Joan was his and that was that. He was lost without his sister. He'd never really gotten over Joan dying. She wondered if he really knew she was dead. Over the years since she died, he'd ask, ask when his sister was coming home. 'Is she still asleep, Mum? he'd ask her. 'Yeah, son, she's still asleep.'

'Mum, is Joan home? She should be home now.'

Alice didn't reply. She slowly walked back to the living room and sat down, tears running down her face. She reached across to a small table that was by her armchair. She felt for a picture. The picture was of Joan and Norman as young children. She held it close to her chest, lost in her memories, memories only a mother could have of her children.

'Yeah, son, she's still asleep,' she whispered softly.

Alice knew what she needed to do. She knew it would be for his own good. She had to tell Johnny Allen the truth. It was the only way to help him.

'Dad, I'm scared. What if this person, or man, you know—' she stopped and looked at him, tears running down her face. She reminded him so much of Jane, more so when she was upset. Both when crying would bite their bottom lip.

'You have to trust me, Missy, nothing will happen. I promise you that,' he said giving her a kiss on the forehead.

He knew he couldn't show her that he was as scared as she was. For once, he was lost. He had no idea what to do next. *Where the hell is she? Who has her? Is it Billy?* He couldn't think straight; his mind was a mess with all kinds of thoughts. *Jackson and Grace, I need to speak to them. They'll know; they must know,* he said to himself.

'Right girls, I'm going to leave you with Becky. She'll look after you.'

'I'll ring my mum; she'll come and get us. Missy can stay with us,' Maddie replied.

'Okay. Becky, I'd like you to go with them. Stay with them, please.'

'I will, Sir, I will.'

Chapter 12

The back of her head felt wet. It wasn't water or sweat, but it hurt like hell. *Blood,* she thought. She tried to loosen the rope that was around her arms and hands, but it was done up too tight. *If I could just find something sharp,* she thought. Sitting down, she could just use her hands to feel around on the floor. She gingerly started feeling with just the tips of her fingers. The floor was wooden, but felt damp, as if something had been spilt on it. *Blood,* she thought in horror. The smell from the room was strange. She'd smelt something like it before. *Dad's whiskey, it's the same smell,* she said to herself.

She carried on feeling around on the floor, but nothing came to hand. She shuffled back towards the metal bed. She felt helpless. She screamed at the top of her voice, but no one heard, no one knew she was there. She started sobbing uncontrollably. She wanted Johnny, *please find me, someone please help me.*

He felt the same way now as he did when his father died. He dropped dead outside Marks and Spencer's in Reading Town Centre, massive heart attack. He spent the next few days just walking the streets. He drank heavily for months after. It was the same when Jane married Alex; he went into a drunken stupor. Again he walked the streets for days after, morning, noon and night. He couldn't lose her, not now, not like this. It would finish him, destroy him.

'Peter, it's me. I'm going to see Jackson and Grace. I think it's Billy that's got her. It has to be him.'

'Okay, I'll meet you there when I've finished with Mr and Mrs White. I'll see Catherine Clarke later. Johnny, you okay?' he asked.

'No, I don't know what to do. I can't lose her, Pete, not now.'

'We'll find her, okay. Just go careful and keep calm.'

She was the most gorgeous girl he'd ever seen. He fell in love with her right there, right then. Truth be told, he'd been in love with her ever since. He would watch her for hours, especially if she was outside playing in the back garden. He never told anyone this, not another living soul, but the day she married Alex, he sat at the back of the church watching. He'd no idea if Jane had seen him that day or not. Truthfully, he couldn't remember much about it as he was drunk. He wanted out after that. He couldn't stand being in Reading and seeing her with him. He often thought he'd never see her again. It was strange she rang him at work right out of the blue a few weeks later asking to meet up.

He always knew Megan was his, but he never admitted it to himself, let alone anyone else. The first person to ever ask him about Megan was his father. He said to him one day, 'She's yours, Johnny; Jane's daughter, she's yours.' It shocked him, to be truthful. He had no idea his father knew the truth.

Inspector Walsh pulled up outside the house of Mr and Mrs White. Both aged seventy-six years old, were out walking their dog, when they found James. He had somehow managed to walk about a mile or so to the park. How long he'd been there no one really knows. Walsh walked up the White's garden path and knocked on the door.

The front door was answered by a small grey-haired lady, wearing silver rimmed glasses. Standing behind the lady was a gentleman, about average height, and like his wife, he had identical silver rimmed glasses on. Walsh smiled at the elderly couple. They reminded him of his grandparents on his mum's side of the family.

Inspector Walsh showed the lady his warrant card. She smiled and showed him into the living room. The house was immaculate, which was something else that reminded him of his grandparents.

'This will be about that young man we found the other morning?' she asked him politely.

'Yes,' answered Walsh, 'So you know him at all?' he asked.

'Oh, yes, I've known Catherine for years. I was friends with her mother, you know,' replied Mrs White.

'I didn't recognise him at first. It was our dog, she ran over to him. I must admit, I thought he was dead. Lucky Pam was with me, she's an ex-nurse,' the old man said as he sat in his armchair.

'Was he unconscious when you found him?' Walsh asked.

'He wasn't unconscious, but he was drifting in and out, if you see what I mean. He was trying to say something. It sounded like, Megan, sleep, then he'd say nothing for about ten to fifteen seconds. Then he said, Megan, then wakey, wakey, sleepy,' said Mrs White, looking confused.

'I take it you knew his girlfriend, Megan Davis?' he asked.

'Yes, such a lovely girl, very polite, well-mannered. She would help me with the shopping, you know, carry some of the bags for us. Such a shame.'

'Did you see either James or Megan hanging around with strangers or someone who looked suspicious?'

'Well, the other week…' Mr White said looking over at his wife. She nodded as if to say carry on, it's okay. 'Well, I saw James talking to this man and lady. At first, I didn't think too much of it. It wasn't until this lunchtime, then I saw the lady again. She was waiting outside Jane Davis's house.'

'Can you remember what she looked like?' he asked the old man.

'She was about average height, slim-build, dark-haired. She looked about, well, I'd say no older than mid-thirties,' he replied.

'Can you remember anything else?' he asked the old couple.

'The man she was with the other day looked a lot older. He was tall, grey-haired, looked very pale. He seemed very much on edge.'

'This lady, was she driving a car or standing by a car?' asked Walsh.

'Yes, a red Vauxhall Astra. I can't remember the registration, but it was definitely a 62 plate.'

'One last question, would either of you recognise this man and lady again?'

Mr White looked at his wife, both nodded to each other, then both said yes at the same time. Walsh smiled and thanked the elderly couple. On leaving he mentioned about doing a photofit picture and that he'd send an officer around to do so.

He wanted answers. He needed answers. But he wasn't sure if either Grace or Jackson would be that truthful with him. He wanted to remain calm, but he wasn't sure he could. What if they gave him an answer he didn't like, then what? The frame of mind he was in, trouble that's what.

Maybe he'd wait for Peter, that would be the best thing to do, he said to himself. He pulled up outside the block of flats were Grace Reynolds lived. He sat in his car just staring into space. He was lost in thought. He held her close to his body, kissing her tenderly on the lips. She smiled at him, the light making her beautiful blue eyes sparkle like diamonds. He kissed her again, laying her softly down on her bed.

Allen jumped as a car pulled into the car park. He didn't really look at it or the people in it. Pulling his phone out from his jacket pocket, he dialled Peter's number.

'Hi, it's me. I can't do this on my own, I need your help.'

'Okay, I won't be long,' replied Walsh.

Allen hung up. He felt strange. The anger started to build up inside him. For the first time, it hit him. Finding out that Megan and Melissa were his daughters was hard enough to take in. But losing Megan before he'd even got to know her, was tearing his mind to bits. He knew she wouldn't answer it, but he tried anyway. He knew what would happen, nothing. The phone was dead.

He started thinking about Kevin and Sian Van Dalen. The scene that greeted him that day has lived with him ever since. It took him and anyone who witnessed it months to get over. Since the start of this case, he couldn't get one thought out of his mind, Jackson or Jack didn't act alone, someone was with him.

He'd almost fallen asleep, when a car pulled up next to him. He almost jumped out of his skin when Inspector Walsh knocked on the window.

'Wakey, wakey sleepyhead,' Walsh said smiling, as Allen stretched and yawned.

'Peter, sorry, I was miles away. How did it go with Mr and Mrs White?' he asked, as he climbed slowly out of his car.

'Good. About a week or so back, Mr White remembered seeing James talking with a man and a lady. Well, it wasn't until this lunchtime that he thought anything of it. You see, he remembered the lady. She was standing outside Jane's house.

'Grace Reynolds, and I'll put money on it that the man was either Jackson or Billy, more likely Jackson.

'Do you remember what Grace said the other day, I don't know him. I've never met him.'

'Oh, she knew him alright, and she knew Megan. That's how Megan ended up with my gold chain. Come on, I want answers. If we don't get them here, then I'm taking them in.'

Allen and Walsh walked across to the main door to the flats. A red Vauxhall Astra was parked on the other side of the car park. Walsh walked over to it and quickly tried the doors. The car was locked. He placed his hands on the front bonnet. The car was still hot, only recently driven.

'It's still warm.'

'Tell you what, that car wasn't there when I got here. Hang on a minute, I can just about remember a car pulling up,' he replied.

'When?' he asked.

'About a few minutes before you got here.'

Walsh checked the registration plate, a 62 plate, 'That's the car that Mr White saw outside Jane's house this morning. One more thing, James tried to tell the Whites something. It sounded like, Megan, sleepy, then Megan, wakey, wakey sleepy.'

'What did you say when you knocked my car window?' asked Allen.

'Wakey, wakey sleepyhead.'

'Where have I heard that before?' he asked. 'That's it, Beth Reynolds. Remember, she would always wake Grace up by saying, wakey, wakey sleepyhead. Grace must have said that to James. Norman then met up with James again after he'd found Megan. He must have said to him that Megan was asleep. Norman then must have helped James to the park. That's where Norman was abducted.'

'If you think about it, that's how both James and Norman came to have their fingerprints on the knife. Norman would have been easy, and James was so far out of it, he wouldn't have remembered.'

'Makes sense. I just couldn't figure out how James ended up where the Whites found him. And one more thing, that car,' he said pointing at the Astra, 'Its owner is one Grace Reynolds.'

The main door was slightly open. Walsh pushed it and turned to Allen. The two detectives slowly walked up the stairs. The front door to Grace's flat was wide open. Allen could hear raised voices, one was Grace and the other sounded like Alex Davis. Walsh and Allen stopped by the front door and listened to the pair arguing.

'That brother of yours is a fucking idiot,' he shouted.

'Which one? I've two, and they're both idiots,' she replied sharply.

'The older, thicker one, Jackson or Jack, or whatever he calls himself,' he shouted again.

' Oh, I thought Jackson was your best mate. I did warn you what he was like,' Grace replied.

'Yeah, but I didn't expect a bloody kid to go on a drug-crazed rampage—drugs that he sold him.'

'Oh, Alex, you don't believe that James murdered Megan, do you?' she laughed at him, 'Now who's the idiot.'

'Fuck sake, I don't know what to believe. Why not? Got any better ideas?' he asked her angrily.

'I've got a good idea. Why don't we finish this down the station?' Allen said as he walked into the living room of Grace's flat.

Grace and Alex stood in shocked silence. Allen could see that Grace was angry. She stood glaring at him, raised eyebrows, arms folded.

'Well, well, the great detective and his sidekick,' she said sarcastically.

'Oh, Grace, you really need to shut your front door. You can get all kinds of people listening. No Jackson or Billy?' he asked looking around the room in mock jest.

'Oh, the two said idiots you mean? I've no idea. Out exercising their one brain cell.'

'Alex, this is going to be twice in the space of two days. What will Simon Woods say about that?'

Alex said nothing, smiled at him sarcastically, shrugging his shoulders. Allen walked over to Inspector Walsh and whispered to him. Walsh nodded and disappeared outside.

'He's so obedient, Johnny. You've got him well trained,' Grace smiled. 'How's Jane? She seemed so upset earlier,' she added.

Allen didn't want to let on that Jane was missing. He wanted to try and trip Grace and Alex up. He wanted them to make a mistake.

'Cars are here, Johnny,' Walsh said popping his head around the living room door.

Allen nodded. He stood by the living room door, looked back towards Grace and Alex. Saying nothing, he held out his left arm and pointed towards the front door.

'Come Alex, the great detective wants a few words with us,' she said grabbing him by the arm and walking towards the front door.

Allen and Walsh watched as Grace and Alex were placed into separate cars. Grace blew Johnny a kiss and waved at him from the window as the two cars sped off.

'Do me a favour, separate rooms. I'll talk to Grace first, then Alex.'

Allen knew something was wrong. Davidson would never come down to meet him in the station lobby. His heart started beating faster and faster. What had he found out? He feared the worst. He couldn't tell by his facial expression. Davidson was very good at not giving anything away. Allen stood in front of him. Davidson said nothing. He handed him a large brown envelope.

'It was placed on my car,' Davidson said.

Allen looked down at the envelope. It had nothing on it, no name, no blood. Slowly opening the envelope, he felt his hands begin to tremble. Inside was a large photograph. The picture showed a blacked-out figure standing over the body of Alison Woods. Allen looked confused, unsure what to make of it. This picture's over thirty years old, why keep it? Why take it in the first place?

'I don't understand, why this? Why now, thirty years later?' he asked looking at the picture.

He handed the picture back to Davidson. He looked at it with the same shocked expression that Allen had.

'Bloody hell, that's him. That's our killer,' Davidson said.

'Two people; same killer but different killers,' Allen said.

'Johnny, what is it? What have you seen?' he asked.

'Oh, this is clever, very clever. The person taking this picture is dominant; the blacked-out figure is submissive. No, he's dominant as well. Megan's killer was submissive. There should be another photograph, same as this, but of Megan's murder.

'Only the one Johnny, that's it.'

'Sir, Sir, there is another picture. This one is addressed to you, it was hand-delivered, well, placed on the desk anyway.' The desk sergeant handed Allen another brown envelope. Allen opened it. This time, along with the picture was a note. The picture was the same as the other one, again a blacked-out figure standing over Megan's body.

'What does the note say, Johnny?' asked Davidson.

'You're a clever man, Allen. I'm sure you've worked this out by now. But pictures can be misleading. Did you like me finding your Saint Christopher? Just a little present for you.'

'You okay, Johnny?' asked Davidson.

'Yeah, yeah, I'm okay. I need to think.'

'Chief Inspector, one last thing, why have you brought Grace Reynolds and Alex Davis in?' Davidson asked bluntly.

'Answers, that's why. No lies this time,' he replied sharply.

'Johnny, by the book.'

'Yes Sir,' he replied walking away.

Allen walked up the three flights of stairs to his office. Pictures, he said, where's the other pictures. He found the other pictures and placed them on his desk. The first two pictures that were sent were of Megan's ripped-up body. Then of him and Peter with the necklace they'd found with Megan's teeth on it.

The next two pictures sent were of him and Billy when they were younger. Then the one of himself, Jane, Billy and Alison, with the note look into the background. The next picture sent was of him and Jane standing in Jane's front garden.

Look at the pictures, think, think. He closed his eyes and started thinking. First picture, murder, look at me, I've murdered someone. Not just anyone, your daughter. Second picture, I know she's your daughter. Teeth, parents keep their children's teeth, teeth sent to Jane. Necklace with teeth on it, my necklace, my Saint Christopher, look at me, I had it. I sent it to Megan, now she knows who her real father is, I'm her father. Picture of Jane and myself standing in Jane's front garden, love, forbidden love, our sin. I know your sin.

Next picture, me and Billy, best friends, like brothers. Brother, Billy and Jackson are brothers. Look into the background, Jackson's in the background. Myself, Jane, Billy and Alison. Come on, come on, think, think, what do you see? Jane and me, Billy and Alison, but Jackson in the background. Pictures, friends, children, brothers, lovers, pregnant. He opened his eyes and smiled. *Of course, now I know,* he said to himself, *but surely not, can it?*

'I take it you've been using that brilliant mind of yours,' Walsh said smiling at him.

'I needed to understand these pictures. He's giving us clues; these pictures are clues. He knew I'd work this out. But I need more evidence. I need more proof.'

'Davidson just told me you've had some more photographs.'

'Yes, two. A blacked-out figure standing over Alison's body, then Megan's body. Same killer but different killers. It's the same person, dominant killing Alison, submissive killing Megan.'

'Who took the pictures, any idea?'

'Dominant, controlling, planning. You see it's the same as with the Van Dalen murders. I couldn't work out who the murderer was, Jackson or Jack. Now I know the answer.'

'Which one?' asked Walsh.

'Both; same killer but different killers. Jack killed Kevin; Jackson killed Sian.'

'Jack's dominant, Jackson's submissive,' Walsh said.

'Correct. Although both personalities are dominant, one has to be more dominant than the other. Jack is a stronger personality than Jackson. Right, I'm going to speak with Grace.'

'No problem,' said Walsh.

Okay, right then, Grace Reynolds, then Alex Davis. No lies, no half-truths, I want answers, he said to himself. He walked back down the three flights of stairs. He knew Grace would be harder to crack. She's always been very good at bending the truth. Grace Reynolds, as a child, would make up stories. Things like, 'Help, help, there's someone in the back garden.' Or she'd come home from school crying, 'I've been followed by this strange man.' Of course, it was all lies. She was also very good at manipulating people, especially her two brothers. He was probably the only person who could see through Grace. He, in many ways, understood her. He knew what her real problem was.

Grace was bullied and teased a lot at school. Most of it was Jackson's doing. He would tell the other kids stories about her. When they were younger, Jackson was just plain nasty to her, but when she got older, that's when she started playing games with people.

She would in some respect get her own back on Jackson. He would get so wound up and angry. He often wondered what part, if any, Grace played in the Van Dalen killings. Did she play on Jackson's already fragile state of mind? She, in some way, had already played with his head when she had an affair with Sian, who at the time was Jackson's girlfriend.

He stood outside the interview room. He took a deep breath. Just as he was about to open the door, a very out of breath, very red-faced Sergeant Miles came running up to him.

'Sir, Sir,' he shouted.

'What's wrong, Richard?' he asked the out-of-breath desk sergeant.

'You've just,' he said panting, 'had a phone—' He stopped again, trying his hardest to catch his breath.

'Richard, slow down, deep breath,' Allen said laughing.

'Oh, bloody hell, I've been up and down those bloody stairs all day long. The Chief Super's had me up and down, up and down about ten bloody times. Then you get a phone call. I run all the way up to your office, and you're down here.'

'Who's the call from?' he asked.

'Alice Denman, she wants to talk to you.'

'Did she say what about?'

'No not really, she just said, 'Johnny will know,' that's it.'

'Thanks Richard.'

He wondered why Alice wanted to tell him now. He knew what she wanted; he'd always known. Norman Stephen Denman's torment, his sin. The only two living people who knew the truth were Alice and himself, and that's how it would stay.

He entered the interview room, sat down in front of Grace, reached over and turned the tape recorder on. 'I'm Chief Inspector Allen. Also present is PC Wilkins. The time is 16:50, date is September 29th.'

Grace looked at him and half smiled, 'You okay, Johnny?' she asked.

'You are Grace Maria Reynolds of flat 12, Bensons Gardens, Newbury?'

'Yes, that's me,' she smiled.

'Where's Billy?' he asked, 'Seen him today? He stays in a bedsit, is that right? It's somewhere in Reading, I believe?' he asked her.

'Oh, very good Johnny, you know he's here.'

'Where's he staying, Grace?'

'Yes, okay, in a bedsit in Reading, if you can call it that, more like a flea sit.'

'So you know where he's staying then?' he asked her bluntly.

'Yeah, I know where he's staying—some old flats along the Oxford road, town end, near where the old cinema was.'

'Okay, so he's here and not in New Zealand?'

'Oh, you've got me on that one. Sorry, wasn't thinking straight the other day,' she said smiling. 'Oh, is the said idiot in England? Oh sorry. You see, I've got a bit of a drink problem, and when I drink, I forget things like where my brother is.'

Allen stood up and walked over to PC Wilkins. 'Find Inspector Walsh for me. Tell him to come down here,' he told him.

'Yes, Sir,' he said as he left the interview room.

'PC Wilkins leaves interview room 16:54.'

'I say, Johnny, he's a big boy. Big secret, I do like men with muscles. Truth be told, I like women with muscles as well,' she smiled.

'Where is she, Grace?' he asked sitting back down.

'Who?' she replied sharply.

'Oh, come on, you know. Where's Jane? You know who's got her and where.'

'Sorry, you've lost me on this one, Johnny. I know you're clever, but you've lost the plot here,' she said smiling.

'Jane was abducted this morning, and you were the last person to see her. You were seen outside her house.'

'Okay, yes, I went to see Jane this morning, as a friend that's all, nothing else. Look if she's missing, I'm sorry, but I've no idea.'

'You can do better than that Grace.'

'So you think Billy has abducted Jane. Well, he's in love with her, madly in love, has been for years. I did tell him years ago, leave it Billy, just leave it, it won't end well.'

'James Clarke and Megan Davis, you didn't know them, is that right?' he asked her.

'I know of them, of course I do, but no, I've never met them,' she replied.

Allen fished around inside his jacket pocket. He pulled out his gold chain and Saint Christopher. He held it up in front of Grace, then laid it down in front of her. 'Remember this?' he asked.

Grace smiled. 'Oh, very clever Johnny, very clever indeed. I suspected something the other day when you were looking at my photograph. Then this morning when I went to see Jane, there's this picture of Megan wearing your Saint Christopher.'

'How and when, Grace?' he asked her with a touch of anger in his voice.

'Oh, let me think now. New Year's Eve party 1990, I found it on the floor. I knew it was yours, lovely inscription on it.' She smiled at him. She could tell by his facial expression he was angry.

'And you've kept it all this time. Why give it to Megan?'

'I didn't. I've no idea how Megan ended up with your Saint Christopher, and that's the truth. You see, I lost it, or should I say someone stole it.'

His mind flashed back to the New Year's Eve party. He could remember now, remember what happened. 'How long have you known about who Megan was?' he asked her.

'About nine or ten months or so. It's not hard to work out, is it? She looked so much like you.'

'You and Jackson met up with James about a week or so back. What was the reason?' he asked.

'Look, my eldest brother is an idiot. In fact, both of my brothers are. But with Jackson, he just goes way too far, so I warned James about him. To be truthful, James didn't seem that bothered about his past. Jackson was, well, not best pleased. Let's just say both were making good money out of selling sweeties to the young and the stupid. But I'm telling you the truth, I've never met your daughter.'

'You don't believe James murdered Megan, do you? I heard that part of your conversation with Alex. Come on, Grace, who killed her?'

'My bet would be on Norman Denman. Now there's a secret I could tell you,' she said with a wicked smile on her face.'

Allen was just about to answer when Inspector Walsh entered the room. 'Inspector Walsh enters the room at 17:02.'

Walsh walked up to Johnny and whispered something to him. Grace tried her hardest to hear what was being said, but without much luck. 'Take Wilkins with you as well.'

Walsh nodded and disappeared out of the interview room, closely followed by PC Wilkins. 'Inspector Walsh leaves interview room 17:03.'

Allen turned his attention back to Grace. 'Go on then, what secret?' he asked.

'Like father, like son,' she replied.

'What's that supposed to mean? Norman's nothing like his father. I know the story you've told, and how Norman attacked you. But that's the problem, no one really knows when you're being truthful, tell me about it?'

'Well, it was soon after his sister died. I was walking down by the river, you know, just daydreaming the afternoon away, as you do. I'd walked as far as the old boat house. I must have been there, I don't know, say half hour or so, when Norman showed up.' She stopped and wiped the tears from her eyes. 'He tried at first to just kiss me, but I pushed him away. I said he wasn't my type; men really aren't. He seemed angry at first, you know, that I pushed him away. Then he seemed to get very excited. He grabbed me, pinning me to the floor. After a brief struggle, I managed to free myself from him. Then I just ran.'

'Look, Grace, I know this may be very hard for you to relive this, but did he touch you in anyway?'

'Well, not really. He did try and touch me between my legs. That's when I got free from him. Look, I know in the past I've made up some stories, but you have to believe me Johnny, this is the truth.'

Allen wasn't sure what to make of it. He'd heard this story before and from, let's say, someone who wouldn't lie.

Inspector Walsh pulled up behind one of the squad cars. The flats in this part of town looked old and run down. *You wouldn't want to stay here,* he thought to himself.

The building itself looked as if it was built sometime early 1900s. It was three stories high, with twelve flats in it. Each flat had a small living room and even smaller bedroom, and a bathroom that PC Wilkins would struggle to get into.

'Why in hell's name anyone would want to stay here is beyond me,' he said out loud.

'If you're short of money, maybe, but even then I'd think twice.'

'Oh, yeah, I could just see your Misses staying here, Arnold,' he laughed. 'Didn't she once say that the Hilton hotel was like staying in a timeshare.'

'She's got high standards,' he replied.

'And she married you,' Walsh said shaking his head at the rest of the lads.

Inspector Walsh walked around to the side of the building. Two men were sitting on some steps that led down some stairs to a basement.

'Hello, I'm Inspector Walsh, Reading CID. I'm looking for Billy. Anyone of that name staying here?' he asked the two men.

The two men, both aged around mid-fifties, one was small in height and build with greying long unkempt hair. The other man was a large man with his arms and upper body covered in tattoos. He had short grey close-cropped hair. The larger of the two men looked over at the other and laughed. Looking back towards Walsh, he said, 'What of it?'

'So you know Billy then?' he asked bluntly.

'We might,' replied the larger man.

'Problem is, mate, does Billy know you?' laughed the smaller of the two men.

'Look, just answer the question, does Billy live in one of these flats?' he asked, pointing towards the old building.

The larger of the two men placed his can of lager on one of the steps and stood up. Not only was he of large build, he was also very tall, over six feet in height.

Inspector Walsh took four or five steps backwards and shouted, 'Wilkins.'

PC Wilkins placed his very large frame in front of Walsh and smiled at the two men. He was a good four inches or so taller and a lot bigger-built than the larger of the two men. Both men looked at Wilkins with wide eyes and a lot of fear. The smaller of the two took a deep breath, swallowed hard and mouthed, 'Bloody hell.'

Inspector Walsh peered around Wilkins' very large frame and said, 'Look, I don't want any trouble, and neither do you, okay. My friend here hasn't had any dinner yet, and he's hungry, so I'd answer my question. Billy?'

'Flat 8, top floor. Not sure if he's in. Haven't seen him for a while,' the smaller man replied.

'Thank you, that wasn't so bad, was it gentlemen?' smiled Walsh.

Inspector Walsh took three officers upstairs to flat 8. He stood outside the door which, to be fair, reminded him of the Denman's garden gate. Knocking the door and fearing the worst, he took a step or two backwards, but nothing, no answer. Walsh banged on the door again and waited. Again, no answer. Turning to one of the officers, he made a hand gesture to the officer to take the door off. To be fair, it took a bit of knocking down. At one-point, Walsh almost called Wilkins up to come and lean on it. Once the door was off, Walsh took two steps inside and stopped dead in his tracks. On the wall in front of him were hundreds and hundreds of pictures, all of Johnny and Jane. Most of the pictures were years old. Some of them amused Inspector Walsh; Johnny looked so young. He picked up one picture that was lying on the floor. Walsh looked closely at the photograph. He, to start with, believed it to be Jane, but looking closer it wasn't Jane, but Melissa.

'Bloody hell, this is a shrine,' Walsh said shaking his head. He placed the picture of Melissa into his jacket pocket. It worried him. Was she the main target?

'God, this person's a bloody stalker,' said Arnold.

Inspector Walsh took a quick look in the bedroom and the bathroom, but nothing, no sign of anyone. 'Right lads, let's give this place a once over. We're looking for anything that will lead us to the whereabouts of Jane Davis.'

The three officers and Walsh looked around for any clues that would lead to finding Jane safe and sound. Walsh started to get the impression that no one had been here for quite a while. *Good God, what a mess,* he said to himself. He stood and took a better look at the pictures. He believed most were taken by Norman Denman. But if this was Billy Reynolds, how the hell did he end up with Norman's photos?

'Sir, Sir, I've got something,' shouted Sergeant Arnold.

'What is it, Stephen?' Walsh asked as he walked over to the sergeant.

'It looks like directions. I know where this is, Peter. It's going over towards Lower Early.'

Inspector Walsh took a look at the directions, which were written on a scrap piece of paper. 'This is over near the A329. It's about a mile or so from Reading Town Centre.'

'Yeah, and if you go in the other direction as if you were going into Lower Early Town Centre, you end up by an old print factory,' added Arnold.

'Brilliant, great work lads. Come on,' he shouted.

Allen looked at Grace, she seemed genuinely upset. If what happened was true, it must have been hard to live with.

'Did Billy ever marry when he was living in New Zealand?' he asked her.

'Yes, I've never met her, but I've seen pictures of her. Her name's Jessica. From what I can make out, all seemed pretty good to start with; he seemed settled.'

'Any idea what happened?'

'You and Jane, that's what happened. He's never been able to get the two of you out of his head. Sorry, but I've no idea if he's got Jane, or if he's mixed up in this murder. All he's done is either come to see me or sit in that flat drinking, that's it.'

Allen turned the tape machine off, thanked Grace for her time. He watched from the interview room door as she left. Was this the truth? Could he believe her? His thoughts turned to Jane. *Time to give Peter a ring,* he said.

'Peter, it's me, any news?' he asked.

'Yes, I was just about to ring you. We've found what looks like Billy's flat, but no sign of Billy or Jane. But some good news, we've found directions to an old factory, it's over towards—'

'Lower Early,' Allen said before Peter could tell him. 'Of course, it's where Tom Reynolds worked. It was an old print factory, closed down some ten years back. Okay I'm on my way.'

'One last thing, that old flat, the walls are covered in pictures of you and Jane, hundreds of them. Also, I found a picture of Melissa. At first, I thought it was Jane. I'm worried, Johnny.'

'She's safe, don't worry. Right I'm on my way. See you in a while.'

Allen ran out of the station, his heart and mind racing at a hundred miles an hour. What would he find? Was she still alive? He started to fear the worst. No, no way, he wouldn't kill Jane. Not Billy, not if he loved her.

'Help me,' she screamed. 'Someone please help me,' she cried out. She'd just about given up hope of ever being found. She was starting to get cold. She had no idea what the time was; the room was dark, blacked out. Sitting on the floor, she tried to loosen the rope tied around her legs by trying to kick her legs to the side, but she couldn't free herself. She started sobbing as her thoughts turned to Melissa. *My poor baby, she must be so scared,* she thought. She cried out. 'No, no, he'll find me,' she said. 'Johnny will find me. please find me,' she cried.

She could hear footsteps getting closer and closer. She curled up as close to the bed and the wall as the ropes would let her. The door slowly opened. The shadowy figure stood in the doorway.

'He won't find you,' he laughed.

'Yes, yes, he will,' she screamed back at him.

'The great detective and the bitch. What makes you any different from anyone else? Johnny Allen's going to lose this game,' he sneered.

'No, no, you're wrong. He'll find us. That's what he does. That's all he does.' came another voice.

'Oh, bloody hell, just leave me alone,' he screamed.

'He's going to take our daughter, Jane. He's going to kill Melissa, but I won't let him,' said the other voice.

'No, no, leave Melissa alone. She's not our daughter. She's mine and Johnny's,' she screamed at him.

'Oh, bloody hell, why did you have to tell her? Why? Don't you get it? She's not your daughter, she's mine,' he shouted back.

'Who are you speaking too?' she asked him. She was confused. There was no one else in the room. No one stood at the door, just herself and him.

'What the fuck has it got to do with you,' he screamed at her.

The figure now seemed angry. It walked over towards Jane and stood over her holding a chain and a padlock. He wrapped the chain around her legs and padlocked it to the bed.

'Just in case you get any bright ideas,' he shouted at her.

'Leave my baby alone. You don't hurt my baby,' she cried.

'I'll do whatever the fuck I like to her. After all she's our daughter; I'm her father.'

'No, you're not,' she screamed, 'She's Johnny's, mine and Johnny's.'

'You seem to forget, I killed yours and Johnny's little bitch.'

'You killed Alison as well, didn't you?' she screamed at him.

'What? No, no, I didn't kill her,' he said laughing.

'Who did then?' she sobbed.

'He did,' he shouted at her. Then he was gone.

Allen pulled up next to the squad cars that were parked outside the old factory. He didn't care how he got her out; he just wanted her back. He was almost too scared to even get out of his car. *She'll be fine,* he said, trying to reassure himself. He'd never felt like this before; angry yes, but fear, no that was something almost completely new to him.

'You alright?' Walsh asked Allen.

'No, I'm not. What if she's—'

He stopped him; he knew what he was going to say. Truth be told, he felt the same way, but he had to remain strong, stay positive. Walsh didn't speak, neither of them did. Both knew, both could see the fear in each other's eyes.

'Right, Wilkins, Arnold, Peters, with me, the rest of you with the Chief Inspector. Johnny, I'll go around the back, see if there's another entrance.'

'Okay.' He watched as Inspector Walsh headed off around the old factory. From what he could remember, the factory was an old print works. The factory itself had been left empty for around ten years or so. He pushed open an old wooden door that looked as if it had seen better days.

'Right. Miles, with me. We'll search over to the left. You two search the other side. Keep your eyes open, and keep on your toes, lads.'

The old factory was just an empty shell; no machines, nothing, just empty rooms. *What a waste of space,* he thought to himself. You could do so much with this space: houses, flats, all kinds of useful things could be built on this site.

'Sir, Sir, over here,' shouted Miles.

'What have you found, son?' Allen shouted over to him.

'Someone's been here, look.'

Allen looked into what was once an old office. The room was small but had two old tables and a chair in it. On one of the tables was a mug, a glass and some cutlery. Over on the other slightly smaller table were some newspapers.

'These newspapers are dated within the last two weeks or so,' shouted Miles.

'He's been here. He's definitely been here,' replied Allen.

Allen turned around quickly and looked at Miles, 'What was that?' he asked.

'Don't know, Sir, I didn't hear anything,' replied Miles.

Allen listened carefully, it sounded like someone crying. 'Everyone quiet,' he shouted.

The old factory fell silent. *There it goes again,* he said to himself.

'I heard it this time, Sir, Miles said.

'Jane, Jane,' shouted Allen.

She could hear someone shouting her name. She cried out again, 'I'm here. I'm here.'

The cry seemed to be coming from above. The old factory had its offices upstairs. Allen ran over to an old staircase that led up to the old offices on the second floor. He called her name out at the top of his voice.

'Johnny,' she screamed out, 'Johnny, I'm here.'

Allen ran up the stairs, followed by Inspector Walsh and the rest of the team. The police officers franticly opened doors, shouting Jane's name. She cried out again, shouting his name out.

'She's here. She's here,' Walsh called out. 'Jane, Jane, don't worry. We're here, we're here. You're safe,' Walsh called out to her.

Allen tried the door, but it was locked and bolted, it had three padlocks, and four bolts on it. He turned around and looked at Wilkins. 'Gary, just take this bloody thing off its hinges,' he shouted.

Wilkins stood in front of the door and sized it up. He took four steps backwards and then launched his six-foot seven-inch, three hundred pound plus frame at the door. The door, the room and the factory, and probably the whole town shook. Seconds later, there were broken bits of door, padlock, bolts, screws, door frame; the lot were in bits on the floor.

Wilkins stood and looked down at his handy work and at was once a door. He turned and looked at Jane, smiled and said, 'Sorry about the mess, love.'

Allen ran into the room and over to Jane. He held her in his arms kissing her, whispering, 'It's okay, it's okay.'

She looked at him and sobbed, 'I knew you'd find me. I knew you'd come. How's our baby? Is she safe? He said he killed Megan.'

'Don't worry, Melissa's okay. She's safe,' he said, reassuring her.

'Johnny, I don't understand. He said he killed Megan, but not Alison. He was talking to himself, a real conversation. He said he killed Alison.'

Allen started untying the ropes from around Jane's arms and legs. He more than understood what Jane meant. He could see it all now, dominant and submissive.

'Johnny, I've got a chain that's wrapped around my legs and padlocked to the bed,' she cried.

Allen looked at the chain and the padlock, 'I don't think it's going to last very much longer, do you?' he said looking over at Wilkins.

Wilkins knelt down, grabbing hold of part of the chain that was padlocked to the bed, and pulled hard, very hard, breaking the padlock and the chain.

Allen looked at Jane, then at Wilkins. He smiled and said, 'Jane this is Gary, Gary this is Jane. And as you can see, when he hits something, it stays hit.'

Jane smiled at Wilkins through the tears that were in her eyes. 'Thank you,' she said.

'No problem. All in a day's work,' he said smiling.

'What happened?' he asked her, helping her to her feet.

'I was walking back towards Catherine's house. Next thing I remember is I'm in the boot of this car. Only thing I can think of is he hit me on the back of the head.' Allen checked Jane's head. She had a massive lump and a three-inch gash.

'Did you see him at all?' he asked her.

'No, not at all. It was just too dark. I didn't even recognise his voice. Like I said, it was strange. It was as if he was speaking to someone else, but there was no one else around.'

'Come on, let's get you to hospital. You need to get this head sorted out.'

She seemed a bit wobbly on her feet and a little lightheaded. Allen and Walsh slowly helped Jane down the stairs, out of the factory, and into Allen's car.

'Johnny, do you have your mobile. I've lost mine, and I want to call Melissa, tell her I'm okay.'

Allen handed Jane his mobile. Her hands seemed very shaky. She could barely hold the phone properly or even dial the number. Allen took the phone off her and dialled Missy's number.

'Hi, it's dad. You okay?' he asked.

'Sort of. Have you found mum yet?' she asked hopefully.

'Well, I've got someone here that wants to speak to you.'

He handed the phone to Jane. With her hands still shaking, she just about managed to hold the phone and speak to her daughter. 'Hi darling, you okay my baby?' she sobbed.

'Oh Mum, oh Mum, you're safe. I was so scared,' she cried.

'I'm okay. Look, I think I need to go to hospital. I've got a three-inch gash on my head, I better get checked out.'

'Okay, I'll ask Catherine; see if she'll take me down to the hospital.'

'Okay, let me know. Love you.'

'Love you too.'

Chapter 13

He felt on top of the world. He'd won, beaten the great Johnny Allen. He pulled up and parked his car in a car park behind the old block of flats. He jumped out of his car. He didn't want to spend any time here. It was a quick in and out. All he wanted was to pick up two photographs and he was gone. He ran up the two flights of stairs to his flat. As he reached the top stair, he stopped dead in his tracks, 'NO, NO, NO,' he screamed.

He stood looking at the broken door that was just about hanging onto its hinges. He slowly walked into the room. 'Who's here?' he shouted, 'Come on, show yourself,' but no reply.

He slumped down in an old chair. He knew what had happened. He believed he knew who'd been here. How? Who told them? Who knew he was here? *Someone's bloody told them,* he said to himself. *Alex Davis, I'll put money on it,* he thought.

He slowly stood up, looking around at the mess. 'Pictures,' he shouted out loud. He started searching franticly through hundreds of pictures. 'Where the hell? Who the hell's got my picture?' he screamed. He slumped back down in his chair and held his head in his hands, tears streaming down his face. He looked down at a piece of paper with the address to the old print factory. It hit him, hit him hard. He knew what had happened. He knew Allen had found her.

'Told you, I told you Allen would find us. That's what he does.'

'Shut the hell up. Just leave me alone,' he screamed hitting his head with his hands.

He slumped back in his chair just staring into space, when a voice came from behind him. 'You alright, mate?'

He stood and turned around to see who it was, 'Oh, it's you. What the hell happened here?' he asked angrily.

'You had visitors,' the man said as he examined the door.

'Who?' he shouted sharply.

'Police. We just went along with it. Asked for a Billy, but as I don't know your name, we just played along with it.'

'So the police did this?'

'Yeah, sorry,' he said as he disappeared.

He sat shaking his head. He was desperate, on edge, his thoughts flitting from one personality to another. He couldn't control it any longer, it was becoming too powerful.

He slowly got out of his chair and stood in front of the wall. He looked at the pictures in front of him. He felt the anger building up inside. In a frenzy, he started ripping at the pictures. He stopped, almost out of breath. Tears running down his face, he looked at the ripped-up picture in his hands. The picture was of Jane when younger, aged no more than eighteen years old. His tears and sobbing turned to laughter as he ripped the picture up.

'You won't win. You won't beat me. Now it will end. The final piece of the puzzle, the last game, and it ends with our daughter,' he laughed.

Melissa felt relieved that her mother was safe and sound, but she still had an uneasy feeling. She had the feeling over the last few days or so that she was being followed. She wanted to tell her mum and dad, but now didn't seem the right time. She didn't want her mother to worry.

She had to tell someone, anyone who'd listen. Maybe Maddie and her mother would listen to her. It was times like this where she'd talk to Megan. She missed her sister more than ever; she helped her with so many problems. Many times, over the school holidays or at weekends, the two would stay up until the early hours of the morning talking. She smiled to herself as she remembered the chats about the usual things teenage girls talk about. Melissa knew her mum and dad would listen, but at the moment it all seemed so strange. The last week had been so hard, with losing Megan then finding out who her father was. She was glad that Johnny was her father. He was really nice, and funny.

'You okay, Missy? You were miles away,' Maddie asked, as she sat next to her best friend.

'Yeah, sort of. It's just been a strange week. My feelings are all over the place.'

'I know how you feel. Look, I argued with James morning, noon and night, but he was still my brother. I still loved him.'

'You two made me laugh. He had two ways of calling you boghead. One would be really nasty, 'Oh go away, boghead,' then the other would be all sweet and kind, 'Oh you okay, boghead?' Melissa said laughing.

'I started signing his birthday and Christmas cards, "love boghead"; became a bit of a joke.'

'You gave me my nickname,' smiled Melissa.

'Missalot. With a name like Melissa Charlotte, what else could I call you?' Maddie laughed.

'You girls okay?' asked Mrs Clarke.

'Yeah, sort of,' replied Missy. 'I was going to tell my mum and dad, but it doesn't seem the right time.'

'What is it? You can tell me,' said Mrs Clarke.

'Well, I'm scared. I don't know if I'm imagining it or not, but I think I'm being followed,' she said. The tears started to flow. She just couldn't hold them back any longer.

'Any idea who?' Maddie asked.

'No, not really. Every time I turn around or go to the shop, or the other day, I went for a walk in the park, there's this lady standing there. I've drawn her.' Melissa reached for her sketch pad. 'It's only a rough quick sketch,' she said showing Maddie and Mrs Clarke her drawing.

'Okay, that's a rough sketch, is it? You're amazing Missy,' smiled Maddie.

'Your mum's brilliant at drawing, but you're another level,' said Mrs Clarke. 'I'm sorry, I've never seen this lady before. What about you, Maddie?' she asked.

'No sorry, no idea,' she replied looking at the drawing. 'Wish I could draw,' she added.

'I'll teach you,' Melissa said smiling.

'You need to show this to your dad. He may know who it is.' Said Mrs Clarke.

'I will,' Missy said looking at the picture.

'Come on then, you two, let's go and see your mum.'

'There is one more thing. You see, I found something out ages ago. I read Alison's…my mum's cousin who was murdered, I read her diary, and I found out who the father of her baby was. I was at my grandfather's house and I found it. I didn't read much of it, only who the father was, that was it. I didn't know who to tell. Megan knew as I told her. But I lied to my mum and dad. I lied as I was scared.'

'Oh Missy, look, don't worry darling. I'll come with you, and we'll tell your dad,' she said giving the young girl a hug.

He stood outside Mrs Denman's house. He knew what Alice wanted, what she was going to tell him. This was going to be hard for Alice, hard for any parent to admit what a child had done. He slowly walked up the garden path and stood in front of the door. He rang the bell and waited.

'Morning, Alice,' he said.

'Johnny, I'm glad you've come. Do come in,' she replied.

He could almost sense sadness in Alice's voice. He could see the pain in her face. He watched as she slowly sat down in her armchair. She reached over and felt for her photograph of Joan and Norman as young children. He took a seat in the armchair opposite to Alice. He reached out and took her hand. She could tell by the touch of his hand that he knew what she wanted.

'Over thirty years, I've kept this to myself, never told another living soul. You know though, Johnny, you see everything. I know what he did was wrong, and for a mother to keep a child's secret for all this time, that's my sin.'

'He raped Joan, didn't he?' he asked her softly.

'Yes,' she said with tears in her eyes. 'Like father, like son. I believe she grew to hate him as much as she hated her father.'

'But there's something else, isn't there?' he asked.

'Yes,' she said nodding.

'Someone else knew Norman's secret. They overheard Joan and Norman arguing, moments before she died, and this person has told you?'

'Yes, they have. As I've told you, you see everything. You know who it is, don't you?' she asked him.

'Yes, I do. It all makes sense now. How much does Norman understand?' he asked.

'Nothing, he doesn't understand any of it. She loved her, you know; I truly believe that. I'd accepted my daughter was gay years ago, a mother knows. She hated men because of what her father did to her. Norman just did what his father told him. He was so scared of him.'

He sat and listened to what Alice told him about Joan and this other girl. He started to wonder if Norman knew who she was.

'This young lady friend of Joan's, now I know who she is, and as you know, she's clever, very clever, and very manipulative. Does Norman know who she is?' he asked.

'I'm not sure, maybe. After all, he found her, didn't he. They were together, Joan and her friend. I believe they met up at the old boat house. Norman found them together. What happened after that, I'm not really sure.'

Allen sat half listening to Alice, half thinking about Joan. She was so kind and caring. She was also a very gentle person. He knew what Norman did was wrong, but it was his father's fault; he scared him stupid. Norman Senior would beat him almost every day, and if he didn't beat him physically, he would mentally abuse him. He thought it strange. Norman would do anything for his sister. When he found out what had happened, it surprised him greatly.

He didn't want Norman to get into any more trouble. After all, twenty years for a crime you didn't commit, that's punishment enough. He started thinking about the day Joan died. What if Joan and Grace, the young lady friend—he laughed to himself—what if Norman had seen what the two were up to, had an argument with his sister, did he then rape her? Grace, what would she have done? Maybe run? No, it doesn't make sense.

He thought back to what Grace told him about that afternoon. She said she had her first sexual encounter, who he now believed to be Joan. Maybe they didn't meet up at the old boat house. They'd met up before that, then Joan told Grace about Norman. But why did she go to the old boat house? Argument, she had an argument with Grace, then ran down to the boat house. Did Grace follow her straight away? After all, it was Norman that found his sister, so he had to have witnessed her running down to the river. Norman didn't know his sister's secret. He didn't know back then that Joan and Grace were in a relationship.

'Is Norman here?' he asked.

'He was. Not sure where he went, probably out somewhere with his camera.'

'Joan's lady friend, it was Grace Reynolds?'

'Yes, yes, it was,' she replied, holding her photograph tight to her chest.

He tried not to make a sound. He didn't want Johnny or his mother to know he was there. He had sad thoughts about Joan and angry thoughts about Grace. He tried to stop the voice in his head, but he couldn't. It was too strong.

He slowly and quietly went towards the back door. He was confused, angry. He didn't understand what had happened. He stopped at the back door. Turning back towards the kitchen, he saw it, but he knew it was wrong.

'We don't like Grace, do we, Norman?' the voice said.

'No.'

'You know what you have to do, don't you?' it said.

'No, I don't want to.'

'You have to. Go on, take it. Take it.'

'Thank you Alice, I'll leave you now. Ring me if you need anything.'

He stood by his car, thoughts running through his mind. It was now starting to make some sense. He looked up and down the road. He had that feeling again, the feeling he was being watched. He could sense someone was watching him, but this time he believed he knew who it was. He took one last look around, sat in his car and started the engine. Just as he did, his phone rang.

'Hello, Allen,' he answered.

'Hello, Johnny, sorry to call, but it's Roger, Roger Woods. I need to speak to you. Can we meet up?' he asked.

'Okay, yes, no problem. Where and when?' he asked.

'Look, I'm going over to the cemetery. I'll meet you there, say, in about half hour.'

'Okay, no problem, Roger.'

Melissa wanted her mum to sleep in; she needed to rest. Her dad had gone out to work early this morning. He'd left a text message saying, 'Let mum sleep in, maybe breakfast in bed.'

She slowly walked up the stairs, making sure she didn't drop the tray or what was on it. She balanced the tray on the bookcase and opened her mother's bedroom door. She looked so beautiful when asleep. She was the most beautiful person she'd ever known. She always found it strange when people would say, 'Jane Davis is beautiful, but her youngest daughter is even more so.'

She carefully placed the tray on her mother's bedside table, then walked around to the other side of the bed and lay down next to her. Jane slowly opened her eyes and smiled at the angelic face smiling back at her.

'Morning, sleepy head,' Melissa said smiling.

'Morning, Missalot,' Jane replied placing her hand on her daughter's arm.

'I've made you breakfast, well, it's sort of brunch really.'

'What's the time?' Jane asked.

'Five to eleven,' she said smiling at her mum.

'Oh my God, I haven't slept in for so long in years.'

'You need to rest, Mum.'

'I didn't even hear dad leave this morning.'

Melissa wanted to tell her mother about being followed, but she didn't want to upset her in any way. Maybe she'd wait until later, maybe when her father got home tonight.

'Do you have any idea who this man is?' she asked her mother.

'No, no idea at all. I didn't see his face or even recognise his voice.'

'You must have been so scared. I would have been.'

'I was, I was terrified, but I knew dad would find me.'

She wondered what her father was like when he was younger. 'Mum, what was dad like when you were younger?' she asked.

'Oh God, he was very shy. I liked him from the first moment I saw him, and he liked me. It took him over a year to ask me out.'

'So love at first sight then?' she asked smiling.

'Well, yeah, sort of. It was funny; when we first met he would fall over his own tongue,' she laughed. 'Do you know what the first thing he said to me was?'

'No, go on then.'

'Oh my God, you're so gorgeous. He said that in front of my parents, his parents, my brother, his sister.'

'What did you say?' she asked smiling.

'Thank you. I was glad. As I've said, I really liked him, so I knew he liked me back. God, I gave him so many opportunities, but he was so shy. I would answer the door wearing just a bath towel, or I'd wear really short skirts.'

'Mum, I'm shocked. Sometimes though, boys need a helping hand.'

'If you got it, flaunt it, that's what Alison and I would say. I miss Alison, always have. She was so lovely. We were like sisters really.'

'Why was she killed?' Melissa asked her mother.

'I'm not really sure, to be honest. She was pregnant, that I only found out the other day. Not sure if that had anything to do with it.'

'So you wouldn't have known who the father was then?' She wanted to be truthful, but as with being followed, it didn't seem the right time.

'No, no idea. She was going to tell me, that I'm sure of, but she never did.'

'You've been through so much in your life. Losing Alison, not being able to marry the man you love, then losing Megan. It must be so hard.'

'I won't lie. I've had many days when I didn't know if I could carry on. It's strange, I didn't know how to grieve for Alison, and to be truthful, I don't with Megan.'

'I feel the same way. I was talking with Maddie yesterday. She said the same. What are we supposed to do? How are we supposed to feel? He will find the person who killed Megan, won't he?' she asked wiping the tears from her eyes.

'Your father is just about the cleverest man I've ever known. Oh yeah, he'll find them alright, you have my word on that.'

It was cold, but then again cemeteries always did feel that little bit colder. He placed the flowers he was holding on his father's grave. Five years; *God, time passes so quickly,* he said to himself. He thought back to the day his father passed away, hardest thing he'd ever done, sat by his father's bedside watching him slowly die.

Strangest thing about his father's death was the dreams he had after he'd died. One of the dreams he had was, he went to see him in the chapel of rest. On entering the room, he saw his father sitting in a chair with his back to him, but however hard he tried he just couldn't see him. He entered the room, walked over to his father and stood in front of him. But by then his father was again sat with his back to him. He didn't understand his dream then, and to this day he still doesn't.

Another dream he had was, he was standing beside his father's coffin, but as a young child. When he looked inside the coffin, he saw himself as an old man and not his father.

Allen knelt beside his father's grave, kissed his fingers and placed them on the gravestone, 'Sleep well, Dad,' he whispered. He stood up took one last look at his father's gravestone and started walking over to meet Roger Woods. He could see Roger sitting on a bench near Alison's grave. What did he want? What had he found out?

'Morning, Johnny,' he said shaking his hand.

'Roger, hope you're well?' Allen asked as he sat down next to him.

'Johnny, thanks for coming. Look, I'm not sure how far you've got with this case, but knowing you, you'll work it out. I spoke to my brother yesterday. He as good as admitted that he got it wrong with Alison's case.'

'The evidence has always said that. Norman Denman didn't murder your daughter. It was just wrong time, wrong place.'

'What I'm going to show you should make things a little clearer.'

Allen could see that even after thirty years, this was still so hard on Roger; so many painful memories.

'I should have shown you this a while back, but I've only just brought myself to read it.' Roger picked up a white plastic bag and pulled out a black diary. 'This was Alison's. I only found it again the other day. When she died, I gave this to my brother as I believed it may have helped. I'm not sure if he read it or what he did with it. You need to read it, Johnny. It will give you some answers.'

Roger handed Allen the black diary. He could see the pain in his eyes. Roger stood up, thanked Johnny for coming, then disappeared into the distance.

He sat for a while looking down at the diary that lay on the bench next to him. He slowly picked it up and opened it. Inside was a note written by Roger, addressed to Johnny Allen.

'This, I hope, will give you answers. I know you of all people will understand, Roger.'

Allen started reading through the diary. It was normal teenage things: who likes who, who's going out with whom, that sort of thing. He continued flicking through the pages until he reached the date June 4, 1988. He read with some interest and surprise what Alison had written.

'God this is so hard. I like Billy, but Jackson is so much more interesting. I know he's bad, but that's what makes him so appealing.'

Allen turned to the next page and carried on reading. 'Feeling so guilty, but making love with him was heaven. Don't know why I feel so guilty. It's not like I've ever let Billy make love to me.'

He flicked forwards to 23 July 1988. 'Oh God, I'm in so much trouble. Found out today I'm pregnant. Have to tell Billy the truth, but I just don't know how. I'm really scared.'

Then written in black capital letters was, JACKSON REYNOLDS IS THE FATHER OF MY BABY.

Allen's mind started racing. This can't be true. They hated each other. If he was the last person on this planet, she wouldn't have been interested in him. He carried on reading through the diary. He stopped on Friday, 23 September 1988, the day before she was murdered.

'Oh, that fucking little bitch, why the hell would she go and tell Billy? How the fuck did she find out? I need to tell Jackson; Billy knows about me and you. He knows I'm pregnant and you're the father.'

Allen sat back on the bench and stared out into the distance. It made sense, as unexpected as it was, that Alison and Jackson would become lovers. He knew why she was murdered and how. He fished around inside his jacket pocket for his phone. He wanted to make sure Jane and Melissa were okay, but first, he needed to speak with Peter.

'Hi, Peter, it's me,' he said.

'Johnny, I was starting to get worried about you. Where have you been?' he asked.

'I've been to see Alice Denman. Then Roger Woods rang me, asked to meet up. Look, I'm on my way back. I know what happened to Alison and why Joan Denman took her own life.'

'Okay, how long will you be?' Walsh asked.

'Not long, about half hour or so.'

'Okay, see you soon.'

Grace was starting to worry about Billy. She hadn't seen him for at least a day or so. He wouldn't even answer his phone.

'Jackson, Jackson,' she shouted.

'What the hell are you shouting at?' he asked her angrily.

'Have you seen Billy at all today?' she demanded.

'No, not since yesterday morning. Why?'

'God, you two are something else; bloody idiots the pair of you. Am I the only one out of the three of us with any brains?'

'Oh, look at Miss goody-goody. You're no angel, little sis. Remember, I know your secrets.'

'And what's that supposed to mean?' she shouted.

'That's your problem. You seem to forget what you've done.'

Grace looked at her brother and smiled at him sarcastically. 'I've done nothing wrong, brother dear. After all, it was you that got banged up for murder.'

'Oh, I knew you'd bring that up. God, you do it all the time. I've done nothing wrong; you got banged up for murder,' he said angrily.

He knew in some respect she was right; she'd done nothing wrong. He accepted she was the clever one out of the three of them. She'd always been able to twist Billy and himself around her little finger. It really got to him. She annoyed him sometimes, well, most of the time, to be truthful. She was bossy, more so when younger. He, out of the three of them, was always the one in trouble. Truth be told, some of it was Grace's doing, not his.

'I'm worried about him as well, you know. I'll go out and have a look around, see if I can find him.'

'Okay, I'll come with you. We'll check his flat first,' she said.

'Have you ever been there?' he asked.

'I've waited outside, but no, no I've never been inside,' she replied.

'No, I haven't either. Truthfully, he wouldn't let me in.'

'Same here. It seemed to me he had something to hide. Come on let's go.'

Alex Davis was angry, very angry. He sat in his ex-father-in-law's house. *Three hours I was kept there,* he said to himself, *three bloody hours, and for what? Nothing.*

'He can't do that, can he?' he shouted angrily.

'Alex, look calm down. Jane was missing, and Johnny found her. Even you must be thankful for that,' replied Simon Woods.

He never thought he'd see the day Simon Woods praising Johnny Allen. 'Come on then, did you know about Allen being Megan and Melissa's father?'

'No, I didn't. I only found out when Jane told me the other day. You must have known?' replied Woods.

'Yeah, I did. After all, she wouldn't let me anywhere near her. Come on then, who murdered Alison? If it wasn't Norman Denman, then who?'

'You should know the answer to that better than I do,' he replied.

Davis didn't respond. He wasn't sure himself. It was something that never came up in conversation with Jane. She never really spoke much about Alison, maybe too many painful memories. He wondered if Woods knew what he felt for Alison. He always knew he married the wrong cousin. Alison didn't really feel the same way. She liked him, yes, but not in that way—more like a brother than a lover. Something else that crossed his mind; Alison had her secrets, big secrets as well.

'Alison was pregnant? I'm right in saying that?' he asked.

'And how did you find that out?' Woods replied sharply.

'I have my ways,' he said smiling.

'I suppose you're going to tell me who the father is next?' he said, not bothering to look up from the book he was reading.

'Well, it isn't me, if that's what you think. I told Allen that, remember?' he snapped angrily.

'Alex, we've been through all this on more than one occasion. Just leave it.'

'I can't just leave it. I'm not taking the blame for this. I had nothing to do with her being pregnant or her murder,'

'Do you have any ideas who the father might have been?' Woods asked, looking up from his book at last.

'Yeah, I do, Billy Reynolds, only logical answer.'

'How sure are you about that?' he asked.

'I take it by that reply you know more than you've made out.'

Woods said nothing. He looked over at Alex, then back to his book. Davis was puzzled. If it wasn't Billy, then who? Only other person it could be was Jackson, but surely not, could it? Maybe he'd question Jackson on it. Alison hated him, hated him with a passion. She couldn't even stand to be in the same room, let alone become lovers.

Allen ran up the three flights of stairs to his office. He was still in a state of shock about Jackson being the father of Alison's baby. He was finding it hard to take in. Truth be told, it was always in the back of his mind. He would sometimes catch Jackson looking at her.

He entered his office, threw his jacket on top of a filing cabinet. Inspector Walsh was nowhere to be seen. He noticed a note on his desk that Walsh had written. It said, 'We're in trouble. When you get here, Davidson's office as soon as possible.'

He looked at the note, struggling to work out what he'd done wrong. He slowly walked back down the one flight of stairs to Davidson's office. He knocked on the door and waited for an answer, still trying to work out what he'd done.

'Enter,' shouted Davidson.

He entered the office which, unlike his, was spacious with a new desk and new table and very comfortable chairs. Inspector Walsh was already sitting in one of the comfortable chairs waiting. He looked up at Johnny and half-smiled, a smile which said, you're going to love this.

'Johnny at last,' Davidson said looking up from his desk. 'We've been waiting for you. Okay, first things first, we've had a complaint from Alex Davis. Remember him?' Davidson asked bluntly.

'Oh, I forgot about him. Had other important things on my mind like finding Jane alive,' Allen replied sharply.

'He's not happy Johnny, three hours you left him sitting there.'

'Look, I'm sorry, but he of all people would want Jane back safe and sound.'

'I know what happened was unexpected, but you should have told me. Where have you got to now? Any updates?' asked Davidson.

'Well, today I've found out who the father of Alison Woods baby was. And Peter, you were right, it was Jackson Reynolds. Sir, I'm off to find Jackson and have a little chat.'

'Johnny, if you bring someone in, don't just leave them sitting waiting, let me know.'

'Yes Sir. Sorry Sir,' he said, standing up to leave.

Allen stood outside Davidson's office. He turned to Inspector Walsh and smiled and said, 'Come on, I've got some news to tell you.'

'What, about Jackson being the father?'

'Yes, and more besides.'

Walsh followed Allen up the flight of stairs back to his office. He knew they were close, close to solving not one murder, but two, and a miscarriage of justice.

'Right then, I met Roger Woods this morning, and he gave me this.' Allen placed Alison's diary on his desk. 'This is Alison's diary. Roger told me he gave it to his brother soon after Alison was murdered, but Simon did nothing with it.'

Inspector Walsh picked up the diary and started flicking through it. 'I suppose it makes some sense in a way.'

'I'd never have believed it, if I hadn't read it myself. The two hated each other, or that's how it seemed.'

'Maybe that's what the attraction was. On the surface, they hated each other, but truthfully they were in love.'

'There's one more thing to all this. This is what caused the argument between Jackson and Billy. In her diary, Alison wrote on the day before she was killed, 'Oh, fucking little bitch, why would she tell Billy? How did she find out?' She was talking about Grace. She found out about Jackson and Alison, then told Billy the truth.'

'What else have you found out?' Walsh asked.

218

'I went to see Alice Denman this morning as well. First off, Norman abused his sister; he raped her, but it's my belief he was forced by his father. Then, you see, Joan was gay, and she had an affair with Grace Reynolds. I believe Joan and Grace had an argument on the day Joan died. Joan then ran off down to the old boat house, Norman may well have seen his sister and followed her. Then by the time Grace had got to the old boat house, it was too late; Joan was dead. Grace you see, had a hold over Norman. I now believe he accidently killed his sister. He knocked into the chair she was standing on. Grace witnessed this and held it against him. I also believed Joan told Grace about what her brother had done to her. That's what they argued about.'

'So if Grace knew about what Norman had done, surely she could get him to do almost anything. What if she witnessed Alison's murder, she by then had such a hold over him, told him he'd have to take the blame.'

'Knowing Grace as I do, she would have taken great delight in letting everyone know about what he did to his sister. She also did it to protect someone.'

'Who?'

'Her brother Billy, she was protecting him.'

'Billy, so Billy murdered Alison?' he asked.

'I'm not one hundred percent sure, but he had something to do with it, as did Jackson. Billy had no intention of murdering Alison, none at all. He was angry, yes, but that was with his brother more than Alison. Her murder was an accident. It started as a fight between Jackson and Billy. When Jackson was younger, he sometimes carried a knife, made him look hard or so he thought. Still can't work out how she ended up with so many knife wounds.'

'What about Megan? Anything on that?' Walsh asked.

'Well, finding Alison's diary has had me thinking. Megan knew something about Alison. I believed to start she may well have found and read this,' he said pointing at the diary. 'But I received a text from Melissa. She found and read the diary, told Maddie Clarke, then she told her brother. Then when James and Megan were in the taxi on the way home, that's when he told her; that's what they argued about.'

'What next, Johnny?'

'Well, first off, I want a word with Jackson. I'd also like to find Billy, before he has any ideas of disappearing again. Something's not right; it bothered me from the start.'

'Like what?' asked Walsh.

'All this. I know these people. I grew up with them. I thought I knew them; they were like family. Billy, Norman, even Jackson, none of them were killers. Okay, Jackson murdered Sian and Kevin Van Dalen, but he was pushed, told what to do. One name keeps coming into my mind, this person knew about Norman and Joan, knew about Alison, even had a link to the Van Dalens.'

'Grace Reynolds.'

Allen looked at Walsh and nodded, 'Yeah, Grace. But there's nothing, no evidence whatsoever to pin Grace to any of this.'

'What makes you believe this is all Grace's doing?'

'She's clever, very clever. Like I've just said, what have we got on any of these murders? Nothing, nothing at all, sins of our past, that's it. If she planned all this, then she knew, she knew I'd work out the sins of people. Norman abusing his sister, Alison and Jackson, Billy's love of Jane, my love of Jane, Sian Van Dalen and Grace, Joan and Grace, even Alison's diary. But the biggest sin of all is mine, my sin, the sin of believing I knew all these people, and she knew that, knew I'd be blind to their sins. Look, both her brothers have dissociative identity disorder, neither can control their other identities, but Grace can. You see, dominant and submissive, Billy and Jackson have one dominant personality and one submissive. Remember what Doctor Richardson said about Jackson's personalities both being dominant, but he'd still have one stronger than the other. Submissive can't control dominant, but Grace on the other hand can control both sides of her brother's identities. She then becomes the dominant one and her brothers the submissive one.'

'So it doesn't matter which personality her brothers are in at any given moment.'

'This is something I'm not sure about. If someone has two personalities, one submissive, one dominant, then the dominant one wouldn't let submissive kill.'

'But what would happen if the submissive side of a personality crossed over, tried to take control?'

'Submissive would try to kill the dominant partner. So as this is two personalities in one person, maybe it could happen, submissive becoming stronger. But surely then it would be dominant but a different personality. But either would be submissive as they're being controlled by a dominant person.'

'How would Billy and Jackson react to being controlled by their sister?'

'Jackson or Jack would just do it for the fun of it. It wouldn't have much effect on either personality. Billy on the other hand, I don't know. You see, sometimes people with this disorder can't remember what the other personality has done. I believe, I may be wrong, but with Billy, I'd be surprised if the submissive side, his real personality, would even know what's happening.'

Allen stopped, his facial features conveyed fear. He seemed worried as if something had hit him.

'What's wrong, Johnny? What is it?'

'Submissive would and could kill dominant. This went through my mind earlier when I was listening to Alice Denman. If Norman knows who Joan's lover was, then Grace Reynolds could be in deep trouble.'

'Submissive killing dominant,' Walsh replied.

He understood now what it meant, but there was something else, another thought. He closed his eyes, a flashback. He could see Grace standing by her front door. She nervously brushed her hair around her right ear, earrings, he'd seen them, of course. Submissive, dominant; two personalities, two killers; same killer but different killers; Billy and William. Billy killed Megan; William killed Alison. Billy is in love with Jane; William was in love with Alison. Billy believes he's Melissa's father; he believes he married Jane. William was dominant; Billy was submissive. Now William is submissive, Billy dominant. That's what pushed Billy over the edge. That's why he became dominant; he was tormented by his other personality. Look at me, I've murdered someone I love, now you have to murder someone you love to prove you're stronger than me. I can do better than that, I'll murder my own daughter. You idiot, she's Johnny's daughter, not yours. You've killed the wrong one.

Another flashback, he could see himself as a small child, standing in a playground. A young boy comes over to him.

'What's your name?' asked the young boy.

'I'm Johnny, but my real name's Jonathan. What's your name?' he asked.

'My name's Billy, but I sometimes get called William, that's my real name. But I don't like William, he's horrible.'

'I'll call you Billy. Billy seems really nice.'

'Johnny, you okay?' asked Walsh.

'Yes, sorry.'

'Go on then, what's that massive brain of yours seen now then?' he asked.

'Two killers; same killer but different killers, dominant and submissive. Now I understand what it means.'

'You've just had a flashback, haven't you?'

'Yes, two. One was Grace Reynolds the first time I met her at her flat. The other was of two small boys standing in a playground meeting for the first time, one named Jonathan, the other named William. Come on, we need to find Jackson, Jack, William, Billy and Grace. I need to find something as well, and I know where it is.'

Chapter 14

Grace parked her car outside the old block of flats where Billy lived. *How the hell anyone could live here is beyond me,* she said to herself.

'He could have stayed with me. I did offer,' she said looking over at the two drunks. She laughed out loud. The two could barely sit up, let alone stand up or even walk.

'I know. He said he needed his own space,' her brother replied.

Jackson paused at the bottom of the staircase and looked up. Grace could see that even her older brother looked a bit scared.

'Lost your bottle,' she said, smiling at him.

'No, no, just making sure,' he replied, as he slowly took one step up the stairs.

'Yeah, making sure of what?' she asked, laughing.

'Go on then, ladies first,' he said stepping to one side, and letting his sister go first.

'Oh, some big brave older brother you are. And there's me thinking you were a hard man.'

Grace slowly walked up the stairs. She'd just about reached the top stair when she turned to find Jackson still standing on the first stair. 'Jackson, for fuck sake, Jack the Ripper doesn't live here, you know.'

'I'm not so sure about that,' he said with some fear in his voice.

Jackson slowly walked up to where his sister was standing. Grace turned and looked him in the eyes, and said, 'Scared are we, brother dear?'

'No, just checking that no one else was going to come in, that's all.'

'Really.'

'Yeah, really.'

'Like who?' she asked angrily.

'Those two drunks sitting outside for one,' he said, nervously checking that no one was behind him.

'Those two drunks? Okay right. They couldn't even sit up, let alone stand and walk.' Grace turned away shaking her head as she carried on up to the second floor. She then stopped dead in her tracks two steps from the top.

'Jackson, someone's been here. Look the front door's been smashed in.'

'He had a visitor yesterday,' came a voice from across the landing.

Grace turned around and looked at a figure standing in a doorway to the flat across the hall. 'Who? Who was it?' she snapped angrily.

'Old bill, you know, police. He did come back, the man living there, but only for a few minutes, then he was gone.'

'When was this?' asked Jackson.

'Yesterday, about a couple of hours after the law came calling,' replied the man.

The man disappeared back into his flat. Grace, followed nervously by Jackson, walked inside her brother's flat. It was cold, dark and damp, with a heavy smell of whiskey.

'Bloody hell, what a dump. Prison was better than this,' Jackson said, looking around the flat.

'You should know, brother dear,' Grace said looking at the ripped-up pictures that were littered all over the floor. She bent down and picked some of them up. 'Bloody hell, Jackson, take a look at these,' she said, handing him some of the photos.

'God, this is Johnny Allen and Jane Woods. I knew he had it bad, but this? That boy is sick in the head.'

'A shocking statement coming from you of all people.'

'Yeah, alright, so I've had my problems, but—'

'Shut up, for God sake. We need to find him, and quickly,' she said, snatching the pictures off her brother.

'Any ideas?' he asked.

'No, she replied. 'Yes, I do. Remember the other day he said about going to have a look at that old factory where dad worked, worth a try.'

'Bloody hell, I haven't been over there in years; not sure it's still standing.'

'Come on, let's go. I'm worried, Jackson. What's he done?'

'Look, don't worry, we'll find him.'

Alice walked up the stairs to her son's bedroom. She as good as knew he wasn't up here. 'Norman, Norman you in here?' she called out, but as she expected, no reply. *Oh, that boy, where's he got to now? How can I keep him safe if I don't know where he is?* She thought to herself.

She sat on the edge of his bed. She had as good as expected he'd get himself into more trouble again. Why doesn't he just let Johnny deal with it? But that was Norman, she thought. He tries to help people, but he's the one that always seemed to get into trouble. It was the same when he was younger. He'd follow the crowd, then they would just leave him. He was just way too slow to work out what was happening, then he'd be the one in trouble. He would get an idea in his head and that was that. He always believed he could help people, but sometimes, he couldn't even help himself.

Alice stood up and slowly felt along Norman's bedside table. She knew that's where he always kept his camera. She knew before she started feeling for it that it wasn't there.

'Out taking photographs again. Let's hope he's safe and not in any trouble,' she said out loud.

Allen pulled up outside Grace's flat. Quickly jumping out of his car, he ran over to the main doors. He pressed Grace's door buzzer, but nothing, no reply. He pressed it again, but again no answer. *Come on Grace, for God sake,* he said to himself.

'She's out, mate,' came a voice from behind him.

'How do you know that?' Allen replied, turning around to face the man.

'She went out about an hour or so ago,' the man replied.

'Was she with anyone?' he asked.

'Yeah, her brother, I believe.'

'Okay, thanks,' Allen said as the man disappeared into the building.

Allen looked over at Inspector Walsh and shook his head, 'No one in,' he shouted, as he got nearer to his car.

'Out finding Billy, maybe?' Walsh said, as Allen got into his car.

'Right, let's get over to his flat. If no joy there, then we'll try the old print factory.'

Grace pulled up near the old print factory. She stopped her car and climbed out. She looked around at what was once a thriving business. What a waste; waste of a business, waste of space, she thought. You could build so much on this waste ground. The old building was just an empty shell, the waste ground was overgrown with weeds and littered with rubbish that people had over the years just dumped.

'God, this was so nice around here once. I used to like coming down here, and waiting for dad to finish work,' she said turning to her brother.

'I know, right. This has been like this for what? Ten years or so,' he replied, kicking an old beer can like a football.

'At least,' she replied. 'Can't believe they would just leave it like this,' she said, holding her hands and arms out, almost in protest.

'Come on, let's see if we can find Billy.'

Jackson walked up to an old wooden door and pushed against it. The door didn't take much pushing to open. It as good as fell off its hinges. Jackson, not expecting the door to be so easy to open, fell through the door and ended up lying flat on his back. He half-expected his sister to come to his rescue, but then again, he also half-expected the response he got from Grace. Jackson sat up, dusted himself down and looked over towards his sister for a helping hand, only to find her leaning on her car in fits of laughter.

'That's the funniest thing I've seen in years,' she said laughing uncontrollably.

'Ha, ha, I'm glad you found it so bloody funny,' he said in a huff.

Grace walked over to her brother and helped him up, still finding it hard not to laugh.

'Sorry Jackson, that was just brilliant. The look on your face was a picture. Have you hurt yourself?' she asked.

'Yeah, my bloody back,' he said gingerly getting to his feet.

'You'll live,' she said, dusting down his black fleece jacket.

'Who's down there?' a voice shouted out. The voice sounded nervous and anxious, almost childlike.

'Billy, Billy, it's me and Jackson,' shouted Grace hastily.

'It's not Billy, I'm William. Billy's not here. Can't you two just leave me alone? I want to be alone, is that too much to ask for?' he shouted.

'We just want to help you, that's all,' Grace replied. He sounded desperate. She knew that this was a cry for help. She deep down realised that the whole situation was hopeless.

'You can't help me. No one can,' he cried out desperately.

'Why not?' Jackson asked sternly.

'I don't know what he's done. I can't remember,' he screamed out in fear.

Grace and Jackson walked over towards an old staircase that led up to the offices. Grace turned to her brother. He took her hand and said nothing. The pair walked up the stairs hand in hand. Each step was taken almost in fear of what they'd find. Grace looked into the first office they came too. She found her brother sitting on the floor, knees drawn up to his chest, hugging them tight. His gaze was one of pure fear. Slowly he lifted his head and looked at her. She could see the look of helplessness in his eyes. Tears ran slowly down his face.

He looked at his sister and brother, then back to the floor. 'She was here. He brought her here. I know he did,' he said. 'But she's gone. I just can't remember what happened. I don't know how or even why he brought her here.' He cried, pulling at his hair and face with his hands.

'Who? Who was here?' Jackson asked as he sat on the floor next to his brother.

William turned and looked at his brother, then up at his sister. 'Jane, Jane Woods,' he whispered softly. 'Billy brought her here, but he didn't say why,' he said looking back at the floor.

'You mean Jane Davis, don't you?' Jackson replied.

'No, no, she's Jane Woods, always been Woods. She never took Billy's surname or anyone else's. He, Billy, he told me that. She said to him, I want to keep my own surname, so she stayed Jane Woods.' He carried on muttering it to himself, over and over, 'Jane, Jane Woods.'

'It's okay, it's okay, that's fine,' Grace said, giving him a kiss on the forehead.

'You said he brought her here. When was this?' Jackson asked.

William didn't reply. He just sat on the floor staring into space. 'William, come on. If you don't try to remember, we can't help you,' Grace said pleading with her brother.

'He'll tell you; Billy will tell you. He thinks he knows everything, but he won't tell me.'

'William, you know what happened to Alison, don't you?' she asked him.

He looked up at his sister, tears streaming down his face. 'Yes, yes, I, I, murdered her,' he cried out.

William turned to his brother. He seemed angry with him. He tried to stand up, but the drink, even for an alcoholic had affected him. He slumped back down. Quickly turning back to his brother, he grabbed him by the throat. 'It's your fault. All this, it's all your fault. If you had just left her alone, but no, no, you had to have her, didn't you? DIDN'T YOU?' he screamed. 'Then he stepped in, took control, made me out to be the weak one, the stupid one. I didn't mean to kill her. He told me to do it.'

William released his hands from around Jackson's throat. He pulled his knees back up to his chest, hugging them again. He sat staring into space, rocking backwards and forward.

'I'm sorry, truly I am. It was a mistake. We made a mistake,' Jackson shouted angrily at his brother, as he got to his feet.

'Who found Jane?' Grace asked, knowing what the answer would be.

'Allen, Johnny Allen. Yes, yes, he found her, it was Johnny. I told him he'd find her. He's coming, isn't he?' he asked his sister.

'Who? Who's coming?' Grace replied, with some confusion in her voice.

'Johnny Allen, of course. He knows. He knows the truth. He sees everything. But he, he still believes he can beat the great Johnny Allen. No, no, Allen's too clever. He'll find us. I told him he'll find us; that's what he does. Billy hated Johnny once we met Jane Woods, but I liked him. I told Billy, I warned him not to kill her, not to kill Johnny's daughter.'

Grace looked down at her brother. He was right, Allen knew the truth alright. The moment she entered Jane's house and saw the photograph of Megan wearing Johnny's Saint Christopher, she knew then what he'd seen. As her brother had just said, Allen sees everything.

'Lovely part of town, isn't it,' Allen said as he pulled up outside the old flats.

'I'm surprised the local council haven't pulled it down,' replied Walsh, nervously eyeing the two drunks he met yesterday.

'You can't pull it down. It's got character. It's part of the history of the town. Anyway, I know who built most of it, so it may well just fall down.'

'See the two characters sitting over on those steps? We had trouble with them yesterday. But we did have Wilkins with us,' Walsh said.

Allen looked over towards the two men and smiled, 'Don't worry, Peter, they won't give you any trouble, not with me here.'

Walsh glanced at Allen then over towards the two men. He raised his eyebrows and puffed out his cheeks. He walked over towards the main doorway where the men were sitting.

'Look here, it's the old bill. Where's your big mate then?' the bigger of the two men laughed.

Walsh turned around to see what Johnny was doing, but he seemed to have disappeared. *Oh, great,* thought Walsh, *great timing as ever, Johnny.*

'On your own, mate,' the man said standing up, just.

'No, he's with me. Hello, Jimmy,' Allen said, as he appeared from behind a big green wheelie bin.

'Bloody hell, Johnny Allen,' the man said almost falling over. He seemed shocked and scared at the sight of Allen.

'That's Mr Allen to you, Jimmy. What's this then, you been giving my lads a hard time?'

'No, no, sorry Mr Allen, just a bit of fun, that's all,' he replied nervously.

'You see, Peter, me and Jimmy here are old mates. We go back years, don't we, Jimmy?' Allen said smiling at him.

'Yes, yes, we do, Mr Allen,' he said nervously.

'Who's your mate then?' Allen asked, looking at the other man.

'This is Legs, Lee Legg, to be truthful.'

Allen looked at Legs. He knew him more by sight, but to be truthful he knew his name. It made him laugh really. He gets called Legs, and he's no taller than about five foot.

'Bloody hell, Fingers and Legs. Don't know anyone called hands and toes by any chance?' laughed Allen.

'Funny that, I like that, Mr Allen.'

'Jimmy, one thing, tell Peter here your surname and how you come to have the nickname fingers, and Jimmy be truthful.'

'Umm, my surname is Fingleton. That why I get called fingers,' he replied sheepishly.

'Truth be told, Peter, it has nothing to do with his surname as such. It's more to do with, one, he's very light fingered, and two, come on show Peter your right hand.'

Fingers held up his right hand which only had three fingers and a thumb. The little finger was missing.

'You see, Peter, one evening in the late summer of 1992, Jimmy here was trying to break into this house. He somehow managed to trap his right hand in the letter box, and a bloody great big Alsatian bit his finger off. The dog did manage to survive the ordeal of eating one of Jimmy's fingers. After all, the dog had no idea where it had been.'

'Bloody dog, I was lucky not to lose my whole hand.'

'Well, you shouldn't be sticking it in somewhere where it shouldn't have been. Jimmy, Legs, when and if—and they will—my lads come calling, no problems.'

Allen turned his attention back to the matter in hand and Walsh's problem opening the main door to the flats.

'Having trouble, Peter?' he asked.

'No,' he replied as the door finally opened.

'Don't worry about Jimmy, he's harmless, and by the looks of his mate, he's legless. That's a good one, Legs, legless Legs,' Allen said laughing.

Walsh took a sideways glance at Allen and shook his head, 'You knew all along what their bloody names were, didn't you?'

'Okay, yeah, I knew,' he smiled.

'All that for the world's worst joke, bloody legless Legs.'

'There's something else you should know about Jimmy Fingers, he's Sydney Yates' nephew.'

'That answers many questions,' replied Walsh.

Allen followed Walsh up to Billy's flat. It surprised him, Billy living somewhere like this. He must have been desperate. He entered the small cramped flat. The two things he noticed, one was the smell of whiskey, the second was the hundreds of pictures of Jane and himself.

'What a surprise, pictures of me and Jane,' he said, picking up a ripped picture of himself as a teenager.

'Something I don't understand is, where did he get all these pictures from?' Walsh asked.

'Norman, Norman would take the pictures, then Billy would take the negatives and make copies. Norman took hundreds of pictures; that's what he did.'

'So Norman knew what Billy was doing?'

'What with his photographs? Oh yes. You see, Billy would tell Norman, 'You need to show more people your pictures. Let me get some copies printed up and soon you'll be famous.' All he did was keep them for himself.'

'So saying that, he must have planned all this years in advance?'

'I don't know to be sure. I believe he just wanted pictures of Jane. Have you checked right through this flat?' Allen asked.

'Truthfully, no. Once we found out about the old print factory, that was it, we left.'

'Come on then, let's give it the once over.'

To be truthful, there wasn't much in the flat to go through. Allen started in the bedroom, a small cramped room, no bigger than a small third box bedroom in an old terraced house. The room itself had a bed and a small old wooden bedside cabinet. He sat on the edge of the bed and looked down at the wooden cabinet. It had three drawers in it. He slowly opened the top drawer. The drawer itself was just about ready to fall apart. It was stuffed full of pictures and old newspaper cuttings.

One of the newspaper cuttings took his eye. "Couple found dead with multiple stab wounds." *Sian and Kevin,* he said to himself. The next newspaper cutting had the headline. "Chief Constable's niece found murdered." He managed to shut the top drawer and just about opened the middle one. He looked at what was in the drawer. *Oh my God, I knew it. But how the hell did I miss this?* He said to himself. Grace must have placed them here. She knew, the second she tucked her hair around her right ear, she knew I'd seen them. The drawer contained just two items. He picked them up and carefully placed them in the palm of his left hand. Reaching down inside his jacket pocket, he pulled out a handkerchief. He carefully wrapped the two items up and placed them in his pocket. Slowly and carefully he shut the middle draw. He reached down and opened the last drawer, but nothing; just more photographs of himself and Jane.

'Anything?' Walsh asked.

'Not much, I'll show you later. Come on, there's nothing here. Let's check out that print factory. You drive. I need to think.'

Inspector Walsh sped through the traffic out of Reading Town Centre and over towards the old print factory. He turned quickly and glanced at Allen. He was sitting upright, hands folded, resting on his lap, eyes closed. He knew what he was doing. He knew he was thinking.

Walsh remembered what Davidson once said to him about Johnny Allen. 'Peter,' he said, 'this man has an astonishing mind. He has information and knowledge far beyond all our capabilities.' Walsh knew Allen could see things other people couldn't. He seemed to be able to get inside the mind of people and work out what they were thinking. Something else that always amazed him was, he never wrote anything down, yet he could just about remember everything he was told, or had seen.

'Okay, we're nearly there,' Walsh said.

'I know,' Allen replied opening his eyes.

'Go on then, what have you been thinking about?' he asked.

'Nothing much really, just all this,' he replied.

'You know what's happened, don't you? I've guessed it's not as straightforward as it first seemed.'

'I wish it was. You see our murderer has planned almost the perfect crime, four murders and not one piece of evidence. We've got nothing.'

'How can you murder four people and not leave any evidence?'

'Easy, someone else commits the murders.'

Chapter 15

Walsh pulled up near the old print factory. Both detectives noticed a red Vauxhall Astra parked nearby.

'We're going to need backup, Johnny,' Walsh said.

'Okay, all three of the Reynolds are here. Come on, let's get this over and done with.'

'Might be better to wait for backup, Johnny,' Walsh added.

'No, don't worry. This is something best left to me. Just keep everyone out here when they arrive.'

'Go careful.'

Allen turned looked at Walsh and nodded. He slowly and carefully walked through the remains of the old broken wooden door that was hanging on just by one screw. He could hear voices coming from the old offices. Slowly, so not to make any noise, he crept up the stairs.

'I can't stay here, he'll come, he'll—' William stopped midsentence. He staggered to his feet, eyes transfixed on the figure standing in the doorway.

Allen barely recognised him. He looked old and broken, a pale shadow of the man he once called his best friend, his brother.

'I knew it wouldn't be long. Have you come for me, Johnny,' he said holding his hands out.

'You knew I would, Billy,' replied Allen.

'I'm William. Billy's not here. Come on then, just the four of us, no one else. This game we play, it's time to end, no more.'

'I don't play games,' he responded.

'Oh Johnny,' he screamed. 'You've been playing this game for over thirty years. Every day, all I can see in my mind is her ripped-up body in front of me. Do you know, he, he always wanted to take control from that day onwards.'

William stopped. He put his hands to his head and screamed, 'NO, NO, just leave me alone.'

'I am in charge. I'm the dominant one, not you. I KILLED JOHNNY ALLEN'S DAUGHTER. What the fuck did you do?' Billy screamed out.

Tears ran down his face. He was starting to struggle with it all, unable to control his other personality.

'Why did you have to tell him?' William screamed.

'He already knows,' Billy laughed.

'Neither of you are dominant,' Allen said as he turned to look at Grace.

She didn't reply. She just stood glaring at him. Truthfully, she didn't have to say a word. She knew what he meant.

'You see, for thirty years my mind would turn back to that day in September 1988. Norman Denman, Alison, William, Billy, Jackson and even Jack. But you Grace, I must admit I couldn't see how you fitted in to all this. You know, you made one mistake.'

'Which was?' she asked.

'You murdered the wrong person. Megan didn't know, well, not to start with, who the father of Alison's baby was.'

'No, no, you idiot, Megan knew. She knew the secret. Once she found out who the father of Alison's baby was, I knew it would get back to you. She had to be silenced,' Grace replied angrily.

'Like I said, you murdered the wrong person. You killed Megan to stop me from finding out the truth. But it was Melissa who found out about Jackson and Alison. She found Alison's diary, read it, found out about you, Jackson, being the father, but she didn't tell Megan. Oh, I strongly believe she was going to tell her sister, but she ended up telling one person.'

And who was that?' Jackson asked.

'Her best friend, Maddie Clarke. Yes, James's sister. It was James that told Megan. You see, when they were coming home that night in the taxi, they had a massive argument. Now I may be wrong, but that doesn't happen too often. You, Jackson, had either a little conversation with James, or he sent a text message, but you received or were told something that made you panic. So you rang the one person who you believed would help you. Neither of you wanted your brother to go to prison. You, Jackson, then waited for James and Megan to leave the nightclub and followed them. You then rang your brother and sister telling them where they'd gotten out of the taxi. But you had one good piece of luck in Norman Denman showing up and one bad piece of luck.'

'Which was?' asked Grace.

'Billy showed up. All was good with William. He didn't want to murder anyone, he never did. But with Billy, that was different. You, Grace, got inside Billy's head. You can be the dominant one Billy. No more being second best. William will be the weak one.

She laughed and shook her head, 'Oh, Johnny, must be so good to be you. You said you couldn't see how I fitted in to all this. Go on, enlighten me,' she said arrogantly.

'Grace, this all started on the day Joan Denman took her own life.'

'Oh, come on Joan, why don't you want me to make love to you?' she asked her softly.

'You wouldn't understand. No one understands,' she cried.

'Try me,' she said, as she knelt down on the floor in front of her.

Joan looked into her lovely big brown eyes. She sat up on her bed and smiled through the tears, 'It's my brother, he's, he's abusing me. He raped me.' She was finding it all too much. She lay back down again on her bed, burying her head in the pillow.

Grace sat on the edge of the bed, unable to take in what she'd just been told. She tried to comfort Joan. She stroked the side of her face gently, but Joan just pulled away.

'Just go, just leave me alone,' she screamed.

'Joan, please, I love you. I'll help you through this,' she sobbed.

'No, no, sorry Grace. I don't want to hurt you. You're so lovely, but I can't.'

'Okay, fine, I'll go then. Trust me, one day I'll make your brother pay for what he's done.' She quickly dressed and stormed out of the bedroom, running downstairs and slamming the front door as she left.

'Joan, Joan, what's wrong with Grace?' he asked.

'Oh, Norman, just leave me alone,' she shouted at her brother.

He stood at her bedroom door. He didn't understand what was wrong. He was just about to open his sister's bedroom door, when she opened it and pushed past him. She paused at the top of the stairs turned and glared at her brother.

'This is all your fault. I love Grace, but it's all gone wrong, and it's your fault. You stupid, sick idiot,' she screamed at him.

'Sorry, I'm sorry Joan. Dad hit me. He made me do it. Joan, please.'

She didn't respond. She just ran down the stairs crying. She turned around as she paused by the front door, 'Norman, tell mum I'm sorry.' Then she was gone.

'Look Grace, I know you loved Joan and she you. But she just couldn't live with what her father and brother had done.'

'You don't miss much do you, Johnny. I was so in love with her. I was slowly walking home after we'd had that argument, I saw her running off towards the river. To start with, I just stood and watched her run away from me. I got to the front gate of my parents' house when I changed my mind, so I ran after her.'

'You knew what she was going to do, didn't you?' he asked.

'Maybe, yeah. I must have spent about half an hour, maybe even longer, trying to find her. I'd just about given up. I had thought maybe she'd gone home. I started walking along by the river over towards the old boat house. I was lost in my own little world. Truthfully, I never even saw Norman. First time I realised something was wrong was when I heard arguing and shouting coming from the old boat house.

'Joan, Joan, oh, where the hell are you?' she cried out.

She felt lost, almost heartbroken. God, I'm going to make Norman pay if anything happens. 'I want her back,' she cried out.

She stopped dead in her tracks. She could hear shouting and screaming coming from the old boat house. She quickly ran over to the old boat house and hid just below an old broken window.

'Joan, Joan, what are you doing? Are you playing swinging?' he asked.

'Norman, just go, please just leave me alone,' she shouted at him.

'If you stand on that chair, you might fall off, and you'll hurt yourself.'

She just wanted him to leave her alone. She was desperate. He stood up and started walking closer to her. 'NO, NO, OH MY GOD, NORMAN,' she screamed. Then she was silent.

'Truthfully, I wasn't sure back then, and I'm still not that sure. I believed he walked into the chair. Joan didn't want to take her own life. You know, I believed she wanted me to find her, you know that don't you? The rest you know.'

'You then set about finding a way to punish him. Alison's murder was an accident, started off as nothing more than an argument between your two brothers. You had found out that Jackson and Alison were lovers. I'm not sure you knew at the time that Alison was pregnant.'

'You never did tell me how you found out about me and Alison?' Jackson asked his sister.

'Easy, I caught you in bed together. As for whether I know if Alison was pregnant or not, well, we all have our little secrets.'

'By telling Billy what you'd seen, you knew what was going to happen. So you followed him down towards the river. Jackson was already down there with Alison and Alex Davis. Then you had, as I've already said, a massive stroke of luck, the opportunity you'd been waiting for, Norman Denman. An argument, a fight started between your two brothers. You'd guessed as much that Jackson would have a knife on him. But one problem arose, it wasn't Billy that went after Jackson, it was William. And even you couldn't have foreseen that.'

'Jackson, Jackson,' he screamed out after his brother.

'Oh, no, Billy,' he said. 'Alex run, okay, just run. This is between me and Billy.'

Alex didn't answer, he knew what was coming, and to be truthful, he wanted nothing to do with it. He was scared, even frightened. He'd seen the knife Jackson was carrying.

'Oh, I might have known, you'd be down here with lover boy,' he shouted at her.

'Billy please, I'm sorry,' she cried out, trying to stop him.

'I'm not Billy, I'm William,' he screamed at her.

He walked up to his older brother, pushing him to the ground. 'Come on then,' he screamed at him. 'Come on you bastard,' he screamed at him again. Jackson jumped up and pulled a knife on him. 'You want some, do you?' he shouted. He lunged at him, just missing stabbing him in the left side of his stomach. William grabbed hold of Jackson's right arm. The two struggled as William tried to snatch the knife off his brother.

'Will you two just stop. Please, please stop fighting,' she screamed.

'Get fucking dressed,' William shouted at her.

William managed to grab hold of the knife handle and Jackson's wrist. It all happened in slow motion. Alison tried to help William grab the knife off Jackson. Jackson let go of the knife. The second he did, William swung around to his left, stabbing Alison in the stomach.

'She was dead. I knew she was dead the second it happened. I could see it in her eyes. That's all I see, every second of every day. She just looked at me and fell to the ground,' said William. He sat on the floor and cried out in horror; this personality unable to take in the horrors of what happened.

Allen looked down at William. He was broken mentally. This moment, the second he stabbed Alison was the moment William couldn't remain dominant. The horror of what he'd done was just too great to comprehend. He knew that William's last act of dominance was the frenzied attack that was to follow.

Allen turned to Jackson and asked him, 'What did you do? As if I need ask.'

'I'm ashamed to admit, I ran. I just ran.'

'He, he did it, stabbing her over and over again. He just keeps on and on. I just had to get him to shut up, so I killed your daughter. I KILLED YOUR DAUGHTER,' he screamed.

'What happened after he stabbed her, Billy?' he asked.

'I don't know, I wasn't there. He, William, he was there. He told me what he'd done that afternoon. I just couldn't understand why he'd murder someone he loved.'

'Why murder Megan?' he asked him.

'Oh, come on, Johnny, you know the answer to that question. You had to have her, didn't you? No one else could have her, but I loved her as well, you know. I hated you for loving Jane. William, he's weak, he didn't want to go through with it, but I knew, knew that this was my time. I'm stronger. I'm now dominant, not him.'

'You see, if Megan hadn't had been murdered, I wouldn't have found any of this out.'

'Oh really,' she shouted at him. 'Johnny Allen, the greatest mind the police force has ever had, and you really expect me to believe you wouldn't have worked all this out. Johnny, now be truthful, you'd worked all this out years ago, but you just couldn't prove any of it.'

'Well, we all have our little secrets Grace, maybe that's mine. You'd seen William murder Alison, hadn't you, and that's where you fit in to all this.'

She slumped down by a tree, tears running down her face. 'What has he done? Not Billy, not my brother,' she cried out.

'What's the matter, Grace?' he asked.

She looked up at the figure standing in front of her. 'Nothing. Nothing, Norman. I need your help. You'll do that for me, won't you? You'll help me?'

'I'll help you, Grace,' he smiled.

'Norman, thank you,' she replied. 'You know what would happen if you don't.'

'Yes,' he replied nervously.

'And if you tell anyone the truth, I'll tell. I'll tell everyone what you did.'

'No, no, don't tell. I'll help you. Grace, is Alison asleep?'

'Yes, yes, she is. So we have to move her before she wakes up, just make sure she's safe.'

'It was so easy to get him to do what I wanted. All I had to do was threaten him. He willingly carried her body up into the woods. He even handled both knives. The other knife was what William had brought with him. But he threw it away, before his fight with Jackson, so I picked it up.'

'Easy really, and Norman spent twenty years locked up for a murder he didn't commit.'

'But he didn't pay for his sin, did he?' she replied.

'I received two photographs, one of a blacked-out figure standing over Alison's body, and the other was the same blacked-out figure standing over Megan's body. I, to start with, believed this to be our murderer. But it wasn't, was it?'

'Clever, Johnny. No, it was Norman Denman. I was hoping you'd realise who it was.'

'I did, once I looked at the pictures closely.'

'As I said, it was so easy to get him to do anything. I know by sending you these photographs, I gave you help. But since when have you ever needed any help?'

'It helped me to understand who murdered Sian Van Dalen and who murdered Kevin Van Dalen.'

'Go on then, tell me,' Jackson said angrily.

'Jack murdered Kevin; Jackson murdered Sian.'

'Your daughter, she was a right little madam. Sorry, Johnny, I didn't like her one little bit, way too full of herself. You see, until you said about Melissa finding out about Jackson and Alison, well, we believed Megan had been telling stories, but now it turns out to have been James.'

'He never said anything to me, not directly. He would come out with one or two sarcastic comments. Then when I had left the nightclub, I got this strange text, didn't recognise the number, to be truthful. Turns out to be Megan's number, but as it turned out, it was James that sent the text.'

'What did the text say?' he asked.

'It said, 'You're a dark horse, you and Alison Woods, that's a secret from the past.' I panicked after that. Yeah, okay, so Billy and I had our arguments and fights, but he's still my brother; couldn't see him go to prison. But I just told Grace and Billy. I didn't know she would end up murdered. I had nothing to do with it, nothing at all.'

'Oh, thanks brother dear. Billy and I will take the blame. I mean, look at him. He has no idea, not a clue,' she said looking at her brother.

'James Clarke, now it wasn't just grief that made him take his own life, was it? Someone got to him,' Allen said, glaring at Jackson.

'After Megan was murdered, the little prick tried to, fucking, blame me. So Billy and I put the frighteners on him. It wasn't too hard. He couldn't remember what happened. Didn't want him to take his own life, no, not that,' Jackson said.

'You planned the Van Dalen murders, didn't you Grace?' he asked her, confident in the knowledge he already knew the answer.

She nervously bit her bottom lip, glancing pensively at her older brother. She knew lying wouldn't be a viable option. After all, this was Johnny Allen asking the questions.

'Scorned by love again, we both were, and we wanted to teach them a lesson. But Jackson, or shall I say Jack, didn't follow the script. Threaten, intimidate, yes, maybe even put Kevin in hospital, but not fucking rip them to bits.'

'God, how many times do I need to say it, I'm sorry. Couldn't control him, okay,' he said in mock empathy.

'So Jack murdered Kevin, so you Jackson just went along for the hell of it,' he said.

'What's good for him is good for me. I knew I had only one chance. You see, Kevin was way bigger than me and a lot stronger. Jack took over. As I've said, at the time, he was just way too strong, just couldn't control him.' He replied.

'Were you there?' he asked her.

She laughed at him, 'Oh you're clever, trying to catch me off-guard. You can't get me that easy. No, I wasn't.'

'Do you want tea or coffee, darling?' she asked her husband.

'Tea, God that's so English. Coffee, I need my coffee first thing in the morning,' he replied.

She smiled to herself, he has no idea, I mean coffee first thing in the morning. Tea, we have tea first thing, I'm English, she laughed. She was happy. Life was good, great loving husband, a brilliant job. Working with children was something she'd wanted to do since childhood. Only thing left was to start a family of their own. They could afford it. Kevin was doing well. They had enough saved up. Maybe she'd bring it up when he was drinking his coffee.

She skipped down the stairs and into the lounge. She didn't notice a figure standing at the large bay window. Blissfully unaware of the horror that was to follow, she unlocked and opened the front door. It happened so fast; she didn't even have time to scream.

The blow came out of nowhere, a wooden baseball bat crashed down on the back of her head. She slumped down just inside the hallway. She tried to scream out for help, but unconsciousness came all too quickly. He looked down and smiled at the crumpled heap lying on the floor in front of him.

'Fucking bitch,' he laughed sarcastically.

Had he heard a thud? He wasn't sure, but it sounded strange. 'Sian, Sian, you okay, honey?' he called out to her, but nothing. She didn't respond. 'Sian, what's wrong?' he called out again.

He climbed out of bed. He could sense someone else was in the house. He slowly and very carefully opened the bedroom door. Again, like his wife, he didn't even see it coming. Two blows, one to the stomach, the other to the back of the head. He tried to struggle to his feet, but the pain was too great. He started to lose consciousness, briefly managing to look up at the figure standing over him, he recognised who it was. 'Jack-Jack-son,' he said, then like his wife unconsciousness.

'Like I said, Jack took over, just lost control. Truthfully now, you knew straight away it was me, didn't you?'

'Yes, the moment I walked into that house, it had revenge written all over it. One question that's stayed with me for years was the written message on the dressing table mirror, FACELESS BITCH. You wrote that, didn't you, Grace?'

'If you believe so, Johnny, that's for you to prove I was there.'

'Oh, Grace, I can do better than that.' He reached inside his jacket pocket and carefully pulled out his handkerchief. Carefully unwrapping the handkerchief, he held out his hands and showed Grace.

'Okay, clever Johnny. I did wonder how long it would take you to find them.'

'Our first meeting, your nervous habit of tucking your hair around your ear, I, in my subconscious mind, noticed the earrings. It was then only a matter of time before I recalled the memory.'

'It must be so good to have a mind like yours. Johnny Allen, the man who sees everything,' she smiled at him. She was jealous of him. She was clever, but Johnny was just something else altogether.'

Allen turned around and stepped out of the old office. He rang Inspector Walsh and asked him to bring four officers up with him. Neither Grace nor Billy put up much of a fight; both seemed to accept their own fate. Allen knew all too well he had nothing much on Grace. She was way too clever to leave clues. Billy or William, well, they seemed to have no idea what the other personality was doing.

He turned to Jackson and said, 'At the moment, I'm not interested in you and your little side lines, but trust me, I will.'

Jack smiled, 'I look forward to it,' he said.

Allen watched as Grace and Billy were led away downstairs. He was shocked at how ill Billy looked. He had no idea what would happen to him. The two detectives followed and watched as the pair were driven away. He found this all too hard to take in. These people were his friends, his childhood.

'You alright?' Walsh asked.

'I will be. All this, thirty years, and we've come to this. These people were my friends, my childhood, my family. How did I not see all this? Come on, let's get this over and done with.'

'Tell me, when we were at Billy's flat, you found something. What was it?' asked Walsh.

'Earrings, they belonged to Sian Van Dalen. Jane and I bought them as a present just before Sian married Kevin. Then they turned up twenty-odd years later being worn by Grace Reynolds.'

'How did you find that out?'

'The first meeting with Grace. You see she has a nervous habit of tucking her hair around her right ear. Subconsciously, I remembered seeing the earrings. It was just a matter of time before I recalled the memory.'

'So unless Jackson took them, which I find very unlikely, Grace had to have been there with her brother. Did she write the message on the dressing table mirror?' Walsh asked.

'I believe so, yes. And that's when she took the earrings,' replied Allen.

'Why murder Megan? Why not just warn her?'

'Truthfully, that's what Grace intended, just a warning, same with Sian and Kevin. But Jackson and William couldn't control their other personalities. William's submissive personality, which was Billy, wanted to prove he was as strong as his dominant personality. In the end, it took over, it became dominant.'

'The Van Dalen murders, you didn't suspect Grace had any involvement at the time?'

'Yes, I did. But as ever I was overruled, you could say. I was told it didn't matter at the time. You see, I was still a sergeant at the time. It was Davidson that led the investigation. I didn't become an Inspector until a month or so after the murders.'

'You found the Van Dalens, didn't you?'

'Yeah, I did. I knew in an instant who it was and why. It had revenge written all over it.'

'What pushed William in the first place? Okay, Alison, I take it, was already dead, but why rip her apart?'

'He snapped, once it had hit him what he'd done. At the time, he couldn't control William, that personality was then, just too strong. Up until then, he'd always seemed in control. Seeing her dead pushed him over the edge. I only ever really knew him as Billy. As Billy, he was quiet, never in any trouble. He hated arguments and fights. William was the total opposite. He was angry, would get upset very quickly. It was strange, I was best friends with Billy but not William, if that makes sense. But in the end, Billy grew to hate me.'

'I guess that only happened once you met Jane?' asked Walsh.

'Oh yes. I tried to convince myself that wasn't the truth, but deep down I could see it back then. He totally changed. We ended up seeing more of William than Billy. As strange as it was, when William was around, that personality made it easy for me and Jane. The reason for that being William wasn't in love with her, he was in love with Alison. At the time, I believed Billy to be in love with

Alison. Back then, as I've said, I tried to convince myself, I didn't want to see the two different personalities for what they were. But thinking back, truthfully I knew the truth back then.'

'Grace witnessed what her brother had done. She'd seen it all played out in front of her, didn't she?'

'Oh yes. She didn't want to see him go to prison. They were always very close, that was something she wouldn't be able to take, seeing him locked up. So as ever with Grace, she manipulated people, Norman more than anyone.'

'Tell me, she was hell bent on revenge. She wanted Sian and Norman to pay for what happened.'

'Yes, very much so, driven by love and hate. Grace couldn't get over what had happened with Sian and Joan, the two people she loved more than anyone else. Sian, in Grace's mind betrayed her by falling in love with Kevin Van Dalen. Joan couldn't love Grace the way she wanted because of what Norman had done to her, so she took her own life. Once Grace found this out, she never forgave Norman for what he'd done. He only did what he did out of fear for his father. In the end, he paid for his father's sins.'

'James Clarke, they convinced him he'd murdered Megan, I'm right in saying that?'

'Yes, one hundred percent. Billy and Jackson just played games with his head. The poor lad just couldn't take it. He couldn't remember what had happened. I believe after a while he'd had a false memory; he saw himself murdering Megan. Drink and drugs played a part in that.'

'He became paranoid.'

'Norman's secret, his sin…oh no, what have I done? No, not like this,' he shouted out.

It flashed through his mind. He knew once he'd left Alice Denman's house, he was being watched. It was Norman, he was there. He listened to every word he and Alice had been saying.

'Johnny, what's wrong?'

'Norman, we need to find him.'

He closed his eyes, the image of his sister's lifeless body flashing through his mind. He angrily banged the side of his head with his fist. 'I'm sorry Joan, I'm sorry,' he cried out.

He reached out and touched her name on the gravestone, 'Why did you have to be dead? I don't like dead; I like it when people are asleep. What's dead?' he screamed angrily.

He stood up, and looked down at his sister's grave, 'I don't like Grace, I don't want to help her. Alison was my friend. I want to see Johnny.'

He quickly started running, tears streaming down his face, the events of the past running through his mind. He ran fast, uncontrollably, knocking into people, his mind in a state of confusion.

He stopped and stared at the police station in front of him from the other side of the road.

'Johnny will help me. He's my friend.'

'Grace must go to sleep.'

'No, no, I don't want to.'

'Why? She must sleep. You want to help Grace, so she must go to sleep.'

'No, no, I don't want to help Grace anymore. Not sleep, she must be DEAD,' he screamed.

Inspector Walsh cut through the traffic in a vain attempt to catch the other cars that had Grace and Billy in them. But it was hopeless, just way too much traffic.

'Bill, it's Johnny. You have to stop Norman. Please keep a look out for Norman Denman.'

'Already on it, Johnny. Beth Reynolds rang about half hour or so back. She said Norman was standing outside her house. What's he got in mind, Johnny?'

'He's going to kill Grace Reynolds. She's in a squad car. They're only about a couple of minutes away from the station.'

'What about you?' Davidson asked.

'We're about five minutes or so behind.'

'We've so far seen nothing. No sign of him as yet, Johnny.'

'Fuck sake, this is hopeless. Come on move,' shouted Walsh.

Inspector Walsh sped into the station car park. It all happened in slow motion. Allen and Walsh jumped out of his car and watched in total horror.'

'Norman, Norman, NO,' he screamed out.

Grace was led out of the squad car, hands handcuffed behind her back. No one saw him until it was too late. He ran over towards Grace, screamed out her name. She turned around. In a split second, he plunged a knife into her stomach. She looked at him in horror as she fell to the ground.

She whispered as she fell, 'Oh, Norman, what have you done?'

He dropped the knife, turning to Allen as he did, 'She's dead, isn't she, Johnny? He wanted her to go to sleep. Is she asleep?'

Allen watched as four armed policeman surrounded Norman. He just stood staring at the lifeless body of Grace Reynolds.

Allen turned just as Billy was led out of the car screaming his sister's name in horror. Allen walked over towards Norman, telling the armed police to back away with a hand gesture.

He looked Norman in the eyes and said, 'Yeah, she's asleep.'

'I wanted her asleep, but he said no, she must be dead.'

Allen stood staring out of his office window. Norman had it in him to kill always, one personality anyway. He couldn't see it. He couldn't see that Norman Denman had two personalities; he didn't want to see it. Hell bent on proving Simon Woods wrong. He said Norman Denman had it in him to kill, and he was right.

'Johnny, Davidson wants you, his office.'

'Okay, thanks Peter.'

'You okay?' Walsh asked.

'No, not really.'

He walked slowly down the flight of stairs to Davidson's office, the events of the past flashing through his mind. Davidson would want answers, but the one question he didn't have an answer for was why? Why did Norman do what he did?'

He stood outside Davidson's office door. He was just about to knock when Inspector Walsh stopped him.

'Don't blame yourself, Johnny. Even you couldn't see what was going to happen.'

'Couldn't I? That's the problem, I could and I did. But you know what? I just couldn't see it. I didn't want to see it. I was so hell bent on proving Simon Woods wrong. That's my sin, hatred. I hated that man so much for not letting me marry Jane. I'd do anything to prove that I was better than him, better than Alex Davis. These people, Grace, Jackson, Billy, Norman, Alison and Joan, this was my childhood. I often asked myself this one question, is our future shaped by our past? I didn't know the answer before. I do now, sins of our past.'

Even the darkness seemed peaceful, respectful of its dead. He looked out over towards the river. The moonlight glistened on the water. He couldn't believe that a place of such beauty could be the scene of such horrors. He loved it down here as a child. It was fun. They would spend hours down here, especially in the summer.

His mind turned to the moment he first met Jane.

Had he dreamt her? Was she real? It took him a while to realise she wasn't a dream, she was real alright. He hadn't just dreamt her up. He checked the time, 10:35 am, but hey, it was Saturday and the start of the summer holidays. He slowly climbed out of bed his mind turning back to the evening before.

He watched the new neighbours move in with, once he'd seen her, greater interest. The conversation he and his parents and sister had with their new neighbours started flashing vividly through his mind. *Oh my God, did I really say that?* he thought with some horror and not to mention embarrassment.

She stood in front of him. She seemed nervous, even a little shy. The first thoughts that entered his mind was, heaven must be missing one of its angels as that angel was stood right in front of him. She had long golden hair that curled up at the ends and sat on her shoulders. She looked back at him with two diamonds that passed for her eyes.

She smiled nervously at him as she bit her bottom lip. Her light blue diamond eyes lit up and sparkled. He could hear himself saying it in his mind, telling himself don't say it out loud, but too late.

'Oh my God, you're so gorgeous.'

He could just see the look on everyone's faces, embarrassment, even shock, but mostly embarrassment.

Allen smiled to himself and shook his head as he remembered that early summer's evening and his first meeting with Jane. He stood in the same place Megan and Alison's bodies were found. Images flashed through his mind of the unspeakable horror that had befallen them.

'I'm sorry, I'm so sorry, Megan. Did you know who I was? Did you know I was your father? I hope so,' he whispered.

He knelt down and touched the ground where she lay, his daughter, his little girl. Tears streamed down his face. For the first time, it had hit him. He looked down at the lifeless body that lay before him. She seemed at peace, at rest with the world and its sins. He touched her face. In that moment, the image was gone.

He didn't want the image of her to go. He wanted it to stay in his mind forever. The one image that he wanted to rid his mind of was that of Billy. But however hard he tried, he could see him stabbing her over and over again.

'No, no, leave her alone,' he shouted, but Billy didn't hear him. He carried on ripping her apart.

'Why? Why Billy? She's my daughter, mine and Jane's,' he cried out. He opened his eyes. The image had gone.

He stood and looked over towards the river. The watery moonlight was starting to give way to first gleams of sunlight. He walked slowly down towards the old boat, lost in his thoughts. The blooded images of Sian and Kevin Van Dalen flashed through his mind. The shock of what greeted him that day had lived long in his memory. His nightmares for months after were of Sian. She was so badly beaten facially, even her own mother had trouble recognising her.

He stopped by the old boat and closed his eyes. He could see Alison standing in front of him. She seemed, as with Megan, at peace.

'Thank you, Johnny. Don't worry about Megan. I'll keep her safe for you. Tell Jane I miss her so much. Tell her I love her, always.'

'I will. Thank you, Alison,' he whispered. He opened his eyes, and the image was gone.

He looked over towards where the old boat house stood. The image of Joan flashing through his mind, and what she and Norman said.

'NO, NO, OH MY GOD, NORMAN.'

'She was playing swinging.'
'Is she asleep, Johnny?'
'Yeah, she's asleep,' he said.

He could see the figure of an old man walking towards him. As the figure got closer he recognised who it was, his father. Neither said a word, both knew, he always knew his son would understand. He held out his hand, trying to touch his father's face, but the image was gone.

'I was going to send out a search party.' came a voice from behind him.

'Jane, God, you made me jump,' he replied.

'I had a feeling you were down here. I woke up and you were gone.'

'This,' he said pointing all around him, 'all this was our childhood, our friends, our family. I just didn't want to see it with Billy and Norman. I knew the truth, your father told me Norman Denman has it in him to kill. Even Doctor Richardson said the same, but I didn't believe it; I didn't want to believe it. You know something? I had a dream soon after my father died. I went to see him in the chapel of rest, but he wasn't lying in his coffin, he was sitting in a chair with his back to me. And however hard I tried, I just couldn't get him to face me, he always had his back to me. I didn't understand it, but I do now. He said to me once, don't lose the people you love as they will end up turning their back on you; you will die a lonely old man.

'Johnny Allen, you're the best and the cleverest detective the police force has ever had. Without you, we'd have never found out the truth, so none of this is your fault. I know you see things differently to other people. That mind of yours, I could see it in you from the first moment we met. You seemed to just understand, it was like you were reading people, like we'd read a book. Come on you, we've a wedding to plan.'

The End